OUR LADY OF DEMERARA

ALSO BY DAVID DABYDEEN

Slave Song (1984)
Coolie Odyssey (1988)
The Intended (1991)
Disappearance (1993)
Turner (1995)
The Counting House (1997)
A Harlot's Progress (1999)
Molly and the Muslim Stick (2008)

Non-fiction

Hogarth's Blacks: Images of Blacks in Eighteenth Century English Art (1985)
Hogarth, Walpole and Commercial Britain (1988)

OUR LADY OF DEMERARA

DAVID DABYDEEN

PEEPAL TREE

First published by the Dido Press
in hardback in Great Britain in 2004.
This paperback edition published in 2009
by Peepal Tree Press Ltd
17 King's Avenue
Leeds LS6 1QS
England

ISBN13: 978 1 84523 112 5

ARTS COUNCIL
ENGLAND   Peepal Tree gratefully acknowledges Arts Council support

ACKNOWLEDGEMENTS

Grateful thanks to Wilson Harris for his inspirational advice, Michael Mitchell for his literary support and to Rachel Knowles for her forbearance and abundance of spirit. Thanks to Marjorie Davies, Kim Trusty, Lynne Macedo, Jon Morley and Glenda Pattenden for their meticulous work.

DEDICATION

For Wilson Harris and Derek Walcott

PART 1
ABORTIONS (THE OLD TESTAMENT)

"THE INFINITE REHEARSAL" (WILSON HARRIS)

★

"Amerindian and Hindoo Beliefs in the sudden abduction/
disappearance of people, and their reincarnations in apparently
different and unconnected forms and personalities, challenge
our Christian expectations of the linear, the stable, the steady
and reasonable development of plot and character, the logic of
Divine Plan which is the sure journeying to death and salvation/
damnation."

Edward Jenkins, social reformer in British Guiana, c.1869

★

"Amerindians! Don't mention those crazy people to me! You
ask them something and they start to tell you, then they break
off in the middle and tell you something else. The second thing
they tell you is meant to have some connection to the first
thing, but to my ears it is completely different."

Benjamin Rogers, English missionary, c.1895,
in a letter to his wife in London, shortly before
being killed and cannibalised by Amerindians.

Thirty found me single. I lay in bed for most of the day, thinking of all the money I'd spent on Corinne. There were countless others before her, but none during my marriage to Beth. A thousand journeys through the same back streets of Coventry, searching for one whose breath was not a chowder of cheap food and alcohol, whose arms were not pockmarked, whose thighs did not bear the telltale signs of blisters. Always the fantasy of coming upon a first-timer, shy to the point of deliquescence. But hardened women lean forward as you approach, offering themselves up for a cull, so you drive past, turn this corner and that, wishing you had true talent, the ability, whilst on the move, to make a split-second decision to stop for a particular one, a girlish figure partially glimpsed in a doorway or darkened mouth of an alley. You voyage through your featureless life awaiting a moment of vision in which you penetrate the shadows not with your eyes but with the intuition of a saint. You ignore the dozen gaudily dotting the end of this or that trail, refusing the smile stitched to their faces, the jiggle of waists, you turn left or right at junctions, drive a hundred yards or two, turn again at a roundabout, and at another, guided by nothing more than a vague hope that something worthwhile waits in the distance. One night you will suddenly see her and you will stop, astonished (admonished) by your good fortune. She will step out of her shelter of darkness beside a disused factory or closed public house, and you will know, by her gait, or the way she grows her hair, or a missing button on her blouse, or by some other innocent sign, that you will achieve contentment that hour, be masterful in her lap and in the loveliness of her giving. Afterwards you will curse Beth, words cankering your mouth.

Thirty found me single and in self-pity, Beth's cursing

returning to trouble me. "You're a-a-a," Beth used to scream at me, searching for something hurtful to say, but her breeding let her down. "You're nothing but a cur." A cur! How sweet the antiquity (iniquity) of the word, how becoming uttered from the mouth of an actress! If only Beth knew the appropriateness of her curse! I was indeed a dog, having dribbled over countless spots in Coventry, marking them out as mine. Go to the corner of Stoke and Mayfield Street, beside the Stag and Hind Inn, and by the first lamp post on the left you may scent my very first encounter with a whore. A young face peeping out of an oversized winter coat, her hair pasted to her head because of the rain. I stopped out of compassion for her slightness but when she unbuttoned herself to expose a belly I was appalled. A black man was responsible for her disfigurement. "It'll be our first baba, we are saving up for a few things," she said proudly, unconscious of the wrong done to her. I turned her on her back, pinned her against the seat of the car, wrapped my arms around so she couldn't flutter out of my embrace, and thrust into her ruthlessly, refusing to stop even when she cried out in pain, begging me to be more gentle. I paid her, let her out into the darkness and the rain to miscarry.

Go a quarter of a mile down Godiva Street, turn left into the Cooperative Supermarket car park, drive past the over-brimming bins and empty cardboard boxes, ignore the rats mesmerised by your headlights, proceed to the far end shaded by silver birch trees, and there you will locate my second and third and fourth and numberless expenditure with all manner of women, for I lacked the intuition of a saint, gathering instead to me those blemished by drugs, black men and more drugs. Their small talk whilst undressing told me this much, and I calculated what to pay and in what mood I would take them according to their stories. Those who were simply beguiled by the Negro and then enslaved by his gift of drugs were recompensed with extra money and apologetic climax. Those who boasted of their keepers and willingly handed over their earnings at the end of each night were treated as no more than the slum creatures they had become. Such women provoked in me a need for hurtful ecstasy.

Exit the car park, turn left, then left again, to the Shell petrol station, drive into its carwash, and you will have arrived, within its secluded walls, at another of my destinations. There I was beaten and robbed by a pimp. I had picked up a woman and taken her there by her instruction. As we drove to the place I took her nervousness to be a measure of her relative innocence, for she was well dressed and well spoken, her finger displaying a wedding ring. I took her to be one with infants, recently abandoned by her husband and forced into occasional prostitution to supplement the welfare cheques. I resolved to be kind to her and readily agreed to her price, asking for no more than straight sex. When we parked in the carwash, she said she wanted to relieve her bladder, opened the car door and wandered off. Her thug appeared from behind the brushes, dragged me out of the car and gave me a sound hiding, emptying my pockets afterwards. I drove home with a battered ego, yet oddly respectful of the success of their scheming. She had, after all, preserved her body whilst profiting from my lust, a crafty slave.

It must have been admiration (abomination) for such methods of deceit which made me return to the place with another whore the very next night. This time her ploy was obvious but I let it happen. She was tiny, almost dwarfish in proportion, and no more than eighteen. Her bony face suggested years of malnutrition and heroin. "I can't, I can't, it's that time of the month," she said as I tried to enter her. She pushed me off and began to sob. "It's not you, it's me," she said, wiping away tears with one hand and stroking my manhood with the other. "What's wrong with you?" she said with sudden spite, staring accusingly at me. Her weeping had dampened my desire for her and she took advantage of my impotence. "Why doesn't it get stiff?" she asked, rubbing me perfunctorily for a few seconds before leaving off. "It's twenty pounds whether you get it up or not," she said sternly, pulling up her panties and recomposing her dress. I handed over thirty pounds, the extra ten in acknowledgement of her brazenness.

Half a mile from the petrol station are the Heartland Towers with their rows of disused garages, for only the most foolish of tenants would dare park their cars in them, the area a haven for petty criminals. It was there that one woman bending towards my lap dislodged her wig, her bald head giving me such a fright of lingering disease that I pushed her off, zipped up my flies with the panic of a novice ambulanceman zipping up his first body-bag. I drove home under the clean light of a full moon, resolving to give up my lifestyle, to start anew, to focus on my profession, to seek out a normal relationship. No more for me the nervous dodging of police patrols or the melancholy which assailed me as soon as I had done with a whore. And yet, the very next night saw me with another, who, as soon as I tugged at her nipple, burst into tears. It was as if that simple preliminary gesture had uncorked her, for she let out in gusts of sorrow the story of her baby, her first and only, christened Jade, cared for like a rarity, shown proudly around the neighbourhood, greeted with gifts, compliments; busy their council flat, with the coming and going of family, friends, and the advice flowed solemnly, then drunkenly as the hours passed and the bottles were drained, advice on when to breastfeed, what new benefits she could claim from the council as a single mother, how to cope when the infant began to teethe, all of which stopped one morning when she went to wake the baby, but it wouldn't, she shook it but it wouldn't, it just lay there still and blue like the morning, and the doctor came and said cot death, and the ambulance came to remove it, then the police, then the neighbours, at first making noises of pity, soon falling silent as she passed by in the street, gossiping behind her back, one of them spraying 'mudderer' on her door. At the climax of the story she bawled aloud. Fearful that a passer-by would shout 'rape' I pressed my hand to her mouth but she bit it so savagely that blood flowed. Hurriedly I reversed out of the garage and returned her, driving as steadily as I could, to the spot where I had met her. She howled at the sight of my bloody hand offering money, opened the car door and ran off into the darkness, the denial of a fee finally convincing me of her lack of cunning and that her grief was real.

After that experience, any sensible person would have left off lechery. Not me. There were other garages, other car parks, alcoves, cul-de-sacs, Meadowview Street in particular. It was a street of derelict houses which ended abruptly at a patch of land mostly overgrown with weeds, in the midst of which a few cherry trees persisted in surviving at the edge of a pond. One spring morning, a woman walking her dog discovered Corinne there. The woman screamed and screamed, but the dog was unperturbed, sniffing ordinarily at the cherry blossoms that had fallen on Corinne's body, licking the dew that had settled on her face.

★

It lasted for nine months. In the end I had to go. Always, periodically, the same insults. "Middle-class cunt." "Bourgeois empty-headed cunt." "What do you know about anything, you fucking rich cunt." I put up with it. It was not such insults which made me go. I was Elizabeth ('Beth' to Lance's kind, I resented the common abbreviation). I was middle-class, that was that, why bother to excuse myself? I even pitied Lance's obsession with class. Which of course made him more furious, that I wouldn't answer back. Plus I knew that it was exactly my social background, my life of privilege, which made him yearn for me. No, it was his constant self-loathing which so exhausted me that I was obliged to annul our marriage. And it was only at the very end that he brought up my racial ancestry in language unbecoming, unseemly, to say the least. Even then I refused to answer back, for it was the mixtures of blood in me which first fascinated him and kept him wedded to me, though he never admitted it. Except at the very end, when, by referring to race, he exposed the secret of his desire for me.

Sometime in the nineteenth century Indian blood entered our family history. My great-grandfather, a sugar planter in Demerara, a province in a country called Guiana, took up a local as his mistress, a young widow who had arrived on a coolie boat from India. A child was born, my grandmother, who married an Englishman. She was shipped off to a private school on the outskirts of Coventry at the age of eight, and ten years later, on the death of her father, she inherited a fine mansion there, and a considerable annuity. My mother in turn was bequeathed the property in Coventry and made a fine marriage to a local dealer in motor accessories. One day all their wealth would pass to me, their only child. Over time my family had increased and consolidated their wealth, in the process becoming lighter of skin, eventually reverting to our original colour. Like raw sugar, pungent in its brownness, becoming an aromatic white through the processes of refinement. My skin was perfectly white, the only memory of an illicit past being the darkness of my irises and profuse black curly hair.

It was the colour of my eyes and the wildness of my hair which Lance commented on shyly at our first meeting, having stared at me as if afflicted by vision. I had long grown accustomed to men staring at me in wonder at my unusual beauty but the look in Lance's eyes was a matter of sadness and so I chose to thank him for his compliment and to engage him in conversation. Difficult, for he seemed at a loss for words, and I had to strive to initiate and prolong the conversation.

"My great-grandmother was Indian," I found myself saying at one point, to my own surprise since I rarely disclosed this aspect of my past, not out of shame, but because it was utterly irrelevant to my life.

"Oh," he said, and took a nervous sip at his glass. We were at a reception held by a local theatre group following the first performance of some comedy or the other. I was struck by the redness of his lips, well soaked in cheap wine.

"She came originally from Bihar, in northern India. Have you been to India?"

"No," he said and muttered something about being a local born and bred, attempting self-deprecatory witticism by suggesting that one of his sort was sent to, and not from, Coventry.

"The English shipped thousands of them from India to Demerara, to work in the canefields. She must have been glad to sign up, being a widow. In those days it was a badge of shame to be a widow. The Indians blamed you for surviving your husband, so she upped and fled for greener pastures, poor thing!"

14

Lance looked at me ignorantly and I cut short his attempt to apologise for his lack of history.

"I know next to nothing myself," I said, "I never bothered to enquire, what's the point, what's gone is gone, don't you think?"

He agreed, but without any conviction, glancing timidly at my dark hair. I stayed a little longer in small-talk, then left him to his confusion and furtive desire.

★

The Belgrade Theatre, summer of 1990, Beth playing the donkey in some pantomime. "You bray well," I said to her at the reception afterwards. "Trust me, I am Lance Yardley, the arts critic for the *Coventry Herald.*" Or perhaps she was Emilia, Desdemona's faithful maid, and I went up to her to praise her for the way she raged against her diabolical husband. I cannot remember. I might have uttered something sparkling like, "Your face blackened with fury in the final act, for a moment you became the vengeful Moor. In all my years as theatre critic for the *Herald* I've never seen that aspect of Shakespeare." And Beth might have replied in a tone of false modesty, "Really? That's so kind of you," and looked at me uncomprehendingly.

In any case, whatever was said or unsaid, we went to a restaurant that night, she drinking red wine and me picking morosely at my chicken tikka and telling her stories of the cultural desert that Coventry's district, Albion Hill, was; of being held prisoner in that world inhabited by the maladjusted, the crude and the criminal. "Stranger creatures you'll not meet," I said, expatiating upon their habits, arousing her curiosity. And when I told her of the dying of my father a tear ran naturally down her cheek and she dabbed at it like an accomplished actress.

That night, to bed, and drowsy alcoholic sex. We both awoke, not knowing what we had performed. "I must go to my father today," I said solemnly as I dressed. She yawned, threw off the blanket and stretched out her body, opening her thighs to draw me back to her. I remember being astonished at the sight of her stiff candy-red (tandoori-red) nipples, but when I lowered my mouth to them she suddenly turned on her stomach, offering me vile impersonal sex, burying her head in the pillow and braying in anticipation of my Moorish fury.

Hours afterwards she insisted on accompanying me to Albion Hill where my father lay dying. I thought the street of boarded-up houses and graffitied walls would make her nervous but she appeared eager to experience the dereliction of my childhood world, stepping out of the car without the least chill of self-consciousness. The door was open, jungle music blasted out, loud enough to herald the dead to their time of judgement. "Slash me bitch up, slash the black motherfucker," the lyrics announced repeatedly. A black youth, fifteen years or so, was stretched on the front room sofa, hugging a stereo player to his chest and kicking his feet to the noise.

"Oi Dave, turn that wog-box down or fuck off out of the house," my sister Miriam shouted, but he pretended not to hear, continuing to kick the air as if he was a wind-up doll not in control of his movements. "That's Dave, never mind him. His mum and him moved in last month across the road. He keeps an eye on Dad sometimes when I'm at the shops," my sister said, nodding perfunctorily to Beth when I introduced her, not seeming to notice Beth's delicate appearance, her expensive clothing.

"Hi Dave," I called out as Miriam led us past him into the kitchen. Dave stretched out a hand for me to slap my greeting, but seeing me hesitate he sneezed instead and wiped his nose on his shirt.

"Don't get me wrong, they're black and all that but his mum's well nice," Miriam said by way of apologising for Dave's presence.

"No she ain't, she's a scrounger," Dave said, suddenly switching off the music. "She's like all you lot, scrounging off Social." He spoke of his mother with pride but Miriam took offence.

"You little baboon, and she gets you new trainers and all and in rasta colours too. Don't speak of your mum like that, you ungrateful sod." She lifted her hand in admonition but Dave was obviously accustomed to her pretence at violence.

"Cho! You don't frighten me man!" he said, sucking his teeth, ejecting the CD and putting in another. "Kill the pig, kill the motherfucking pig," he sang along with the lyrics, rolling his hand the way black pop musicians did on television to signal their youth-rebel status.

Miriam went on the attack again. "That David Attenborough gave you your name didn't he? Don't lie, I saw the two of you on telly. You was eating bamboo, he tickled you under the chin and named you Dave because you was an orphan ape, the hunters killed your folk for food, so he took you in, tell the truth." Before Dave could retaliate I called out to Dad.

"I'm in 'ere," he answered in a surprisingly strong voice and I ushered both women into a room adjoining the kitchen where Dad lay on a makeshift bed.

"He's a good lad and I like the noise, it makes me heart race. And he goes down to the Paki shop to get me sweets," Dad said, and to prove his case he shouted above the music, "Oi Dave, be a good lad and get me some Halls from the Paki, and get a Coke for yourself and tell Paki to put it on the slate."

"Alright geezer," Dave shouted back, willingly abandoning his song to serve Dad. "Want any crisps or cream-cakes from the shop fatty-batty?" he called out to Miriam as he left and Miriam swore at him.

"This is Beth," I said to Dad.

"Watcha Beth. Nice to meet you."

"Nice to meet you too," Beth lied.

"Sit where you can. It's a bit of a mess but I'm sick you see. Did Lance tell you?"

I cleared an armchair of stale clothing for Beth. She sat down crossing her legs politely. "Yes. Lance mentioned you were under the weather," she said, the understatement testifying to her class.

"Tea luv?" Miriam asked her, not bothering to wait for an answer, going to the kitchen to put the kettle on.

We sat drinking thickly sugared tea, Beth taking tiny sips, disguising her disgust at its sweetness. Dad slurped at the mug, more out of memory of happier days for he could barely retain any liquids other than water. After a while he gave up and reached for a cigarette.

"He must be feeling better today, he's already had ten fags," Miriam said, lighting up one for herself.

"I feel a bit numb, I'm waiting for me circulation to come back," Dad said, almost happy in his advanced stage of decline. "I think I'm on the strongest morphine patch," he added, a note of pride in his voice.

"You've done well Dad," Miriam said, "you'll use up all the doctors have to give, you'll last the course."

"True," Dad agreed, "I started off on the number one patches, but now I'm at full strength. You can't keep a good man down, eh?" He tried to laugh but shook with coughing instead. I handed him a towel to wipe the froth at the side of his mouth.

"Don't trouble yourself with him, he'll be alright," Miriam said but in a lowered voice as if she had spoken the words to comfort herself. The froth oozing from him gave her a fright.

Dad began to cry, then remembering the presence of a stranger drew violently on his cigarette. "So what you do then girl?" he asked Beth, staring disconsolately at her but before Beth could respond Miriam thrust a glass of water at him.

"Down it all, water's good for your peripherals, nurse said." Miriam explained his peripherals to me. In the months caring for him she had picked up medical terms relating to his cancer and was always ready to show off her specialised knowledge. "When you're on your way it's your peripherals that goes first, fingertips, tip of your nose, your toes, that kind of thing." She was addressing me, the only educated one in the family, the one who grew up to be witty and erudite and wrote newspaper articles on Shakespeare while she, Miriam, got herself pregnant at fifteen, and by the age of nineteen was mother to three children by three different men; none of them with money or class, none of them staying around to claim fatherhood. The first was the predictably spotty virgin boy she packed shelves with in the local Tesco. The second serviced the local pub with tablets and potions – it was he that gave her a gold chain as a way of lowering her defences, an extravagant and unnecessary gesture since her defences were already at floor level, and a kind and flattering word would have sufficed. The third sold plastic goods from door to door and left her a set of buckets and a hosepipe. After the third birth Miriam forswore all sex, settling down to her life as council house tenant and recipient of Welfare.

"The social worker bought Dad all of this," Miriam said interrupting her talk of peripherals to rummage through a plastic bag. She took out a shaving set, a packet of cotton wool, a soap-dish and a pair of ear plugs.

"Think Dad, if it was December you could have put in for balloons and a train set," she said. "The Social comes ever so often so he can put in for his special needs. I missed her on Monday otherwise I'd put in my own order. I fancied some new tea-towels for me own house, a bath mat, maybe a bathrobe, matching colours, green I'd go for. But you never reminded me that she was coming on Monday, did you Dad? You must remind me, otherwise we'll miss out on what you're due." She turned to Beth conspiratorially. "When you're dying the Social give you whatever you ask for, they're scared shitless in case there's a scandal in the papers. 'Man Left to Die Without Washing Powder.' Ha! Just think of the headlines. 'World War Two Veteran Dies Without Benefit of Loo Paper and Green Bathrobe.'" Beth looked suitably horrified.

"Don't push your luck Miriam," Dad said, stubbing out his cigarette. "They'd cotton on from my birth certificate that I was only twelve when the war was on. And by forty-five me and your mum was shacked up in Birmingham, we missed out on all the bombing."

Mention of Mum made Miriam glum. She lit another cigarette and puffed continuously at it. Dave returned empty-handed, accompanied by Mark, Steve and Sarah, Miriam's children. "Paki won't give no more credit," Dave announced slamming the door violently to express his disgust at man's inhumanity to man.

"Hi Grandad," the three teenagers declaimed in unison. Steve reached to his ear for a cigarette. A trainee carpenter on the government's Youth Employment Scheme he signalled his upward mobility by keeping things like pencils and chalk behind his ears.

"Hi Lance. Hi Lance's bird," Steve said. Beth returned a greeting, holding up a limp hand.

"That's a nice amethyst you've got, I bet it's not from Argos," Sarah gushed in a tone between admiration and envy. Beth held out the gaudy finger for Sarah's finer inspection.

"Can I try it on?" Sarah asked excitedly, taking off her own ring.

"Tom gave me mine, cheap sod." She turned to the landing and shrieked, "cheap sod, my man Tom. More a boy than a man, our Tom." Tom hearing his name called made a reluctant appearance at the death scene. He had nodded off upstairs in Dad's old bedroom. Dad had been brought downstairs so that he could he nearer to the kitchen where friends, family and neighbours trooped in at all hours to pay their respects and gathered greedily around tea and sandwiches. In the closing stages of his illness my sister Miriam had left her own house and moved in to play host to the well-wishers.

"Why did you get me up bitch?" Tom growled at Sarah when he saw that Dad was still alive.

"Mind your tongue young man, she might be a slag but that's for me to say, she's my daughter," Miriam chided him.

"She's a fat fucking useless cunt of a pig," Tom said, deeply irritated at being woken up for no reason.

"He loves me really, we're getting married one of these days," Sarah said to Beth, rubbing her hand with the newly adorned amethyst over her pregnant belly. "We're deciding on names, aren't we Tom?" Tom suddenly looked sheepish as if self-conscious of his immaturity in the face of fatherhood.

"Ain't the Paki doctor told you whether it's a boy or girl?" Miriam asked.

"He did a scan, the sprog's big enough in my belly to tell but Tom don't want to know. He wants it to come out as a surprise, don't you Tom?" Tom squirmed at the betrayal of his romantic secret. Mark and Steve giggled at him, their best friend who had seduced their sister, taken her to McDonald's and curry houses, exhausting all his dole money, and now penniless with another mouth soon to feed. Forced to seek employment, he had just got himself a job as a butcher's apprentice. Work didn't suit him though. He much preferred to laze in bed.

"Don't look so shamefaced lad," Dad said in a kindly voice. "I was just like you when I was your age. I didn't bother with what popped out, so long as it was healthy and kicking and bawling. Get yourself back upstairs and have a kip, get all the rest you can now, there'll be nowt once the bastard shows up."

"Go on Grandad, tell us about when our mum was born," Sarah said, but her brothers groaned at the prospect of hearing the stories again.

"Your mum was a strange fish when she broke your grannie's water and popped out into the world. Your mum was a blue – " A chorus of sighs and guffaws interrupted him. "Now listen to me, your mum was a blue – " but they would not relent, ending their grandfather's effort at storytelling. As he lay dying Dad must have thought it his duty to construct the family saga, giving them the details of their infant biographies, reminding them of later childish pranks and accidents. It was his way of making amends for his long absences from home, occupied by bookmakers or Her Majesty's keepers.

"I was doing time in Winston Green when Miriam was born," he said, looking tenderly at his daughter. "I was in for – "

"Eighteen months for burglary," Mark chipped in.

"But they let you out on a day release for the birth," Steve added.

"And granny was in St. Paul's hospital in the Blue Ward," Mark continued.

"The Social give all the bitches blue nightgowns, that's why they call Maternity the Blue Ward," Steve explained.

"Shut up boys, show some respect to your grandad," Miriam shouted. "Give him a chance to tell the story himself. Your time will come don't worry, one day you'll be stretched out like him and then you'll have your chance to babble."

"That's all it is, Grandad's babble, we've heard it all before," Mark said rudely and he and Steve left to join Dave in the front room.

"Tell us Grandad, tell him Lance, tell him to tell us," Sarah turned to me for support, for Dad had fallen back on his pillow, partly exhausted by our presence, partly seduced by the morphine sweetening his blood.

21

The doorbell rang. "Send them away, whoever it is, say your grandad is resting," Miriam ordered. "It's that Paddy who used to live at the end of the road with the Lada," Steve said, peeping from behind the curtain.

"That'll be Geoff," Miriam whispered to Beth, "a right spanner. As bog Irish as they come. He lives in the Mental now. We better let him in."

Geoff entered bearing a parcel of herrings which he dumped unceremoniously on the kitchen table, seemingly relieved to be rid of them. "Frederick's sleeping then, is he?" Geoff said nodding in Dad's direction.

"That's good-looking fish you've got there Geoff, they've got a nice colour on them," Miriam said. Beth leaned forward to take a look, nodding politely to show agreement with Miriam. As she leant back her breasts pressed against her blouse, reminding me of our morning's excitement. I glanced at my watch, calculating an early exit from my father's house. I would take Beth back to my flat, we would spend the rest of the day having loveless sex. The beginning of a relationship was always the most pleasurable, the sheer selfish indulgence in the other's flesh. Hour upon hour, days and nights of plundering, before the inevitable exhaustion, the inevitable boredom. Thereafter human emotions took over, the awakening of conversation, the unveiling of the other's character, the discovery of flaws, the flow of compassion, the making of tacit agreements to ensure a tolerable relationship. Then the outings to the cinema, restaurants, shops or else nights spent together watching television for want of something more meaningful to do, or else to avoid human intimacy. The sex would always be available, but the original savagery of it would never be recovered. The sex would be mannered, for consciousness of the other's personality would rein in the desire for swift brutish triumphant repeated orgasm.

I looked at Beth's breasts, foreseeing a future which would dignify (calcify) our lovemaking. Miriam interpreted my sudden glumness as sorrow for my father's condition. She put the kettle on for a fresh round of tea. "What happened to your Lada Geoff?" she asked, hoping to spark up a conversation which would distract us all from Dad's dying.

"Swapped it, but I got robbed."

"Robbed?" Miriam's face lit up with concern and Beth took her lead, a little sigh issuing from her lips.

"Well and truly robbed, right royally robbed. Buggered me up proper, I stopped thinking straight after that."

"Who robbed you Geoff, tell us who did it," Miriam tutted, stirring an extra spoon of sugar in Geoff's tea to compensate him for his loss.

"I loved that car," Geoff said, struggling to contain his emotion.

"I know, I know... you were always washing and polishing and repairing it... you used to shoo children away if they came too close to it, in case they scratched the paint or something."

"That car was sweeter to me than any wife, and a good little runner, come shine or sorrow. Put in the key, give it a bit of choke and the engine turned over first time, regular as clock-work. That car had faith in me, and I let it down when I swapped it. It's probably in a knacker's yard right now..." His eyes misted over.

I looked at my watch again, this time with deliberation, hoping to catch Beth's attention but she was focused on the tale of the fool.

"Tell us more," Miriam said, giving Geoff his tea and gazing at him with great kindness. "Get it off your chest, you'll feel better for it."

"Well I was weeding my allotment one day when this man comes up and says, 'The name's Arthur.' 'Yeah? I says. 'I've got some seeds.' 'Seeds,' he says winking at me. 'What kind of seeds? I says. 'Seeds, but nothing you've ever planted,' he says, winking at me again. 'What's wrong with your eye Arthur?' I says. 'Nothing's wrong with my eye,' he says. Dodgy bastard I thought, probably a poof, winking at me like that! 'I don't want no seeds,' I says."

"Bloody right, good on you," Miriam said, encouraging him to continue. "You sent him packing, eh?"

"We must go soon, I've got a few things to do this after-noon," I said to Beth, anxious to get away.

23

"Stay put for a minute. Let the girl hear out Geoff," Miriam chided me. Beth smiled gratefully at her and turned again to Geoff in a pose of studiousness.

"He came back next day, and the next, and the next, sometimes winking with his left eye, sometimes with his right, till I got all confused and took the seeds from him and gave him keep of the Lada."

"Oh Geoff you didn't!" Miriam exclaimed in disbelief, her lips quivering at the injustice of it all.

"He wore me down, didn't he. You don't know what it's like, all that winking. If it happened to you you'd empty your house and hand all the furniture over just to get rid of him. It was all so... so... confusing."

"It was, it was," Miriam agreed. "Here, let me fetch you a biscuit to soak in your tea. I would have done the same Geoff, don't trouble your head over it. What's done is done, never mind the car. Plus walking is good for you, fresh air in your lungs, and you see things in the streets, you notice little interesting things when you're walking which you miss if you was in a car."

Sarah, entering the kitchen to fetch a packet of crisps for her boyfriend, caught the end of Miriam's tattle. "That's true Mum, I found a twenty pound note once."

"You never! A whole twenty!"

"Yes, I just looked down and there it was lying on the pavement."

"Give over Sarah, no one is lucky as that."

"No, true Mum, twenty pounds it was, ask Tom. He took me down to B & Q and bought some wood and tins of paint with it and a new saw. He said he'd make a cot with his own hands for when the baby is born and decorate it all nice in different colours." She giggled nervously, opened the packet of crisps and crunched on them, hoping that the noise would disguise shyness.

"He's such a sweetie that Tom," Miriam sighed. "Never mind his butchershop language, it's all a front. Deep down he's a marshmallow."

"Mum! You promised!" Sarah groaned.

"Promised what?"

"You promised never to mention that word, you know how it gets me going and I'm fat already."

"She's got this craving for marshmallow," Miriam confided in Beth. "It's the pregnancy. You get all kinds of cravings when you're like how she is." Beth blushed with embarrassment and Sarah groaned again at the mention of the word.

"I've never found a twenty pound note, though I must say I do enjoy walking nevertheless," Beth said, recovering her composure. "I tend to notice things like doorknobs when I'm walking past people's houses."

"Doorknobs?" Sarah asked, her face a picture of incredulity. "Bugger me, you mean you don't look out for the money?"

"Leave off Sarah, everyone to their own, that's how the world is various," Miriam said, frowning at Sarah to prevent her bursting into cruel laughter.

Beth needed no protection. She appeared not in the least perturbed by Sarah's response. "Doorknobs suggest so much about history. The brass ones are best, especially when they're a little dented or the sheen has worn off. You find yourself meditating on all the hands which have turned that knob over years, decades, centuries even, and you wonder about those people, who they were, whom they opened the door to – wives, husbands, children – what greeting or rejection they received. And it comes to you in a flash that one day sooner or later it would be your time to die, to leave off fumbling at the doorknob, like all the others have." She stopped and put her hand to her mouth. "Oh I'm so sorry," she apologised to Miriam, remembering my father. "I didn't mean to speak of death."

"That's deep Mum, Beth is deep. Do you really look at doorknobs?" Sarah asked, her voice quietened in admiration. "I wish Tom and me could go walking like you do."

"I'll put the fish in the fridge before it goes off," I said to Miriam, embarrassed by the direction of the conversation.

Geoff, lapsed in memory, started at the mention of his herrings.

"It's the only fish that grows from the earth, though that man Arthur promised others," he said apologetically. "I would have brought your dad some trout, something better than common fish, but the man cheated me."

"Don't trouble yourself. Geoff, you don't have to bring anything, we're just glad to see you and Dad loves herrings, he'll soak them in tomato sauce and wolf them down, wait and see."

"No but still, trout is more... you know, more special. Any Lada should be worth a shoal of trout but I was robbed you see."

"Go on, tell us more," Miriam said to humour him.

"He swore the seeds were magic like in Jack and the Beanstalk."

"Oh yes... the Beanstalk, a good story that," Miriam said turning to Beth for support. Beth, pleased that Miriam had taken her on as a fellow conspirator, irrespective of her superior class, nodded to confirm that Jack and the Beanstalk was indeed a good story.

"He said the cabbages and tomatoes I grew was rubbish, once I planted the seeds it would be out of this world."

"Definitely Jack," Miriam said. "You remember how the beanstalk grew and grew touching the sky and beyond? In the end Jack did alright out of that plant, didn't he Beth?"

"He did indeed," Beth agreed. "It's a long time since I read it though, I can't recall all the particulars."

"Arthur told me I'd grow rich with foliage. 'Rich with foliage', his exact words. It struck me at the time as a strange thing to say. I still brood over his way of putting it. He looked at my little cabbages and tomato plants as he said it and laughed as if to accuse me of being a useless planter. That hurt, I can tell you."

"Some people, eh? Can you believe it, how heartless some people can be, can you?" Miriam asked.

"True," Beth agreed. A silence befell the two women as they pretended to contemplate the ill will of humanity.

"He could have just taken the Lada keys and just gone his sinful way, no need to mock Geoff's handiwork. Ever since I was a child I remember Geoff coming to our house with lettuce and tomatoes and runner beans. The whole street knew he had green fingers. Dad used to be proud of you. Poor Dad, he was always trying his hand at planting things in the garden but they all died on him. Once an apple tree grew to a foot's height. 'Geoff,' he said, 'you're the greatest at green things but I'm catching up.' But the apple tree died, which made Dad admire your gardening even more."

"That's why I'm ashamed to bring Frederick herrings now," Geoff said, his face creasing with distress.

"Oh Geoff!" Miriam exclaimed extravagantly to stop his tears. "We're just glad to see you, honest, you don't have to come bearing gifts."

"You don't understand," Geoff said. "I hate the taste of herrings, but that's what came out of the ground. I planted the seeds and waited. Nothing happened for days until it started to rain and the land was waterlogged. Then I saw a strange thing poke through the mud, slowly, head first, then the body, then when all of it was out it flopped into the water and lay still. Talk about fright, I was well gone, I nearly soiled myself, but somehow I got hold of myself, took up a stick and poked at it. That's when it flickered and blew bubbles from its mouth. I ran, I don't mind telling you what a coward I was, I just scarpered for my life."

For once, Miriam was speechless, looking to Beth for inspiration, but Beth too was in want of a proper response.

"Next time I went back and God's truth, there were five herrings swimming where I had planted the seeds, the rain had flooded my allotment well and proper, a good six inches in depth. One of the buggers swam up to me and nibbled at my ankle as if I was its father or something. Weird it was. I kicked it away. I don't like herrings. 'I don't like herrings,' I said to it, for I now saw it for what it was, but it came back to play with my ankle and followed me all the way to the gate of the allotment, not wanting me to leave, and the others came up, but I shut the gate on the lot of them and left anyway. Who wants a bunch of fish for company, I'd look a right plonker walking up the road with a family of fish trailing behind, wouldn't I?"

"I suppose if they were trout or salmon or something rich you wouldn't mind," Miriam said, recovering her senses.

"That's the point, you got it right first time! Herrings are ten a penny, not worth a farthing much less a Lada," Geoff said in an aggrieved voice.

Sarah should have been shaking with laughter but she was so enraptured by the thought of doorknobs that she heard nothing of Geoff's story. Each time it rained he returned to his allotment hoping for special fish but the earth only yielded the common breed which he gave to friends and neighbours for nothing, apologising as he did so. In the dry periods his cabbages and tomatoes failed to flourish as once they did. In the dry periods he was left with barren land, and when it rained ruinous fish. He was bankrupt. He was Ladaless. He moved out of his house and the social worker put him into the nearest psychiatric ward to cure his depression.

Sarah heard none of this though. "Do you really love doorknobs?" she asked Beth, awakening from her reverie, her eyes glazed with admiration.

★

I grew up like that, day after day, the same grubby conversations, the lack of ambition beyond Dad's fantasy of winning on the horses. Miriam and I went to school, came back, never wanting to learn anything, for we knew we'd grow up and become what every child in Albion Hill aspired to – council flat and the dole, the income boosted by a little burglary, a little trade in stolen goods, a little job on the side cleaning, plastering, decorating.

Until Mum did something stupendous. I was ten, Miriam four years older. Mum loved us within her means. Dad was in and out of prison. He made little provision for us. But Mum had Irish in her, born in Ruddlestone, on the east coast; Mum was accustomed to scraping together a living and surviving on potatoes. We were content with the second-hand clothing Mum acquired for us from various charity shops. We never complained about the unvarying diet of grease she reared us on. We resented Geoff's occasional gifts of home-grown vegetables, for they had an alien fresh taste, and the odd caterpillar was to be found in the folds of his cabbages. I believe my repugnance at the sight of insects can be traced back to Geoff's cabbages.

There was no understanding of change, hence our disbelief that our lives could change, much less that we could have ambition.

It was on the day of Dad's fourth release from prison that Mum disappeared. I remember it was the fourth release because I remember the bounty he brought home on each occasion. The first was an enormous leg of cured ham which we fed on for two weeks, Mum cutting it up expertly, lavishing mustard on each slice and making up our school lunch boxes with new pride, knowing that we would be the envy of other children, for the ham was from foreign climes (the wrapping bore strange words on its label, which I used to puzzle over, my first curiosity at the nature of language), and would set us apart from those with their usual soggy bacon sandwiches. I believe she may have even overprimed each slice with mustard so that we would sneeze on eating, thereby drawing attention to the novelty of our food. The second release saw me with a battery-operated water pistol which lit up in different colours whenever the trigger was pressed. The third, an electronic watch which played a jingle at the changing of the hours, again a state-of-the-art device. Rapid advances in science and technology could be measured by such gifts, though at the time we had no inkling of the notion of progress. Albion Hill was timeless in its pattern of ordinary inbred goings-on, until Dad did his time and returned with new gadgetry (Miriam once received a pocket calculator which had only recently been invented). Dad may have been cloistered in a cell but the gifts he brought home introduced us to a world outside of Albion Hill, for their boxes bore the statements, 'made in China', 'made in the People's Democratic Republic of Germany', and inside were instructions in various languages.

All this I appreciate now, but at the time we were merely joyous at the anticipation of his homecoming, awaiting the toys. After a month or so we were impatient for him to be newly incarcerated, so that we could be replenished with gifts on his release. The late-night knocking on the door and the sight of police cars with flashing lights queued outside our house may have stopped our mother's heart but the commotion excited us. She wailed when he was being handcuffed but Miriam and I were practised in the routine of his arrest. We'd stuff some of his socks, vests, underpants into a plastic bag and run to the car as the police van was preparing to drive away with him. He gave us the same final forlorn apologetic look, but we were glad to see him off.

The day of his fourth release left me with an abundance of toys but motherless.

★

"Don't get me wrong Beth but you two are not cut out for each other," Miriam said as she rearranged the pillows under her father's sleeping head. "Hay don't grow until the sun shines, know what I mean?"

I looked at her in surprise.

"You know... oil and water don't mix. And it don't rain fish, never mind what that madman Geoff says, like and unlike is contrary, get it?"

I pretended not to understand so that she would twitter on and, in the process, let slip something truly revelatory about Lance. It had been a full month since our being together but Lance always changed the conversation when I inquired about his past. He refused to talk about himself yet he permitted me to visit Miriam on my own, as if I should find out for myself the essential details of his life. Access to the scene of his father's dying, however, yielded little except the obvious: a childhood of poverty in a working-class or welfare-dependent district of Coventry. Sarah prattled on about doorknobs, marshmallows and jewellery whilst her partner was mostly asleep upstairs, waiting for the previous night's alcohol to leave his body. The two boys, Mark and Steve, played cards in the front room and had next to nothing to say to me. Steve would rub his finger behind his ear and mutter something about carpentry when I inquired after his work. Mark, unemployed, would light up a cigarette as an excuse for not speaking. Lance's father, in despite of his decay, was a farcical figure, awakening periodically from his coma and calling for the newspaper.

"It's all right Dad, I've put a few bob on what's-his-name, in the two-thirty at Newmarket," Miriam would say, dabbing his forehead with a wet towel.

"Did you get the odds? You sure it's Goldfinger you've backed?"

"It'll come up trumps, don't worry your soul, we'll be millionaires by tomorrow," Miriam comforted him. "Look who's come to see you Dad, it's Beth, Lance's friend. She brought you flowers and all, say thank you to Beth." But her father had sunk into sleep again, his breath barely indicating life but his feet twitching alarmingly.

"He's not having a fit," Miriam assured me, laughing at my troubled face. "He's dreaming of Goldfinger pounding the turf to the winning post, a fifteen-to-one outsider. Isn't that true Dad? Tell Beth about your dreaming, do us a commentary like they do on telly."

Banal talk in a shabby council house with a set of semiliterate people of Irish breed, and the father dying without dignity. I had thought this was all I would harvest of Lance's character until Miriam startled me with her efforts at metaphor. "Water off a duck's back, that's what you are to our Lance, know what I mean?" I maintained my look of incomprehension. She paused to gather her thoughts for one final assault on the English language. "Mud don't turn into porcelain just so, water don't make wine except by miracle, but I'll still pray for the two of you. Don't get me wrong, I don't go to church and that but I'll still pray for you lot."

"But it's hardly fair to compare Lance and me to plain water and porcelain, don't you think Miriam?" I protested, putting her on the defensive. Her father's feet stopped twitching as if Goldfinger had met an insurmountable fence. I immediately regretted my questioning of Miriam's assessment of my romance with Lance. The race was lost, tomorrow they would not be millionaires but as poor as ever, and without a father, as they were already without a mother.

31

Miriam read my thoughts with the cunning of a woman of her class and condition; a woman who had spent her life manoeuvring men to her bed and when they had failed to provide for her, getting all the government benefits due to her and the illegitimate children the men left behind. She gave up on the possibility of romance, settling instead for the welfare cheques, investing her energy and emotion into accessing more and more services from the social security system. Or so I read her character, her seeming pessimism about my relationship with Lance. I read such pessimism as a simple show of jealousy, a possessiveness over her brother and a reflection of her own failed affairs. I was wrong. What I initially deemed to be cunning on her part was in fact a more troubled psychology. She wanted to save him from hurt. She read my thoughts not cunningly but with a sisterly concern for Lance's frailty.

"Oh he's porcelain all right," she blurted out, her eyes shining with admiration for his achievements. "He's in the papers every week, he's famous, our Lance, the cleverest Albion Hill ever produced. I always knew he'd grow up to be special-like. There was that star in the sky, wasn't there, when he was born, Dad used to say, a comet called something or other." She paused and giggled in self-consciousness. "I'm stupid aren't I, tell the truth."

"No you're correct, I was born in 1962, the same year as Lance, and there was a comet in the sky."

"Dad was right then, except that no Wise Men came with gifts. Oh there was noise all right, in the middle of the night, commotion and flashing lights, but it was the police come for Dad, not the Wise Men. I bet you was born with gold and goblets of frankenstein around you, and the manger was a posh ward in a private hospital."

I would have risen to the challenge, but her father began a fit of coughing at that very moment, distracting both of us. "I'll do it," I said, taking the towel from Miriam's hand and wiping the phlegm from Frederick's mouth. She allowed me to tend to her father, but then she snatched the towel from my hand.

"It's not for you and it's not my duty neither. Mum should be here to clean him up, to put a last spoonful of soup in his mouth, to rub his ankles, to whisper in his ears the Newmarket results, and tally all his winnings, not me and you. He needs Mum, but where is she? Lance needs Mum, but where is she?" She sat down at the edge of the deathbed, staring at her father and speaking to herself. "Lance is porcelain, born under a bright star, but Mum turned him into mud didn't she, turned him into mud. Talk about a miracle! Jesus don't have nothing on her, our mum!"

★

"My mother and father have gone to Italy, they'll be away for the rest of the winter," Beth announced, throwing her winter hat onto my bed and flouncing down after it. She kicked off her shoes and slid under the blanket. "Gosh, your flat is soooo cold," she complained, feigning a violent shivering.

"I keep it cold whenever I'm writing," I replied calmly, disguising my irritation at her presence.

"I know. Miriam told me something or the other."

"Oh did she? What else did you winkle out of her?" I rose from my desk and lay beside her, more out of duty than desire. The ease with which she occupied my bed disturbed me. Women visiting my flat always did so with prior warning, or by appointment, or by my summoning.

"I didn't get very much out of Miriam. You know how she rambles, it's near impossible to make sense of her. Plus she's mostly shy and silent with me. She's ashamed to talk because she feels her words are common."

I took a sudden dislike to Beth, resenting the hint of arrogance in her attitude to my sister. "I have enough words for my whole family," I said curtly, resolving to have coarse and painful sex with her the moment my anger peaked.

"I know, Miriam said as much. She's exceedingly proud of you and your writing."

"They're only newspaper reviews, hardly a great fictional tome on the condition of Britain."

"I know, but that will surely come, you'll be a star one day, believe me." There was coquetry in her voice and in the way she slackened her thighs, inviting me to play with her body as a reward for my potential genius. Once more I felt wounded by her insincerity and the assurance with which she announced my future. Her attempt at intimacy alarmed me, I withdrew from the bed and took up position again at my desk. She seemed unconcerned by my going, for she puckered the pillow to make her head more comfortable. "Do you mind if I move in for a while? My parents' house is awfully huge and all the more lonely when they're away."

"Poor you," I said, unable to disguise my contempt, but she was blithely dismissive of my mood.

"We have two gardeners and the maid sleeps overnight but they're hardly company, are they? How long can I sustain conversation about secateurs and hedges? In the spring and summer I can admire their flower beds and ornamentation but the land's dead at this time of year and there's nothing more boring than evergreens. As for Alice, she's only a moron, poor dear, it's not her fault that she was born practically deaf and dumb, and therefore ideal for service. She talks to me in sign language but I can't make out head or tail of her gesturing. I merely wave at her and she seems pleased at that because she resumes her work contentedly. Oh Lance, have pity on me, let me stay awhile among your shelves packed with books. I wouldn't disturb you, I promise. I'll just lie here forever listening to the banging of your typewriter keys and the sound of the bell at the end of the carriage. Say yes, darling, and make me a fulfilled woman!"

Of course I said yes, immediately regretting my weakness. The mornings thereafter were taken up with repeated acts of sex, none of them enjoyable because of her steadfastness. I was unaccustomed to a perennial presence in my bed, for that is where she spent most of her time, getting up only to browse through my library, to make food for herself or to cleanse herself of stains in preparation for more spillage and frenzy. I returned from my office to a flat strewn with books and a lavatory choked with discarded tampons, for she would not relent in spite of her condition. It was neither her untidiness nor aristocratic attitude to hygiene which affected me, but the simple fact of her being there, day and night. Such loyalty, if I can dignify her sojourn with such a word, was an alien and distressing experience to me. The women – whores, or ambitious actresses to be more accurate – I invited to my bed left as soon as I was finished with them. The pleasure of sex was precisely because it didn't last beyond an hour or a drunken night, but would be renewed when the next one was plucked from the streets or the cocktail circuit. The thought of having to cope with a solitary faithful and persistent presence was unbearable. "When exactly are your parents returning to England?" I asked one night, but as usual she was not alert to the melancholy and desperation of my questioning.

"He'll return when he's surfeited on Marinetti, not an instant before," she said in the irritatingly highfalutin voice of hers. "Marinetti – the Italian fascist, the Manifesto man who – "

"I know who Marinetti is," I interrupted.

"Of course you do darling," she said serenely, "that's why you'll understand why a motoring merchant like my father is obsessed with Italy. He simply adores Marinetti and all that reverence for machinery. Cogs and wheels and pistons are heavenly to my father, especially if the contraption thunders out of a shell and is engulfed in smoke afterward. My father is a connoisseur of tanks and gun turrets and screaming metal. He's translating into English every word that Marinetti ever uttered or published, it will be a masterpiece of a volume, fatter than your first novel." She turned over and lay on her belly, inviting me to enter and fire between her buttocks.

"And your mother?" I asked, embarrassed at the softening of my voice, for her brazenness was a blow to my ego.

"Mother is equally queer. She goes to Italy to snare butterflies. You'd think she'd go to Italy for the Sistine Chapel, the cypresses, the cappuccino, but Mother is a fanatic collector of butterflies. She nets them, dips them in a special poison of her own preparation, preserves them in all manner of fluids, dries them out, pins them up on velvet boards, displays them in glass cabinets scattered throughout our house. It sounds frightful, I know, but there's a certain artistry in the pursuit of her hobby. Mother is not a scientific authority by any means, she arranges

35

her collection not by species but by hue. Each cabinet is dedicated to a particular colour, the reds for example arranged from top to bottom, starting with a dark crimson, then descending in shades until petering out in a pale pinky specimen of a butterfly, poor thing! Poor thing meaning my mother, not the insect." She giggled like a spoiled child relishing the impunity with which she could insult her mother. "Come to bed Lance, I'm fed up with the smell of Mother's formaldehyde and Father's cordite. Sniff me instead and forget all about parents." She spread her legs, awakening all my canine instincts, and I went to her willingly, putting aside my theatre review for another evening.

★

"That's when he started to write, when Mum went. Well, she didn't 'went', if you see what I mean Beth, she did a runner if the truth be told, she deserted us." At last! It took considerable effort to conceal my excitement at Miriam's confession. I had to steady my breath and wear a face of mild concern. "Letters. He'd read them out to me. 'Dear Mum, today on my way to school I slipped on the icy pavement and bruised both knees, you should see how they've swelled up.' 'Dear Mum, I was helping Dad to peel potatoes when the knife slipped and cut one of my fingers deep, so much blood you'd think I was wearing a red boxing glove (like the one you promised to buy me for my birthday).' Letters like that, full of invented bruises, cuts, sprains, toothaches, as if Mum would feel sorry and come back home to look after him. Did she ever! Months passed, no replies, so he changed tack. 'Dear Mum, I have made up my mind that when I am big I will study to be a lawyer.' 'Dear Mum, I told the teacher today that I want to be a surgeon.' Imagine an Albion Hill boy becoming one of them! But Lance wrote this to Mum calculating that she would feel so proud that she'd want to come back home. Especially when he wrote to her saying he'd decided to take holy orders and become a priest when he grew up – appealing to her Irish side. Dad took each letter, addressed an envelope, went down to the post office –

but of course he didn't really, he was only making a show, he nipped into the pub or the betting shop instead. Dad must've got fed up with the pretence because one day he said, 'Your mum has left the country, she's gone abroad, I don't know where.' Lance's letters ended but a new phase in his life was starting. He took up geography big-time. Dad had to buy him an atlas full of pictures. Before too long he could tell you the capitals of a hundred countries and who owned them – the French, the British or the Dutch. Our mum was in one of them, somewhere, so he was going to learn everything there was to learn about those 'abroad' places. And he started to take his French lessons seriously, and was the best in his class, and everybody started calling him Kermit, you know, after that frog in the telly cartoon. They'd go 'croak, croak, croak' in his face or pinch their noses and fan the air, complaining about the smell of garlic. Pig-ignorant Albion Hill boys and girls, the lot of them. We had a saying in Albion Hill that if you wanted to hide your money from burglars you should put it in a book, since no self-respecting person in Albion Hill would open one. Lance turned out different didn't he, reading and study-ing and going to university, all because Mum scarpered. Dad was in and out of prison, the Social put us with this and that foster family, but Dad always applied for us when he was out and would go to court with a lawyer and win the case, so every two years or so we'd all be gathered back home, except Mum of course. We must have gone through four or five foster families all over Coventry – Stoke, Earlsdon, Foleshill. All the foster mothers treated us well. They were envious of Mum, and still glad for her, because she had escaped whilst they remained slaves to Welfare and their marriage. They didn't want Mum to come back... Anyway, though we were hopping here and there Lance still had his head buried in his books, dedicated like how you imagine a priest would be, all serious and red-eyed from reading. He had no mates but words, how he liked to play with them! Me, I went the other way, traditional, you know, I was always ready for a laugh and a lager and a bit of thieving and a bit of necking with the boys. Traditional Albion Hill person, me. You've got to fit in to

open your mouth again!" Miriam's outburst shocked all of us into silence.

"I'll take it back," Steve offered, to becalm his mother. He went to raise the box but its weight overcame him. The box fell to the floor and spilled its contents. Miriam stared at the tools scattered at her feet. I expected her to explode once more but as she stared at Dad's belongings a smile softened her face and she began to laugh. Steve giggled in relief, and I found myself joining in the conspiracy of humour.

"What's so funny?" Beth asked, tugging at my elbow, not wanting to be a stranger to our family secret, but I was too amused to answer. "What's so funny?" Beth asked, turning to Sarah, but as usual Sarah was oblivious to her surroundings, engrossed idiotically with the play of light on Beth's bracelet.

"I'll carry on Grandad's memory by using his tools but more honest like, in carpentry," Steve said to further appease his mother.

"You're sure you're not going to flog them?" Miriam asked, sternness returning to her voice.

"Mum! Come off it!" Steve protested.

"That lot will go in five minutes down the pub, the Albion Hill thieves will be bidding for them like nobody's business."

"That's true and they're in top nick, Grandad really looked after the tools of his trade, didn't he?" Steve picked one up and looked admiringly at it. "This is a wire-cutter. It's so sharp and strong it can cut into barbed wire, no matter how thick. He's got a whole set of cutters, some for delicate jobs, like the electrics in a burglar alarm, some for more heavy-duty jobs like wire meshes around factory windows. Wrenches for padlocks or bolts, hammers, metal saws, he's got the lot."

"Your grandad was no two-bit thief," Miriam said proudly.

"Shame you never showed him any respect when he was conscious. Now put his things back in the box and lock them away in the shed. If you behave from now on you can inherit them, but mind you, only for your carpentry."

"Mum! Leave off," Steve protested his innocence again, eagerly gathering up Dad's tools.

"He didn't do nobody any harm bless his soul," Miriam said,

leading us into Dad's makeshift chamber. "God'll preserve him for a while yet. He never did houses, only factories and premises. He'd never rob from a family home or anybody with a face and a name." Dad was sleeping peacefully in his bed. "Don't he look a right angel Beth? He was in a horrible state earlier, that's why I called. He was wheezing and struggling but he's settled now."

Beth, invited to peek at my father did so bravely but I could sense her discomfort, not at the thought of his criminal lifestyle but at my seeming approval of it.

"Don't get us wrong Beth," Miriam said, coming to my rescue, "we're common or garden robbers, but Lance will tell you it's the other lot who do all the damage, the ones with suits on and secretaries in offices. Lance works with the newspaper, he moves with the clean hands but he can tell you about their scams and frauds involving millions, can't you Lance? But never mind all that, just the two of you sit down and make yourselves comfortable. Dad don't want to be hearing of the posh gits and their clever crimes, it will only bring on a fit. Go on, read him from the Bible, Lance, I've put one under his pillow."

I picked up the Bible with a feeling of impurity. Beth and I had been making love when the phone rang, Miriam summoning us to the deathbed. We had rushed from the house without cleansing ourselves, Beth spraying on some perfume and reaching for jewellery – she did so with the naturalness that came with her class.

"I've been reading the Bible to him this last week," Miriam shouted from the kitchen. "Lovely stuff, all of it. I flick from one book to the next, but it's all the same, Jews fornicating behind every bush and sand-dune." She returned bearing a tray of tea and shortcake. "Until I came to the book of Job! I stopped in fright. All those sores and plagues, God really had it in for Job didn't he? What a bastard, I thought, turning Job into a piece of dirt, I'd never believe in a bastard like you. You should have heard me swearing at God. More like ruler of my arse than the universe, I cursed him, but then Dad started to rasp and rattle as if God was working strings in his lungs and I shut my mouth right away and started on praying and crossing." She burst into fresh laughter and nudged Beth so heartily that the tea spilt into her lap. Beth rose automatically, brushing the hot liquid from her dress. She clenched her teeth, not so much because of the scalding, but in disgust at my sister's vulgarity. In her many visits to the house she had kept her composure, tolerating Sarah's gawking at her jewellery, the incoherent grunting of the boys, Dave's wretched music, Dad's raving, the smell of fish in the kitchen (Geoff, as if anticipating her coming, would turn up with rotting herrings), the endless gabble about Albion Hill's citizens and their useless doings. Miriam's cackle and the soaking of her thighs with cheap tea were her breaking point.

She should have stayed for Dad's death. I resented her departure, her not witnessing the drama of his final moments. She, an amateur actress in pantomime and provincial theatre, missed out on the universal drama of his going.

The doorbell rang. It was Geoff. Beth brushed past him, hurrying from the house, shameless in spite of the tea staining her front. Geoff had brought scampi. An expensive parcel, as if he knew that Dad would die today and therefore was in want of a special gift. Geoff told no story about magic seeds which hatched into fish. He merely stood at my father's bedside, a look of normality on his face. He had regained his sanity for this special moment. "I bought it from the market," he said, handing over his parcel to Miriam. Expensive no doubt, but stale all the same, in no time suffusing the room with a familiar rankness. The smell must have aroused Dad. He raised his head from his pillow and sniffed the air. Seeing Miriam bent over him he smiled. "Blue as a porpoise breaking the sea, that was you being born," he said, and he looked immensely relieved to have got the words out, like a man exiting the dark canopy of the confessional. "Blue fish you was Miriam, and in all my time in prison I used to dream of escaping to the sea, to watch the porpoises lifting and plunging beside you." Thankfully the boys were not present to interrupt him. He lay back, satisfied with himself. Miriam began to weep. No one had ever described her in such pretty language. Dad closed his eyes, preparing to die, but the doorbell rang again, demanding a little more time with him. Dave came in, followed by his mother. Dave had in his hand a tube of Dad's favourite cough pastilles, freshly shoplifted from the Paki's. Seeing that Dad was beyond appreciation of the gift, Dave unwrapped one, popped it into his mouth and sucked loudly and rhythmically. It was his way of bidding Dad goodbye. His mother stared at the stranger on the deathbed, a resigned grief on her face. An African woman prematurely aged, I thought. Pockmarked skin. Sleepless eyes. I wondered what calamities she had seen, what wars or drought, what hacked or wasted bodies, that made her look upon Dad with such familiarity. He was a stranger, an Englishman, but she had met him before in different guises. Dad opened his eyes and gasped when he saw her as if recognising a long lost, long missed relative. He stretched a frail hand to greet her but then recoiled from her in horror, and his mouth spewed forth obscenities for the last time. "Fuck off nigger. Fuck off death. Kill the fucking nigger before the nigger fucks you." The strength and clarity of his voice and the bitterness in it so stunned us that we didn't realise that it was his final expression. Except Dave, who was so moved by Dad's lyricism that he spat out his sweet as if preparing to sing, and he wrung his hands, but in distress, not with the vigour that usually accompanied the beat of his music.

The doorbell rang a third time, but Dad would not awaken to it. I was glad for I knew it was Beth dried out and waiting to be let in. Too late. For all her curiosity about Albion Hill life, for all her kindness to Sarah and patience to Miriam, she could never gain access to our family, our past. Miriam sobbed when the doorbell rang and she called out our mother's name but I knew it was Beth come back, hungering for knowledge of our past which would always be denied to her.

★

I ran to the end of the street, turned the corner and ran again, not caring that people were staring at me, for I was crying all the time and rubbing my belly where the tea had spilled. Then I stopped, composed myself and walked back to the house, slowly, deliberately. I would tell Lance of my pregnancy and my decision to terminate it. He opened the door, refused to meet my eyes, looking down at his feet with a guilty expression like a boy expecting to be chided for a misdemeanour. His glumness and the unusual hush in the house told me that Frederick had died. I went to comfort him but he avoided my embrace and my sympathy. I felt that if I hugged him he would disintegrate into tears, exposing himself as frail, human, scarred by his childhood, in need of a mother's love. I wanted to tell him that there was no shame in his father's death, no shame in the way his family conducted their lives in Albion Hill, but he would have brushed off such reassurance as further evidence of the condescension of my class. So I remained quiet and lowered my head, if not in an attitude of prayer, then at least in deference to the mood of the house. We were both in pretence, he assuming the role of a man whose achievements could not be denied by the miserable and banal circumstances of his father's death; I, feigning sympathy with alien people in an alien environment. I remained quiet, wanting to formulate a prayer in my mind but all I could hear was his hiss of accusation, the repetitive charge that I was a fake, lacking true and spontaneous warmth. *Calculating bitch! Upper-class twit, you only want to slum it with us, Albion Hill is a little underclothing excitement for you, that's all.* He was always denying me entry into his world. After a while I grew tired of his outbursts. I accepted my status as a scion of privilege. I no longer bothered to argue my sincerity in craving a relationship with him, which meant a relationship with his past. I surrendered to his word, which was that I was a counterfeit, an outsider.

They were gathered around the bed staring at the corpse. I was moved to cry out in the presence of death but I restrained myself, for Lance's insults boomed in my mind. It was their tragedy, not mine. I longed for communion with them, all of us immersed in one grief, oblivious of anything existing outside of that grief. Instead, I found myself detached and oddly perceptive of the quirkiness of their behaviour, as if I was a spectator of some dumb-show. Sarah kept rubbing her neck as if irritated by cheap phantom jewellery. The gay orange ribbon woven into her hair seemed inappropriate for the occasion. Her boyfriend, freshly awakened, yawned continuously, insensible to the solemnity of the moment. The two boys looked nervously to their mother for guidance, but Miriam's hands shuttered her face. She did not want to witness anyone else's distress but her own. All her life had been devoted to caring for her family. Now she needed to reclaim herself. Geoff took out his handkerchief in anticipation of tears, but seeing it caked with dirt he put it back in his pocket and kept a tight rein on his emotions. Lance appeared deep in thought, his lips moving occasionally as if he was already rehearsing the funeral oration. Only the African woman displayed obvious feeling. She collapsed dramatically on the floor. Dave prodded her repeatedly but she refused to rise. There was a trickle of blood from her nose, the sight of which and the sudden realisation of the process involved in terminating my pregnancy, making me nauseous. I felt faint and reached for Lance, clinging to his side. He mistook my action as the consequence of grief and his mood softened. He held me upright. I buried my head in his arms wondering whether marriage to him would redeem me from the sin of killing the baby, or, if not redeem me, then punish me. Of course my parents would shun me for marrying into a lesser family. My life would shrink to Albion Hill proportions. It would become hardened to abuse. I would learn to tolerate the restrictions of language. Miriam would be visiting our house regularly to borrow money, Sarah to gawk at the furnishings and to show off her swollen belly incubating an Albion Hill thief and thug. The boys would insist on helping us to decorate, when what they really wanted was a handout from me, their rich aunt, in return for not disfiguring our walls. Or they would kick a football in the garden, trampling the flowerbeds like hooligans, and Dave would call out some insult or another to provoke Lance, for he sensed Lance's dislike of his race ("Hey Lance, know why your daddy named you so?" he once taunted him. "It's because you're a big prick, that's why."). I would be forever shackled to the clichés of Lance's past.

★

Dark-haired beauty raped and drowned, the headline heralded the dawn. It had promised to be an uneventful day. I arose early and slipped out of bed, careful not to awaken Beth. As soon as her eyes opened she would turn on me, tugging and clawing, ravenous for morning sex. A series of porcine grunts and then a long howl of delight signalled that she had done with me. I was freed. I could go as I pleased for the rest of the day. She cared nothing for my office work so long as I returned early from it to gratify her for another hour before midnight when she turned into a sow heavy with sleep, lying on her side and snorting. Nine months into marriage and the same routine, no sign of the waning of her appetite.

Dark-haired beauty raped and drowned, the headline announced to the world but I read it knowing it was addressed exclusively to me. I went to the newsroom which was unusually hectic. Half a dozen reporters, normally sleepy-eyed or hung over at this time of the morning, were speaking into phones whilst their fingers danced excitedly over their keyboards.

"Here, Lance, take a look at these," one of them shouted, barely able to contain his elation as he shoved a handful of photographs at me. "It's my story this, my big break. You're our theatre man, give me a few phrases about the setting of the murder scene, how it's composed and all of that type of baloney you arty-farty types are always spouting. It'll give a bit of flair and je ne sais quoi to what I'm writing."

The face was unrecognisable, defiled by blows, but its masses of black curls told me right away that it was Corinne. I had no need to look upon the rest of her body, to recognise her by her small, almost malnourished breasts, her black nipples, the tattoo of a Hindu deity on the inside of her thigh, partially covered over with pubic hair in an act of mockery. She refused to shave and used to laugh sacrilegiously, daring me to ejaculate over it. I used to refuse her, fearful of being drawn into the mystery of a foreign culture, even though it was the exoticism of the pagan which first attracted me to her community.

"He tied her up to a tree with barbed wire, you can see the barbed wire still wound around the trunk. And when he finished he dragged her half-dead to the nearby pond and drowned her. Then he sprinkled cherry petals over her and placed some stones over her face in mock burial. He must have panicked because he then tried to set light to her, but the fire didn't catch, she was barely burnt. The mist must've defeated him, or the twigs were too damp. That's how the police found her, covered under stone and a floral tribute. It's all there, in the photographs, the most bizarre murder of the decade. Poor wretch, but still, it'll make a cracker of a story and it'll make my name. The nationals will be calling me up soon, I'll move away from this shitty backwater into a proper newspaper."

Of course I'm caricaturing the reporter. He did not say as much, but he might well have, given the callousness in the way he pressed the photographs upon me, insisting that I examine them and come up with a florid phrase or two to drape over her sensationally tortured corpse. I refused him as I used to refuse her. I handed back the photograph and made my way to my office where I threw up violently into the wastepaper basket in a fit of morning sickness.

★

I ran a bath, pouring scented balms into it. I cleansed myself thoroughly and afterwards put on new undergarments and a new dress. I prepared my face with mascara, powder, lipstick. I brushed my luxurious black hair, staring proudly into the mirror. The taxi arrived on time, and by 10 a.m. I was at the most exclusive private clinic in Coventry, the nurses fussing over me with no less than two doctors in attendance. By 4 p.m. it was done. It took a few minutes to realise where I was. I peeled off the cover to go to the toilet only to be shocked at the pool of blood on the bed sheet, fresh, liquid, too thick to soak through to the mattress. I drew the cover back over me and pulled up my legs. It was in this childlike attitude that the nurse found me, as Mother used to when I cried out to her because of the thunder and lightning outside my bedroom. Mother would come to me bringing a newly treated butterfly to comfort me but the sight of the pin and the smell of fluids on her hands only made me more terrified.

The nurse found me weeping for by then I had recognised the blood as mine. A doctor came, examined me, pronounced me fit to leave. The nurse helped me to dress and took me outside where the taxi was waiting. I was glad for the winter darkness, for I could return home unseen.

I was too dazed to take the tablets given by the doctor much less run a bath. I collapsed into bed fully clothed. I came to hours later, Lance shaking me awake. There was great concern in his eyes. I wanted to raise my hand to touch his face, to stroke it, to banish all distress from it, but my body was drained of all strength. "I'm fine," I assured him weakly. When I awoke again, he was sitting beside me, a glass of milk in his hand. He raised my head. I drank a little from the glass. There was a tray of sandwiches on the bedside table. I made an effort to eat one, to please him, but then I immediately vomited.

For three days I lay in bed sweating with fever. Lance insisted on summoning a doctor but I refused, for I did not want him to know the cause of my sickness. For three days he tended to me, feeding me soup, milk, changing the stained sheets, giving me napkins to absorb the blood. I pleaded with him to return to his office work. I would send for Alice, our deaf and dumb maid, but Lance would not allow this. He was determined to care for me on his own, and he did so with such abundance of patience and tenderness that by the time I recovered at the end of the week I had made my mind up to marry him. We had been cloistered together for a week, with no company but each other's and I desperately wanted the solitude to last.

The baby would have been a hindrance, I was glad I had it killed. Lance and I would marry and live differently from my parents. We would be inseparable, in thrall of each other. My parents made me out of boredom, sending me away to board-ing schools at the earliest chance, so they could lose themselves in their hobbies; hobbies which appeared different and mutu-ally exclusive, one to do with machines, the other with butter-flies, but which were truly the same in terms of their obsession with death. Father's head was always buried in Italian books. At the close of day Mother would sit in her laboratory cleansing her fingernails of the dust of butterfly wings.

She loosened and scraped away the dust with a pin, from afar it looked as if she was mutilating herself.

★

It was only a matter of time before the police would come knocking on my door, inquiring about my relationship with Corinne. I spent each evening in my study, composing the statement I would submit to them. I discarded many drafts in the effort to arrive at a final script which I would then rehearse steadfastly, so that no amount of questioning by the police would unsettle me. Beth left me alone to get on with my composition. She probably thought I was working on a novel, the achievement of which would redeem me in the estimation of her parents. Not that I was overly concerned as to what she believed about my seclusion in the study. Our marriage had gone flat in less than six months. The marriage was out of her insistence, and I acquiesced, thinking that I could work up a passion for her which could be sustained over a few years, if not a lifetime. It would be a novel experience compared to the passing excitement with a succession of whores. When Beth abandoned me it was to Corinne that I clung as a substitute and means of revenge (or rather, to Rohini, for that was her true Indian name).

I began simply and tried to maintain an evenness of prose, purging it of emotion or individual flair. I sketched out a historical context, seeking to delete (secrete) myself at the outset by the provision of cold data. The Asians arriving in large numbers in Coventry in the 1970s, expelled from Uganda, Kenya and other parts of Africa out of sheer envy of their intellectual and commercial talent. 'The Jews of Africa', the newspapers called them. Fifteen thousand inhabiting the Foleshill area, setting up temples, gurdwaras and mosques. By and large peaceful hardworking enterprising people, rarely making the news except when the odd one was stabbed or the odd house torched by resentful Whites. Their slow accumulation of wealth, and with it social influence and visibility. Hence twenty years after settlement they could command the *Coven-*

48

try Herald's headline, albeit comically. *Hindu divinity bleeds milk from forehead. Thousands flock to witness miracle.* It was a measure of Asian success that a story which would previously be ignored as ethnic superstition could dominate the Coventry news scene for a whole week. July 10th, 1991: the end of that week the editor summoned me to his office. "We're running out of material, the story is drying up but their god is still pouring forth, he'll put the local dairy out of business! Pilgrims and worshippers are flying in from all over the world. It's pure theatre – go cover it from your angle. Mention their *Mahabharata* and *Ramayana* – didn't the Royal Shakespeare Company drama-tise some of their scriptures recently?"

There was a queue of hundreds at the temple door. All dressed in colourful cotton garments, some in what I took to be outlandish ceremonial costumes. The local florists must have made a killing (I crossed this out as soon as I typed it). Each devotee carried a garland of flowers. Altogether a scene to ravish the senses (again, crossed out). A true spectacle, the air powdery with scents and dyes. Spoilt only by periodic pushing and shoving, for only forty were let in at a time. They surged forward, dropping their flowers and all pretence of dignity. The pathway was a carpet of crushed petals, buttons loosened in the scramble, even the odd wig dislodged and abandoned, the owner not able to retrieve it, swept into the temple by the torrent of bodies.

I decided against joining the queue. Racial pride? No, more fear, being the only white man at the scene. I stood at a respectful distance outside the temple gates, avoiding their Hindu gaze by writing into my notepad. "Ah, I espy a kindred soul," a voice hailed me loudly from behind. A hand rested intimately on my shoulder. I turned around to be greeted by a tall stout fair-skinned Indian who immediately struck me, in spite of his informal, even shabby clothing, as a man of substance. Perhaps it was the imperiousness of his bearing – he stood like one accustomed to the ceremonies of soldiery, his body taut, his shoulders raised as if to display epaulettes of rank. Perhaps it was his extravagant moustache, circling up-ward at the tips, which gave him an Oriental military look.

Whatever it was, he was an impressive figure, and I found myself paying attention to him, like one of subordinate status. "My niece," he announced, stepping aside to reveal a small creature hidden by his bulk, wrapped from head to foot in eastern cloth like a freshly wound mummy. Only her small smooth hands indicated her age. After this perfunctory introduction he moved in front of her again, blocking her from view. "A kindred soul," he repeated, and when I looked puzzled he nodded at my notebook. "I too am a man of reverence for the authority of the written word" (as he said this he looked contemptuously at the line of pilgrims). "Indeed somewhat of a bibliophile if I may so confess." I was so taken aback by his sociability that I was speechless. "Samaroo's the name, of ancient Bengali stock," he said, offering his hand. I found myself admiring, against my will, a chunky gold ring he wore on his small finger, and I suddenly felt foolish, remembering the way Sarah would gawk at Beth's jewellery.

"Lance Yardley, reporter, *Coventry Herald*," I said automatically, like a captured soldier declaring name and rank.

"So, Mr. Lance, you're here to chronicle the antics of the natives. A sorry lot. Rogues, rodomontaders, recreants, and among them a sprinkling of wife beaters and practitioners of incest." His loud voice should have alarmed me (some people in the queue were beginning to look in our direction) but its cadence, its impeccable English accent, impressed itself upon me. "It's Hanuman, our monkey-god, Sita's saviour and protector. He's been set in stone for a millennium or two, in the temples of India, but all of a sudden, transported to Coventry, he bleeds milk to bring some mystery and glory to our otherwise quotidian existence. Come to my premises, I'll gladly instruct you in the esoterics of the East. Allow me monopoly over your notebooks and you'll be rewarded a rare anthropology of our heathen ways." He reached for his wallet, which bulged with bits of paper, mostly tatty. He searched through it with excessive deliberation before extracting a dog-eared business card. I received it with a strange sense of gratitude. I had thought the day's excitement would have been the sight of a deity issuing milk, but as Samaroo handed me his card I felt on the brink of a more fateful adventure. "Come Rohini, enough of this imbecility. Goodbye, but only briefly I trust, Mr. Lance." He strode off and she trotted behind him, clumsily, for the cloth was bound tightly around her feet. Then for no more than a moment or two, she turned and looked towards me. She slipped the shawl from her head, but before I could take in her beauty she covered herself again, leaving me with a fleeting breathless impression – a mirage almost – of her lush black tresses.

That very afternoon I found myself in his shop, a little embarrassed by my haste to visit him – and to gain sight of his niece (this sentence, and the previous one, and many others, I purged or reinstated in different forms). It was a shop choked with old English crockery, brass ornaments, pictures, vases, hand-woven rugs, candlesticks, antique lenses and microscopes, books from a bygone era (you could tell by their solid stitched binding, which revealed the confidence the previous generations of readers had in the permanence of the British Empire), all laid out haphazardly on the floor, on shelves, on walls or dangling from the ceiling (only the clocks I remember in any detail, a dozen or so which, during our lovemaking – Samaroo on business elsewhere, relinquishing his niece to me – would chime in unison, as if gossiping sensationally among themselves). He poured me tea sweetened with Indian spices. He talked about Indian philosophy, rising constantly from his chair to search the shelves for the relevant books. I admired his eloquence, his enthusiasm. There was something thrilling about the technical terms he introduced me to – not so much their meaning as the exoticism of their sounds. It was the presence of his niece though that sustained my interest throughout, her every movement a flash of nakedness, an incarnation of his obscure talk. Outside the shop she was wrapped like an alien parcel but indoors Samaroo allowed her to wear what she desired, a blood-red English dress which exposed her neck, her arms, and the rest of her to my cunning eye.

"Outside the shop I'm called Rohini," she told me on the first occasion we were by ourselves, Samaroo gone for the day to the auction rooms. "Inside, I call myself Corinne." She spoke with fierce pride about her adopted name.

"Why Corinne?" I asked, drawn to her passion.

"I found it in a book of English fairy tales, that's how. I hate my Paki name. I hate everything Paki about the Pakis. Look what I've had tattooed on my leg. I made a white man tattoo my leg, look! She raised her dress to show me a picture of a monkey which I took to be the deity Hanuman. "I wanked him whilst he was doing the tattoo, warning him to keep the needle steady and sure, otherwise no Indian wild-meat for him." She looked at me brazenly, keeping her dress raised. "He was the real McCoy, is that how you say it, a real English bloke. Kept his hand straight for a whole hour and not a smile on his face. But as soon as the tattoo was done he fell on me, raped me almost. A Paki would've botched the job and still wanted a fuck and even want to charge me the money. India is full of them, greasy little shits, corrupt and useless."

Her foul language was only bravado, I decided, for our lovemaking was shy and awkward. It took place on a sofa in the kitchen, a small room at the back of the shop. We practised the same routine throughout our relationship. On Tuesdays, Samaroo would be away from Coventry and, upon Corinne's phone call, I would hurry down to the shop during the lunch hour. She would greet me with some obscenity or tart remark about nothing in particular – the weather, the state of the shop – swearing as if to perfect her English which was still tainted by an Indian accent. I followed her to the sofa. She would not undress until I paid her. She took the money without the least acknowledgement of its magnitude. Then she lay down on the sofa. She fondled my penis which was swiftly aroused in spite of, or because of, her half-hearted efforts. She showed not the slightest sign of curiosity or amorousness at my stiffness. I tried to kiss her but she moved her head to one side. Still, the sight of her slight body – she was eighteen years or so but her body was that of a child – was sufficient to madden me, and though she squirmed in protest I fastened my mouth on her nipple as I entered her, imagining the taste of blackness. She closed her eyes to me as I laboured over her and I took pity on her frailty, finishing quickly to spare her further indignity. Afterwards I wanted to lie ten-

52

derly with her, to run my hand through Eastern black hair, but she eased me off her body, got up and dressed, leaving me with a sense of disgust. Disgust at having spent a day's salary without being satisfied. Disgust at my humaneness in not prolonging the sex. I never blamed her for the brevity and lovelessness of the act. She was only a child, and for all the vulgarity of her speech, she remained an immigrant, a stranger to our ways.

It was on the same sofa that I would sit with Samaroo listening to him talking about India. His father, an officer in an Indian regiment, died in North Africa fighting the Nazis, one of thousands of Indians who had lost their lives in the war but whose efforts were largely unrecorded. There was nothing left of him – he was killed by a landmine and his body parts left behind as his regiment drove on towards the enemy. Samaroo, a boy of sixteen, had only one letter to remind him of his father, an undated letter posted from an unnamed desert camp, the details of time and place censored for security. In it his father wrote heartily of the war, describing the sight of hundreds of tanks speeding across the desert sands, their guns thundering forth in unison. He strove to convey battle as exciting and picturesque. He spoke of the manliness of it all, of the bonds of friendship forged between soldiers of all nationalities.

Samaroo joined the British army after the war, inspired by the example of his father. India was in a ferment of political and ethnic strife, but the welfare of his mother and his two brothers was secure, for they were a family of wealthy land-owners. He could leave them behind without feelings of guilt. The British trained him, sent him to Malaya to fight the insurgents. It was there that he encountered men with their faces blown away, men shorn of limbs, so that it was difficult to distinguish them from the carcasses of animals. He returned to India chastened. The violence there in the name of religion, the daily massacring of Muslims by Hindus, Hindus by Mus-lims, sickened him. He voyaged to England, to seek out the source of the mayhem. He arrived in the middle of the winter of 1959, but it was not the incredible cold which depressed him, nor the grime of the city, its air thick with coal dust. It was the ignorance and spite of the English. Landladies were reluctant to rent him rooms, little boys threw stones at him in the street and scooted off in merriment. No one seemed to recognise his status as an Indian of respectable background and ample means. No one seemed to remember his father's sacrifice and that of thousands of his countrymen. The radio kept reminiscing on the war and cinema newsreels reported on rebellions in the colonies, but no one mentioned his father's role, nor indeed his. One day, walking across Westminster Bridge he paused and took out from his wallet, where it had been carefully folded and put in its own compartment, his father's letter. He separated himself from the crowd, leant against the railing and read it. Then he tore it up and let the small pieces fall from his hands into the river. It was a melodramatic moment, wasted on the crowd which flowed away from him, driven by their own concerns.

"And what of Rohini?" I asked when he fell silent. I didn't want him to brood on the indignities he experienced in England. I asked after her as a diversionary tactic but also to feed my curiosity.

"My eldest brother died whilst I was in London wandering through its cathedrals and churchyards in search of the nature of the place. It used to perplex me that such a godless people as you English are would have built such magnificent edifices and maintained them with such devotion! Of course I learned very quickly that the cathedrals and the splendid libraries were the concern of a few, the inheritors of a past which they revered and were determined to preserve for the sake of their own class. The living spirit of England was the high-street shop. People were fervid in the aisles of clothing, the tills sang with joy, it was the equivalent of the crush and noisiness of our temples and your cathedrals in olden days. But when I returned to India to attend the funeral rites for my brother I began to appreciate the secularism of the English. The constant fog of London must have blotted out parts of my mind, the chimney soot must have smeared the eye of memory, for I was shocked at the condition of the temple. Peeling exterior. Broken stonework. Beggars defecating on the pathways and entrances, goats lapping up the mess. Cripples displaying their wiry limbs, those without arms raising garlands of flowers between their toes, imploring you to buy. And a multitude of children waiting to sell their lice-bitten flesh, their mothers pushing them forward whenever a worshipper passed by, bawling out their price."

He came back to England in 1960, resolving to purge himself of India. He moved to Coventry because of its reasonable property prices, purchased a lease on a derelict shop on the fringes of the city, which he restored to a tolerable standard, living abstemiously on the floor above. He cultivated no friends, he sought no partner in marriage. He kept fastidious distance from the Asians who had settled in the north of Coventry, finding security by huddling together in a dozen streets or so, converting abandoned cinemas and factories into places of worship to maintain their ethnic identities. In their breeding patterns they were unaffected by their new environment, and the streets were soon littered with children. Samaroo wanted neither community nor children, concentrating instead on stocking his shop not with saris, chutneys, curry powders, as others did, but with English goods of a previous age. His only gesture to Indianness was an assortment of spices he kept to flavour his tea, and a small library of Eastern philosophy. He spent his time indoors except for Tuesday mornings, when he set off for the auction room to select no more than one or two items, careful to restrain his admiration for the beautifully chipped and battered artefacts on offer. It was not the method of the miser but that of the connoisseur. He cared little for money – his annuity from family lands in India was sufficiently large to enable ten times the purchases he made. He chose from the auction to enhance his previous collection. The slow process of acquisition was pleasing to him. It removed him from his fellow Asians, in the pace of his living. They scurried here and there, one job to another, working day and night shifts, obsessed with the quick heaping-up of money. They scrimped and saved and when they spent it was done cheaply and craftily. He chose to buy according to the beauty of an object, not its price. Profiteering held no satisfaction for him.

He had only a few customers, three or four a week, and it gave him no pleasure parting with his stock. He only sold out of a sense of duty to his business: he was after all the proprietor of a shop. And when an item was removed from his possession he felt a little pang of loss, but no more than that, determined as he was to discipline his emotions.

On the same Tuesday, in the afternoon, his purchases made, he spent a few hours visiting a church. German war planes had reduced much of Coventry to rubble but some churches, like St. George's, had survived. It was invariably empty. He loved the solitude of the place. He loved the ancient wooden beams supporting the roof, the ornate oak pews, the delicately sculpted figures of saints on the marbled altar. Above all the memorial tablets on the walls with their inscriptions in elegant and felicitous language, some of which he committed to heart and would declaim to me in accents which mimicked perfectly an eighteenth or nineteenth century decorous English voice. He would linger over antique words and phrases, relishing their poetical flavour.

Afterwards he would go home, eat a little supper, then take up English books – novels, poems, biographies, essays, it didn't matter – and read late into the night. He began to regret destroying his father's letter, not for the loss of its sentimental value but because he remembered how beautifully written it was, how poetic its description of war. His father was a soldier but he was also an educated man, the descendant of scribes and scholars; men who had been accorded the highest places in the courts of princes. Samaroo's garret in Coventry was a far cry from such a refined ambience, but downstairs in his shop, he sought to replicate the world of learning he had grown up in.

In 1979 his mother died of a brain tumour and he was called back to Calcutta to bury her. Once more he was distressed by the squalor and dereliction of the temple, especially its throng of prostitute children. He had picked Rohini out from the massed bodies. Saving her from brutality would be his way of thanking the gods for his mother's privileged life. He had done it on impulse and even now he was uncertain as to why he had selected her from the others. They were all equal in their wretched nakedness. There was nothing to recommend her, no peculiar beauty, no air of mystery.

"Perhaps it was fated to be so, but I've long since lost sincere belief in Providence. I teach you Hindu religion as history, not as a living faith. In India the scriptures are monstrously alive, weapons of war against the slum dwellers, to keep them manacled in fear, enslaved in ignorance or to free their wrath against Muslims. At least in England your empty gorgeously crafted churches and the 'yeas' and 'thees' of your Bible confess to a dead or inert religion, apart from your Catholics I suppose who still maintain their drinking of actual blood and eating of actual flesh. At any rate I brought Rohini to England as an act of thanksgiving, part of me still sown with the stubborn weeds of religion. I sent her to school, but instead of reforming her character she only learned to swear and gratify herself with the slang of her English classmates. I despaired of her and as soon as she turned sixteen I removed her from school and isolated her in the shop, under my scrutiny. I thought she'd improve if surrounded by fine and ornamental objects, and if she conversed with customers like you who are refined and discriminating in their tastes, don't you think?"

★

My marriage to Lance was bogus and fated to come to a rapid end. I had insisted upon it, unreasonably, for I had only known him for a few months. He was equally impulsive in his acquiescence. It was a shabby affair in the registry office. I wore the same dress and undergarments I had bought for the abortion. Lance wore his normal workday suit. My parents were not present. I had written to them in Italy the day before the event, a plain letter to begin with, giving them the barest of information about Lance's family – their names, their ages, their occupations, or rather, lack of occupations. I tore this up and composed another, embellishing all the characters. I wrote of Miriam as a domestic nurse, giving her clement and tender qualities. I described her boys as honest, respectful, of inquiring minds, and invented charm for Sarah, upping her age to

57

make her pregnancy more respectable. I had total freedom to remodel them, knowing that it would not matter in the least to my parents who cared nothing for their character, only for their social status. Saintly they may have been, but they were poor, and that was that. My parents would never have the slightest intention of meeting with them, much less deeming them family. I imagined them opening the letter and sighing over the contents. 'There she goes again,' I could hear Mother saying, more in tiredness than despair, and Father would put on a sage and sympathetic look, agreeing with her not out of conviction but because his mind was elsewhere, on the infernal machines of war. They had done their duty, giving me an expensive education, providing me with money and a mansion to live in. That I failed most of my examinations and left school at eighteen with few qualifications did nothing to unsettle their self-confidence as parents. They were never particularly ambitious for me. That I spent the next five years drifting in and out of part-time secretarial jobs neither pleased nor displeased them. When, at the age of twenty-four, I discovered the pleasures of the stage – not just the acting but the short-term dalliances with actors and men in the audience – Mother gave me mild encouragement, offering to send me away to drama school in London but not persisting when I declined her money. I spent the next few years with different amateur groups in Coventry. We toured various theatres in the West Midlands, and I slept with a dozen men, none of them memorable. I went with them because it was the done thing in amateur dramatics. There was no money to be made from our performances, only the excitement of putting on costumes and, the play over, gallons of alcohol drunk, undressing for casual sex with whoever was available. There was unconcealed competition among my fellow actresses but more often than not I won the man because of my gorgeous dark eyes and black hair which gave an alluring sheen to my white skin. He would be giddy at the prospect of my nakedness. I was otherwise of mediocre appearance, a little over five feet in height, slightly overweight, with a nondescript face. My fellow actresses were striking in their slenderness of waist, or fullness of breasts, but the man would come to me. To begin with, I shrugged off their envy, their gossip and backstabbing, but they eventually wore away at my spirit of resilience. They expressed their malice by demoting me to lesser roles, finally rendering me invisible by making me play the bear or donkey or cow, even inventing animal characters and forest and farmyard scenes when the original pantomime contained none. It was as the front legs of a mule or suchlike that Lance first encountered me in the theatre, but still I won him. My part was to loll or prance around occasionally for the amusement of the children, but mostly I was to stand still, at the edge of the human drama. I was present to fill in space on the stage. There was little to do so I amused myself by inspecting the audience through the eyes of the mask, selecting my man for the night. I noticed Lance immediately. He was in the second row, yawning, looking at his watch. Occasionally he would take out a notepad from his pocket and scribble something into it. It was not handsomeness on his part that attracted me to him. Far from it – he looked clerkish in his tie and jacket, with notebook in hand, like any number of minor bureaucrats you would meet in the town council or local government offices. I chose him because of his air of agitation and irritability. He was as bored as I was by the ridiculousness of our play. I made my mind up to seduce him, should he attend the reception afterwards. I would leave the theatre with him for good. My foolish resolution was perhaps affected by the absurdity of the surroundings, the ranting and overacting of the group, the gaudy costumes, the exaggerated brush strokes on the backdrop canvasses of rural scenes, which still could not disguise the dinginess of the theatre. Perhaps it was because I was standing in one spot for too long and my blood had drained away, leaving me light-headed. Whatever the reason, I decided there and then that I would seek other employment as his wife.

Alice was my only invitee to my wedding. She didn't seem to appreciate the nature of the occasion, for she looked neither serious nor happy. She was in her maid's uniform. As soon as the ceremony was over she gestured anxiously to me, wanting to return home to her domestic duties. Her behaviour was true to character. She had turned up unexpectedly at our house, many years ago, at the very moment that Mother had grown apathetic to housework, craving more time with her butterflies. We had had a succession of servants, none of them staying long because of the meagre wages Father paid. His parsimony was deliberate. He was envious of Mother's hobby, her passion, which gave her a certain independence. He would stifle her individuality by forcing her into domestic drudgery. Such cruelty gave life and emotional charge to their marriage for they had long grown numb to each other. Alice was a godsend to my mother. She set about her work with fanatical energy, dusting and polishing as if born for such activities. She took whatever money Father offered. Mother was grateful for her silence, her lack of complaint. Mother was freed to pin her butterflies without interruption and distraction.

Alice stayed for months on end, venturing out of the house only to buy groceries a few minutes away, returning as soon as she could. I used to wonder about her background, but given her disability it was impossible to arrive at any understanding of her. Nor had she any possessions which would yield up a biography. Though I guessed her to be thirty or so, the blankness of her expression made her appear ageless. There were no telltale wrinkles, no unusual scars or stretch marks on her body. I tried many times to take her to the park or a city centre. I would draw pictures of our destination, grasp her by the hand and lead her to the door, but she would pause there, withdraw her hand abruptly and turn back to the kitchen. When I blocked her path, insisting that she left with me, she would panic. Her body trembled and her mouth opened to let out a phantom whisper.

The house was her refuge and security. She lived chastely and contentedly in the basement, among sacks of coal and storage boxes. She would not take up my mother's offer of a better room, preferring the darkness of the basement, even in winter when only a paraffin heater provided was feeble defence against the chill, and the damp snuffed out her candles. But just as we were getting accustomed to her strangeness, she surprised us by disappearing. A search of the house and its grounds revealed nothing. The gardeners did not see her leave. Father made a perfunctory report to the local police station but didn't press for action, so none was undertaken. Weeks passed, the house accumulated dirt, and at the very moment that Mother began to fret and agitate, Alice returned. She was in her maid's uniform, which was as neat as ever. She went straight to the kitchen to resume her work. She behaved as if no time had passed between her going and coming, no troubling and mysterious interruption in all our lives. Her fierce attachment to the house lasted for four months, then a second disappearance and a second reappearance. Our wonder ceased as we came to accept her ways. There was even something reassuring in their predictability. She gave a pattern to a household which would otherwise have been unruly. Father would leave his office at a whim, at any hour, and come home bristling keen to indulge in his Italian translations. Mother was collapsed on a couch, in another part of the house, sleeping late into the day, for she had worked throughout the night. Only Alice connected the two, fetching coffee for one, fresh clothes for the other, keeping the spaces between them calm and clean. The time of day didn't matter, for it was replaced by Alice's presence. She was a different kind of clock, silent, without sensation or alarm.

I exploited her regularity to get her to the wedding, turning up in a taxi on Thursday at 11.15 a.m. as she was about to enter the grocery shop. I whisked her away to the registry office. The truth is that I had chosen the day and time of my wedding according to Alice's movements. A peculiar decision maybe, but as she sat dumbly and unconcerned by the proceedings I was struck by the meaning of what I had done. My future with Lance was written on Alice's vacant face. His invitees – his sister and her children – shifted excitedly in their chairs, chatted loudly, clapped when we signed the wedding certificate. They were pleased with themselves, pleased for the chance to show off their best clothes and fashionable footwear. They were eager to depart for the champagne reception in a nearby restaurant, where they could mingle with Lance's generous friends, people of a superior order to them. I envied their festive spirit, their innocent enjoyment of free food and drink, their ready consumption of the fruits of other people's labour. Their lives would be disorderly, changeable. They would experience crises and revelries, one moment crying in desolation, the next in joy, without seeking a logic to their experiences. Sarah would bear children by different men, or abort, her brothers would spawn their own bastards. They would behave towards each other with vulgarity and tenderness. They would squabble and share, riot and reconcile. They would sniff at their own instincts and chase after them like dogs from lamp post to lamp post. They would be outrageously alive whereas my life would be as predictable as Alice's comings and goings, at first mysterious but quickly becoming a routine.

★

The sex with Corinne was swift and silent but different from that of my previous whores. There was crazed delectation of her dark skin and child's body. Shame should prevent me from confessing it but I was wildly excited by the imagining of her past. The squalor of sex in undergrowth, in the shadow of the temple, the stench of beggars' sores and dogs' excrement defiling the air; above all the image of a coolie fastened greedily inside her, for he himself was poor, pulling a handcart piled high with bricks, timber, hardware, whatever his employers burdened him with, and the rupees he was paying Corinne represented several hours of backbreaking work, meaning that he would go without his curry that day. The moment I was done with her I was overcome by self-disgust and bewilderment at having fantasised over her meagre body. Even so I knew I would keep returning to her, craving her vulnerability. Over time my conscience would diminish, I would take her with the same prolonged brutality of the coolie labourer, and worse, even haggle over the money, wanting to cheat her of her dues.

"What will you do with the money?" I once asked her, making small talk as I dressed.

"I'll save it all up and when it reaches three thousand pounds I'll run away."

"Run away where?"

62

"Far, very far. I'll go on a plane that will take me across the seas to America."

"Tell me when it's time and I'll go with you," I said absentmindedly, anxious to get back to work. She looked scornfully at the colourless flanks of my face and gave a shrill laugh like a child blowing into a reed. "It'll take years, I've only given you a couple of hundred pounds so far," I said, my voice edged with malice, for I felt wounded by her youth. She laughed again, this time darkly.

"I'll steal Uncle's huge ring. He hates gold, he says we Pakis are obsessed with gold. We even plate our teeth with it. It's his mother's, that's why he wears it, to remember her. Being the eldest boy he's meant to pass it on to his wife. But Uncle has no wife, he'll not miss the ring. Anyway, I don't have to steal it. I've got nearly two thousand pounds already. I'll be off soon, and that will be the end of all of you, except my Jew."

"Jew?" I asked, and she relished my confusion. Her face lit up as she told me I wasn't her only client (cunt).

"What do you think I do on Tuesdays when you're not here? You don't think I wait, biting my nails. I call up another, and if he can't get away from his desk, I'll call up another. I've got half a dozen of them, plus the night-time ones. When Uncle sleeps at ten, I tiptoe out of my room to a waiting car for a quick ride. He speeds me off to somewhere dark, then speeds me back, then speeds off to his wife. And they pay more than you, and besides I make them come to the shop and buy Uncle's things, so Uncle makes a living too."

"Who's the Jew?" I asked, suppressing the jealousy in my voice.

"Oh, he's special," she said, putting on a faraway dreamy look so as to goad me. "He just comes to the shop to be near me. He spends hours examining this and that book or picture, and when he buys he does it honestly, because he likes what it is. He likes me too for what I am. He never touches me, he's too decent for that, plus he's in his seventies, but he slips me money when Uncle's not looking, and when Uncle's not around he tells me how lovely I am, how he'd like to take me away to another country, America, because he hasn't got any

63

relatives, so he can go as he pleases. He speaks with truth in his voice. He swears he'd never never do anything to me, he just wants me to be with him, he says he just appreciates lovely things like the things in the shop. Shame half of them are fakes! I know because my Jew tells me so, he shows me how the trademarks on many of the porcelain bits have been painted on to make them out to be older than they really are. 'Never mind,' my Jew would say. 'They're still beautiful, they're like you.' And he'd dust down a vase and hold it up to the light so that it gleams. When he goes from the shop he leaves me bright inside. I forget how old I am, I forget that I am a Paki, I even forget my true name."

"Of course some of them are probably fakes," Samaroo said when I visited him later that day and broached the topic of how difficult it must be for him to authenticate his purchases. "I don't trouble myself with provenance and the like, which is the plague of our profession, people giving value to things only by their dates, overlooking the artistry at hand."

"You sound like Mr. Goldberg, one of your regular customers, I think that's his name," I said, hoping to verify the existence of Corinne's Jew.

"Goldstein," he said, correcting me. "Enoch Goldstein. So you met the gentleman?"

"Only briefly. I had a free hour today, at lunchtime and came around to the shop to browse. Mr. Goldstein was there, we exchanged a few words."

"Enoch Goldstein's a remarkable man, don't you think? He washed up on these shores a refugee from Nazi Germany. His parents sent him ahead, they stayed back to keep guard over their business, hoping for a change, but it was Treblinka for them. He told me this much, and I don't persist in inquiring after his past. He ended up in Coventry for much the same reason I did." He halted abruptly as if he had given away a secret. He rose from his chair and went to the kettle, to create a diversion. There was no need to, for I had long guessed why he had chosen to settle in Coventry. He was drawn to the smell of death which was still raw in the 1950s and 1960s. The burnt-out shells of houses and the crowded graveyards were testimonies to the German bombing which had given Coventry international fame. The council had placed an orchard of cherry trees in the city's main park, with a plaque at the base of each bearing the name of a victim. Each spring, when the trees blossomed in pale pinks and whites, a ceremony for the dead was held. The blossoms gave a semblance of freshness to the city, a charmed lie, for the grime and drabness of Coventry's streets were ancient and stubborn. It would take the lushness of the Hanging Gardens of Babylon to disguise its nature.

"Listen to this," Samaroo said, replenishing my cup with Indian tea. "I memorised it as soon as I came across it." He closed his eyes and declaimed in a sonorous voice: "'This marble transmits to posterity the virtues of Elizabeth Christian Pinder, wife of the Honorable Francis Ford Pinder, and daughter of Jonas and Christian Mercy Maynard: who animated by the unfading example of her excellent Mother, shone forth thro' life one of its brightest ornaments: distinguished by unaffected piety, Christian humility, and active benevolence. After ten years of uninterrupted felicity, passed in the endearing society of her beloved husband, her tender frame and delicate constitution fell a victim to the slow but fatal progress of a disease, which undermining her invaluable health, and yielding neither to the tender assiduities of an adoring husband, the united skill of the most experienced physicians, nor the influence of a more genial climate, removed her in the bloom of youth to the regions of eternal bliss, on the 9th of December, 1799, aged 30 years.'... Isn't that magnificent? And that's the conundrum about fakes, it is no simple matter of black and white proportions. The epitaph is exquisite, whereas the individual may have been a despicable creature. Is the language therefore fake or should we not simply marvel over it and disregard the character of the corpse? Our *Gita* dwells on such mismatch between word and flesh." He went to search his shelves for the relevant passages. I watched him in the midst of his inkwells, vases, crockery, bric-a-brac, and it came to me that just as he had voyaged to Coventry to be near death, so had he set up shop and filled it with the belongings of the departed. Each artefact was no more than a memorial to the dead. His shop was as much a graveyard as the church cemeteries he wandered through each Tuesday afternoon, amassing their epitaphs in his mind. Like the Jew his life was determined by war. His father had died in battle, and when he grew up he had seen war first-hand. In Malaya he must have even participated in the odd massacre on behalf of the British. The artefacts he now possessed made death bearable by giving it a genteel appearance. Slightly chipped Victorian or Edwardian vases were the elegant remains of great wars and their sordid colonial aftermaths. The poetry of the epitaphs disguised how nasty and brutish and prolonged the pain of the life was.

Corinne entered the kitchen to offer a plate of biscuits. I was struck once more by her lustful presence. The sight of her fledgling breasts as she leant in my direction only darkened my thoughts about death. She sensed my dolour and challenged it by quickly putting her hand into her underpants, withdrawing it and smearing a biscuit with her wet forefinger. "Eat," she said in a mock-authoritative voice, then satisfied at the effect her vulgar act had on me – the blood had risen to my skin and a light sweat formed on my brow – she turned away hastily, making sure her dress swished high up her thighs, advertising her readiness for sex with me at the next available date.

I nibbled on the biscuit awaiting Samaroo's lecture on the *Gita*'s wisdom about being and non-being, about the concreteness of abstraction and/or vice versa. Such alien lucubrations were beginning to exhaust me. I wanted a more direct admission from Samaroo, a plain account of the bayonet's tip working open a native's veins, the whirling fire balls that were Muslim flesh lit up by Hindu neighbours, the moaning of women gone mad with manhandling. His mouthings from Eastern scriptures were almost dishonest, for he was secreting all of what he had witnessed of war in their ethereal conceptions. He must have anticipated my mood for he returned not with the *Gita* but with a sheaf of papers tied with a string. "I want you to have this," he said, unpicking the knot. "I bought it a while ago, part of an auction lot. I read odd parts but the handwriting is so fine that it confounded my eye and I gave up in exhaustion. Your younger eyes will devour it, I have no doubt of that. Take it, and use this lens to magnify the handwriting."

"What is it?" I asked as he handed me lens and paper which had printed on its head in crude lettering, 'Benjamin Rogers of Rogers Groceries, Falmouth, England...' I held the lens to the paper and began to read but Samaroo would not let me. He embraced me instead, unexpectedly. I felt small against his body, even shocked by his sudden intimacy. Corinne and my child whores must feel this way, I thought, but before I could dwell on this realisation, Samaroo freed me.

"Take it away and dwell on it in the solitude of yourself. When I started to read I sensed that I should do so in some isolation. I would have to withdraw a little from the world. Oh it's no Dead Sea Scroll or any such divine intervention in human affairs, no need to gaze in wonder at it. From what I can discern it's a patchwork of autobiographical notes from a young hand, I believe a priest's hand, though written on a grocer's notepaper. It's something of a curate's egg you can say, helter skelter, upside down, inside out. A jigsaw, the edges not quite matching, and you'll be intrigued by it because it's dense with puns – there's a garden and a guardian... but see for yourself. Take it and remember me by it."

I knew as soon as I received it that I would never see Samaroo again. He gave it to me in that spirit, placing it in my hands without meeting my eyes. "You know Lance," he said, turning from me, taking up a vase and inspecting its base. His voice slowed, losing its personality. He held the vase up to the light, turned it this way and that. He spoke haltingly, acting out the connoisseur assessing the quality of the vase but not committed to acquiring it. "You know Lance, some of our philosophy says – that a man is always confronted with choices – even though the decision he makes is preordained by the gods. We are not unfree but we are still – bound to act in obedience to a divine will. Some of us are destined to be saints, others to be brutes – and only the gods have an overarching understanding – as to why we must behave as we do. Is that shallow Hindu philosophy, or does it bear thinking about?"

There was a strange calm in his eyes as if he was unconcerned with his own question. He stared at the vase, to read the inscription on its base but not seeing the words. What was he trying to tell me? Was he forewarning me of the consequences of an act as yet unpremeditated? I left the shop for the last time, as baffled by his distant behaviour as I was shocked by the intimacy of his giving.

★

Predictable, the stages of our relationship. Firstly, the efforts Lance made to behave like a married man – a week's honeymoon in a Cambridgeshire country hotel, the breakfast trays, the presents, the prospect of other holidays, the breathless lovemaking. He redecorated his flat, allowing me generous space though I had wisely left most of my belongings at my parents' house. Then the slow unpicking of the knot he had tied himself in – excuses to stay late at the office, a reluctance to come to bed, the occasional quiver of irritation when I tried to embrace him. Then the odd hostile remark which eventually turned into a maelstrom of abuse, and the abject apologies and self-flagellation afterwards. I could have told him that it was his mother who was still tormenting him. He had wanted to escape Albion Hill, as she did, but it remained in his shadow and conscience. He had failed to transform himself into the powerful figure he yearned to be, a man whose fame, wealth and professionalism were such that his mother, in whatever obscure spot she found herself after abandoning him, and howsoever many years later, would come to hear of his translation. As it was he was a by-line in a provincial newspaper, allowed twenty paragraphs a fortnight to hype some insignificant play. I had boasted at the beginning of my great-grandfather who in the 1880s owned a thousand acres of Demerara canefield, with as many natives beholden to him for their livelihood. He had listened with great respect, chastened by a sense of his lowly background and small achievements.

In the final weeks he was hunched over his typewriter, working the keys furiously, ripping the paper from the barrel, tearing it up, inserting another sheet. I was amused by this sudden surge of activity. I resented his pretence at irate genius. For all his rage no work of art would materialise. He would remain an Albion Hill boy, thwarted, unfulfilled. He used to curse my father, calling him a fascist, but I came to appreciate the steady writing of my father, the complete devotion to Marinetti which one day would be given body in a series of leather-bound gilded volumes, privately printed for a select readership.

There was no need for an elaborate farewell. "I'll be back in a few weeks, I'll soon tire of my parents," I told him before setting off for Italy. He was visibly relieved by my decision to visit my parents. He made a fuss, buying me a new suitcase, pressing money into my hand, taking me by taxi to the airport. Miriam turned up a few hours before my departure.

"I brought you a gift for your mother," she said, fishing out a parcel from a plastic bag and opening it with pride. "It's ham. It's foreign, none of your rubbish from a Coventry pig farm. Lance used to like it, didn't you Lance?" She carefully rewrapped the silver foil around the meat. I took it from her, thanking her, assuring her of my mother's gratitude. Lance was sullen throughout our taxi ride, knowing that as soon as I got to the airport and bade him goodbye, I would deposit the ham in the nearest bin.

★

Thirty found me alone. I lay in bed for most of the day, thinking of all the money I had spent on Corinne, wondering where she had hoarded it, and how much she was worth in the end, what with the offerings of her other lovers, including the generous Jew. Did she achieve her three thousand pounds? Were the notes stuffed in her uncle's vases or hidden under a floorboard? Thirty found me trying to still my heart by dwelling on such banalities.

Beth had been gone for three weeks. The police had not turned up to question me about Corinne, though I had edited and polished my statement in readiness, reducing it to two pages of tepid prose.

I bided my time until darkness fell. I set off for the red light district of Coventry as a birthday treat. Apart from Corinne I had been faithful to Beth during the nine months of stifling marriage. The urge to tour the streets returned, and with Beth gone and given it was my birthday, I set off without being laden with guilt. The truth was I had spent the day resenting Beth's sudden departure. She had come too easily into my life, I should have been more defiant. And she left as casually as she had first met me. As to Corinne, I had denied my grief, and my pity for Samaroo (to whom I had not even sent a letter of condolence), by focusing on the composition and inner recital of my statement. Writing in a factual, even forensic, mode made Corinne disappear as a person and made my sexual relationship with her a simple matter of commercial transactions. Which is what it was, I admitted this much to myself. I wanted more. I wanted her exclusively and resented her favours to other men, especially the Jew, impotent and decrepit as he was. When I realised I was one among many I wanted her at least to show some enthusiasm for our lovemaking, but there was not the least flicker of delight. She merely took the money, lay down and stayed quiet during the act, moving or moaning only when I thrust too heavily, discomforting her. Afterwards, if I spoke tenderly to her, her eyes would light up with scorn. I was a plain-looking, overweight Englishman, hardly the paramour of her dreams. She must have been disgusted at the hoary colour of my skin, the freckles like dried-out sores. "You're beautiful, so beautiful," I once said to her, euphorically pleasured by her body in spite of its quiescence. I stroked her face and combed her hair with my fingers but she responded ungratefully, sliding away from me and, as she dressed, boasting about the Jew who would elope with her to America.

The streets were practically empty, which I thought strange, until I realised it was terror at the news of Corinne's murder. The whores had decided to migrate temporarily to another city which was what they did in situations of distress – when the police, for example, conducted their occasional purges or when an unsuspecting girl had been picked up by a client, taken to a derelict house only to find a gang there ready to batter her. The body – for that was what was left after her ordeal, a body alive but permanently bereft of mind – was eventually found, hospitalised, sensationalised by my newspaper. A comatose body now and then but there had not been a literal murder in living memory. I had come out to spy the new faces which was always an exciting prospect, especially after a lengthy absence from the streets. The new ones gave me hope that my appetite would never become exhausted. I fully expected to spend the rest of my life in the embrace of Coventry whores, and the new faces reassured me of the constancy of supply, whatever the actions of the police or the monstrous deeds of the odd client. As to the old faces, there was equal gratitude for their longev- ity, their loyalty to their trade. Of these I had half-a-dozen favourites whom I had known over a decade, going to the streets once or twice a week to choose between them. It was intriguing, sometimes disappointing, to notice how they changed with the years, invariably becoming more foul of aspect and speech. They had their regulars – men too nervous or fright- ened to go with other whores – so they no longer kept up appearances even though they gave the same satisfaction. "Better the devil you know than the angel you don't," one of them explained when I asked after the health of her trade. "My punters keep coming back. They know I don't cheat, which is more than you can say for that lot." She nodded contemptu- ously in the direction of some youthful competitors as we drove off. "That lot take your money and give you a quick shag and whilst they're doing it they're rifling through your pock- ets. You go home and there's no wallet. They've got your dosh, credit cards, address book, pictures of your wife and kids, and their pimps take it off them and start blackmailing you. Or the pimps sell all your credit cards, they end up in Bulgaria and all those nasty foreign places, and before long the Fraud Squad's banging on your door. Better to bang me, love, my pussy is clean, and my conscience, and all my punters swear by me. I never rob and I go to the doctor regular-like for a check up."

I spent an hour cruising, disappointed at being abandoned by my familiars, when I caught sight of a figure emerging from a block of council flats. I drove towards her as did other cars in my desperate situation. She was obviously very drunk or drugged for she swayed as she walked. The glare of headlights must have unsteadied her further for she staggered against the lamp post, hit her head and fell onto the pavement. I drove on, in my rear mirror seeing her grasp the lamp post in an attempt to rise. She fell back on the ground and fluttered like a maimed bird. The other cars sped past, seeking more appetising flesh. No one, including me, stopped to help her. She was only a whore, it was to be expected that she would experience such collapse. We all told ourselves that she was hardened to the cold, hardened to bruising. We could not be held responsible, neither for the causes nor the consequences of her chosen profession.

How often had I seen such figures beating themselves or wrapping their arms around their bodies to ward off the cold? Or sipping constantly from a liquor bottle, to keep alert? There were always one or two, ugly beyond desire, or of dubious reputations, who never attracted a client but who would stay out all night, alcohol their only companion. Driving round and round the streets I found them in the same spot. I admired their faith – there was no other word for it. I would see them eventually making their way home, empty-handed, dizzy of head. They too would sometimes stumble and fall, and I would drive past unconcerned, thinking that sooner or later a police car would stop for them.

Why then was I disturbed by the woman from the council flat who had slumped onto the pavement? I could have loitered in the area but I gave up my quest for sex and returned home. I felt hopeless and depleted. I switched on the television and switched it off immediately. The manuscript that Samaroo had given me stuck out from the magazine rack. I had put it there, promising myself to examine it soon, but Corinne had been murdered (mothered) that very night. I had forgotten the manuscript, occupied as I was with my defence against police questioning. I took up Samaroo's lens and read the opening paragraph. I was immediately drawn into the story, but the writing soon lost direction, becoming an agitated scrawl, recovering a few pages later. There were chapters of clarity, then sudden deterioration into notes, doodles, haphazard sentences, and what appeared to be words written backwards in the light of a mirror. The fine handwriting sometimes dwindled to a point where it became unreadable, even under the thick lens Samaroo gave me. It was as if the writer was secreting himself by such acts of diminution. I flicked through the pages, picking up the story here and there, but though suffused with passages of astonishing beauty, it made little ordinary sense. After an hour or so all I could gather was that it was the autobiography of a young Irish Catholic priest, set around the time of the First World War. Part of the story was placed in Guiana, where the young priest, a novice, had been sent, to assist the work of one Father Jenkins, an elderly missionary. The word Demerara kept recurring, as if to remind me of the promise I had made to Beth, to take her there for a holiday. It would have also been a mission to trace her ancestry, the scandal and intrigue of her Indian great-grandmother. Our relationship faltered, the promised journey was forgotten, until the idea was resurrected by the priest's manuscript.

Demerara, Guyana: at our first meeting Beth had talked of it as the place where her great grandmother had mated illicitly with an English planter. I remembered it from my school geography books as an obscure colony at the other end of the world. Sir Walter Raleigh had gone there looking for gold, but in more modern times it was the destination of English people fleeing from shame, failure or the attention of the authorities. What better place for me to escape or delay possible investigation by the police over Corinne's murder? But my desire to visit Demerara perhaps had a more idealistic motive. The spectacle of the whore staggering homewards had troubled me to the point of self-loathing for my nocturnal appetites. A few months' sojourn in Demerara would remove me from the scene of the grime, perhaps provide space for some form of cleansing. And I would have the priest's manuscript as inspiration and solace, for it seemed to tell of his quest for a purified faith. 'The Peace that passeth all understanding': the phrase was a recurring feature of his writing.

The next week found me impulsively at the airport, laden

with no more than money, the manuscript and a few belongings. I posted a note to my employer, stating that I would be away for an indefinite period. I put the pages I had prepared for the police into an envelope and addressed it to Samaroo. There was no covering letter. It would be his burden to read between the lines of the bald statement to discover my innocence or my guilt. On second thoughts I tore it up, depositing it in the nearest bin.

★

I came back as I had left, on impulse. Three months had passed but I was glad not to have heard from Lance. Nor did I seek to communicate with him. My parents made a show of welcoming me to their holiday cottage on the Mediterranean coast. They fussed over me for a day or two, and I lied about the state of our marriage, saying that Lance would be joining me as soon as his workload lightened. They soon returned to their selfish ways and were unconcerned when Lance failed to turn up, accepting whatever excuses I offered.

Three months of idleness and isolation, occupying myself with a little gardening, reading, the preparation of meals, but mostly walking to a favourite spot of beach where I would just sit and stare at the empty sea, wanting to clear my mind of the memory of Lance. At the end of each day I was healed a little more. His cursing and accusations grew dimmer and dimmer. I had arrived at the end of October. The chestnut trees were bleeding colours, a last rebellious stand against the onset of winter. Autumn berries shone in gay defiance of their fate. Everything seemed hectic and rapacious, a last fling at life, a last sucking of whatever nutrients remained in the soil. I thought of the ending of wars, when soldiers facing certain defeat would rampage through villages and towns, wanting to deflower, feast, behead, mutilate. The beauty of autumn, the frantic and spectacular burst of colours, took on a frightening aspect. I stayed indoors, glad for the darkening clouds, for the rain which veiled the landscape. The year ended in a comforting gloom in which I could lose sight of my marriage.

Then, to the alarm and delight of the country the winter ended abruptly. There was much talk in the media about the effects of global warming, the maiming of the spirit and the rhythm of the seasons. Father, deep in his books about war machines, paid no heed to warnings about natural catastrophes. Mother eagerly prepared her nets and jars for spring's harvesting of flamboyant species. I watched the slow resurrection of shoots in the winter garden, fledgling buds opening up into tiny flowers. Soon it would be the first anniversary of my marriage. It was a date I could not deceive myself into forgetting.

I returned to my parents' house in Coventry to discover that Lance had gone to Demerara soon after I left for Italy. There were many letters waiting for me which Alice had carefully set aside from the dozens of others for my parents. I wondered whether, in spite of her illiteracy, she had somehow intuited their importance, hence her safe keeping of them. I quickly banished such a thought from my mind. Alice was an idiot and would remain so for the rest of her life. There was nothing mysterious about her behaviour. She was attracted to the overlarge colourful stamps on the envelopes, that was all, I decided.

I read and reread his letters, and with the help of an atlas I was able to trace his journeying within Demerara. That was the easier part for the true challenge was to reconstruct his state of mind and his purpose in going abroad. I could never take what he said at face value. He was something of a shape-shifter, adapting to other people's moods or to other people's expectations of him. One moment he was an Albion Hill boy made good; another, a writer frustrated by the small tasks demanded by a local newspaper; another, a devoted or a hostile husband. The first letter started cryptically enough and I could imagine how much he had rehearsed the opening line to impress it upon me: 'December 20th 1991 – I have come to Demerara to find the priest in myself, and so be cleansed of sex.' I laughed aloud, not so much at the attempt of solemnity, but at the reference to sex, for he was a novice at this. Touring with theatre groups had initiated me into carefree sex. There was an easy transition from playing rogues and slatterns on stage to enacting fantasies in bed, and we had the costumes, blindfolds and thongs to hand. Lance was innocent of such erotica. He was shy, even apologetic in his reaching after me, and the sex was a swift spending of energy. I guessed that sex with prostitutes was like this, an awkward silent tussle before ejaculation, but I quickly dismissed my suspicion that Lance was a frequenter of whores, even though he never spoke of a normal relationship, or indeed of any relationship, prior to ours. His father had had such a reputation and there were hints that his mother had fled in disgust. No, Lance's whole life was in resistance to his father's failures, and if he was inexpressive in bed, it was perhaps because he was burdened by his father's doings. I forgave his inexperience, more drawn to his literary mind and the pathos of his past. I sensed his unease afterwards, his disappointment in his sexual performance and resentment at my superior competence. Later, in attacking my social class, I used to wonder whether his rage was not in truth fuelled by his sense of sexual disadvantage. But it was the romance of marriage I wanted, not the raging of flesh. I imagined us moving from Coventry to a city like Cambridge, where the theatres were intellectual, where he could fulfil his talents by reviewing classical plays and I could find more serious roles than panto-mime characters. He would be my entry into a life of the mind, into dramas that were fusillades of poetic language.

'I have come to Demerara to find the priest in myself and be cleansed of your sex...' the second letter began.

★

The National Archive promised much, if one believed the hugeness of the signboard announcing its existence. This was but one aspect of the oddity of the place, the bombast of signs. Businesses announcing themselves as 'Pillai & Sons, Suppliers of Building Materials' or 'Inshanalli & Co. Ltd., Dealers in Industrial Goods' and the like, turned out to be ramshackle shops, the few goods watched over by suspicious Indian proprietors. I was to learn from Manu that the Indians were on the lookout for quick-fingered Negro customers. "Negroes, oh god!" Manu said, "they just steal like they born to do so." He looked up to the heavens with melodramatic despair and made the sign of the cross (to curry favour with me, knowing me to be a Christian), first wiping his hand on his grocer's apron.

The National Archive was a row of dusty shelves tended by an elderly Negro. "We don't know nothing about a priest," the Negro said, as if denying a crime.

"He left England some time in 1914. He was not a priest then, but a boy of sixteen or seventeen. He came to work with one Father Jenkins, a Catholic missionary. Do you have records of ships arriving in Demerara in that year?"

"We only keep lists of slave ships," he said, malice exciting his face, giving it a momentary youthfulness. I glimpsed in it the courage and the rage of his slave rebel ancestors. Manu was to tell me later: "They quick to take offence. Just mention slavery and their minds go berserk and they want to smash and burn and kill. Slavery done two hundred years now but the Negro still feeding on the past. He too lazy to make effort for the present and the future, so he save up the past like a hoard of saltfish, and when he chew his mouth go sour and he spit. Negro does put a parcel of saltfish in the bank for savings, whereas everybody else – Chinese, coolie, even one-two buck people – put proper money."

The archivist was not only reluctant to help me but seemed to take delight in deflating my ambition. "You'll never find the boy, we don't have ship records and we don't collect private papers from that period except from Governor Generals. We don't have newspapers either, and even if we did, he would have to commit some crime to come to notice, and from what you say he was a Catholic missionary. A lot of them must have done crime but then in those days a white man could get away with murder, and it wouldn't get reported. And no point asking the Catholic church, all their papers burn up in the great fire of 1947."

The Librarian of the National College was similarly unhelpful, if more courteous. "A waste of time, people in this country just don't keep records, or else cockroach and moth eat them out. It's hard to preserve anything in this heat you know. But you must excuse me, we all busy with the Columbus exhibition which is going on show in a couple of months." He gestured to a heap of books and bundles of posters behind him.

"I wasn't aware that Columbus visited these shores," I said, puzzled by news of the exhibition. My first act when I arrived in Guyana was to seek out a history book. The two bookshops in the city had none, except for a slim text for schoolchildren. It told of Walter Raleigh's expedition into the interior to search for the fabled city of gold and its great chieftain El Dorado. He was the first of countless adventurers over the centuries, most of whom had perished in the Amazonian jungle from disease or hostile native arrow. The jungle interior of the country was littered with the bones of foreigners.

"Columbus didn't come this far if you go by the records, but you can never tell. He could've stopped off for a while on his way to somewhere more important. Just because it's not written down doesn't mean it didn't happen. Anyway, soon it's Columbus's five hundredth anniversary of discovering the New World, and an American foundation has given us money for a Columbus exhibition, and all those books you see, so we have to do one. Thirty years ago, when we were a British colony we'd have to obey whatever you told us to do, now it's the Americans who give the orders."

I thought I could hear a rising note of resentment in his voice. He too was a Negro. I left the library convinced of the futility of my task. I should have known, from the time I landed, that I had embarked upon an impossible quest to discover the priest. The sight of dilapidation – the tumble-down houses and the stinking canals – of the capital city, Georgetown, should have told me straight away that intellec-tual pursuits would be rare in such a place. People were too occupied with the immediate grind of living to contemplate the past, much less preserve its records.

"You can't blame we. We too shame to remember and when we do, we just feel guilt and anger," Manu explained. "All-you have castle and ting to mark time, and what we have? Mud huts that wash away with the rain and vines that choke and cover over burial ground, so no trace of the dead left." The Librarian, no doubt to get rid of me, had suggested I visit Mariella Settlement, twenty-five miles or so up the Demerara River. He remembered – though he could not swear upon it as a fact – that a Catholic mission station had been set up there countless years ago. From the information I had given him about my Irish visitor, it was likely he would have made his way there.

He was, of course, lying, or at the very least, misleading me. When I arrived, after a three-hour speedboat journey through jungle and rapids, there was only Manu and his company of malefactors. A huge signboard, 'Manu's Leisure & Hotel Services', met my eyes as we turned a bend in the river and headed towards a clearing on a high bank. The freshness of the lettering suggested that the sign was continuously maintained against the ravages of the weather. It was spectacularly odd and wholly unnecessary, for it was inconceivable that, after miles and miles of monotonous jungle, any traveller could overlook the clearing. The boatman grew agitated as we approached, chattering to me in an indecipherable tongue. He was reluctant when I tried to engage him in Georgetown, and I had read his hand signals as a demand for more money. We had settled on a sum but he still looked uneasy as we set off, remaining silent throughout the long journey. On arrival he helped me off the boat quickly, and no sooner had I steadied my feet on firm ground than he revved up his engine and sped away. I panicked and wanted to call after him but it was too late. I was on my own, in the middle of nowhere, waiting to be greeted. It was late afternoon, in an hour or so it would be dark. I thought of my whores in the alcoves and shadows of lonely streets. I thought of Corinne gagged and bound to her silent tree. I remembered them against my will, for my priest was failing me even before I had found him. It was he whom I sought to distract and redeem me from the past. I had come to this godforsaken spot hoping for a miracle but the boatman had abandoned me to the memory of my sinning.

★

"All-body here is foul, we is one spirit, no high or low, top or down, all is thief or abductor or bugger-man," Manu said, as if to excuse the filthiness of the room that was to be my accommodation until I could get back to the relative comfort of Georgetown. There were no sheets on the bed. The mattress was coated in stains. "Big hefty man come here, named John or Lewis, but after a month of pumping their seed their hand tired and they longing for a hole, any hole. They fall on each other so by the time they leave they name Joanna or Louisa. Eh eh, this place does really change you from the worst badman to whining pussy and bugger-battie, if I was you I'd watch me back! Not with me though. I is an Indian regular as rainfall and sunrise, I don't buck nature, I does just make money from bushpeople."

His was the only building in Mariella Settlement, a two-storey wooden structure. Upstairs there were four bedrooms, downstairs a grocery shop and a space containing a few tables which passed as a bar and restaurant. It was downstairs that I had my first evening meal, a stew of rice, black beans and pigtail (although a vegetarian Hindu, Manu's clients were mainly Negro pork-knockers – the local name for gold miners – so whatever religious sensibility he possessed gave way to the need to make money). Manu sat with me out of boredom rather than curiosity as to my origins. A white man in the midst of Demerara jungle should have provoked obvious questions but in the weeks I stayed he never once inquired of my life.

"They all run away, long long time back," he said when I asked about the emptiness of the place. "The native people," he explained when I looked puzzled. "They call Arawak. Bow and arrow folk, cassava eaters." He told me a dismal tale of how the once thriving village had been set upon by a gang of Spanish explorers and burnt to the ground. Those who survived the massacre hid in caves in the interior but the Spaniards, believing them to have escaped with the gold of the village, combed the forest until they were found, naked, shivering, half-starved, empty-handed. The Spaniards, cheated of treasure, hacked them to pieces, then returned to the village which they made into a base camp from which to launch raids upon other Amerindian communities along the river. "That was centuries ago, but like yesterday for Arawak people, time don't pass for them like for we, and that's why they hardly come back, though Spanish long pick up and gone. Arawak believe this place cursed, even today they 'fraid to land here. It hard doing business with this curse lying over the place. Only when fuck-time come, when the Negro pork-knockers emerge from the bush with gold, that one-two Arawak women turn up for a share, the more brazen ones who don't fear man much less jumbie spirits. I telling you, business really bad."

I awoke at dawn to the shriek of parrots, a noise as dreadful as the death cries of the Arawaks cornered in the caves. Manu was already in his shop, sitting behind the counter with a towel in his hand. The shelves behind him bore tins of food, mostly corned beef and ham. There was a row of rum bottles. Another section housed the hardware necessary for bush life: scissors, knives, thick two-inch long tarpaulin needles. "They get spoil overnight," he said, spitting upon the knives and polishing them one by one. "Rust, dust, cobweb, bat-spit, insect-shit, all of them does sour and soil the goods if you not vigilant." I watched him working on a needle, trying to restore its sheen. He was a small man, a dwarf almost, with a child's tiny eyes and face that appeared immature in spite of the greying bristles. He wore short pants and a vest, and his feet were unshod. He was totally bald and the sunlight trickled around his head, giving it a sparkle lost in his merchandise. "The bush turn things to mange," he said, fretting as he focused on cleaning the point of the needle. Then his mood lifted unexpectedly, he looked up at me with bright eyes. "But it's so beautiful, eh, all of this." He gestured outside to the river glittering with sunlight and the trees a wall of shimmering green. "They call wallaba tree or hackea, taronira, hayawa, dukaballi, the names sound like music, no? Best of all is the mara tree when a toucan sitting on its crown showing off its beak to God as if to give praise for making it more radiant than any other bird and promising to keep the colours fresh as on creation day. You see any when the boat bring you from Georgetown?" The sudden revelation of soulfulness confused me. Up until then his talk was common, even heartless. He had described the Arawak massacre in a matter of fact way, with no hint of pity or terror in his voice: "You see toucan? Any sakawinki monkey hopping from tree to tree follow you up-river?"

I had seen nothing on the journey. The jungle was stupendous in its vastness but I had closed my mind to it and to the spectacle of a sky gorgeous with tropical birds. It was surprisingly easy for me to put on my Albion Hill blinkers and dull my vision. I had done the same in Georgetown, refusing the enticement of its slums and its bars swarming with whores, safely cocooned in my hired taxi or in my own thoughts. My priest would have done the same. He would have arrived in a country of vice and hatred. He would have quickly discovered its brutal history. The English had shipped over Africans as slaves and worked them to the bone in their plantations. Then, short of labour, the English had imported countless coolies from India. The planters set African against Indian, Indian against African, the English excelling at the training of fighting cocks, fighting dogs. Above all, my priest would have realised the real origin of evil, which lay in the clearing of spaces in the jungle, the draining and ploughing of the land for the growth of sugarcane. The planters had to suppress Christian conscience, take up whip and drive their slaves and coolies to work. The jungle was as unruly as it was vast, hundreds of thousands had to be sacrificed in the effort to tame it. Only a murderous heart and a mechanical will could bring success to such an enterprise. And the bush would muffle the sounds of the killings, making them more bearable. And the planters would be absolved of guilt for the news of the killing did not travel abroad. My priest would have seen the spite in the planters' faces. He would have been appalled at the sight of Africans and Asians made mad by labour and quick to resort to violence against each other at the slightest call. He would have left Georgetown as soon as possible, seeking the sanctuary of a monastery up-river, far from the cesspit of human emotions. I had followed this path, dwelling not on the journey through awesome landscape, but on the prospect of arrival at a state of simple piety. I had landed instead at the house of a hypocrite, one who saw no contradiction between deceit and cleanliness of heart.

"I keep my place spick and span, every month I paint the signboard to make it fresh as toucan-beak. Look at the ceiling, not a trace of cobweb, it clear as the sky because every day I brush and re-brush it. You can tell a good shop from how the ceiling is."

"Oh, how is that?" I asked, pandering to his pride, for I was totally dependent upon him for my welfare, being in the middle of the jungle.

"If the top not clean, what about the cock, what about the bottom, what about the space between my toes?" He rubbed his shiny head in mock self-congratulation and giggled. I too found the gesture comic and shared in his vulgar mirth. A bond developed instantly between us and I knew I could be relaxed in his company.

"What about the bedrooms though, they're crawling with fleas and my mattress stinks," I said, confident in my boldness.

"That's nigger space up there, I don't bother disinfecting it. When the pork-knockers come all they want is rum, pigtail stew and buckwoman pussy. They smell like fowl-coo and vomit everywhere. Flea cleaner than they. If I was flea, I would move out without even taking one suck in case I drop dead with poison. And the Negroes insist on drinking from bone, no glass or tin mug for them. I keep a set only for them." He reached into the drawer beside the counter and drew out six bone tumblers. "Each is a goat-skull which I hack and shape to make cup. Imagine the savages! The trouble I have to put up with, the business not worth it!" He opened a new bottle of rum and poured me a drink (in a glass, out of respect). I reached into my pocket and drew out some money. "No, no, take it free, drink, food, lodging, I never charge whiteman when they stay here." I was taken aback not by his generosity (though this was surprising in itself, having grown up in Coventry where the Indian proprietors of corner shops gathered in every penny) but by his mention of previous white visitors. "Once in a blue moon they come, scraven for God, more hungry than wild dogs tearing at a deer. If you see their white faces you frighten, they so hot with fever! I does feed them fish stew and wait for them to go. Only last year one of them show up. He stay for a whole month and try to convert me to Catholic, and I use to pray and make sign to please him because I feel sorry for him, how he look so desperate like he is a convict break out and running from the devil. Thank God when Arawak pussy arrive, followed by a gang of Negro pork-knockers, like Mary coming to the manger and Wise Men turning up. The whiteman take one look at them sinners and flee. He pay me for my boat and paddle off, and he so hurry that he left book behind. Look, I still have it." He reached into the same drawer beside the counter and this time drew out a Bible.

"Who tore out the pages?" I asked, flicking through it and noticing the stubs of several missing sections.

"I sell to the Negroes to roll tobacco in, the paper so fine. But mostly I wrap eggs with it, it keep the shell clean and the insides too. If I wrap egg in any other kind of paper, the egg turn gander in two-three days, but with Bible book-paper the egg stay fresh, is a magic, eh? But tell me Mr. Lance, you too come here looking for God?"

I went upstairs and returned with the priest's bundle of notes. I showed a page to Manu. He stared at it with great curiosity, prodding a finger at the heading. "What it say there, tell me, I not shame to admit I stupid with the English." I read it to him: 'The Falmouth Relief Society for Heathen Guiana. Secretary: Benjamin Rogers of Rogers Groceries, Falmouth village, England, purveyor of the finest quality of affordable goods.'

"Is a man like me then who write that, a man in business? So you not come for God but to look for your dadee who had shop in colonial days, eh?"

I explained to him that though the notepaper belonged to some English grocer, the writing on it was the story of a priest's life, or rather, that of a young man destined to become a priest who journeyed to Guyana in 1914. I had no true answer as to why it was so. One of the notepapers had scrawled on it, in a hand uncertain of literacy, 'Dear Father Jenkins, hear is some donnations from the people of Falmouth for use among the savagges. May God keep you safe from there spears.'

Manu laughed heartily at this, as if recognising his own

condition and the jungle state in which he existed. "Paper short in old-time days, so when priest come Guyana he take whatever he find, which is grocerpaper of good whiteman who collect candle and cloth and send it for the natives."

"Perhaps so," I said, not wanting to hurt Manu by telling him my own version of events, which is the priest had deliberately written his life on a grocer's paper in contempt of those who worshipped at the altar of commerce (I thought of Beth's father and her wealthy forebears) or else to redeem such people from their meanness of spirit. "But why do other white men come here in the first place?" I asked.

"Cause big church used to be here. In the middle of the bush a church with tower and bell."

"So there was a monastery here after all," I said excitedly. "How do you know about it?"

"Me dadee tell me. He read it in a book. He read plenty book, Bible too, and he tell me Bible story. Me dadee clever like that. Is he put up the sign outside and though I can't read it and he long dead, I does keep it fresh to remember him. Like how some people does put flower on grave, so every month I does paint the sign, to honour me dadee. Is he name Manu, is he set up the shop, and it pass to me when he dead. Me not name Manu, is me dadee name so. Me really called Rajah. Rajah is me true name but I answer to Manu cause of what write on the sign. When me dadee come, years back, only wall left, you could never tell it was a church, but me dadee read it in a book, and he build shop on the same spot." His eyes glistened as he remembered his father's initiative. He wiped the sadness away with the towel he used to polish his goods. "Me muma dead when I was boy, me not know she, me too small and me dadee heart break. He burn she, sprinkle the ash on this same river and leave Georgetown forever. He come here because it far and lonely, but it still close to the river, so every morning he wake up and stare at the river and remember me muma face, and he take flower and fruit and throw it into the water to bless she spirit." He dabbed his eyes again, unable to continue. When he eventually recovered he told me, haphazardly, the life of his father. Manu had come to grieve in the isolation of the jungle, forsaking his brothers and sisters in Georgetown. He became a mother to Rajah. He told him stories at bedtime. He made him soup when childhood fevers seized him. Took him to the riverbank every morning, soaped and scrubbed him, until he was big enough to bathe himself. Taught him to count money, so one day he could run the shop. Taught him how to make a slingshot out of wood, twine and pieces of rubber. How to whistle loudly by rolling back his tongue and blowing around his fingers. How to imitate bird cries and monkey chatter. Two of them by themselves mostly, Rajah like a shoot to a bigger tree. One day, for no reason at all, the father died. He went to bed as normal but just didn't wake up in the morning. Rajah took him to the riverbank, soaped and scrubbed him, then laid him on a pyre of hayawa wood. Beautiful, the name of the tree, and it gave off a perfume when it burned. He scraped the ashes and sprinkled them into the river where they could mingle with his mother's.

Rajah loved the river, the receptacle of his parents' ashes and he spoke of it in terms of magical revelations. "When tide low all kinda tings does wash up, as if the riverbed convulse and cough up what does choke it. Sometimes knives and guns, sometimes pieces of chain wrapped round bones, and when you put them together you get a picture of longtime Negro slave-people breaking chain and running away from plantation, and whiteman chasing them all the way in the bush, but when whiteman go to catch them, they jump into the river and prefer to drown. Or else they grasp whiteman weapon, wrestle it from he and throw into river. Mostly glass bottles, which you can tell from the strange shapes is from another age. Dutch soldier, Spanish soldier, English soldier, everybody had fort here and there along the river, and when they drunk they throw bottle in the water. Put it to your nose and you can still smell the rum and beer which is like jumbie – what we does call ghost – in the bottle. The river full of jumbie from the past which suddenly appear and shine in the mud like silver fish, sunlight flick off the glass so they look as if they living. You believe ghost people does come back and live, or you believe they dead-dead?"

"I don't know what I believe," I said. Sensing a weariness in my voice his own mood changed and his talk was tinged with sadness.

"We is Hindoo folk, we believe when we dead we turn into cat or crocodile or centipede. Every morning my dadee drop a few grain sugar on the grass outside the house for the ants to feed, in case me muma come back small and brown like one of them. So me dadee feed she. But I believe me dadee come back bright and royal. Whenever toucan settle on the crown of mara tree, I know is me dadee I seeing. And he keep watch over me. I is a prince, that is what Rajah mean in English. But all the whiteman I tell this to sigh, just like you." A huge black butterfly flew into the shop as if seeking refuge from the blinding sunshine. It settled on the top of a rum bottle. Rajah immediately flicked his towel at it. Stunned, it fell to the ground and Rajah mashed the life out of it. He wiped the top of the rum bottle of any traces of the butterfly. Obviously Hindus were not reincarnated as butterflies, or else his goods were more precious than the soul of some migratory coolie. I gave him a look of disgust but he was oblivious to it, resuming his storytelling with an innocent air.

"Just so you sigh, whiteman sigh too who pass this way. They're running to God or running from God and they get so confused with the to and fro that they don't know what to believe, what not to believe. Seven days pass, they pack bag and go back to Georgetown. But not the last whiteman, he was one mudderass madman. He go the other way, take my boat and paddle toward Pillar." His voice trailed off in a frightened whisper as he explained to me the perverse behaviour of the man. Pillar was a spot a few miles upland, watched over by huge black rocks which the Arawaks believed to be eggs laid by the deities of another tribe. The water beyond Pillar was suddenly treacherous but the worst of it was the spirit inhabiting the bush. "It call Kanaima," Rajah said, spitting as soon as he spoke the word and scraping his tongue clean with his teeth. "It come to the stranger – the weary, the hungry, the lost traveller – in the shape of a child bearing cassava bread or an old man holding up the lines of his palm as a guide to the forest's pathways, or

87

a woman with stiff nipples and a song on she lips." According to Rajah, Kanaima befriended the traveller, fed him, danced for him, slept with him, but when he woke up he found his throat slit though he was still alive. They cut out his heart, his kidneys, his liver, unspooled his guts. They ate all of his insides, left him a husk to wander through the bush howling, begging to be favoured by death. The odd traveller who by some miracle refused the beguilements of Kanaima stumbled out of the bush in a state of complete imbecility. "Big big man turn toad, hop, hop, hop, like salt sprinkle on they back and they torment. If you pin them to the ground and ask them what happen, they open they mouth and croak. You can't get sense from them."

"Have you ever come across such a man yourself?" I asked when Rajah paused to contemplate the dread of what he had uttered. But he squinted at me without seeing the ridicule on my face.

Manu, the great maker of ancient Hindu laws. This much I knew from Samaroo who had lectured me on Manu's attempt to tame (maim) human appetites. I envisaged Rajah's father, also called Manu, as a lesser reincarnation of the legendary Lawgiver. A cunning coolie, he had migrated from the city, unable to compete with the shopkeepers there. He had found a niche market in an abandoned settlement upriver, catering for the pork-knockers who paid in gold. In his business he maintained a semblance of order, painting and repainting his signboard, polishing his bottles and tins, laying them out neatly and precisely on appointed shelves. The Lawgiver as grocer, regulating his life by adding and subtracting figures, raising or lowering his prices according to the shortage or surfeit of particular goods. When he died the property passed to his son, but the son lacked the discipline of the father, lacked the chastity involved in the calculation of sums. The son kept the shop methodically, but he was seduced by the forest. This was evident from the state of the bedrooms, the unclean sheets, the stained mattresses, the fascination with the debauchery of the pork-knockers and their whores which was connected in some peculiar way with his delight in Arawak myth.

The next day, as if wanting to reveal some aspect of his

character, he insisted on taking me on a river tour. "Pi-pi-you. Pi-pi-you," he called out imitating the whistle of a bird. "Look she there, look," he said, pointing to the treetops but I couldn't spot it, though it called at us constantly as we rode past. "Listen," he said, raising his paddle from the water to bring the canoe to a stop. "Listen, you hear that? Crat-crat-cratak-crat-cratak. Is a crow, what we call blanbie-bird, you does hardly hear it and never see it because they black and merge into the shadows of leaves and keep quiet quiet like they is stuffed birds. When you hear it, is good luck will come to you, a lot of good luck I tell you. Listen, it calling again, a whole heap of good luck will happen for we!" I strained my ears to catch the crow's call, but the previous bird was pi-pi-youing so frantically that I missed it. Let good fortune come to Rajah, he was blessed with hearing attuned to the noises of the jungle. I did not begrudge him the solace of superstition.

"Arawak people believe that everything get magic in it, more than we coolie," he said looking at the flowers and fruit floating down the river, palm nuts, yellow hog-plums and clumps of water hyacinths making their way to a suitable shore. The open river glowed with a fervent heat and the water was warm to touch. In parts not a ripple disturbed the surface which was like a polished mirror, reflecting a peacock-blue sky. Rajah explained that the heat made the fish retire to the depths below, hence the stillness of the water's surface.

We swung left and turned into a creek. Huge trees greeted us, towering to a height of more than a hundred feet, from which hung festoons of creepers decorated with spectacular flowers. The smaller trees came as near to the bank as they dared, and then stopped, allowing a crowd of prickly shrubs to extend themselves into the ooze. We paddled past thickets of ferns and mangroves with their branches extending outwards and downwards like the legs of the spider without its bloated abdomen, to a point where the creek was almost closed by a lattice of bush-ropes. We tied up the boat and I waded through the muddy foreshore, careful not to step on crabs scurrying for shelter, and followed Rajah into the jungle arcade. I was immediately jolted by the gloom and chill of the air.

"It surprise you, no?" Rajah asked, seeing me shivering.

"I thought the jungle would be a cauldron of tropical heat and light."

Rajah laughed at my naïveté. "Treetops hem out the light. Look how them vines like thread sewing all the treetops in one so that they can stay the sun."

My eyes grew accustomed to the masked and filtered light, and I was even more startled by the profusion of vines. They hung from all heights, some taking root as soon as they touched the ground. Others sent out parallel, oblique or horizontal shoots in all directions, making bridges and pathways in the sky. Strangest of all was the sight of a huge tree uprooted and dangling in mid-air, still alive though not grounded in soil, its trunk still sending forth new branches. A thunderstorm must have toppled it but the vines caught it before it could fall. It lay suspended in a cradle of vines, some of which took root in its trunk, like feeding cubes, and I thought of my father in his final days attached to drip-feeds. I was suddenly overcome by the frightfulness of the scene, the frenzy of life in the trees, the evidence of death beneath my feet where the earth was soft with the dust of rotted leaves, rotted insects. Armed with a cutlass, Rajah wanted to go deeper into the jungle but I feigned illness and went to sit down on a log. It looked solid enough but crumbled immediately under my weight. Rajah laughed again as I lay sprawled on the ground.

"Never trust what you see, the thing dead years now and insect eat out the inside, but the bark still look fresh like woman does brighten she face with powder to hide she sickness." He pointed to a mora tree which towered to the sky, straight as a pillar, its branches high and ornamental. "The tree dying in truth. Come back six months and you will see it fall over. You know why?" He took pleasure in his superior knowledge, explaining to me in an excited creole the infirmity visited on the majestic giant mora by a solitary bird, a tiny featureless bird stopping to take breath, depositing on a branch an undigested seed, flying off a few seconds later. Out of the seed a wild fig tree was born, rooted in the thick branch of the mora, usurping its resources, raising itself into full bearing on its sap. Soon the fig tree so thrived that it reared out of the topmost branches, seeking the sun first. It drank up the light even as it sucked up the juices of the mora. The fig tree burst into fruit but this very moment of triumph contained its downfall. Birds, eager for its fruit, were drawn to it. They deposited the seeds of different species of vines in its branches. The fig tree became infested. Vines sprouted from it like a haemorrhage.

"Mora nourishing fig tree, fig tree nourishing vine, too much. Mora bound to die, too much burden to feed everybody, never mind woodpecker and woodlouse. Look, you can see how some branches already droop. First mora will dead, then fig tree, then vine, but don't fret, some other seed will fall on the funeral heap and a new growth come out of the rotting belly. Nothing ever dead-dead for true."

We took to the boat again, heading homewards, leaving behind the tangled brake of tropical scenery. Rajah made one last stop at the mouth of the creek, climbing up a tree overlooking the water. Lodged in a fork was a great clump of an orchid, its flower stems loaded with yellow butterfly-like blossoms hanging over in every direction, with panicles rising to an astonishing height. It was a picture of graceful beauty but Rajah climbed the tree and hacked it off. It fell thickly into the mud. Rajah shoved it into the water and held it under with a long bamboo. The orchid's roots soaked and I watched with dreadful fascination ants rising to the surface, covering the water in black patches. Several larger forms could be seen swimming through the patches. These turned out to be cockroaches but not all the occupants of the orchid were dislodged, for soon I spotted a centipede, a full foot long, struggling in the crowd. Satisfied that the plant was purged of all parasites he brought it to the surface and heaved it into the boat. "Orchid like this one fetch plenty dollar in Georgetown, but I go plant it in front of my hotel, it so pretty. When I in the shop and look out I will see the orchid and the river beyond." There was an unexpected tenderness in his voice and I began to believe what he had declared earlier to me in the forest arcade. "I love all this, I is priest in this land," he said, gesturing to the trees around us. Their tops were joined together like a cathedral's dome, light slanting and fanning out as through a prism of stained glass. "I love tree more than woman," he whispered and I was convinced by the tremulousness of his confession. Perhaps he was not the small-minded grocer I suspected him to be. Perhaps the strangeness of the place had got to him. I remembered Geoff, his story of magical seeds germinating into fish, which caused us such merriment. Here, in the midst of the jungle, Geoff would find a home. Indeed, Rajah would think of Geoff's story as a trifle, for Rajah knew that you could plant a seed and in a little time it would surge upwards to breach the sky. Rajah knew, from Arawak sources, that giant creatures lived beyond the clouds, that if you climbed to the top of a vine and peeped over the ledge of a cloud, you would be flabbergasted at the monstrosity of what you saw. There would be no words to describe it. When the giants spoke, even in hushed tones, the earth beneath shook with thunder. In the daytime when they fought they bred hurricanes, blizzards, tornadoes. At night when they made love, lightning came out of the mouth of darkness, tongues of gold licking the tresses of the forest.

The blanbie-bird had indeed brought Rajah good fortune for when we reached the hotel an Arawak woman had taken up residence, slinging her hammock between two posts. Stone in hand she knelt on the ground surrounded by what looked like a collection of chrysalids. She cracked one open with the relish of an English child opening up a hazelnut.

"They does eat caterpillar from special palm tree," Rajah said twisting his face in disgust. "Look at she necklace – it make from peccary teeth, and she bracelet is beetle-wing." I gazed upon the bizarrely decorated woman, at her gleaming black hair. She had a creased face but youthful, almost immature breasts. I kept a respectful distance but Rajah stood over her as she sucked at the insect cases, explaining to me the habits of her people as if she was an animal at a marketplace and he the owner anxious to point out her body of value. She remained silent, seeming not to notice us, chewing on her food. "She don't talk. They stay dumb even if you kick them. Is because they know what we can't even imagine. They see and dream things which still them." As if to prove his case Rajah raised his foot in a threateningly manner but the Arawak woman (or girl) didn't flinch, concentrating on the nature of stone and shell.

Her presence announced the coming of the pork-knockers. They would arrive the next day, Rajah said gleefully, retiring to his shop to prepare his goods, not bothering to take the orchid out of the boat even though it was certain that it would wilt and die before morning. He had promised to take me to the caves, the scene of the Arawak massacre, but in the coming days he would be preoccupied with serving the appetite of the Negroes in return for their gold. Other Arawak women would turn up and the hotel would be a bacchanal of sex and rum. I withdrew to my room and unwrapped the priest's bundle of papers. In the fading light I read them for the umpteenth time. I struggled to decipher the handwriting, to arrive at his troubled self. My priest's story was broken and haphazard. Cryptic lines. Gnomic paragraphs. Obscure notes. Doodles. Impossible puns. I would mend the sentences, make them flow, give them purpose and direction. I would design his life and where there were holes and gaps I would conceive of incidents and themes. My landfill would be my imagination but I would draw too on actual people I knew, give them places in the story. Miriam, her children, my father, Geoffrey, Beth, Corinne – they lived ordinarily, purposelessly, even stupidly. I would revise their existence on the page, or originate a new existence for them. As for me, I too would subject myself to the alchemy of writing, hoping for some measure of renewal, some fulfilment of potential or else a complete transformation of self. The priest's autobiography would at times become mine, populated with my Albion Hill relatives whom I would resurrect in different forms so that hidden aspects of their character could come to light. Or if in real life they had no depth, nothing to be revealed, then I would reinvent them altogether. If, because of my superior education, I owed them anything, then it was to rewrite them.

I lit a flambeau, took out my typewriter, wiped its keys, put on a fresh ribbon and fed it paper. Gnats and flies drawn to the light fell into the open flame, creating a litter underneath it. Smaller moths burnt their wings and dropped, whilst now and again a great sphinx came fluttering along, seeking its death. I typed and typed, pausing to listen to the creaking of hammock ropes downstairs. The Arawak woman was lying beneath me, an unexpected revelation and muse. Rajah's explanation of her silence was deceitful. She was no creature awed into speechlessness by the mysteries of the spirit world. Years of abuse by pork-knockers had reduced her to her condition. She kept returning to them, out of ordinary poverty. I resumed my opening up of the priest's history, keys striking paper like hailstones, for I suddenly hungered for the chaste flesh and sacredness of his being.

★

'I came to Demerara to cleanse the priest of your sex and lose my own self...' It was the final variation of the opening line of his first letter. The other letters prepared me for his eventual disappearance. He spoke of Demerara's past – wars, plunder, slave rebellions, coolie riots. The memory of death was everywhere he said, even though the Whites, Indians, Negroes, Chinese and Amerindians had long stopped slaughtering each other. The idols – and there were hundreds of them in temples and thatched huts – bled routinely and there was no flurry of excitement when they did, no crowd of curious reporters. The Guyanese saw in the bleeding the nature of their past. If their gods reminded them of violence, so did creatures at the other end of the scale of existence.

'Your mother would be in her element here among the insects,' he wrote contemptuously. 'Even as I type ants are rummaging out of every chink and cranny of my room. They've caught a cockroach. In vain it tries to run or even fly, several ants have taken hold and will not lose their advantage. Soon every particle of soft flesh will be eaten, and nothing remain but the two wing-sheaths and the covering of the thorax.' His fascination with such killings was betrayed by the detail of description, but his mood changed abruptly to despair. 'My priest left Coventry hoping to escape war but landed here, amidst people afflicted by history. The English, the French, the Dutch, even whilst warring with each other, shipped all manner of people from Africa and Asia, setting black against brown against yellow, dividing and ruling, making money from the squalor. My priest would have been bewildered by the universality of killing. The insects of hatred would have eaten away his tenderness. My landlord Rajah swears that a whiteman like him would have soon grown corrupt, like a carcass left out in the tropical sun. Rajah says the whores would have swarmed over him, picked him clean of virtue and money.'

He lifted himself from his depression by turning on me. 'Who knows, perhaps your great-grandmother was one of those whores. When I first arrived I thought to search her out but people don't keep records here, not in terms of paper anyway. They preserve the past in the way they act, so the place is overrun by light-fingered whores. Your great-grandmother has appeared to me in different forms. Sometimes she is gaily frocked and powdered, a hibiscus threaded in her hair. She speaks softly as she offers to pour my drink, but as soon as another woman approaches my table she snarls, bares her teeth like a common dog, dropping all pretence at good breeding, good grooming. Sometimes she is in a maid's uniform, sweeping the pavement with a pointer-broom, pausing to smile and wink as I walk by, and when I ignore her, hurling some comment after me in broken English. Sometimes she peeps out at me behind jalousied windows, housebound by Hindu marriage, hopeful that by some magic I would remove her to happier climes. Mostly your ancestor sits on a market stool behind a tray of mucous fish, calling out like a wounded forest bird, "Banga-mary, mary, come buy me banga-mary." She is torn and gaunt. She has bad teeth and lice. Her arms, thin with malnutrition, bear pagan tattoos.'

Such vindictiveness made me doubt the veracity of his description of Guyana. The stench and sickness he found there were aspects of his self-disgust. Especially his final letter, the rage and the sadness of it, which was exactly as I remembered him. In it he cursed Rajah as a high priest of debauchery, feeding the bush Negroes a communion of pork stew and rum. To be sure, Rajah was chaste. He had no desire for a wife, gratified instead by the sexual brutishness of his tenants and the gold they left behind. Rajah stood by as the Arawak woman was abused, or else he suggested even more ingenious tortures. On their last day, to strengthen their spirits for the return to the bush, Rajah suggested they smear molasses over the woman's body, stake her to the ground and watch in enjoyment as insects were lured to her. 'She should have screamed as ants and marabuntas bit and stung her but she kept her mouth shut literally and barely twitched. Was her silence an act of defiance, a refusal to surrender to these brutes? Or was it a necessary price to pay, given her need? For they will let her go with a boat full of food and some gold nuggets. They could cheat her, but in the end they will be fair-minded, even generous. Who am I to judge them? Am I any better than them? And what of your father who stakes his workers to the ground of poverty, screws them with low wages? No, I do not engage with them. In the seven days they have stayed here I've kept my distance. They were initially curious about my presence but their hunger for Arawak flesh quickly took precedence over me. You have to understand their loneliness, weeks upon weeks panning for grains of gold in a jungle stream, not a woman in sight, and the rum running low. Monkeys steal their food supplies, snakes invade their camp, vampire bats, alligators. Demerara makes devils of them. In the daytime they sleep, for the sun is cruel sovereign of the sky. At six the sun slips behind the trees, slips off the horizon in a blaze of colours, like a grand abdication. The devils awake, Rajah becomes prince of their ceremonies, bringing out their goat-skull vessels and bottles of rum.

I light a flambeau, take out my typewriter and focus on my priest's story. The more they curse and lash out and fornicate in the darkness, the more I close my ears and eyes to their doings. Instead I cleanse my priest of the jungle, untangling him from vines, washing his body of the mud of a mangrove swamp. This brothel was built on the ruins of a monastery, but I will restore the sanctity of the air by writing of my priest.

When my task is done, I will be free to set off for Pillar. As soon as I've looked upon the cleansed face of my priest I will depart in peace. You may say that I am suffering from sunstroke or gone mad with jungle fever. Say what you will, but I will go to Pillar and beyond. I believe the priest travelled there and returned whole. I will take the Arawak woman as my guide and spirit and intuition.'

"Lance's run off with some whore in Demerara," I told Miriam, baring my jealousy. Miriam looked at me in disbelief. "It's all in here," I said, showing her the letters, wondering whether she was literate enough to read them, for she looked dutifully at the envelopes' bright stamps before handing them back. "He's seen the light, or rather the darkness, hallelujah, and he's departed in peace!"

"But he hates black people, ever since some boy at school teased him, said that our mum run off with a darkie," Miriam said protesting his innocence.

"Oh he's with a darkie alright, a nasty little lawless clod. The letters strive after purity but beneath all the poetical flourishes there's only filth."

Miriam sighed in hurt and I remembered the good manners of my upbringing. "But I've not offered you anything, forgive me. I've been so worried about Lance." I signalled to Alice to bring in some refreshments. "And how are Sarah and the boys?" I asked as Miriam bit anxiously into a sandwich.

"They're all right. Sarah's sprog'll be out any day now. She's as rounded as one of your doorknobs. That's all she talks about, doorknobs. Day and night, doorknobs. They get obsessed that way when they're pregnant you know."

I didn't know but smiled sympathetically.

"If it's a boy they'll call it Lance, Ethel for a girl, old-fashioned like. Steve is still doing carpentry, Mark is looking for work."

"I can ask my father to employ him," I offered reluctantly.

"He'll be chuffed when I tell him. But don't worry yourself, you've got Lance to think of, poor dear. Will you go to Guyana to fetch him back?"

She was in such distress that I wanted to please her. "I'll go,"

I lied. The prospect of Guyana was appalling. Not just the savagery of the place but the journey into my own past. Lance was always backward-looking, tethered to the hurts of his childhood. No, let him lose himself in the darkness of the jungle, in the lap of some primitive. My marriage was an error, I would annul it as soon as possible. I was young and foolish, thinking I could find romance with him. I would return to the carefree life of the stage. Or I would chose another career, assuming a position in my father's business. Or I would go to Italy, work as a teacher of English. The future held out manifold possibilities once I freed myself of the idealism that made me marry Lance. Miriam seemed to have read my mind.

"Don't worry about us, we'll be all right. Albion Hill people have gone on forever, will go on forever. And your folk too. They'll go on the same." She gestured to the finery around her, the sitting room with its rich carpet, rich furniture. "Nothing changes. Except for the odd one like Lance. He got out of Albion Hill but I never thought he'd go so far as Demerara!"

"I'll search for him and bring him back," I lied again. My father was a man of power. He would speak to his contacts and before long English detectives would be dispatched to Guyana to locate Lance. I suppressed a desire to laugh as I thought of the detectives coming across a naked Lance in some mud hut beyond Pillar, eating from a bowl of caterpillars and protesting as they hauled him away, as if the English were Kanaima in disguise. I imagined his native spouse suddenly finding her voice, screaming at the white men, raining blows on them, in her agitation tribal feathers falling from her hair, the hut becoming like the scene of a colourful cockpit. Fortunately the doorbell rang, I quickly recomposed my mind. Miriam, obviously uncomfortable at being in such plush surroundings, remembered some task she had to complete and left hurriedly. I would not see her again. Later that day I would put my wedding ring in an envelope and post it to Sarah. The cluster of diamonds in a platinum setting would no doubt delight her for the rest of her life, or she could sell it to provide for her inevitably fatherless urchins. In any case it was Lance's money that bought it, money he should have given back to his Albion Hill tribe.

Alice showed the newcomer in. The presence of the visitor troubled her as if she sensed some impending danger. She was shaking and her mouth opened and closed in a silent jabber.

"Samaroo," he said, bowing. He sat down with a dignified movement, straightening his tie and smoothing the end of his moustache. I was struck by the imperiousness of his manner. He spoke in measured tones, in immaculate English.

"Madam I have brought you a message from Lance," he said opening his leather briefcase (beautifully weathered by age, I thought) and drawing out a package. "It came in the post last week from Guyana. It's somewhat confusing and unfinished but I read it with much interest."

"What is it?" I asked, taking the package, my hands quivering against my will.

"It's a mystery to me but I suspect it's Lance's reconception of his own life, his reincarnation if you like, though it purports to be that of a priest. He has secreted himself in the vestments of the Church. But no, maybe something more queer, a blending of his life with a priest's, a kind of sacred marriage or master-slave wedlock…"

"Why should Lance be writing to you?" I asked.

He brushed aside the hint of jealousy in my voice and recounted his friendship with Lance, the initial chance encounter at the Hindu temple and the long hours of discussion in his antiques shop. "He had a huge curiosity in our Hindu avatars, the different manifestations and resurrections of our gods as princes or beggars or animals, but his hunger came to a swift end when my Rohini died. He stopped coming to my shop. No doubt you would have read of the tragedy in my family, the murder of my Rohini." Alice's distress erupted at the mention of the murder, her hands flailing the air in combat with some unseen demon. As Samaroo rose to leave, Alice backed off from fright and ran from the room.

"Forgive her, she's disabled," I said, but Samaroo didn't seem to notice her, or if he did, his culture must have prevented him showing any sign of offence at her behaviour. The world he belonged to was alien to me. In it, perhaps women behaved as strangely as Alice.

"I am deeply sorry to hear of Rohini's death," I said, lying for the third time that morning. He bowed, acknowledging my condolence. He stood before me gathering his thoughts, struggling to arrive at an orderly statement.

"I believe you will find in the package an expression of guilt," he said at last. "Whether the guilt is real or imagined is a matter which I have not yet resolved. Rohini was destined to die, and if it was by Lance's hand, there is no need for contrition or forgiveness. What compelled both of them to suffer as they did – for to act or react is one and the same participation in suffering – was beyond their understanding. He may have bound and burned her but he himself was inflamed and constrained by urges beyond his recognition. This is the wisdom of the texts I taught him. You may accuse me of inciting him to kill by freeing him of responsibility for the act, blaming the gods instead. But I was thinking neither to abet him nor to discourage him, not even to warn him. I was merely introducing him to the philosophy of our books."

I was dumbstruck at his words, but he would say no more, as if himself confused by the stupidity of his utterance. A murdered Indian girl. Nobody responsible but Hindu gods. Lance dressed in priest's robe and surplice. Lance fornicating with a savage in the bush, beyond Pillar, beyond the vigilance of Christian people. Of course it was all stupid, Samaroo should have prepared a better statement. I began to doubt Samaroo, the care with which he presented himself, the propriety of his words. Behind the façade of order lurked Rajah, grinning, pouring rum into vessels of bone.

"What *really* happened to your niece?" I asked in accusation. "What have Lance and you to do with her murder?" He looked mortified, uttered a polite excuse for his going, bowed, hurried out of my sight. I went to the kitchen to look for Alice but she had fled, probably hiding in some comforting corner of the house. I returned to the drawing room and sat down again, willing myself to calmness. The envelope bore exotic stamps as if some of Mother's butterflies had come to life, shook off their pins and settled colourfully on it. I took out the script and began to read, wondering what role Lance had designated for me. The whole of the day and all night I read and reread it, seeking out Lance's admission of guilt. I fell asleep on the sofa and as soon as I awoke I turned to the script again, but the morning light brought no revelations. Anger swelled up in me as I read, anger at Lance's draping of himself in riddles and allegories, refusing to appear nakedly before me. And his Albion Hill tribe added to my confusion. Lance had written them all into the story but they were infuriatingly unfamiliar. There was Geoff, Miriam, her idle children, and even my dumb maid Alice whom he had converted into a prophetess of doom! Worst of all he had made me into a pathetic mother. I threw the script away from me but found myself hurrying to retrieve the scattered pages from the floor. As I reordered them, it came to me, in a moment of dreadful clarity, that I would be forever pinned and framed within his story. I would become obsessed by it, as if afflicted by a phantom pregnancy. No, I would not surrender. No, I would not allow him to abuse my body, my future, again. I would refuse motherhood and abort him from me. I would take the package to the garden, find some paraffin in one of the sheds, clear a space between the daffodils, dig a hole, place the package in it and set light to the life of Lance, watching with horror as the morning breeze lifts the ashes and settles them against the faces of the spring flowers, corrupting their beauty.

*

The Arawak woman was wearing the same red dress she came in, only now it was more soiled. I could tell, from the way it clung to her body, that she wore no undergarments. We paddled for twelve hours, and all the time she said nothing, though Rajah had assured me that the Arawaks only spoke English, having long lost their ancestral language. We paused occasionally and I offered her water, pieces of cooked meat and fruit. She took these without any sign of grudge or gratitude. When we arrived at her village children dashed to the boat, helping to moor it at a makeshift platform of bound logs. A girl, ten years or so in age, leapt into the woman's lap, followed by a slightly younger boy who wrapped his arms around her neck and dangled like a playful monkey. Her face brightened, she caressed them, and for the first time spoke, though in an accent beyond my understanding. She left the boat with her bundles of tinned foods and other goods purchased from Rajah's shop. The children chattered excitedly as they followed her to her hut. They pulled at her bundles, eager to open them. She spoke again, this time in a harsher voice, and they stopped their scuffling, obedient to her word. It was the first time I had seen her as a figure of authority.

The rest of the village – no more than a few dozen – were hard at work. The sound of sawing and hammering as men repaired their houses or boats drowned out the natural noises of the jungle. I saw women cooking, planting their kitchen gardens, sewing, beating clothes at the edge of the river. The children were in close attendance, forking the ground, mending fishing-nets, filling buckets in the river to replenish the tin drums which were the villagers' reservoir of potable water. The picture of ceaseless industry gave the lie to Rajah's description of Arawaks as sleepy and slothful, bush creatures as yet unaccustomed to the transactions of the modern world. "They live for food and fuckie-fuckie. What they know about making things for the future? They happy in mud-house and string-hammock."

The Arawak woman took me to a hut vacated by its usual inhabitants for my benefit. I sat among their few possessions, their bundles of cloth, straw baskets, cassava graters, pots and pans. The hammock was spotlessly clean as was the rest of the dwelling. The Arawak woman came with a plate of food – fried fish and boiled yams in a peppery sauce, with a generous pile of cassava bread. The children spread a cloth on the ground and the woman placed the plate on it. She poured me a cup of sorrel juice. I ate and drank, watched over silently by them. When I finished, a little boy brought me a bowl of water to wash my hands. Afterwards he gestured to me to hold out my hands and he wiped them with a towel. Then he gave me a shot of home-made liquor, which I drank in one go, wheezing afterwards to his obvious satisfaction. Having properly performed their duties to a stranger, they left. The alcohol worked rapidly on my nerves, I fell asleep without effort.

The next morning, the same ritual of feeding me, this time with fruit scrupulously peeled, sliced and arranged prettily on the plate, with a freshly picked coconut to slake my thirst. It was now my turn to gaze upon the children and to notice, to my amazement, that they were all slightly different in appearance. There were hints, in the shapes of their noses, in the texture of their hair, in the varied tints of their skin, of a history of cross-breeding. Hindus, Africans and even the odd Chinese – traders, adventurers, runaways from plantations or from the city police – had passed this way, sought the company of women (a mixture no doubt of forced and willing sex) and left their mark in the blood and composition of the natives. What was remarkable was the seeming harmony of this mongrel community. The children gathered around the Arawak woman and obeyed her authority, and she looked at them with an equal degree of solicitude. And, given her youthfulness, her imma-ture breasts, the children could not have been hers, though she treated them as her family.

The oddness of Arawak family – that must have struck my novice priest when he passed this way, their ready assumption of the role of motherhood and fatherhood, irrespective of blood ties. And the evidence of racial mixture and the accept-ance of such – that too would have been a troubling experience for him. To the superficial eye the Arawaks appeared orderly in their day-to-day application to practical tasks, building and renewing their houses, patching their fishing nets, but the idea of unruliness was there. My priest would have seen it in the slight variations in their features, the traces of African and Oriental which told of sexual corruption, sexual deviancy. And as he probed deeper he would have discovered the nature of their superstitious minds. Rajah had put it bluntly: "Arawak them is crazy people." Rajah then expatiated upon their pagan beliefs, and he did so with relish. A Hindu who worshipped idols and bleeding monkey gods, he was relieved to show up others as being more outrageous than his people. "Hindu believe when you die you come back as ant, like me muma, or

103

toucan like me dadee, or maybe a prince, a pandit, a pork-knocker, depending on whether Lord Krishna, who rule the universe, vex with you or content. Lord Krishna can make you what He want, by His will and word. Pork-knocker is obviously the worst He can do to you, you got to be bad to Lord Krishna to come back as a jungle nigger. Arawak people different from we – they believe in gods who can change you when you is still living, not bothering to wait until you die. One moment you are a man planting your cassava quietly, when badam-bam-bam! Arawak gods send a spirit that fall out from the sky, topple you, mash your face in the ground till you suffocate, but just as you going to die, the spirit haul you up, fly you to treetop and leave you there. When you come to your senses, rub your eyes and look at yourself, you start scream and you never stop, because you discover Arawak spirit turn you into a howler-monkey. One moment you is a man, the next a monkey, so you let go one scream and you never stop. That's why the jungle so noisy with monkeys, day and night they getting on bad. And soon-soon another man come to take over your wife and work your cassava field. That's why Arawak them don't have stable family, because husband can turn into monkey any morning, or wife into carrion-crow, and whoever left behind go off with whoever else left behind. Monkey and carrion-crow alright though, at least people don't eat them. Worse is when spirit turn you into labba or deer, sweet-sweet bushmeat. Then your own wife and children and her new man hunt you, slaughter, spike, skin you, roast and gobble you. Arawak people is cannibal, is truth I talking."

To begin with my priest would have been excited by such superstitions, since it would have given him an opportunity to proselytise among the natives. I imagined him trying out his missionary voice for the first time, preaching the Gospel of Love, preaching abstinence before marriage, fidelity after marriage. He would have attempted to introduce them to the principles of Reason, explaining that there was only one God who had a definite plan for the universe and all that lived within it. Man/God. Son/Father. Whore/Virgin. Flesh/Word. Earth/Heaven. Sin/Salvation. He would have given them an overview of human history, from the Patriarchs and their pristine world to the doomed fate of that earth because of war among men. He would have told them of the ending of the world, describing aeroplanes, tanks, huge batteries of guns, screaming metal. Of course nothing he said would have made sense to them. His youthfulness and the virgin excitement in his voice would have further discouraged them. From time immemorial they lived according to their own beliefs, they understood their own peculiar ways. They had survived floods, storms, drought, kanaimas, white marauders, African and Oriental raiders, so why abandon their beliefs, their centuries and centuries of existence by the same river carrying hyacinths and hog-plums to the same shores? And as to history, they knew only spear, cutlass, poisoned arrow. The thundering of metal was beyond their conception. Their world was a collection of huts in a jungle clearing, chicken pens, pigsties, vegetable gardens. Beyond it was Pillar and the terror of kanaima. No, what my priest uttered would have been unacceptable to them, but they sung along to his hymns and swallowed the communion bread to keep the peace, in case a gang of other white men descended on the village to take revenge on them.

This much I imagined, for in truth there was nothing in the notes of my priest to suggest the nature of his engagements with the Arawaks. His story, written haltingly, told of his childhood in an Irish monastery and his subsequent upbringing in Coventry in the house of a retired Father of the Church. The Father, despairing of the coming of the First World War, had sent him away to the colony to keep Father Jenkins' company. When he reached the Demerara Mission however, Father Jenkins was nowhere to be seen. His inquiries to the Arawaks who lived in the Mission were met with incomprehension. "Father Jenkins gone. Kanaima take he," they said, looking puzzled when the young man lingered in their hut, wanting another answer. Eventually they ignored him, returning to their domestic tasks. The days of waiting for Father Jenkins's return became weeks.

To begin with the notes my priest made were in a neat handwriting. They were in the form of draft letters to the

Church Fathers in Ireland. They were mostly descriptions of the landscape, naming the birds, the animals, the jungle trees, but he concentrated on the insect life of the place. There were detailed lavish passages on cockroaches, locusts, beetles, moths and the like. He recorded little of his experience of the Arawaks – there was something wilful and deliberate about his reticence, exciting my speculation. Was he concealing some act or acts, or was he merely so alienated by their habits that there was little to chronicle? The continuing absence of Father Jenkins must have affected him for his handwriting grew agitated when he recorded it. The closing notes betrayed signs of extreme distress. The words were mostly indecipherable and the sentences broken, some veering off the page, his hand seeming to lose control of its movements. The name 'Pillar' was scrawled again and again, with variations like 'rape', 'liar', 'pillage', 'lap', 'lip'. Then there were only inkdrops, the pen unable to formulate sensible thoughts, hovering instead over the page and dripping from its tip.

The Arawak woman took me to Pillar. I had thought to paddle there myself but she put aside her superstitions in return for a generous sum of money. As we approached the waters suddenly swirled and foamed. I was glad for her expert steering of the boat. The place was marked by a sprinkling of boulders that looked like eggs laid by some gross prehistoric bird. I tied the boat to one of the boulders and stepped nervously onto the muddy foreshore, cutlass in hand. It was a small island in the river, a soggy patch of land, the topsoil not deep or solid enough to support trees. The Arawak woman stayed behind in the boat as I waded through the tall grass looking for... I had no idea what I was looking for and wanted to turn back immediately, but my eyes were drawn to a clump of bush at one corner of the island. My feet led me to it and when I reached, my feet kicked at the mound of earth against my mind's intention. My feet kicked and kicked until a skull was revealed. The earth gave way and a skull was revealed. No bones, no traces of clothing, only the skull which was broken on one side, a shard of it missing. An act of violence. The body it belonged to had been murdered. I had seen enough photographs of the dead in my newspaper offices to tell me this much. The body had been left there to rot. Animals must have scavenged it, devouring the whole of the skeleton, except for the skull. I dug deeper into the grave with the tip of my cutlass, unearthing something compact. At first I thought it was a stone but when I took it up and wiped it clean on the grass I discovered it was a piece of glass, a lens set in an ornate handle. The inscription carved in the handle was still legible – 'Leitz of Munich, Germany, manufacturers of the finest scientific instruments.' I recognised the lens from the notes my priest had written on his life in Coventry. It had belonged to him, his most prized possession. He had come to Pillar and discovered Father Jenkins's corpse. He had buried the lens with Father Jenkins, for it was no longer of worth to him.

I dug a fresh grave for the skull and the lens. I twined a length of grass, bound it with a strip of my shirt and fastened it to the spine of my cutlass, to make a Cross of sorts. I sat beside the Cross and grave, keeping company with Father Jenkins as my priest must have done. The Arawaks had killed Father Jenkins. The horror of the deed would have so shaken my priest that it stopped his writing altogether. He would have doubted the depth of his Christian faith. He had looked at life through his lens, with superficial eyes. What was he but a callow youth, believing that he could transplant Christian doctrines into the souls of Arawak folk, taming their appetites, corralling them into prayer and hymn? And what of Father Jenkins? Should he not have returned to a Europe on the brink of savage war to preach his Christianity there, instead of interfering with innocent natives, interfering with customs and beliefs he could hardly understand, or made no effort to understand?

I sat beside the Cross and grave pitying my priest, for his superficiality was the result of the innocence of youth whereas mine was beyond forgiveness. I had looked at life through the distorted lens of my own grossness. I had held the lens to the young faces of women, willing the light to scorch them, set them ablaze, turn them into ashes. It was I who had killed the faith of my priest. I was the kanaima who waylaid, seduced and murdered Father Jenkins. I wanted to kneel before the Cross and grave but I knew it would be a hollow gesture. The common thief stayed awake and waited for Christ's dying, under a sky jewelled with stars, so that having borne witness to the miracle of grace, he too could depart in peace. *I* would slink away from the Cross and grave as soon as I could, grieving for a whore and a corrupted mother.

The Arawak woman was waiting for my return and my money. She was eating a chalice of gold, for so it looked from afar and through my superficial eye. It was a yellow pawpaw lit up by the sun. The juice ran like yolk down her face and neck into the opening of her dress. I could tell from the way her dress clung to her body that she wore no undergarments.

★

I closed my shop when Rohini was murdered but not out of sorrow for her, though that came naturally enough. It was fated that her life would conclude in distress. In Malaya, I had witnessed a girl set upon by drunken British soldiers. I watched their actions from afar, as our gods did. I did not interrupt, not because I was the most junior of the group in terms of rank, any protest on my part therefore useless, but because our gods had decreed it thus. The spectacle made me hold the gods in incomprehension, but there was still the necessity of obedience to their will.

The girl's cries and the unrelenting will of the soldiers literally chastened me. By the time I returned to India to cremate my mother I knew I was fated for a wifeless existence. It was then that I adopted Rohini as a kind of fetish or symbol of my abstinence, even as I craved another condition. She was a lonely child abandoned outside a temple but she was fated to become the focus of male disgust. In our religion we wrap our holy books in red cloth, and so I let Rohini wear her blood-red dress in the shop.

I closed the shop when Rohini was murdered because her death marked the end of a phase in my life, and I would become something else, whatever the gods determined. This was what I taught Lance, the Hindu ideas of becoming, of reincarnation, of rupture and startling transformation. I taught him this to guard him against Rohini. Of course I knew all her nocturnal doings with men. And that all the clients in my shop were *her* customers, lusting for the freshness of her living body, not for my dusty artefacts of a bygone age. Except for Enoch Goldstein, the Jew who saw in her images of his carefree youth, otherwise the innocence of his mother before Nazi soldiers settled upon her. And in his own way, Lance too, seeking in Rohini the virginity of his mother even as he entered and raged within her. These two were my only genuine clients, steeped in memories of the past.

I introduced Lance to Hindu philosophy so that he could understand that his urges and his actions were his own, even though plotted and overseen by the gods. I sat him down on the same sofa he dirtied himself with Rohini. I read to him passages from the *Ramayana* and the *Gita* which offered glimpses into the processes of regenerating one's self, of being born anew and in multiplicity, in spite of the determination of the gods, for the gods allowed the freedoms of becoming even as they determined the course of these freedoms. Fissure, crack, abortion and rupture took place in one's lifetime, but from these could emerge utterly different redemptive conceptions of one's self, as incomprehensible as the nature of the gods.

Whoever murdered Rohini did so out of surrender to the past, out of despair that nothing could change, nothing should change. They tied her to a post with barbed wire, which is the devil's rope, burnt her beyond recognition, buried her under stone, all the time securing *themselves* against the terror of change. Someone like Lance. Not necessarily Lance, for such men were legion. In Lance's case he would have found his mother in Rohini, fastened her to a stake so she would never again escape him, disfigured her beyond the desire of other men.

Which is why I gave him the bundle of papers, which was a young priest's testimony. And when it was returned to me as a package from Demerara, how transformed and reincarnated by his imagination! The want of his mother was written into it, but in different compassionate forms. He had made muses of his whores, in the process cleansing his life of the accretions of Coventry dirt. In reconstructing the priest's story from fragments of confession, Lance had crawled out of the crevices of his old self to reveal a person struggling for wholeness and transfiguration. And in so doing, the style of his writing changed, the irony and sour understatements of his journalistic prose sloughed off like dead skin, and in its place a new raiment of lyricism. At first the changing language and style were what attracted me to his autobiography, his novel, but when I reread it I was seized by the religious imagery. I had always taken Christianity in England to be a dead thing, as dead as the relics in my shop, but Lance had resurrected it as divine mystery, even as he had recast himself (and all the inert pantomime characters of his family and acquaintances) as players in a divine comedy.

So where does that leave Lance, if I can put it so crassly? An Albion Hill man gone native, a born again pagan ending his days among Demerara madonnas and Arawak whores? One of the hundreds of thousands of white adventurers and lost souls from Walter Raleigh onward, whose bones were destined for the mandibles of jungle insects? Or a man of his word, a man of His Word, at the beginning of his life of cleansed flesh? And what of me? I have closed my shop, I have closed the past. I have forgiven Lance for sinning with Rohini. I have mothered this story. It was I who gave him the priest's manuscript, a relic from the past, and a Hindu lens through which to read it. That is enough for this phase of my life. What comes after will be a new beginning, even if I return to the past life of India. I wrap Lance's typescript – his imagination – in a red cloth as a Hindu wraps the Ramayana, and I take it to his wife Elizabeth. The typescript is a creature in swaddling cloth, and I give it to Elizabeth as the infant she never bore, or the infant she could still bear out of her virginity.

PART 2
REINCARNATIONS
(THE NEW TESTAMENT)

"Go, little Book; in faith I send thee forth."

Robert Southey

PROLOGUE

In the spring of 1914, at the age of sixteen or seventeen (perhaps less, perhaps more, for I was ignorant of the truth of my birth) Father Harris, my mentor and guardian in Coventry, sent me away to British Guiana, on the coast of South America. I was to assist Father Jenkins who had set up a Catholic mission on the bank of the Demerara river, to broadcast news of Our Lord's existence to the Hindoos, Negroes and pagan bushmen of the colony. War was expected in Europe and Father Harris's intention was to keep me in Guiana until the madness was over when I would be sent back home. "A few months at the most," Father Harris prophesied, but he was wrong. Four years passed before I returned to Coventry, to find Father Harris bedridden. Apart from the infirmity of age, he bore no signs of physical illness. He had taken to his bed out of despair at having survived the war, but with his faith in tatters. "I'll die soon," he muttered, "commit me to paper, just drop me down some wormhole, don't worry to bury me."

I had thought to compose a report on the situation in Guiana, for the benefit of the Church fathers in Ireland who were responsible for the mission there. I would begin with an account of my voyage across the seas, the marvel of whales and flying fish and the passage through islands furrowed, ribbed and riven, lifting up shaggy heads into clear skies whilst below they nourished here and there, in green laps, vegetation as picturesque as Eden's. Lofty peaks, long jagged defiles and in the valleys the prospering of deciduous beauty. Then, when the lightship met the steamer and made its way to Demerara water, the sight of the flats, the stellings, the stores and sheds, the low white jalousied houses over which, everywhere, cabbage-palms spread their wings.

"Ram Ram Englishee" a Hindoo greeted me as I stepped ashore. He announced his name as Manu. He was covered all over in mud, except for his turban which was spotless white. He made to garland me with flowers, as if I was to become a new addition to his pantheon of pagan deities, but I shrunk from him, refusing the fragrance of hibiscus and frangipani. I looked over his shoulder to a spot where his fellow natives were milling excitedly. They were gathered around a goat, and from the flash of cutlasses and the fire they lit, it was evident that they were about to slaughter it. I reached into my pocket for my rosary. A beetle flew blindly into my face, breaking my prayer, and the Hindoo abandoned his mask of reverence and laughed at me as I brushed off the insect. It fell to the ground, landing on its back. I stooped involuntarily to examine it, and the Hindoo stopped laughing, bemused by my studiousness.

I had thought to write up the diary I had kept during my sojourn in the jungle, an irregular diary for there were days and months on end when there was nothing to record, nothing of horror or of fascination, for the solitude of the jungle was rarely affected by the deeds of the small numbers of humans who lived within it. And when the natives did behave in ways worthy of chronicle, I distrusted my pen, in case it surrendered to the lure of the exotic. After long periods of inactivity and boredom the least activity was liable to appear spectacular.

I returned to Coventry and put away my diary, for the dourness of the city and the familiarity of Father Harris's house would only heighten my recollection of the landscape of Guiana, tempting me to false excitements. I focused instead on what I hoped to be a plain account of Father Harris's life, its movement towards doubt. "Commit me to paper," he insisted, refusing to be buried for he said the earth was already crammed with millions of victims of the war and could not contain even a grain of Christian faith.

I made notes at his bedside as he spoke to me of the characters and incidents in his life, of beliefs held passionately and his equally fierce rejection of them. "Drop me down a wormhole

114

when I'm dead," he said, but though I knew his meaning I lacked conviction in my ability to write the passages of his decline. After weeks of his confessions, all I had was a dishevelment of notes. I could not make a clear start until one morning, seeking inspiration in the unruly garden of our house, a crow shrieked at me. I looked up but could not sight it in the elm trees, though long dead and bared of the camouflage of leaves. It called again, mocking me, I searched the trees, but saw nothing, until it called a third time and when I looked up I was suddenly awakened to an image of Lance. He grinned at me devilishly, raised his tongue to reveal a bird's egg, daring me to break my silence.

I

"And how is your grandfather?" Father Harris asked cheerfully as he prepared to teach me chemistry, arranging beaker, pipette, test-tube and candle in his makeshift laboratory. He uncorked a jar of blue crystals and spooned some out onto a weighing scale. I looked on excitedly, not bothering to respond.

"Now, boy, answer," Father Harris rebuked me gently.

"He's in some pain but he eats well. Besides, the almshouse is clean and well-run, he'll be fine there."

Father Harris stopped the chemical experiment he was plotting and gazed at me with pity and fondness. "Geoffrey is an Irishman of unusual suffering," he said. "He is..." He paused, searching for words to say but then changing his mind. He resumed the measurement of the crystals with exaggerated concentration, not wanting to think further on my grandfather's history and present condition. I knew he was satisfied with my conduct, my regular visits to my grandfather to keep him company and read to him. I knew too that he was preparing me for the future by not encouraging me to dwell upon the past. I was now in Coventry, under his protection and tutorship. My past in Ireland was over, the Irish sea I crossed at the age of fourteen being a final dividing line between then and now. My grandfather had removed me from Ireland and brought me to Father Harris's house in Coventry, whilst he

115

took up residence in the nearby almshouse. He would spend the rest of his life there, reminiscing on his Irish past, whereas Father Harris would guide me into the future through moral and educational instruction, so that one day I could be anointed into priestly life.

But the more the past was denied me the more it tempted me to seek it out. I scoured my mind to recall the whispers and the gossips of the servants who worked in the monastery I was placed in as an infant. It was in the east of Ireland, in a village called Ruddlestone, but it could have been anywhere since the monks and the children in their care, me included, were completely isolated from the surroundings. We lived in self-sufficiency, serviced by a well, a small herd of cows, a field growing corn, a vegetable garden, and an apple orchard. Three aged women lodged in a barn in a far corner of the grounds, in the shadow of the high stone wall which shielded us from the world outside. Their main role was to wash us and to mend our clothing. On warm days we wore no shoes, and in winter, strips of cloth wound around our feet. Food was scarce. And yet I remember neither the cold nor the hunger but for the icicles hanging from the rafters of the chapel, their tips gleaming like lit candlewick. Sometimes, when they broke off, and when the monks were distracted by prayers, I would scrabble under the pews for one, bite off a thick piece and await the chanting when I could suck and crunch it secretly and expertly, my mouth moving as if to the words of the song. The taste of icicle in my mouth, the burning dampened by a coating of dirt, is the only sensation that has survived my early years, for the sole purpose of our being then was to arouse our appetite for worship and prayer. Our dormitory was a row of wooden beds, with white sheets, and in winter, white woollen blankets, the three old women utterly scrupulous in boiling and bleaching away any stains. The chapel was whitewashed stone, pews painted white, white altar-cloth, the only shocking colour being blood streaming down Jesus' white body and coagulating at the nails at his feet. That, and the golden light of candles, and the field shining with corn, and apples resplendent in autumnal mist, and the vast sky painted in sunset ochre, vexed scarlet and purple, were the only colours allowed to us, for they spoke of God's suffering, God's wrath, God's benediction, so the monks taught us. And they taught us to read, so that we could read the Bible, and to write, so that we could write and commit to heart prayers and psalms.

Our days and nights were passed in total silence, except for school lessons when we read aloud endless pages of the Scriptures, encouraged by a sudden blow to our backs when we faltered, not delivered with malice but with a shepherd's vigilance over his flock. We soon learnt to persevere, but more to cherish our voices, the sound of which was so rare that we took full and joyous advantage of the time allowed for its utterance. After a while it didn't matter so much what we read as the measure of the cadence of our voices. We learned to start boldly in the clarity of faith, to dip and pause and trail off in the timbre of bewilderment and sorrow and doubt, then to recover strength, gathering the air in our throats in a spirit of defiance and exultation:

Who will grant me that my words be written?
    Who will grant they may be marked down in a book?
With an iron pen and in a plate of lead
    Or else be graven with an instrument in flint stone?
For I know that my Redeemer liveth,
    And in the last day I shall rise out of the earth
And I shall be clothed again with my skin,
    And in my flesh I shall see my God,
Whom I myself shall behold and not another:
    And my eyes shall behold, and not another.
This my hope laid up in my bosom.

Sentences became the road to Gethsemane, or the thinnest of trails guiding our bodies through a dark forest; commas and colons and full stops the serpents, vines, pits and rocks that bruised and trapped our feet, but we shook ourselves free by the power of prayer, bandaged our limbs, moved unsteadily then triumphantly towards the light of Revelation. At evensong our voices soared and soared higher still, happily released from our vows of silence. Afterwards, silence again as we trooped back to our dormitory in preparation for sleep, but a precious silence, guarded fiercely against the temptation of speech, as the grail of God's blood is guarded against Satan's mouth.

But for the three witches the cup of my early childhood would have brimmed over with happiness. If the monks were our absent fathers, these were to be our mothers. Agnes, Agatha and Abigail were their names, and their natures were almost as similar. The three woke us at dawn in a unison of croaks, led us to the stream beyond the orchard. An orderly queue was formed. The first boy stripped. Agnes poured the first bucketful of water over him. He was passed on to Agatha for soaping, then to Abigail who rinsed him down and dried him. He went to the back of the queue. The second boy stepped forward to be processed, then the third and the fourth, until we were all done. In their grumpiness, they handled us roughly, careless of soap-water running into our eyes, rubbing the towels unkindly at our faces, but no one murmured, much less protested. We were compliant to the ways of God, and deep down each of us knew, without need of explanation, that in their treatment of us they were reminding us of our guilt. Not the guilt of mankind the monks preached to us about, which Jesus took upon his shoulders on the road to Gethsemane, but a more private, personal sinfulness.

Then to the salvation of chapel and morning worship, the monks already in place, fixed to altar and pew as forever as Jesus to his Cross, except their faces were puffed with fatigue and twisted in an attitude of distress, whereas Jesus' eyes were lidded in eternal repose and his lips were rich and his body manly strong, blood running in luxuriant rivulets over it, for the sins of the world could not vanquish him. The salvation of chapel: the sight of Jesus' gleaming body which, for all the dourness of the monk's visage, or the sorrowful intonation of prayer, made us open our throats when it was time to sing. After hours and hours of silence we simply opened into hymn, practising our voices, straining and stretching and tilting and modulating to hear what they were capable of, but always in conjunction with each other, a shoal of sounds moving in unison, no one darting off in pride or panic or disobedience, for the body of death hung over us like a shark, the body of Jesus manly strong and sure and streaked in blood as proof of his supremeness, which made us fearful but also certain of another world beyond our present sinfulness, if only we kept in communion with each other.

Except for Lance. He brayed. When our singing rose to a crescendo, he brayed, not out of waywardness to harmony but because his voice had broken. He was older than us. A foot taller and a trace of hair above his lip as evidence of the extra years he claimed to be. And unlike us he knew the details of private, personal sinfulness. Why Lance chose to confess to me I will never know. I can, now, surmise that he sensed in me a devotion to my vows of silence, not just in not speaking out of bounds, but in keeping steadfastly within me my own thoughts. Perhaps he sensed that I would be loyal to him because I was loyal to my own self. But that is almost certainly a foolish explanation, years after the event, for I cannot sincerely remember anything about my childhood character to which words like 'loyalty' and 'steadfastness' could be attached. In truth I cannot remember being conscious of anything but the ritual of waking, washing and worshipping in the company of other boys. We kept silence between us according to the rules of the monastery, so that neither gossip nor idle talk should blunt our contemplation of God. We were to unsheathe ourselves to make space for the sacred. It was simply that, a way of being, practised and perfected over centuries by monks and given to us as the sharpened blade of faith which we must keep in fierce condition and pass on to those to come.

Lance broke his silence in the kitchen with the same innocence as his braying in chapel, and instead of being shocked by the sudden casting aside of our vows I found myself eager to hearken unto him, indeed to encourage him to speak. We had woken early as usual, and made our way to the stream, the light mist curdling at our feet. When it lifted we looked back to see our footprints in frosted grass, an oddly beautiful trail from our dormitory to the edge of the stream, pieces of silver lit up by the morning sun. The branches of the apple trees hunched under the weight of dew. A crow shifted from foot to foot, half-awake, hungry, then with a sullen cry flew off as we approached. The icy water from Agnes's bucket emptied over me like an axe against softwood. Duly chopped and massacred, then wiped on a towel of bramble, we filed obediently into chapel where the sight of the blood of Christ made a different sense and the sermon about Judas (it was Easter week) made me wonder instead at what the devil's silver he got could buy: a year's supply of bread (yeasted, richly crusted, seeded with cumin), cartloads of cheese, lambs slaughtered, roasted, bathed in sauces and served up in huge portions at a table laden with purple grapes, pomegranates, olives, tankards of sweetened milk, feasts such as we read of in the books of Leviticus, Joshua and Judges. Afterwards, Judas would belch and clean his teeth studiously with a thorn plucked from Jesus' crown. I crunched at an icicle, not bothering to pray because all the monks had their backs turned to us.

Lance and I were left alone in the kitchen, for it was our turn to scrub the pots and tin plates. Lance wet his forefinger and prodded at whatever breadcrumbs were left on the plates. When he had gathered enough he put his finger into his mouth and sucked it with relish. He scraped the bottom of the pots for any residue of potato, offering a caked fingernail to me. I licked the potato off it gratefully. I would have drunk the soap-water if he had given it to me, out of a desire to conspire with him. It was not a sudden desire. For as long as I could remember I had stood beside him in chapel listening to his voice soaring to the heavens as if caught in the coat-tail of a honeyed bird. I tried to follow, straining my voice after his flight but could never reach the heights of his rapture. Then his voice broke, abruptly, one morning like every other morning, nothing on earth or in the sky as we trooped to chapel to prophesy it, no strange formation of birds, no trees blackened by overnight lightning, no fruit fallen prematurely to the ground. The three old women had washed us as morosely as before. I took my place beside him with the same expectancy of song, but when he opened his mouth a hoarse noise came. He cleared his throat of imagined phlegm and started again, soon catching up with us, but when the phrases wound to a certain height his voice faltered, fell behind, halted. I looked up to see the puzzlement in his face. The next day and the next, puzzlement turned to distress, then surrender. He started the hymn with a forced boldness, which immediately jarred against our easeful entry, and when our voices began to rise he struggled to lift his own. He stopped out of a shame of failure. I felt we were betraying him by our show of melody. I too ceased singing the highest notes, out of fellowship with his maimed wing and spirit.

We washed the pots in silence, but in a rebellious mood, both of us on the brink of speech. Silence was enforced on us to prevent the formation of friendships. We were a gathering of godly children, but isolated from one another by silence. The Bible and Hymnal bound us in a community of worship, there was to be no deviation such as would occur should one boy speak to another of the most trivial or the most distressing of matters. The troubling details of a dream for instance, or the sudden longing for sight of whatever lay behind the high walls of the monastery. Whatever pain excited or tempted us was to be found in Biblical passages. The sores of Job. Jonah's loneliness in the belly of a whale. Daniel in a den of raging animals. Jesus fasting in the desert, refusing to stomach Satan's sweetmeats. Zachariah clinging to the branches of a sycamore tree. Paul blinded by God's lightning. Above all, Judas with his shameful bag of silver. All these were to address our childhood anxieties, but how could they be of relevance to Lance's situation?

"You know why your name is Lance?" I asked, committing the sin of speech out of kindness to him, for any answer he made would be a lesser act. 'Easier for the victim of temptation to find forgiveness than the tempter': it was one of the 'eternal truths' the monks made us write down repeatedly on our slates. Was it out of fear that Lance refused to respond? Or something kinder, the wish not to encourage me to damn myself more than I had already done? There was no one present but the two of us and the eternal God and since God chastised and punished us only through the deeds of the monks, I was willing to take a chance on His oversight.

"You don't know, do you!" I persisted. Still he kept his

mouth shut, though by the way he turned to the pot, inspecting its inside and outside, I knew he was thinking loud thoughts. It suddenly and cunningly came to me that I could make amends to God by holy utterance.

"You are the pointed stick that a Roman soldier poked into the side of our Lord on the Cross," I said, wisely, as if I were a monk giving instruction. I felt momentarily justified in speech but the years of practised piety made me bow my head in sorrow of what I had said. The wounding of Jesus was not something to be spoken of lightly, over a sinkful of breakfast plates. We were out of place, out of the order of altar and pulpit and pew and the ministration of monks. I felt like a little boy whom God was calling to, as He called to Samuel, but unlike Samuel, I was afraid to answer, even though I knew that He was calling me to repentance. I fell into dismal silence, my heart racing, then nearly stopping in absolute fright when Lance, in his agitation, dropped a pot clatteringly onto the floor. I fumbled to retrieve it and wash it anew, wash away my own sins thereby, but Lance brushed aside my hands. There was rage in the way his mouth quivered. And then he spoke, thank God! No, don't thank God, I heard myself thinking a fraction of a second later, overcome by a sense of accumulating offences, and yet I was grateful when he spoke.

"And do you know what *your* name means?" he asked. It mattered not one breadcrumb or tiniest scraping of potato to me what my name meant, except that he should ask again, which he did.

"Do you know what *your* name means?" he spoke a second time. I looked up at him with a mixture of stupidity and solicitude, a look I would give a monk when he asked a difficult question and I keenly awaited the blow that followed. A practised look, part of the ritual of obedience to the Lord, willingness to surrender to His wrath. Except that now, nothing Lance told me could hurt more than his refusal to tell me, to go on in audible words. The more he spoke the more we were bonded in friendship, even though it compounded our sins. Or was I a coward seeking to shelter under his greater offence, like an insect scurrying to the shadows?

"Cunt. That's what your name means," he said, and when he saw I was unaffected he leant his face over mine, opened his mouth wide and spelt out the words in a volley of saliva: "C-U-N-T." I had an inkling of the nature of the word but wiped my face mournfully in deference to his mood. More talk would follow, I knew, our friendship would grow beyond the repair of prayer or confession. All of a sudden I understood my previous loneliness and wanted to cry. He, sensing my emotion, mistook it for the distress of a maimed animal. "C-U-N-T," he repeated full in my face, fresh saliva and all, wanting vengeance for me calling him a Christ-killer. A sob issued from me, but from where, I knew not, and even as I uttered it I could hear God calling unto me, as unto Samuel, and though I needed to cry I could not, for God was calling unto me.

★

Lance and I volunteered to wash up twice a week, way above the demands of the rota. The monks allowed it as a sign of exemplary charity on our part. Of course all we wanted was to chatter to each other. Or rather, for Lance to try out his new voice on new matters, since I did most of the listening. "Look at this," he said, fishing out the piece of paper hidden in his underpants. It was folded several times over to shrink its size. He opened it up on the dining table and smoothed over the creases. "It's about Bathsheba," he said excitedly, "I know everything about the whore. I tore her out from the Bible." He paused to enjoy my feeling of alarm, and before I could reply, he said, in a wilful tone of voice, "I took the Bible from the cupboard underneath the altar."

"Stole?" I asked in disbelief.

"Yes, lots of them are there, with pictures. Not like the ones we get to read. I just took one and wrapped it in cloth and hid it in the orchard under three large stones." He smoothed over the ruffled page again in a gesture of defiance. "Go on, have a look," he urged, "your name is in there somewhere."

I wanted to read but resisted the temptation, needing to know first how and why he had done something so desperate.

Talking to each other was wicked enough, but stealing a Bible, tearing out a page and reading it was just plain damnable.

"I knew there was more to what they were giving us," Lance explained innocently, "I had this urge, that's all."

The monks had selected thirty or so passages from the Bible for our instruction. When the Bibles were handed out to us in the classroom, we were directed to a particular passage. The hours that followed focused entirely on that passage. We read it, discussed it line by line, transcribed it on our slates, memorised and recited aloud key sections. At the end of the lesson, the Bibles were handed back to our teacher. It never occurred to us to question why that particular passage was chosen, and we never thought to wander off by reading the verses above or below the allotted paragraphs, or on the opposite page, never mind turning over the page to peek at what lay there. The words we read were bare, it was unthinkable that there would be pictures. Apart from what Lance was to reveal to me the only picture I saw in all my years in the monastery was a small piece of stained-glass on the window above the altar, of a stag, sacred white, being hunted by dark-skinned devils and their hounds. I dwelt on it in moments of boredom, exciting myself by the terror of the stag as the hounds leapt upon it, dragged it to earth, opened it with savage teeth to plunder its liver, its heart.

The monks kept their Bibles in a cupboard underneath the altar. "Lots and lots of them," Lance said with the excitement of an adventurer who had stumbled upon a mountain cave lit up by veins of gold, or a graveyard of elephants, their ivory tusks pushing up through the earth like stalks of a strange plant. "Bibles of all the Fathers who lived and died here, and all the ones still around. I took one of the dead Bibles, it had the name of a 'Father Jenkins' written in it. I'll show you."

He never did show me the whole Bible, only portions of it culled according to his own sense of authority over me. If the monks selected passages of spiritual cleansing and surrender to the will of God, Lance ruled over my curiosity with stories of shockingly novel deeds. *'And they made their father drink wine that night: and the firstborn went in, and lay with her father... and the younger arose and lay with him.'*

"Lay with," he said, addressing my ignorance. "Lay with means what the worm does to a ripe apple."

He still made no sense.

"Think of yourself as the worm," he offered generously, and when I looked doubtful he reassured me it was only playing a part. "OK, so what do you do with the apple?"

"I nibble at the skin."

"And?"

"I eat some more?" I asked.

"Yes, yes, but then what?"

"I eat some more I suppose," I said nonchalantly, as if I could take all day and fill my stomach to my heart's contentment, pausing to take a nap or maybe just to look around at the other apples on the tree in case one took my fancy and I decided to start on it instead.

"Well, suppose you've eaten out the whole skin, what are you going to do?" he asked, a hint of exasperation in his voice. When I fell silent he changed tactics. "Suppose a blackbird sees you on the apple, a bloated and lazy worm, don't you think it'll swoop on you?"

The spectre of terror worked for I babbled, "I'd hide under the skin."

"But you've already eaten out all the skin," he said, incredulous at my stupidity.

"Then I'll just bore a hole and hide inside."

"Ah," he said, "you've got it." He leaned back on the bench in a gesture of relief. "Do you know what the inside is called?" and without waiting for my response he leaned forward with a look of smugness. "It's called the cunt of the apple."

"The cunt," I agreed and spelt it out to indicate my learning, C-U-N-T. I hoped he would now be appeased, but he persisted with the spiritual zeal of a bully bent in converting me to his ways, or at least rousing me from apathy, for I was beginning to get bored of the lesson.

"When you get inside what do you find?"

"Find? What do you mean by find?" I looked at him, awaiting some clue, but his face trembled with anger. I expected a blow at any moment which I would suffer as gladly as I would at the

125

hands of a monk. At least the answer to the question would be provided and I would be absolved of all responsibility to think for myself. I would merely repeat whatever he told me, out of obedience to his will and superior learning. But Lance merely glowered at me, urging me to answer the question by myself. It suddenly came to me that he himself was ignorant of the answer. I was overcome by a charitable feeling for him, almost pity.

"When you bore through the cunt deeply enough you reach appleseed," I said with mysterious clarity; mysterious because it was obvious, and yet unclear because I was unsure as to the purport or conclusion of our lesson. What were Lot and his daughters up to in turning a perfectly healthy apple into a worm-ridden, rotten and inedible thing?

"That's exactly it, don't you see," he said, and once again I knew he couldn't see. He couldn't see but I decided that I would, on his behalf.

"It's like making a hole in Jesus' hand," I said, confusing both of us. And that was that. I could not go on, there was no way that I could explain the connection between the holes in Jesus' palms and the worm's passage through applecunt. The silence that followed was the dark space of a prayer through which I groped to find a saving trail back to the orchard of morning fruit, at the beginning of summer when the trees bore with such strange and careless simplicity, and not singly but in clusters that gleamed to catch the eye, and breathed so rawly that my feet, clogged with sleep, quickly loosened and has-tened past to the stream, and even after the old women cleaned me I still felt guilty. Afterwards, in chapel, I sang loudly and mindlessly, hiding in a bushel of sound, and in the classroom lost myself completely in the text before me – always a piece of Scripture like the white linen of altar-cloth, or the clean handkerchief with which Veronica mopped Christ's brow.

Lance didn't say anything to break the silence. We continued washing up the pots, conscious of a hostility between us. It was late autumn, from the kitchen window I could see the trees bereft of fruit, no longer beckoning. Apples lay on the ground rotting and riddled with insects, and beneath them, beneath three stones was buried Father Jenkins's stolen Bible. Lance had broken its spine to tear out its pages more easily. The damp would get to what was left. All manner of things would crawl into its soggy carrion to lay their eggs. I must always have known the mood of the seasons, having spent all my memorable life in the grounds of the monastery, but only now was I conscious of the presence of the orchard as a living and dying body. Before I broke my vow of silence, the orchard was always there, a space between sleep and the old women at the edge of the stream; or else we ate of its fruit ordinarily, part of our routine diet: bread, cheese, a morsel of meat or fish, apples. Day after day after day. Lance unclothed me of habit. The pieces of paper he fished out of his underpants made me shiver in expectancy. They were crumpled and soiled and tasty. And yet, as soon as it was over – our secret reading on the messy dining table – I hated him. I hated the way he smirked afterwards, knowing that I was shocked by his revelations, yet wanting more.

We resumed washing up the pots, conscious of a hostility between us. Afterwards, in chapel, I sang loudly and mindlessly, and when I prayed I summoned up in the darkness a picture of Christ's unblemished palm; not lined and crisscrossed and marked like mine or Lance's, but luminous as morning fruit.

★

'Now as they were making their hearts merry, behold, the men of the city, base men, took fancy to the taste of their own kind and spoke to the master of the house, saying, "Bring forth the man that came into your house, that we may know him." But the master begged for the man, his guest, saying, "Behold, here is my daughter a virgin and my concubine: them I will bring out now, and humble ye them, and do unto them what seemeth good unto you: but unto this man do not so vile a thing." He brought forth the concubine unto them; and they knew her and swine-drunk and hollering they abused her all night until the morning: and when the day began to spring they let her go. She went bleeding and limping to her master who, seeing her spoilt, took a knife, laid hold of her, and sliced her, together with her bones into twelve pieces, and sent her unto all the coasts of Israel.'

After this there could be no more. I was unable to read with him. I had eaten too gluttonously. I was nauseous with the fear that the monks would pounce upon me, that in my bloated and helpless state I could be pecked over by blackbirds. Lance was proud that he had so fattened me. For weeks he let me be, the two of us cleaning the kitchen in a new silence. He polished the tin plates like knightly armour or trophies of conquest. I thought of Tamar, whom he had previously introduced me to, Tamar in Leviticus begging to be left alone, but being feasted upon by her brother. When her brother slept, Tamar escaped, climbing over the high wall and hiding in the forests; her brother brightening his sword and the bridle of his steed, gathering his lean hounds for the chase. "If you think that's good, wait for this," he said, drying his hands thoroughly and taking out a page not from his underpants but from under his vest. The new hiding place and the unfamiliar shininess of the paper told me immediately that I was in for a special treat.

"Want to try a piece?" he asked and not waiting for my consent he unfolded it with particular care. It was an illustration in red and blue and white showing Bathsheba sponging her body, the starkness of the colours seeming to make her nudity all the more candid. My eyes were drawn to the open-stretched sky, hauled down to the red towel spilled at her feet, dragged up her thighs, then, unable to settle, darted between the sky, the towel and the body luminous and clean as a wafer.

"The man, look at the man," Lance suggested, gladdened by my confusion.

The man? The man? What man? I looked at the picture but the shame that smeared my eyes stopped me seeing anything beyond the suggestion of nude flesh. "It's you, you and me," he said prodding at the corner of the picture, directing my attention to a man hiding behind the stone wall, gazing upon Bathsheba with blue burning eyes. The man, helmeted and dressed in a soldier's uniform, grasped his spear so tightly that I could not tell whether he was preparing for action or whether he was about to collapse and the spear was his only means of support.

"He's me and you," Lance repeated, stabbing his finger at the man to emphasise his point. A moment of puzzlement and then the sudden remembrance of how I had accused him of spearing Christ's side made me babble out a ready apology. "It was only a joke," I said, "I only wanted to hear you talk."

Lance brushed aside my confession with laughter. "You can't be so daft as to think I believed you," he said, folding the picture and putting it back in his bosom before I could protest. "You're too small and stupid to see any more," he said in a mocking tone. "Plus you're going away soon, you can get your own pictures then."

"Going away?" I asked in alarm. "Where would I be going away?"

"Oh, somewhere or the other, far away, anywhere but here, but you're going for sure, and you will see," he said, his voice darkening with prescience.

"I'll never leave you," I said involuntarily, overwhelmed by a sense of discipleship and at the same time a genuine but unspeakable fear of the thoughts he had aroused in me.

"Your mother left you, so don't be silly," he said, not bothering to soften the blow in his voice.

"My mother died, and my father, in a famine," I replied instantly. "That's why we're all here, all of us, and you too, because all our parents died." I arose from the table wanting to resume the cleaning of the dining room, wanting to focus wholly on simple things like breadcrumbs and traces of cheese. I was afraid of his greater secret knowledge of things, that he would disclose to me some final shocking fact.

He placed his hand on my arm and pressed me back to the bench. "I just showed you your mother, you cunt," he said bitterly. "Didn't you recognise her face? Or were you just peeping at the rest of her? Like your father who spied her in a field, fell upon her, and made you."

"Leave me alone," I cried, rising once again, then sitting down by my own fatigue of will or desperation to suffer his revelations.

"Cunts are people who leave, that's why I'm sure you're one," he said wearily as if suddenly burdened by a wisdom he never sought in spite of his pillaging of the Bible. "Do you remember what you left, where you left, or who, before you came to this place?"

I couldn't and I said so without hesitation. How often, as we bent our heads in concentration over verses about Jesus and his father Joseph, his mother Mary, did I let my thoughts loosen, and wonder what became of mine? And surely the other boys must have longed as I did to know about their parents? The monks told us nothing of our past, and if in the freedom of daydream or to the sleeping mind they appeared, we uttered nothing of it to each other, enslaved as we were to silence. My parents never came to mind, however much I sought them out in a branch felled by rain, a chipped bowl, a pulled tooth, and in all the other small happenings which awakened me to the truth of being alive. I tried to find them too in the great stories placed before us for study, of the plagues, earthquakes, floods and famines sent by God to quell the disobedience of men. A great calamity had carried them off. I decided – why, I cannot tell – on a famine. Perhaps it was to explain to myself why I was always hungry, eager to receive the sacrament on my tongue as a supplement to our pitiful diet, disappointed at how insubstantial the wafer was, then washing it down afterwards with wilful sucking on an icicle when the monks were not watching.

"I remember everything," Lance said boastfully as if attempting to put a distance between us, leaving me before I would, or wanted to. He shifted his body on the bench, threatening to go, but this time it was I who put my hand on his arm to restrain him.

"Tell me," I begged and when he wouldn't I begged again, surrendering to his self-pity.

Tell me what? Of course there was nothing to tell. What sin or vision of goodness could a boy of fourteen disclose to me, a boy cloistered from experience but for snippets from the Old Testament? And what could a lesser child like me understand, even if Lance had spoken to me? There was nothing, but I must go on, for the crow called to me. All winter it had worried, even frightened us with its lonely caw and flight as we approached the stream. One morning it was no more. Gone. Where? Why? I daydreamed in the classroom afterwards, quite careless of the scrutiny of the monks, for the empty orchard was more hurtful than the weight of their hands. I imagined that it had fled to

Biblical lands, to cinnamon groves or cedar trees on the banks of the Euphrates, which pleased me deeply for it would no longer cry out so dismally. The loveliness of the names of faraway places would change its cry into song. But as suddenly as I soared within, in the rhythm of its flight, I was smitten with the image of an archer hiding behind a boulder, secretly licking the tip of his arrow in preparation for the killing. Famine. Plague. Wasteland. All creatures had perished except the miracle of a bird, the last, no, the first living thing in the sky which the archer would bring down out of spite for God. After the Flood the rainbow, but the archer would refuse the new Covenant, shooting into the air out of foolish manly pride.

That night I struggled to sleep but when I did I dreamt of a line of boys, led by myself, making our orderly way to the stream. Suddenly I stumbled, my feet coming against an obstacle. I looked down, discovered a dead bird lying on its back, feathers frozen to its body, feet pointing skyward, beak turned towards the earth. My instinct was to stoop, pick it up with cradled hands, place it gently away from the path to prevent us trampling upon it. Instead I was seized with a horror I could not understand. I kicked it away, maladroitly, for it moved only a few inches. The other boys milled around the dead bird, kicking it to each other, until its feathers started to come away. Lance appeared from nowhere, pushing us aside as if to protect the bird from our cruelty, but he stamped upon its breast with such force that its beak opened. We stood around the bird, excited and sickened at the sight of the green and red liquid trickling from its beak. The three old women came running up to break our circle of fascination. They gazed upon the mutilated bird and began to wail as if at the death of family. They took up sticks to chastise us but Lance wrenched them from their hands. He lashed out at the women, a stream of obscene words pouring from him as if he was speaking in tongues.

"I know my mother and my father," Lance said in a voice of devotion, the words sounding like a line from a prayer or psalm. (That is truly all I remember him saying, but just as I once dreamt the contrary fate of the crow, so I now let words trickle from his mouth. I press him to go on. Stories leak out.)

His parents had emigrated to a land across the seas called the Bermudas. The soil was blessed there, fertile, verdant. They owned the plantation, growing figs, oranges and pomegranates. They had left him in the care of the monks, but soon they would send for him. Or else his parents had drowned in the Caribbean Sea, in sight of the Bermudas and all its promises. The ship had been boarded by pirates. Having plundered passengers and cargo, they set light to the ship, but took pity upon him, an infant. The pirates wrapped him in swaddling-clothes, set him adrift in a lifeboat. A British warship, drawn by the light of the fire, eventually found him, returned him to Ireland. The monks, astonished by the miracle of his survival – for he had gone a week without nourishment or water, exposed to the fiercest sun and nightly chill, but was perfectly healthy when found – took him in readily as an infant chosen of God. Or else his parents had arrived in the Bermudas after an uneventful sailing, but within a few hours of landing the savages who lived on the island set upon them with poison-tipped spears. The savages butchered all the newcomers, but took him away to the heart of the forest, for in their religion newly born children were gifts from the gods. The savages intended to rear him as a kind of living idol, awed as they were by the whiteness of his skin, but a British raiding party rescued him, and put him on the next ship sailing to Ireland.

"My mother was a whore," Lance said, shattering my daydream and circle of fascination. "A whore from a village somewhere in Ireland. My father smashed her in, buried her in our garden under a pile of stones. Here, this is what she looked like." He reached into his bosom and took out a Biblical picture which I immediately recognised, from the cowering posture of the woman and the men crouching to pick up stones from the earth.

"Her eyes were just as smitten with fright," he said, scanning the woman's face to identify other aspects of his mother. I expected – or wanted – him to cry but he suddenly crumpled the picture into a ball and threw it to the floor.

"She's dead anyway," he said with wilful finality. I wanted more. I wanted him to tell me that after her husband had accused her of sinning and driven her away, she took the infant

Lance with her. They hurried to the next village, getting there just before nightfall. The mother – I name her Beth – knocked on the nearest door but no one answered. She went from cottage to cottage seeking shelter but no one came out. People were indoors – their lamps were lit and she could hear conversations, arguments, crying as she approached – but as soon as they heard the rattling of the gate they fell silent. It was as if they were forewarned of the coming of a leper. They would not greet her, nor would they chase her off, for to do so would be to arouse the wrath of our Lord, He who moved among sickly prostitutes, giving them succour and a healing touch. A huge thunderclap breached the sky, rain poured down and Beth hurried on, passing the last cottage and entering the forest. Guided by constant flashes of lightning she stumbled upon a cave where she rested. Some animal must have lived there once for she found a lair of dry leaves and the ground littered with the feathers of prey. She made a bed of dry leaves and feathers for Lance, and laid him down and watched over him all night, armed only with prayer against the return of the animal.

The next day she ventured out of the cave to search for food. After many hours she returned with a mere handful of winter berries which she crushed in her mouth and fed to Lance. There was no vessel to fetch water so she had soaked herself in a shallow pond in the middle of the forest. She took off her blouse and wrung it over Lance's mouth. She mixed the rest of the water into the earth, making a paste which she daubed over Lance's body. It would harden soon; encased in clay he would sleep warmly. Again she stayed awake, waiting for first light when she would forage vines and trees for fruit and drench her clothing in the pond. This time she returned empty-handed and shivering. It was the end of December. The forest yielded nothing, barely surviving on its own resources. Lance would have to make do with water.

On the third day she found the pond frozen over. She hacked off a piece of ice which she warmed between her breasts until it was liquid enough for his tongue. That night she lay down beside him, expecting to die, but her eyes opened to morning light flaring at the entrance of the cave, and a wind through the forest like the beating of wings. It was Christmas Day she knew instinctively, and God had sent an angel to deliver them to a room in His mansion, gay with summer flowers and vines with suckling fruit. She shook Lance awake, gathered him and moved towards the light but when she reached the entrance of the cave there was nothing but her lonely self. She stood there shivering so violently that she had to clutch Lance tightly to her, lest she dropped him. The light was an illusion of fire and the wind spat frostily at her. She turned to go back into the cave but a voice arose in her mind commanding her to stay, to suffer, to be converted into a pillar of ice, and she obeyed, out of shame, for the infant she was carrying was not her husband's. And in the very moment of the sorrow of repentance, as she lowered her eyes to the ground, she found the first gift of the unseen angel – a broad feather which she stooped to pick up, and underneath a quail's egg still warm to touch. Footprints trailed away from the cave to the forest – what kind of creature she could not tell.

Each morning the same dazzling light and clamour of wings which drew her to the mouth of the cave, where she found a broad feather covering over an egg; a quail's egg, but sometimes a hen's, a duck's, or some other bird she did not recognise. And the footprints were always different, always unfamiliar. She replenished Lance's nest of leaves with fresh feathers and fed him yolk, crushing the shell into pieces of wafer which she subsisted upon.

It was not to last, this strange and meagre communion between mother, child and forest creature. The soaking of her clothing in water gave her a permanent chill. Her body stiffened into a curve, giving her the appearance of a crouching animal. Unable to stand upright she crawled on all fours towards the light, her hand shaking in cold and guilt as she retrieved the egg.

And as she lay on her side dying, what vision flickered, making her stare beyond Lance's cradle into the gloom of the cave? Seven golden candlesticks and a rainbow wrapped around the Son of Man like a winding sheet? Was the darkness a canvas twinkling with images of her wrongdoing, her surrender to the honeyed tongue of a neighbour whilst her husband was away tending his sheep? Did the voices of the villagers arise, accusing her, mocking her, urging her husband to banish her to the forest?

All this and more I wanted to hear from Lance but he remained glum, staring at the ball of paper on the floor as if he had cast away his mother.

"She was a whore, my father smashed her in, burnt her face, buried her under stone," he said repeatedly, fingering a rosary of self-pity, but I denied him, craving a story of forest creatures – angels – bringing him gifts out of simple compassion, departing without need for gratitude. And when his mother died they howled continually, and so eerily that villagers scavenging the forest for food were drawn to the cave, even against their will. And verily, it was thus he was found and delivered unto the monastery as a miraculous child or spoor, a sign from God that the forest, stripped by winter, would flourish again, soon, so long as they kept faith with the seasons, the taking away and the giving; the surety, even in the midst of hunger and distress, that God was mindful of their fate.

★

In the seven days before my grandfather came to collect me, taking me to Coventry, Lance refused to share stories from the Bible, much less speak to me. He would not rise in the morning to be bathed by the women. The monks, noticing a new sullenness in him, let him be. They even appeared frightened by his presence in chapel and classroom, sensing in his broken voice signs of a troubled mind, troubled body. He glowered at the Gospel passage set before him. When they prayed aloud for souls brought to trial or to the threshold of wickedness I knew they were praying for him. He knew it too, resisting the public exposure of his condition. I, out of solidarity, began to resent the piety of the monks, but especially the cruel solicitousness of the women. I moved away when Agnes reached to soap my body. I went to a private part of the stream to bathe myself. I could feel their contempt splattering upon

135

my back like phlegm. When I returned they scowled at me. "You're not my mother, don't touch me," I said blatantly. I expected them to search the ground for a birch with which to punish me, but Agnes leaned back on her heels and laughed. The other two broke out in a sympathetic cackle. I knew they were laughing at my mother but I could not shield her from scorn, for I was ignorant of her name, never mind the sin she had committed. I envied Lance his remembrance of his mother, fictitious as it was.

I stared out of the classroom window awaiting the return of the crow, and when it did not appear, wondering what had become of it. The three women were in the orchard pruning the trees. I watched them hacking at the branches with the spite of those who would reduce living things to their own decaying selves. I looked across to see Lance glowering at the Gospel passage and my heart quickened for him. I felt a sudden gratitude for the way his body hungered him, the way his imagination supped on the darkest stories of the Bible. It came to me that I would never see him again, or if I did it would be countless years away, he grown into a creature as callous to boys in his care as the three witches, eyeing their young flesh enviously; or else like the monks, slobbering over their prayers, greedy for eternal life, guarding each drop of Christ's blood for their own palates.

In the final days we continued working privately in the kitchen, but no words were exchanged. I missed the communion between us, the way he would scrape off a mite of food from a plate with his forefinger and place it upon my tongue. Nor did his gestures and movements betray any feeling for me. He wiped the table, swept the floor, put away the cooking pots, that was all. He had withdrawn into the solitariness of his hurt body. He was not to be approached, not to be touched.

On the morning my grandfather came to claim me I awoke and as usual went to Lance's bed to rouse him. It was empty. I searched the kitchen, the classroom, the chapel, but could not find him. I wandered through the orchard calling out his name. I discovered the three stones under which he had hidden the Bible. They were upturned, and the Bible was missing. I walked towards the stream but the sight of the three women made me stop. Agnes held out a piece of soap to me, like an oracle. Agatha swung her bucket like a happy child setting off to collect blackberries. Abigail wiped her ankle with a towel as if ridding herself of an obsessive stain. I turned away from this scene of madness and went back to the dormitory to gather my belongings and await my grandfather. On this, my last day, I would neither wash nor feed nor pray.

★

My grandfather comes to me as a stranger and I leave with a stranger. He is a lean troubled man. When he cups my cheeks in greeting I feel the bones of his palms. He brushes back my hair and runs an enquiring hand over my forehead, seeking to recognise me. I look down at my shoes, refusing to face him. A week before, the monks had told me of his coming to remove me to England, but it was as unreal a moment as his presence before me, now; as unreal as the shoes the monks found for me in some hidden store, to set me on my journey. No one comes to see me as I am taken away – the shoes are a sufficient gift of farewell – except the three women who wait by the gate, to close it after us. I ignore them, focusing on the startling lightness of my bundle of belongings – comb, towel, vest, trousers – but from the corner of my eye I see one of them search her bosom and pull out something. I look at her and flinch, thinking I am to be mocked one last time. It is Agnes. She has a piece of cloth in her hand. It is tied into a knot. Her hands tremble as she unties the knot to reveal a coin. She spits upon it and rubs it in the body of the cloth. Cleansed of dirt the coin is held out to me. I do not take it, out of bewilderment, but she prises open my hand and places the bright coin in it proudly. Afterwards she looks foolishly at me, and Agatha and Abigail are fidgety, shifting uneasily on their feet, wanting me to cross the threshold quickly so they could bang the gate shut and padlock it with practised venom.

The sea is choppy and my stomach loosens, but more in loneliness for Lance, though the deck is crowded with people, mostly men, who by now are familiar to me. My grandfather and I had ridden miles and miles on a horse-drawn cart hired for the purpose, until we came to the wharf. The noise of wheels over earthen roads and the constant jolting over pits and ruts made conversation impossible. It was late afternoon before we reached the wharf.

My grandfather unfastens the cart, tethers the horse to a post and goes off to make a final settlement with the owner. He leaves me on a bench in the waiting area in the company of men who prattle among themselves, joking, passing around bottle after bottle of whisky, but for all the merriment they appear to be performing, as we did in the monastery. They swear. We prayed. They tell stories. We recited the psalms. They suckle on the bottle. We ate wafer from appointed hands. My grandfather returns and joins the men, becoming suddenly talkative, drinking with them as if it is expected of him.

Night comes, the moon appears, the sky unveils its stars. Tomorrow a white cloth will be wrapped around them, making them disappear, as the monks with utmost studiousness wrapped linen around the chalice and plate of the Eucharist before padlocking them away. When night fell they would come out again, the moon and stars practising to shine, as we would practise our evensong voices.

The sea is choppy and my stomach loosens, but out of a fear of being set adrift from all the things I have been faithful to, acts of worship, repetition of prayers, obedience to the monks, which Lance tried to tempt me from but when I refused, drawing sacred linen around me, he disappeared. Now I am yielded up to a company of men, swine-drunk and hollering and I search the sky for Lance but there is only the rehearsal of light from the moon and stars.

II

"Geoffrey, an Irishman of unusual suffering": I rehearsed Father Harris's words in my mind as I walked the mile or so to the almshouse to visit my grandfather. Fourteen months of shovelling dirt in Coventry had exhausted him completely and a sudden sickness ended his career on the canals. From now on he would be dependent on charity. The sight of him, of his bedsores and leftover pieces of cake he hid under his pillow for a future time, made me ashamed of our kinship. A boy of fourteen could be forgiven for such feelings. You must forgive me Geoffrey, I addressed him silently, overcome by guilt. I resolved to make amends by reading to him with fresh voice. I looked upon him again as he lay on his piss-soaked mattress, wanting to imagine him differently in spite of the reek; wanting to imagine his Irish garden, the scent of the tomatoes he raised with such loving nurture, and runner-beans, cabbages, peas, all things he tended from fragile seed or shoot to textured ripeness. And the cow, with its peculiar fragrance of milk, manure and bits of thistle snared in its coat, bleeding greenly at the stem. All I could see though was a decrepit Irishman, wifeless, widowed from his garden in Wicklow, sent to Coventry to wait tenderly, at other times furiously, for the moment of his death.

"Will you be wanting Jack and the Beanstalk again?" I asked. He nodded. I started, as usual, by describing the illustration to him. It showed a cottage set in a small plot of land overlooked by a birch tree, and behind that, vegetation indicating a rural landscape. A pair of geese embellished an empty sky. A lamb roped to a post grazed with familiar and contended idleness, and beside it there was a boy in bizarre circumstances, for he was climbing, with a huge and ragged movement, what looked like a grotesquely enlarged stem which stretched to the top margin of the picture and to an imaginary land beyond. I told the scene to my grandfather but he made no response. I was about to resume the story when his feet began to twitch, rubbing against each other as if to kindle into life.

"Arthur, piece of filth, Arthur took my wire," he blurted out. He raised his head and eyed underneath his pillow to make sure the bits of food were still there. The effort exhausted him and he fell back upon his bed. His outburst made his frame appear all the more pained and wasted. I noticed his elbow joints pressing against his skin, threatening to breach it. A bony hand raked the blanket over his neck and mouth, as if he wanted to suppress further speech, but he could not, for Arthur's name escaped from him again in a squirming mournful cry, the kind of noise a dog would make if a loving master suddenly raised a cudgel over it. He began to sob, but only for a few seconds, stopping abruptly in defiance of his grief.

"The thief of my wire. I saved up months and months to buy wire, walked one full day to town, walked back the same day and all night with the wire strapped to my back, coiled around my waist. The worst of it was the digging and biting and scratching into my flesh, like Satan's hounds."

Satan's hounds: the words caused me to look away, and I wondered whether or how my grandfather knew of my daydream, the way the hounds caught up with me, opened me, scratching at my liver, relishing my heart. Guilt wakened me to speech, my mouth hurriedly resumed the telling of the story, but my grandfather stopped me, demanding that I describe the illustration again. And again. And again. Between each telling he stuttered out a wholly unrelated tale of stolen wire, broken with swift vile insults against Arthur, the smelly cunt, the devil's mount, and sometimes more expansively, in images of drowned rats floating in a latrine's porridge, a bird held down whilst its eyes were gouged out, a mule so laden with logs that its back buckled and cracked.

My grandfather, tired of repairing his garden fence against constant damage by his own and his neighbour's cows, saved fanatically to buy barbed-wire. He and my grandmother went without salt in their food, and then without food, to accumulate the money. When it was enough he set off early one morning, freshly scrubbed, hair oiled and cleanly combed, for the town of Castlepoint. It was a proud time for both of them. Wire was expensive; in the village only their garden would be adorned with it, signalling achievement and the hope of future wealth. He wore his best shirt, and his foot was shod, for going to town was in itself a mark of ambitiousness. His money, tied in a clean piece of cloth, was secured underneath his shirt. It brushed pleasurably against his waist as he walked the twenty miles to Castlepoint. A bag stuffed with apples, cheese and a tattered vest and blanket was slung over his shoulder.

He was surprised to be greeted by Arthur as he made his way out of the village. Arthur was waiting by his garden gate. He winked at my grandfather by way of a greeting, slapped him on the back, wished him a happy journey and pressed a florin into his hand. As he walked down the main path leading to the forest and to Castlepoint, Geoffrey puzzled over Arthur's behaviour. Why the intimate winking? Why the unprecedented act of generosity? Of course Arthur owned twelve cows and as many geese, undoubtedly the richest man in the village. His wife had died childless, and he had refused to remarry, not out of romantic attachment to memories of previous happiness but to lavish all his wealth on himself. He was shockingly fat, with a triple chin, and though in his early thirties, the gallons of whisky he downed every week aged his face with permanent pouches under his eyes. He did no work, employing a half-blind idiot to tend to his cattle and geese. The idiot who was simply called 'Idiot' was born with a defective brain – his head was lumpy and elongated like a rogue marrow. His parents didn't bother to give him a name, much less baptise him. Idiot's father drank himself into a rage, cursing his wife for a rotten belly, beating her for the least error of housewifery – a soggy carrot on his dinner-plate, a trace of grease on the doorknob. She was forbidden to leave the house, to prevent her bruises being seen and provoking outrage even in the coarsest of hearts. Nor was she permitted to cry upon punishment, so that the neighbours suspected little beyond the normalcy of domestic strife. At first she sought escape by caring for her idiot infant, cleaning, feeding, lullabying it in a fantasy of fulfilled motherhood. Once, in an act of blasphemy, she pretended the tub in which she bathed it was a font, and she a priest. She dipped it in the water and blessed it, making the sign of the Cross on its forehead, all the while speaking gibberish to imitate the Church's Latin. But the beatings took their toll on her sanity. She began to despise the child, slowly – at first the odd pinching, dressing it roughly, spitting into its milk – then working up to murderous intent. How she rubbed dirt into his eyes regularly, so that one eventually went blind; this, and more, she confessed in court, and in the lunatic asylum afterwards.

Idiot was taken in by a monastery in Kildare, but he ran away as soon as he grew legs sturdy enough for the sixty miles back to the village. Legend had it that he spent years chained in the monastery's cellar, half-starved, eating the very straw he soiled and slept upon. The monks took his misshapen head as a sign of inner loathsomeness and did whatever they could to suppress his potential appetite for devilry. Prayer, the denial of tasty food, solitary confinement for long periods with his hands tied behind his back to prevent self-pleasuring... such was the experience of his childhood, before he escaped at the age of twelve.

★

"Why Arthur's sudden kindness?" Geoffrey mused as he walked home along what felt like an endless path running through fields of corn and barley, which suddenly ended in a thick wall of forest. It was the hour of dusk, there was no one to keep him company, apart from rooks hurrying across the sky to roost before darkness disorientated them. It was a vast sky and a vast plain stretching away, with monotonous flatness, to the forest. He had only his own thoughts to distract him from the lengthy journey ahead, and the weight of the barbed wire on his shoulders and back, biting through the tattered vest and blanket that had replaced his best shirt. The moon was a distant pale disc, unconcerned to watch over his weariness, and the wire punctured his skin in the same places, however much he shifted his muscles and arranged his posture. The wire was fastened to his upper body in such a way that it could not be removed by himself alone. He was trapped in it as steadfastly as a badger or young deer. Darkness trickled around him, then thickened, slowing his pace. The night's insects, drawn to his warmth and sweat, settled in his hair, his nostrils, his mouth. After a while it was too laborious to flick them away, so he took them in his breath and spittle.

Still, for all the discomfort, it was Arthur's florin which pressed upon his mind, the questioning of it keeping him awake. He scolded himself for accepting it, then scolded himself for doubting Arthur's spontaneous kindness. After all, the rest of the villagers had reacted to the news of his intended purchase with approval. Some had even praised him for his feat of saving such a sum of money. Recollection of their words of kindness as they passed him working in his garden gave fresh energy to his feet. Even the Proprietor in the shop in Castlepoint was full of admiration for him. For all his attempt at elegance, his oiled and brushed hair, his one respectable shirt, there was still something about him which betrayed his poverty (popery). Perhaps it was the way he wandered about the shop, astonished at the range of goods, the sophisticated contraption of blades and other machines to make ploughing and harvesting more easeful, obviously destined for ownership by rich farmers, those with hundreds of acres and a flock of labourers. Perhaps it was the way he stood before the Proprietor that betrayed his peasant nature, his feet clad uneasily in his shoes, wanting to be rid of them. At first the Proprietor, stoutly English, in starched collar and braces holding up his ample trousers, had eyed him with suspicion, but as soon as Geoffrey placed his bag of coins on the counter and poured them out, his mood changed into one of surprise. The Englishman counted out a full two pounds and fishing out a pencil and pad from his back pocket, worked out what the sum could purchase. Twenty-two feet and four inches, he announced at last, then began to recalculate the figure. The wire came in coils of eight yards, so Geoffrey was one foot eight inches short of money, the Proprietor said. It was not worth his while cutting one foot eight inches from the coil. But did Geoffrey have an additional shilling and say four pence, the Proprietor asked, a hint of sarcasm in his voice. Geoffrey was overcome by a sense of his foolishness. The figures confused him, he had no knowledge of numerical measurement. He wanted the Proprietor to take the coil outside and unroll it on the ground so he could reckon the length of his garden. He would walk along the wire on the ground, taking off his shoes to gauge better the accuracy of the length of his garden. Then at some point he would stop and order that piece, perhaps taking an extra step to make sure he was correct. Now, with the Proprietor gazing at him, anxiety washed into his mouth, stopping his breath, his ability to speak. "Not to worry," the Proprietor said with sudden pity, "we'll think of something, why don't we? Tell you what, there is a little task I have been keeping for some passing vagrant. They keep coming in, droves of them. Begging, but once you mention work, off they go muttering and cursing." And without further negotiation the Proprietor took him to the tallest ladder in the store and handed him a broom.

Of course he was too ashamed to complain. Of course he was too ashamed to take off his fine shirt or to show sorrow when it soon became soiled with cobwebs and the shells of insects. Instead, he brushed the ceiling with intense concentration, ignoring the shower of dust on his face, ignoring the customers who wandered through the shelves of goods they could easily afford, who looked up at him with pity and contempt or with no emotion at all. He tried hard not to overhear their conversations with the Proprietor, conversations that lacked the nervousness of his opening question about the cost of wire. For they knew what they wanted, and at what small cost to their capacious pockets.

And was the Proprietor full of admiration for him, his frugality in saving up the necessary sum, the ambitiousness of his project, his long walk through potato and barley fields and forest to town, and the care with which he presented himself? Now, as he ventured home, with the ceiling's dirt settled on his face, his torn vest and blanket as clothes, his fine shirt smudged beyond recognition, he doubted. Oh yes, the Proprietor had stared at the ceiling with the astonishment of a magus, for what before was a mess of cobwebs now gleamed with original colour. Yes, so grateful was the Proprietor that he gave the full coil of wire and even two boxes of nails (for Geoffrey had forgotten to account for these). And above all, the paper. The Proprietor had taken the trouble to write out a receipt, detailing length of wire, feet times pence, sum total, deduction for work done, nails *gratis*, all in a scrupulously neat hand, though he must have known that he, Geoffrey, couldn't read what was written down, much less verify its accuracy. But for all this, did the Proprietor really admire him, or was it mere gratitude for cleaning his ceiling, a task which any mindless creature, any shular and stray could achieve?

It was a question which arose again, but more acutely than the wire spiking his flesh, when the wire disappeared. Its disappearance was utterly more painful than the transporting of it home, because of the questions it provoked. Did the Englishman value him, did he, did he, did he appreciate the sacrifice that went into the purchase? Or did he secretly dismiss him, Geoffrey, as foolishly ambitious, wanting to rise above his station when he should have been contented with his Popish Cross of poverty? Is that why the Englishman made him, Geoffrey, ascend a shaky ladder to filthy heights, to confront him with the soil of his being, his endless planting of things in dirt which when they sprouted were the only measure of his being; and when they failed, as they did, left him lesser than a man, lesser than a husband, literally a widower. For all the fine words on the paper, he was left literally a widower.

'Widower'. That is what another Englishman wrote down on another piece of paper, after the famine, when as a desolate remnant and survivor, he contracted himself to canal-digging in Coventry. Name: Geoffrey Malone. Age: Unknown. Place of Birth: Ireland. Marital Status: Widower. When asked about his marital status he had begun to tell the contractor of the circumstances of his wife's death, but the contractor cut him short and scribbled the word down, for there was a queue of similar men awaiting recruitment. Without asking, the contractor seized his thumb, pressed it onto a pad of ink and then onto the paper. Dismissed, he waited on a bench in the depot, in the company of other broken solemn men, for interview and physical examination.

★

Pride. It was what had brought him there, on a bench in a ramshackle depot, awaiting processing and eventual shipment to England. Pride had placed him before Englishmen who would ask him questions and write down the answers half-heartedly, who would probe into his mouth to check the health of his gums and teeth, who would feel his thighs, study his soles, as if he were a farm animal examined before being bid for. Pride in being the first in his village to acquire bucky-wire, ownership evidenced in the Proprietor's paper. Pride in not stripping naked to the waist before cleaning the ceiling. And when the wire disappeared, ripped from the fence-posts one dark night, when it rained so violently that the noise of the theft was drowned out, it was the loss of pride which was the abiding hurt. He felt worthless, not in terms of his wasted purchase, but in the abrupt collapse of self-esteem. Three days he had spent fastening the wire to posts, a far more difficult task than he had imagined, the curl of the metal needing to be straightened out to keep it from dislodging the staple-nails. His hands were bloody and bandaged, but he was proud of his mortification. After a while the pain became addictive, driving him on though it meant the constant opening up of wounds. On the fourth day he had woken up before first light, needing to finish his handiwork. To begin with he thought nothing of the absence of the wire, putting it down to the darkness of the time of day, and the darkness of sleep still obscuring his eyes. He moved closer to the posts and pushed out his hands, his fingers feeling for the wire, delicately, as if milking a cow's teats. He felt again, squeezing the air softly at first, then his fingers became frantic and cruel as saliva curdled in his mouth and his lungs filled up with morning mist. He felt a sudden rush of life within him, a moment of bliss, like the last perverse and defiant blasphemous shudder against the closing down of his muscles, his organs, his breathing, his being. His time had come, by God's design, but he cursed within before surrendering to the futility of his rage. He sat down sullenly by a post, awaiting death and the examination of angels and the transportation of his soul to Heaven.

To Coventry. New canals to be dug to move coal. Pride was to be his ferryman there, he was sure, taking him to a place of foreigners, a town of huge factories billowing smoke. It would cover him over in a shower of dirt. He would disappear, merging into the grime of everything and everywhere. Pride, then the loss of pride, for when he eventually arose from the post and returned to his bed, it was to lie there forever, hoping that the darkness would not lift. My grandmother awoke, went outside to feed the fowls, shrieked when she saw the denuded posts and ripped out staplenails. She stumbled back to the

146

house, careless of mud and cow dung soiling the floorboards the colour of her distress. Shook him. Harder. Pulled at his limbs. Pulled at his hair. He would not open his eyes, wanting her to leave him alone. He could hear the surge of cries, he could smell the filth of her feet, but as a man in a self-induced coma, unwilling to respond.

In the days that followed he worked his gardens like a zombie, weeding and planting, without connecting to the earth, without feeling the hurt of his bruised hands. (Later, in Coventry, he would shovel with brutish automatic effort, caring neither for the aching of his muscles nor the wounds he inflicted on the earth.) At first the villagers kept away, possibly out of respect for his grief, possibly out of guilt at their part in his undoing. When they did approach with condolences and words of encouragement, he merely harrumphed, swallowing his saliva. He stuck his fork in the dirt and turned it over as if gouging out eyes, but with the cold and mindless ritual of an inquisitioner.

Idiot was the convenient scapegoat. The villagers knew that Geoffrey seethed within, from the way he plunged his fork into the earth, the way he wrestled with weeds, hauling them up mercilessly, when before, living plants, however redundant to the pot, were removed with a care close to apology. His faith was always ample, regarding all growing things as deserving of their own life. Was not his own life useless and trifling, sustained only by the mercy of God? His reputation among his fellows was as a meek, quietly spiritual creature, one moreover who possessed the ability to heal, for it was to him that they brought their children suffering from minor ailments. He massaged their bodies, he mixed seeds and herbs into a paste and fed them, he dabbed their lips with his own spittle. Always they left his house with their fevers cooled, their aches attended to and partially becalmed. Now this gentle man was dangerous in his repressed wrath, unable to cure himself. Idiot was yielded up to him as sacrifice.

Idiot lived in a pen behind Arthur's cottage where the cows and geese were kept. Arthur had built him a dwelling of clay and straw at one corner of the pen which in rainy weather dissolved overnight, or at the height of summer cracked and collapsed. Idiot was always restoring his hut, it was impossible to know why he bothered, since he never inhabited it, preferring the openness of the pen and the company of animals. In cold wet nights he would lie down beside a cow, snuggling up against its belly, with such a natural sense of the contours of its body that hardly a drop of rain fell upon him. More bizarre was the way the geese gave him succour from the afternoon heat, draping their wings over him as he slept, every now and again fanning him or rubbing their wet beaks pleasingly along his neck. Ague, pneumonia, chilblain, fevers affected those living in cottages, but the changing of the seasons brought no such maladies to Idiot. Though he worked as vigorously as any man, his skin remained unblemished. Others bore the scars of thorns, sharp rocks, sickles, the usual hazards of planting their gardens or taking animals to the common pasture a mile away along a dirt path made perilous by endless rain or endless sun. Blind in one eye, defective in the other, he sniffed his way safely to the pasture and back again. There was a constancy in his appearance, and though he had advanced in age, he had not changed at all from the time he first arrived in the village six years previously. Very few noticed this curious aspect of his appearance, and those who did gave him only a moment's attention. People were too occupied with the husbandry of their land and livestock to bother with Arthur's cretin. They had nothing to say to him since he could not speak, and anyway, he spent his time in the solitude of animals, hidden from sight behind Arthur's cottage, living on cow's milk, the raw vegetables he planted in Arthur's garden, and going and coming from the pasture, fruit gathered from the ground where they had dropped ripely.

Why Idiot would want to steal Geoffrey's wire baffled everybody. To be fair to the villagers, they did ask themselves the question, but, not being able to provide a comfortable answer, they put it down to the mystery of Idiot's mind. He was the devil's child, some argued, and therefore was bound to do devilish acts, out of pure malice. But those who said that didn't really believe their own accusation of satanic influence. How many of their relatives or forebears, giving birth to defective babies, had not taken them quietly, at first dawn, to the forest pond, to drown them. To be sure, the Church deemed such babies signs of evil, but any farmer knew that once in a blue moon he would turf up the most curious of potatoes, either huge in size, joined up to another, curved into a bowl-shape, flattened like a pancake, or malformed in some other startling way. The farmer, out of respect for the nature of the earth, buried the potato. The same with babies. The odd one came out differently. It couldn't be baptised in the normal way, but dipped headlong into the forest pond until it died, then buried under clean soil, with no stone or bound sticks marking its bed. Satan had nothing to do with it. Things were just so.

They decided to confront Idiot, to search his habitation. They brushed past the drunken sleeping Arthur and entered the pen. The geese immediately arose in one movement, standing their ground and making wild aggressive noises. The villagers backed off. The cows moved towards them en masse, then sensing their fear, stopped, looked at them with eyes all the more threatening because unfathomable. The villagers scanned the pen, looking for Idiot, alighting on a mound of earth in the far corner which stirred slightly, then with more force, then arose slowly and deliberately, shook itself like an animal shaking impediments from its coat, and when the dirt showered from it, the boy-man was revealed, crouching, alert, as if waiting to spring. He was naked, except for pieces of mud which had hardened here and there on his skin, permanently it seemed, for grass took root in them, greening his body, and tiny flowering plants gave it a curious gaiety. The image of a resurrected corpse, bearing about him the bright tokens of a living earth, made a few of the villagers cross themselves repeatedly. Idiot raised his mouth to the sun and mooed. He stretched out his neck in their direction and sniffed, making a sudden honking noise of recognition, then slowly withdrew his neck, curving it to his armpit where his tongue licked as if to cleanse his flesh or feed upon insects. The geese were oddly pacified by his movement, stopping their cries and retreating to their corner of the pen. They pecked the ground or combed their bills through their plumage, neglecting the presence of the villagers. The cows followed their lead, turned around and ambled off to the trough where they drank effortlessly, without enthusiasm. The villagers were left alone, for Idiot ignored them, swaying his flanks as if to ward off flies with an invisible tail, running his mouth along his arm and making sucking foraging noises. After a while, satisfied with all his actions, he lowered himself in a movement of sedateness and fulfilment, rested his face in the earth, fell asleep. The villagers idled by the gate, unsure of themselves, before trickling out foolishly into Arthur's garden, but the last of them upon departing, picked up a heavy stone and flung it mightily at the Idiot-mound. Why he did so he didn't know. Perhaps it was to assert himself against the beast. Perhaps it was to accuse the boy-man of an act more unspeakable than the theft of wire. Perhaps it was in panic, like a man in nightmare bolts upright, punching and flailing at the air to shatter the dream. Perhaps it was innocent, like a boy throwing a stone into water to gaze upon the ripples.

It landed with a lavish thud on Idiot's forehead. His body shuddered as the blood left it. He made tiny squeaking noises as if his lips were rusty hinges to his breath. The cows continued to drink nonchalantly and the geese were only momentarily distracted by his plight, going back to preening their feathers or sparring with each other.

III

"Did Idiot die, did he?" I asked my grandfather, but he would not answer, staring at the ceiling and moaning, as if the stone had landed stunningly on *his* head. When he did speak it was a babble even more disconnected than before, single words, muted phrases, which, inspired by Father Harris's injunction, I have tried to piece together with the care of piecing together a shattered eggshell, even though the life within had splashed and drained away. It had been one of the most puzzling, but joyous, exercises of my childhood, when in Father Harris's writing class he presented me not with pen and paper but with a handful of broken eggshells, glue, brushes, chunks of earth in different hues which I must grind to dust and mix with oils of his own preparation. It was my task to match fragments as best I could, if necessary chipping away at them to form compatible edges, glue them together with utmost concentration, then paint them according to my own mood. "Don't cover over the cracks," he chided me when I presented the first egg to him, gloriously rounded and purple, awaiting his approval. But he crushed it and made me start again, showing me how to dip the finest point of brush in blue paint and run it along the cracks to highlight them. "Always leave a memory of the original," he taught me when I represented him with the egg, pressing his finger into the top to open up a ragged hole. "The memory of the original only comes when you see the breakage, do you understand, boy?" I didn't, or I did, but couldn't utter it except in the felt joy which came after the utter discipline and frustratingly slow process of matching and gluing the pieces together, fabricating a whole but taking care afterwards to distress an area by my own will, then tracing the lines of glue like blue veins alive with blood, lavishing bright paint over the rest of the surface.

Idiot was wounded, mortally or not I never discovered. I learnt, or I believed, or I imagined, that the villagers insisted on his guilt, though Arthur, summoned that very day to their makeshift court, claimed to have searched Idiot's hut and found nothing. He must have buried it, they charged, but Arthur was in no mood or fit state to dig up the pen, nor would he allow them to trespass on his property to do so. "He must have thrown it into the pond, let's go search," a girl offered innocently. The rest of the children stirred with excitement, but their parents hushed them, and the silence that followed was weighed with foreboding.

Arthur eventually surrendered to their need for a sacrifice and agreed to dismiss Idiot the next day. He awoke in an alcoholic haze, took up a stick and went to the pen to drive Idiot away, but Idiot was not to be found. Arthur shrugged, dropped the stick and returned to a fresh bottle of whisky and the warmth of his bed. The day passed, then another, Arthur getting up periodically to check the pen for Idiot's return. But the boy-man was absent. In a fit of panic, Arthur sobered up and went looking for Idiot, though the hour was late, for he needed Idiot's service in minding his cows, feeding his geese, cleaning his house. He lit a torch, stumbling along the path leading to the pasture, calling out Idiot's name in the falling darkness. An early owl hooted back from the direction of the forest pond but Arthur would not venture that far. He stopped in panic, fished an imagined flask of whisky from his back pocket and guzzled it down. The owl called again, stridently this time, but Arthur would not heed. With the mightiest of effort he summoned up all his strength, lifting his leg out of the pull of an imagined quagmire, turned and fled with no sense of shame at his diminished manhood, never mind a sense of his humanity. Or rather it was a sudden sense of his humanity which tangled his feet, the fright of solitariness at the edge of the pasture, under a vast dark sky which mocked the torch glued miraculously to his hand, though it shook in delirium, the owl calling for a third, a fourth, a fifth time, each call more insistent than before, and more close.

Was there ever a story or fairy tale of a bird mistaking a man for prey, swooping down to seize him as he hurried homeward in the dark? I don't remember. Perhaps I read it in a book which makes me dream now of Arthur brushing aside bramble and low branches as he dashes from the security of the village, careless of nature's assault and possession of his human flesh, so that when he reaches home his hair is festooned with leaves and twigs, his limbs scratched like earth in a season of drought.

And it was drought which befell them when Idiot disappeared, a drought beyond all expectations, for the rain had fallen tentatively in the previous week, promising a month or so of regular showers, only to halt abruptly the moment they had finished sowing. Slowly the ground turned to stone, entombing the seeds. The pasture withered, and all the trees along the path which gave shelter to animals, first the birch, then the oak, then the yew. They simply dried up, and, hollowed out by insects, branches broke off or hung pathetically by skeins of bark. One by one the livestock perished, followed by the villagers, then my grandmother, her death hastened by guilt over Idiot's disappearance. "But it was me, not her," my grandfather muttered. "Poor Amy was blameless, it was me who should have died." He was inconsolable on this point, going over and over in his mind, sometimes in snatches of mournful speech, the pride behind the purchase of wire, the pride which needed to be fed by Idiot's banishment. But it was the mention of Amy which aroused my curiosity. I was by now, after the fifth or sixth visit to my grandfather and after innumerable descriptions of the Jack-and-the-Beanstalk picture, bored by the familiarity of his tale, but the mention of Amy renewed my interest. Who was Amy? What did she think of the whole business of the wire? Did she love my grandfather? Where did they meet? What was her age when she died? Was my mother her only child? And what of my mother's disappearance? Was Amy as agitated by grief at her disappearance as by Idiot's? Did she survive that grief only to succumb deliberately to guilt over Idiot's plight? Was her death a deliberate act, a final repentance for her rejection of my mother? Was my mother dead? Who was my mother? Where?

That was the true riddle of my childhood, eclipsing all others, even the story of the startling discovery of the wire at the bottom of the pond, revealed because the drought had reduced it to a slick of mud. My grandfather winced with pain as he confessed the discovery, pain not from the sores eating into his flesh but from recollection at his bewilderment at the sight of the wire, coiled like a serpent in the mud, Biblical in its innocence and in its malice. My grandfather stared at it with a believer's eye, but was yet unbelieving, as on that fateful dawn when he stretched out his hands to feel the nothingness between the fence-posts, the holes, the absence of flesh in Christ's palms which aroused and bewildered the apostle. It was, because it was not, as He was, because He was not. My grandfather stepped towards the pond to grasp the wire or nothing, but stopped abruptly, falling on his knees instead, not out of residual hunger, the aftermath of famine, but out of an overpowering sense of meekness.

It was the same meekness that overcame him as Arthur broke off a piece of potato and placed it upon his tongue. Amy had died beside him, in bed. He was too weak, too confused, to remove her to the garden, to bury her there, underneath the apple tree where he had taken the navel string of my mother and, after prayer, the holiness of which was disturbed by a delirious sense of achievement, of fatherhood, had buried it as thanksgiving to the earth that fed them, strengthened them in love, provided the clay and straw and wood for their shelter, nurture for his hens and cow. Dazed by thirst but memories of their life flooding his mind, he lay with her in bed, unwilling to let go, yet praying for his own end.

He must have been on the brink of final collapse when Arthur entered the house and stood above the bed, calling out his name, shaking him, summoning him back to consciousness. Arthur held a baked potato to his mouth, breaking off a piece and feeding him. His mouth opened automatically to receive it. Desperately he tried to swallow it, but couldn't. He coughed feebly. Arthur took it from him, chewed it to a paste in his own mouth, and fed him again, and as he sucked it into his body, Geoffrey was overcome not by a simple gratitude but by a sudden realisation that it was Arthur who had stolen the wire, Arthur who was the angel of retribution, doing God's bidding by punishing him for his pride, and now that he was on the verge of death, it was Arthur who was the angel of deliverance. He swallowed another serving of potato and choked, not out of the narrowing of his throat through starvation, but out of a delirious sense of failure before the Fatherhood of God, who had sent famine to rob him of wife and worth, but when he was in the throes of misery, sent an angel to redeem him. He grasped Arthur's hand with astonishing firmness, given his feeble state, and his mouth snatched at the potato, wanting to swallow it whole to reveal the depth of his gratitude for the holy gift. After he had eaten and drunk from Arthur's grail of whisky, his head dropped back onto the bed and he fell asleep, dreaming that a light was drawing him towards a forest, a light so intense that he had to shade his eyes as he walked, bumping into rocks and trees, bruising his body all over. He reached the spot and the voice commanded him to remove his hand from his face and stare toward the pond where the light shone. He obeyed, though terrified that he would be blinded by the light. He stood there bleeding, a barefooted peasant, but his eyes strengthened the more he gazed, until at last he could make out the source of the light, which was *his* wire, lying in the mud like abandoned treasure. It had lain there for months, but no rust had gathered upon it. It was as new as the first day he possessed it and the fourth day he'd lost it, flashing at him like the blades of knightly swords, and he let himself be cut deeper than the wounds the rocks and trees had inflicted on him on his lifelong peasant's journey through pasture and woods.

★

The first picture again and again described to Geoffrey. Jack ascending the beanstalk, the cottage, the garden, the geese, the tethered lamb, and my grandfather yielding up scraps of memory in fitful muttering. But it was the second story, of Andromeda, which sustained me through the ordeal of listening to his gibberish. I was ashamed to look upon the illustration yet could not look away from it. It was a picture for myself, for though I read its story to Geoffrey I could not bring myself to reveal its details to him. Andromeda was tied to a post, beside a pond or lake, out of which a monster reared its head, but for all the hideousness of its jaws it had sad eyes as if burdened by appetites it could not understand, much less control. At the top edge of the picture was a Knight on a winged steed, sword drawn, resolute in his nobility. A damsel in torn clothing, thighs spread, ankles bound to stakes, the wind ragging her hair, her flesh gleaming with the stains of rough handling... I knew the instant I set eyes on her that I was the Knight who would defy the monster, cut her free, cleanse her in the pure waters of a forest stream, anoint her in scented oils, marry her and live happily ever after in a cottage like Jack's, with a garden of flowers, trees laden with pears, a pen of milky cows. I was a boy then, knowing only the image of Mary Mother of God sculpted in the chapel I worshipped in. I lit candles before Mary, breathing in the maddeningly sweet incense that powdered her body, the very smell of the Holy Spirit, that made me resolve – without being able to express how or why – to dedicate my life to the service and worship of her. I have since failed, but then I was unblemished, so that the sight of the damsel on the brink of violation aroused in me the deepest longing for peace. 'The Peace that Passeth all Understanding' – the most hypnotic words of my youth, especially when they flowed from Father Harris as he knelt in serene prayer before the Cross, his white priestly robe making him as vulnerable to stain as the maiden. I knelt beside Father Harris, a small boy, but in my mind I was towering over him, mighty in valour as the Knight, my sword drawn to protect him from the demon of the lake.

None of this could I divulge to my grandfather, whose incoherence and sudden eruption of spiteful memories about theft and loss slowly darkened my vision of the damsel, so that my initial guarding of her turned to jealousy and possessiveness. I wanted to fasten her even more securely to the post to prevent her escape. The Knight, at first present to cut her loose, was there to keep her captive with the terror of his sword and to ward off the monster whom she wanted to be captured by, wanted to be sucked into, settled into the slime of its belly in the obscurity of the bottom of the lake. The monster became my rival and adversary, awakening in me a desire to hurt her, so that even if it vanquished her, at least its prize would be a ruined, already taken thing, a virtue already stolen and hidden away.

"That bastard Arthur, he was no angel, he was a piece of dirt," my grandfather exploded, contradicting his earlier portrayal of Arthur as a figure sent by God to test him before redeeming him. The effort of cursing wearied him. He sank into his bed, rubbing his legs to inflame the sores, wanting to punish himself for trusting in Arthur, eating his potato when he should have slipped into death. "And he took your mother's cunt, long before he took my wire," my grandfather said in the hushed tone of confession, the truth of his involvement in sin slowly dawning on him. Cunt. I recognised the word without knowing how or why, as if always natural to me, like my hair or teeth or shadow. Cunt was the smell and shadow of me, I was reared within it and of it. Cunt, canter, canticle, chalice, church: words conjugated and multiplied with horrible natural fertility. The cunt-damsel. The Knight cantering towards her. He will abduct her. He will serenade her with lewd songs. She will drink of the cup of his loins. She will marry him in the absence of the Cross. She will forsake me, as my mother did at my birth.

My grandfather's sudden revelation of Arthur's doing made me dizzy. "What's in the picture?" he asked, recovering his composure and becoming an old man again, wanting to be read to, an old man in his final childhood needing a story to put him to sleep. But I couldn't continue, nauseated by the sense of being on the verge of some undesirable movement in my life. He had reverted to childhood and I was unfolding into adulthood. I closed the book, shutting the picture of the naked Andromeda from sight, not wanting to grow up. I went back to my room in Father Harris's house and lay down before the image of Mary the Mother of God whom I was more determined than ever before to adore as the permanently smallest and meekest of her creatures.

IV

My room, with its picture of the Virgin, was a sanctuary against the mayhem of Father Harris's house. Stuffed birds and women in the loft. Trays of watercress germinating in the cellar among men fleeing from some calamity or the other. People knocking on the door at all hours to confess, to beg for money or for shelter. My duties were prescribed – to cook, clean, sweep, dust, tend the garden pond – but they were never settled, what with the comings and goings of the maladjusted, the crude and the criminal. But how to describe the hectic matted rhythm of this portion of my life? Best to begin with Father Harris's study.

Father Harris's study: never an open Bible to be seen on his desk. There were twenty-five or so on the topmost shelf of his bookcase, clammy with disuse and wedged so tightly that to remove one was to risk ripping off its cover. They bore curious titles, telling of Father Harris's various interests as a young priest, before age – he was many years into retirement – made him put them away at the top of the bookcase, beyond his own reach, especially now that he was too crook-backed and frail of limb to climb the library ladder. *Titles: The Bible for Rustics; The Bible for Mechanics; The Bible for the Weak of Spirit; The Bible for Married Women; The Bible for Rulers of State; The Bible for Nurses and Doctors; The Victorian Imperial Family Bible;* a text it seemed for every human ailment, mood, occupation, class and political persuasion and for every denomination too, for there was *The Bible for Lutherans* and *The Bible for Methodist Laymen, The Amish Testament, The Mennonite Book of Worship,* among the standard *King James Bible* and the *Rheims Bible.* "Don't talk to me of the Bible," he wheezed before I could answer his question about what I had studied in the Irish monastery. He gathered his breath in defiance of his failing lungs and pointed his stick to the other shelves. "Those will be your reading from now on my son, you will sup until you swell and want to retch. Look at me, how meagre I am, age rotting away my brain and bones, but I was a beer-barrel once upon a time, straining against its hoops in a galleon which was one among a magnificent fleet sailing beyond the Pillars of Hercules, to the unknown regions of the earth. Unknown my boy, but you will know it, you must land and plant the flag of Christendom. I was the fattest Admiral, the commonest tar puffed up with rum, the topsail bloated with wind." His outburst, seldom fathomable, was punctured with the jabbing of his stick at the bookcase until the effort of standing alone exhausted him, the stick fell from his hand and he toppled into the sofa placed there for the precise purpose of catching him when words weakened him. I retrieved the stick, eased him up and supported him to the chair at his desk.

The desk: before I get to the desk proper, let me recount a few titles of the books I was being introduced to: Plato's *Republic; The Tragedies of Aeschylus; Greek Myths and Legends; The History of Witchcraft;* Homer's *Odyssey; The Apocrypha;* Grimm's *Fairy Tales; The Lives of the Saints;* Blake's *Collected Poems;* and other texts arranged without any obvious order. Another shelf bore church pamphlets on *The Savages of Polynesia, The Warlike Caribs of the Amazon, Missions in Pagan Africa, Among Libidinous Hindoos, Among the Cannibals of New Guinea, The Igloo Settlements of Eskimos, The Dustbowls of Aborigines.* Lower down still were books on the bizarre and untamed creatures of God's imagination – *Baboons and Their Mating Habits, Whales in the South Sea, Alligators of South America* and so forth. The bottom two shelves, the most accessible, bore strange Latin titles like *De Occulta Philosophia Libri Tres* among which were sprinkled English ones like *Alchemical Formulations, The Gnostic Vision, The Life of John Dee, The Philosopher's Stone,* Newton's *Principia Mathematica,* the last one being Darwin's *The Origin of Species* leaning against a bust of Giordano Bruno.

The desk proper: scissors with yellow handles, a scalpel, a set of needles, a bundle of waxed twine, inkpots, a microscope, lamps, candles, glass dishes or tins containing soil, dead leaves, seeds, feathers, bits of insects, scraps of paper with mathematical drawings or computations; and as if to embellish the scene, a vase of flowers, long dead and dried out in colours of faded orange, faded purple. An empty Cross hacked simply from stone hung above the desk, at the centre of it, overlooking the disorder. Could anything be studied here in rapt concentration without the mind wandering off to the bric-a-brac? The figure of Father Harris seemed to suggest not, in its crookedness but also in the words which escaped his mouth in fits and starts. "What a labial palp; heavens; just look at that jaw feeler!" He fell silent, put down his magnifying glass and looked out of the window, searching his mind for some precise word. "To be sure, a common German cockroach," he muttered to himself before his voice swelled in the passion of enquiry. "You can tell it's a German from the light-brown body and tiny size, don't you know boy?"

I paused from sweeping up the study and looked stupidly at him.

"The oriental kind is twice the size and black. In the Amazon they live in rotting logs, they grow as fat as my thumb." He stuck his thumb out and gazed upon it in wonderment, before shuddering at the thought of the log heaving with infestation. He put his thumb away and turned his attention again to the insect lying stiffly in a cradle of linen. He studied the thing again, seeming to forget me, but as soon as I thought it was safe enough to resume sweeping, he looked up, beckoned to me, his hand a flurry of excitement. "Boy, come and dare tell me that this isn't an exquisite example of cockroach." He thrust the magnifying glass at me. I took it and leant over the insect, peering at its mouth. "There's a word for it," he said, snatching the lens from me, thinking hard, biting down on his dentures as if the pressure would inspire revelation. He spun around with sudden energy and paddled off with his feet on his wheeled chair to a bookcase, paddled back again with a thick volume entitled *The Anatomy of Insects*, which he placed absentmindedly and heavily over the cloth containing the cockroach. He flicked through it, found the relevant page, scanned it, and with a little yelp of delight announced the word 'chitinous'. "A cockroach has chitinous teeth in its stomach, did you notice them boy?" He searched the desk, puzzling at the missing specimen.

"It's underneath the book, Father," I said, sadly, anticipating his disappointment. He lifted the book, gazed ruefully at the crushed insect and then looked at me with dejected eyes as if weighed down with a knowledge so intimate that he was unsure whether it could be imparted to me.

"A German cockroach, light-brown, tiny, not black and Oriental," I said wanting to console him, to confirm my willingness to be his disciple.

"Chitinous," he said, "chit-in-ous. Write it down, learn it well." He fumbled in the drawer of the desk, hoping to find a pencil. I noticed a dribble of froth at the side of his lips. It was a sign of sickness, I knew. The knowledge that he would die one day was unbearable. I turned my back to him in sorrow, in betrayal, and resumed my cleaning.

*

"And how is your grandfather?" Father Harris asked cheerfully as he prepared to teach me chemistry, arranged beaker, pipette, test-tube and candle in his makeshift laboratory, a large cupboard which still housed his clerical gowns of old, more treasured now since they were a nursery for the moth and its enemy. "Ichneumon-fly, boy, mark it well, the ichneumon-fly which is the enemy of moths and the cardinal defender of my sacred vestments!" He chuckled to himself. "Now there's a man to talk about for centuries to come." he said, turning to me and putting on a tutorial face. "Cardinal Newman, boy, memorise the name, and you know why? Because he devours sham, whether of the State, whether of the cynic, whether of the dogged cleric or the doubtful scientist." His voice lifted and he made to stand up to declaim better but agedness prevented him from rising and his throat gave up on him. He dropped back into his chair and looked gloomily at me, seeming to resent the daily steady draining away of his life. And then, remembering the lesson at hand, he brightened, mischief danced in his eyes. He leaned to me and whispered conspiratorially, "Don't believe them when they say good riddance to the moth. Oh I know, it makes holes in your best woollen jacket, but what's a patch or two in return for a miracle?" I smiled at him to signal my agreement, though not comprehending a single word. "Yes, yes, yes," he said, pleased with my response, "you and I know the ichneumon-fly..." He stopped and beckoned to me to speak.

"The ichneumon-fly," I said. "The Cardinal Newman of insects who devours sham."

"Good boy!" he said beaming at his young scholar. "Now where was I? Oh yes, yes, you and I know that the ichneumon-fly is blessed of God, though some people go to extremes in their devotion, eh? I hear there was a nobleman whose furs and tapestries and carpets were so plagued with moths that he was on the verge of despair and ruination until his gardener introduced the – "

"Ichneumon-fly," I said promptly and he stretched out his hand and placed it on my head in confirmation of my status as a bright disciple.

"And do you know what the rascal did?" he said, withdrawing his hand in a motion of agitation. I began to wonder what sin the fly had committed, introduced as a welcomed guest in a nobleman's mansion only to betray his master and host in unexpected ways. Did it infect the household with a strange disease? Did it join forces with the moth to speed up the downfall of the nobleman?

Father Harris must have read my puzzlement in the creasing of my brow for he laughed out loud and drew me tenderly to his bosom. "It was the nobleman who was the rascal," he said, making me sit upright again to receive the moral of his lesson. "The flies bored through the flesh of the moth-caterpillars, laid their eggs, which hatched into grubs, which fattened on the insides of their hosts, eventually gobbling up all their vital organs. The nobleman was overjoyed. He put the fly on his family's Coat-of-Arms. He made the little mite into his personal symbol, painted it upon a golden shield above his porch, sculpted it upon an ostentatious medallion to embellish his mantelpiece. All the latches and doorknobs in the house were removed and replaced by those shaped as flies, done ornately of course, with filigreed bits and bobs. And the gardener got nothing, not even a mention of his name over the dinner table as he and his friends met to celebrate. The drunken swine!" Father Harris had worked himself into a rage. Froth formed at the corner of his mouth with his final exclamation. He lay back on his chair to rest, crossing himself, but the mood of repentance didn't last long, for he sat up and gestured to me to draw close. He looked me passionately in the eye. "Hate the rich, always, hate their smugness and their science."

"I will hate the rich, Father, I will hate their smugness and their science," I said in a serious voice as if speaking a prayer.

"The true science," be resumed, "is the knowledge that all that lives is holy, even the meanest. A cat can look upon a king."

"The true science," I repeated, "is the knowledge – "

He signalled me to stop. "No need to parrot me, boy, though what a lovely creature, what a bird! Do you know it's a shame that only one-eyed pirates have parrots perched on their shoulders? But what can they see? I once did a painting of the Magi kneeling before the baby Jesus, each holding out a parrot, and you should see how Mary had to shield her eyes from the lavish colour of their wings and how the Saints squinted, but Jesus came alive at the sight, stretching out his hands as if to dip them in the glow of their gorgeousness. But there I go again – what was I saying? You should give me a sign when I run on, don't be afraid, add it to your rota of duties – you clean, wash, cook, and now will raise your hand to catch my attention when I'm slipping... but what was I saying?"

"No need to parrot me, boy, though what a lovely creature, what a bird," I said exactly.

"That's right, there's no need to repeat my words, just remember the gist of what I say. Yes, difficult, I know, poor boy, for my gist is like the Cardinal fly-eggs, I lay them everywhere, some hatch into vigorous caterpillars, some barely splutter into life and will never wing. Catch what you can, boy, thoughts are like butterflies." The involuntary mention of butterflies brought him back to his original subject with a jolt. "I was talking about moths, was I not?" he asked, shaking a hand at me.

"You called them a miracle, Father," I said.

"So I did, so I did, and truly so. And do you know why?"

I thought for a while, then hazarded an answer so as not to disappoint him. "Is it, Father, because they have chitinous teeth in their stomachs?"

He looked at me with such adoration that I began to believe in my own giftedness.

"Now, isn't that something to think about, isn't that just something to think about? Do you know, I don't have a clue as to what's inside a moth's stomach, I've never even pondered on it, imagine that, never pondered on it, but now that you mention it a whole new study is opened up to me! Do you really think there's a link between the moth and the cockroach, perhaps hinted at by a similitude of teeth...?" His eyes flared with excitement, he began to parrot my words against his will: "It is because they have chitinous teeth in their stomachs. It is because they have chitinous teeth in their stomachs. That's what you said, isn't it boy?"

I nodded and looked at the bookcase, wondering whether I should fetch the *Anatomy of Insects* to settle the issue with the same crushing authority with which he had placed the book on the desk, but the memory of my grandfather's talk of the sinfulness of pride made me change my mind. Yet it was pride that Father Harris was breeding in me by repeating my words.

"Such wisdom from the mouths of babes," he said with the gratitude of someone who had newly regained his faith. "I was about to tell you that the moth is a miracle in that it never feeds when it's grown except on the fat it accumulated as a caterpillar. It eats itself, then it starves and dies in a short while. And as a caterpillar it drinks nothing all its life, getting whatsoever moisture it can from the woollen threads it devours, which is next to nothing. And you wonder what all that thirst and hunger is about, and what a miserable brief existence, and just as you are about to sink into doubt, you suddenly see Jesus arrayed on the Cross in loneliness and hurt at being forsaken by the Father and by the disciples. But look again. Flies gather to him like notes. When night comes a moth laid by the moon settles on his forehead, beating and breaking its wings against the thorns. The meanest of God's creatures sing and bear witness to and emulate his dying, just as he was born among lowly animals. They keep his only company, and that was what I thought of as a miracle before you mentioned another."

The meanest of God's creatures... the women appeared on cue, pushing through the study door as if summoned up by some miracle. "Ah, our residents in the attic," Father Harris said, greeting them with a beaming smile. "Come perch by me," he said, moving to the edge of the sofa to make space for them. "Birds of prey by the looks of you, or hungry chicks, which are you?"

The women were taken aback by his friendliness. I suspected they had barged into the room to complain of my treatment of them but their boldness waned at the sight of the frail and kindly priest.

"The larder door is locked," one of them eventually said.

"We've not fed for the whole day," a second woman added, glaring at me.

"It's him. He's got the key and won't give us," a third woman accused me.

"The key is where it always is, on the nail beside the kitchen cupboard," I lied, turning to Father Harris to assure him of my proper stewardship of his guests.

"It's never there," the first woman snarled, recovering her aggressiveness.

"You should drink holy water for the lie you've just told the good Father," the second woman said.

"A whole jug, no, a tubful of it," the third woman added, staring me up and down as if in astonishment at my deed.

"Leave him be," a fourth voice squeaked in my defence. "He's done no wrong but protect his master from the likes of you."

The three women parted to reveal a fourth who had been hidden from sight behind them, a wiry creature, pale as a moth, standing unsteadily as if bled of strength. I expected the women to pounce on her for taking my side, but instead they circled her, guarding her from our gaze like a moth needing to be protected from the gleam of thorns.

"See there's enough fish and loaves for them," Father Harris said after they had left the room in lumpen sorrow. "Let them eat, and if there's nothing left for us you and I will be caterpillars and sup on Scripture." He eyed the top shelf of disused Bibles, grinned, bared his teeth in a show of impiety.

*

Father Wilson arrived as usual at lunchtime, on Friday. Fish day. Father Harris was already seated at the table, a sullen figure glancing restlessly at the cutlery, then at the clock, pretending to be still deciding whether to dine, or not. Father Wilson entered the room bearing a gift. Father Harris mumbled a greeting and shifted, signalling the weakest of intentions of getting up to shake his friend's hand, then settled quickly back into his chair. They sat at opposite ends of the table and didn't bother to say grace. I served them baked haddock, baked potatoes and peas. Father Wilson had placed his gift in the middle of the table, a peace-offering perhaps but more, I suspected, a means of marking off the space between them. The head of a house sparrow peeked out of its loose brown-paper wrapping. It was looking sideways, avoiding both of them, and, being stuffed, remained facing in one direction throughout the meal.

165

The two men ate without relish and made a show of ignoring each other. It was their weekly ritual, except that sometimes the bird was a fish or a mouse or some other subject of Father Wilson's experiments in taxidermy. The subject was never raised, until after lunch, when the two of them retired to the study to smoke.

Father Harris picked at the haddock, ate a potato and left all the peas, like a boy determined to sulk, whereas Father Wilson sliced off the fish skin with the subtlest motion of his knife, dissected the flesh then sat back and gazed upon his handiwork. He looked at the untidiness of Father Harris's plate with barely concealed contempt. Satisfied that his deft flourishes of the knife had irked his friend, he leaned over his plate and devoured all that was upon it in a display of hunger. He looked up again and after a moment or two of working up a malice, burped in Father Harris's direction. This declaration of war was ignored, Father Harris refusing to respond with the same resolution that made him refuse his peas.

During coffee Father Wilson spoke on some trivial matter and Father Harris answered vaguely. Father Wilson spoke again, but this time Father Harris pretended not to hear, rubbing a finger at his ear as if to clear it of obstruction. When Father Wilson spoke a third time, Father Harris coughed over his words, and that was the end of their intercourse.

Looking back now, I can conceive of them as a couple who had spent so many years in each other's company, obedient to their Catholic vows of marriage, that they grew discontented with each other, wanting only to irritate or unsettle each other. But that would be too easy an explanation. Better to deem them adversarial twins locked in a passionate but conflicting love for the same and the different revelations of God's presence: a presence seemingly bodied forth in humankind, fish, insect, fossil, whatever was living or had lived, which they hallowed, but from different and frail roots of perception. Their one and the same faith in the presence of God, which was their one and the same reverence for the living and the dead, was confused in its expression, the constantly failing struggle to share through words what they divined or intuited. Their

Catholic scripts – their hymns and prayers – were a stock of images and formulae, but they were to be practised through chanting, they were to be recited endlessly to numb the mind to the gnawing wordless querulousness of the spirit. Father Wilson and Father Harris were twinned in priesthood and in doubt, in ritual obedience and in discontent. This much I believe Father Harris confided in me whilst I lived with him in Coventry, though at the time I understood little. Then I thought they were two slightly mad old men, snapping at each other in a strange ritual of courtship, imitating the behaviour of some of the strange creatures they studied under microscopes.

It was only after leaving the dining room and claiming his favourite sofa in the study, stretching out his legs and looking forward to smoking, that Father Harris lowered his shield and engaged Father Wilson in conversation. I fetched pipes and tobacco for them, like preparations for combat. They sat opposite each other puffing for a while, working out strategies, each man hidden behind his own cloud of smoke, then, satisfied that their pipes were fully and deeply lit, they began. Father Wilson undid his parcel and handed the house sparrow to Father Harris.

"It's never the skinning or the degreasing which taxes me but the mounting," he said, hoping to pre-empt Father Harris's appraisal. "I'm never decided what posture to give it, whether preening itself, or worrying a worm on the ground, or set to take off."

Father Harris held the bird up to the light by its beak, and at arm's length, as if in disgust at the sight. Father Wilson appeared hurt by the gesture of scorn, but before he could recover Father Harris inflicted a second, more uncivil cut, or so he hoped.

"A badly stuffed bird is such an intolerable caricature of the living creature, don't you think?" he asked, handing the bird back to the seemingly wounded priest. He looked at his friend sympathetically as if wanting to elicit a full confession of failed artistry before dispensing forgiveness. Father Wilson refused the invitation, accustomed to the role he was expected to play which sometimes was reversed according to the subject matter, or the mood they were in, or in pure arbitrariness, he becoming the hunter, Father Harris the quarry.

"And why give me such a common bird?" Father Harris complained. "You can stuff a sparrow in your sleep, and by the looks of it you did. Why not stretch yourself and try a pheasant or a golden oriole or a purple heron? I have an attic full of your dull sparrows and martins."

"A bird is a bird is a bird," Father Wilson retorted. "You know full well that the techniques of taxidermy are uniform. It's the same process of lifting off the skin and making the mannequin and applying the binding and wiring the insides. The real craft is in the wiring, but it's always the same technique."

Father Harris drew in his breath deeply, signalling his disagreement, even despair. They had had this skirmish before, Father Wilson insisting that the stuffed creature did not have to convey the special qualities of its erstwhile existence, whereas Father Harris held forth that an accomplished artist could convey, no recreate, even with glass eyes, and the flesh substituted with tow or wool, and the bone substituted with wire, the subtle and the sleeping beauty of the bird's livingness. "When it's alive you see the visible, if that, through glass eyes, because that's the way most of us are, glass-eyed. We only see the visible. It's the artist, the one who dreams oddly but whose waking life is an effort to clarify the dream, who knows the nature of the bird's particular livingness, even in its seeming dead state. Take this pipe..." He held the stem of his pipe between two hands and suddenly, with strength that made him groan like a man giving up his life, he broke it in two.

V

In the silence that followed this act of sudden violence Father Harris lowered his head as if in prayer, and remembered against his will a sky hemmed with sea gulls and a ruffled garment of sea upon which fishing boats clung, each a bead of bright sail. He had left his church in Falmouth, his latest posting, and taken refuge on the loneliest spot of beach to think of Alice, but the gaiety of the scene would not allow it: light sprinkled upon the waves like sequins, the kaleidoscope of sails, these distracted him from inward gaze, so that he soon gave up on his gloom, stretched out his legs, placed his hands behind his head and lay back on the sand, careless of the soiling of his clerical clothes which Alice used to launder with such devotion from the time she washed up on this same beach five years before, hardly a mermaid, given her croaking deformity, but all the same a creature of inexplicable nature.

It was just after dawn when, awakening to the constant ringing of the bell, he opened the door to Alice. She was dripping wet and the morning mist clung to her like a cruel gown, but she stood – or rather stooped – at the doorway without shivering, indeed without the slightest sign of belonging to the cold earth. Father Harris ushered her in, impatient to close the door to the chill and to get back to his bed. He was not in the least troubled by her presence. The church-house had seen the coming and going of the oddest creatures, men and women turning up at all hours seeking coin or shelter, or in the case of smugglers – who all wore scars and a fixed look of anxiety, like badges of identity – refuge in his cellar after their exhausting acts of ducking and evading. Alice was shown into a room adjoining the kitchen where she could find clothing and a bed, and Father Harris went back to sleep.

It was not until after evensong, when he went to the kitchen to prepare a meal, that he remembered her. He had got up, bathed, walked in the church grounds among ancient and new graves, reading inscriptions as they caught his eye. Many had perished at sea, then been hauled out, sometimes by their own fishing nets, brought to shore and buried.

Father Harris paused by a mass grave containing the undifferentiated remains of four men – Stephen Yardley, Mark Yardley, Christopher Reece, John Taylor – who had been the subjects of his very first funeral as a new parish priest in the year 1900, the beginning of a new century, the beginning of his sixtieth year on earth.

The remains of the four men were draped in their fishing nets and given back to the earth like an unwanted catch. Their women wept loudly but Father Harris conducted the ceremony with ritual calmness. Five years of other deaths followed, Father Harris burying each with the same hymns, prayers and sermons, making no distinction of age or sex, for death had made none. Each was a soul destined for hell, purgatory or heaven. In life they were exposed to the certainty of the seven sins, and after death, to outcomes depending on degrees of surrender to or triumph over those sins. Everything was measured and measurable in broad terms, the details of who people were or what they did mattered not. Contemplating the details only served to complicate the ordained scheme of sin and salvation, and yet it was what Father Harris could not fully resist, in spite of his Catholic indoctrination. They were people with quirks, talents, points of view, not just actors in a scheme of sin and salvation; people with passion, grand or useless, no matter, for it was particular to them. The gravestones reduced them to their names and dates and a dutiful verse from the Bible, but Father Harris found himself, much against the grain of his priestly training, trying to resurrect their individual selves, an act of necromancy almost, the most damnable of sins.

But the fishermen were dead and gone, beyond imagining, their true stories buried with them. From the evidence of their wives sobbing inconsolably they were saintly men, but perhaps the wives wailed out of custom before pocketing the charity of the Church. Human affairs were as ravenous as the worms scavenging the grave, this Father Harris knew from his Catholic learning, but he actually wanted to take their side against the accumulated accusations of the Scriptures. He had buried them all as souls to be submitted to God's judgement, but he wished he had taken more notice of them as living fleshly presences. Stephen Yardley for instance, one of the drowned fishermen, used to come each Friday with a parcel of herrings. Father Harris accepted it at the door, perfunctorily, thinking the gift no more than a parishioner's duty to his priest. Perhaps there was more to it, for Yardley would linger at the doorway and shift from foot to foot, unwilling to leave after handing over his herrings. Yardley was in his early sixties, and after a lifetime spent at sea, he may have wanted to talk to the sheltered priest, talk of perilous experiences and scrapes with death, or else about more ordinary and yet beautiful things, like the exultation of porpoises in the wake of the boat and in sudden communion with human beings. Two of Yardley's fingers were missing: Father Harris seemed to remember that Yardley was an occasional carpenter (a noble profession for such was Joseph's). Were his fingers victim to a slipped chisel or saw? To be sure there was a story there but Father Harris closed the door on him, thinking that Yardley was on the brink of confessing some sin, in which case he should wait in church for the appointed hour. It was necessary to maintain the orderliness of his vocation, with specific times for specific activities, so he believed then, and still did now, except that he also regretted not inviting Yardley into his study, and he wondered what mystery might have unfolded from the man, what sea lore or common tale spiced up by his fisherman's imagination.

The regret passed but he knew it would return to nag at him, no matter how rigorously he attended to the reading of Scriptures or to the performance of Mass. It was this quality in his character, the inability to focus wholly on his calling, the 'weakness before temptation' as his superiors called it, that made them dispatch him to Falmouth as soon as a vacancy became available. It was far from Ireland, an insignificant spot of less than fifty Catholic souls. He could be safely banished there. Nothing momentous had occurred in Falmouth since the foundation of the village centuries ago, and it was not likely that Father Harris could disrupt its equilibrium. Still, they took precautions by first sending him to understudy priests in Dunsmore and Flegg, even more obscure parishes, and they made plans to retire him in Coventry, in the south of the city which was so sturdily Protestant that no Catholic church was established there, only an outpost, a dilapidated house where Catholics in temporary need, or in the midst of journeying, stopped for a day or two. There was a small dwelling nearby, an almshouse for the disabled and dying. Father Harris did not resent being purged from Ireland, indeed he relished the prospect of travel and of meeting with ordinary people. They baffled him with their unlettered and slippery lives or else they bored him at Confession, holding back from telling the truth and yielding up petty misdemeanours. It was impossible to know them. For them Religion was a matter of not taking the bait of doctrine but they still nibbled at it to show obedience. After a while he gave up on them, seeing them as travelling souls, their destination marriage, procreation, death, and he a conductor of the ceremonies that gave order to their deeds, guiding them from here to the time of their trial.

One by one, or sometimes in a shoal, they died on him, taking their stories to the grave intact, partly because he had not bothered to attend to the details of their lives, partly because they would not divulge them to him, even at Confession. A truly slippery lot, human beings, but perhaps it was not because they were human beings but because they were fishermen. He merely walked on the shore, on the edge of the sea, but they spent every watchful hour floating on its colossal body, trying to avoid awakening its wrath even as they snared it with nets, hauling up a harvest of bizarre or familiar fish, some of which they kept for themselves (a portion reserved for their priest on safe land), others which they threw back as if to appease its might. To take from the sea and return home secure required from these puny creatures the utmost guile, manoeuvrings of body and mind which Church doctrine was hopeless to contain. Yet, for all the cunning of their lives, for all the fables they withheld from him, they were his in death. He had buried them with song and prayer. He had asked God to forgive them. Death had pinned them down to certain allotments in the graveyard, in the grounds of the church. He could wander among them, knowing they were all there. A shepherd satisfied that his whole flock had returned at the end of the day from grazing; knowing that they were all there, even as he was unsure as to who they all were.

★

Evensong came and went, thankfully a very abbreviated service since no one turned up. Father Harris was relieved. His earlier wanderings among the graves had exhausted and depressed him. He put out the candles with despairing breath, closed the Church doors and went to the house to prepare supper for himself. Afterwards he planned to settle down with Cardinal Newman's *Letters* which he hoped would brighten his mood, its insistent humane prose and unabashed engagement with questions of doubt, reeling him back to the idealism of his calling. To his surprise the pot was already on the stove, and he lifted the lid to the gratifying sight of a fish soup. On the table beside the stove was a note in flowing handwriting: "Eat immediately, but first, heat for four minutes over fresh wood, no longer." He was in the process of rereading it, intrigued as he was by the clarity of its instructions, when Alice entered the kitchen. Without the slightest of greeting she hurried to the stove, and with such determination that he moved away automatically. She sniffed at the soup, then satisfied of its freshness, put new wood to start a fire.

"Sit. Go. There," she said brushing him aside and gesturing to the table. He found himself obeying her command. He sat down meekly, musing over his first impression of her: a woman in her late fifties, from the crinkled skin of her face, whiskers sprouting from her lips like a catfish's, but with hair startlingly black, profuse, naturally curled, defying her age with reminiscence of an earlier beauty, even a certain coquettishness. She blew vigorously at the fire, stirred the pot with an arthritic hand – a curious combination of alertness and frailty. His second impression when he had settled at the table and had taken in her presence more fully, caused him to exclaim, "Woman, what in heavens are you wearing on your body!" She turned around calmly to meet his outrage. A smile warmed her face, her whiskers twitched mischievously. "Cloth. Table. Curtain." She pointed to her head, which was partially covered with a handkerchief. "Dress wet. Wait to dry. Soon. Tomorrow. Cloth. Table. Curtain. Will do for now." She had taken off her morning dress, put it out to dry and wrapped herself in the meantime with a tablecloth and bedroom curtains. A handkerchief wrapped around her head, though much too small to contain her abundant locks, was her attempt at feminine propriety.

Father Harris resisted the deliciousness of the soup. He ate solemnly, resenting not so much her presence in the house but the way she had taken down the curtains and usurped the tablecloth. She should have sought his permission, he found himself thinking in his study afterwards, his sense of injury preventing him from appreciating Cardinal Newman's *Letters*, the charitableness of its contents. He was accustomed to all sorts seeking temporary shelter in his house, but they all kept a strict distance from him, respecting his space and the property of the Church. By the time they left, usually the morning after, before first light, before he was awake, there was no trace of their sojourn with him. Something about her, the ease with which she provided clothing for herself, her assumption that he was needful of a freshly made and filling supper, made him unable to absorb the Cardinal's wisdom.

He slept soundly that night and awoke refreshed and at a later hour than normal. It was her doing, he knew it, but it confused and disturbed him, this change to his pattern of restless insomnia and morning irritability. All his nights in England were a struggle to sleep. Perhaps it was the shock of a lonely bed, for the dormitory of his Irish seminary was communal. Perhaps it was the material he had read before retiring – theological essay, sermon, life of a saint – which his mind was still contemplating. Perhaps it was that he was ageing rapidly, with no prospect beyond the performance of immemorial rituals. But what else did he want, what erosion or rebuttal of the ancient certainties, Catholic pronouncements perfected and repeated over centuries by men more worthy, more sacred than himself? Was not the desire for newness a sign of pride, a foreboding of disobedience? His dissatisfaction with his calling, his disturbance of self, kept him awake, and though he prayed fervently, repeating the ancient and hallowed words of prophets and saints, he still could not dampen the want and the temptation within him which were all the more troubling because his mood could not be explained in words.

The house was unusually warm. The fire in his study was lit. He went to the kitchen to find another blazing. He was normally too lazy or careless of his comfort to heat the house, waiting for the evening when he settled down before the hearth with a book. There was a note on the kitchen table (which was adorned with a new tablecloth, freshly ironed, creaseless). "Father, I have set off early to pick mushrooms before the sun drains them or sheep graze over them. Then to the butcher – the best and most generous cuts are always to be obtained first thing, when his knives are gleaming sharp and his mind alert to the whole animal. This evening you will have a newly baked loaf, so finish off the scraps this morning or leave them outside (without butter) for the birds." The note disconcerted him and at the same time he felt comforted by her solicitude.

That evening he found her bent over the ironing board, pressing his shirt, then dipping into a basket of his washed clothing for a new item. He cleared his throat to catch her attention but she kept her back turned to him. He was once more startled by her rivulets of black hair. She was wearing a plain calico dress, obtained no doubt from the loft which was scattered with the leftovers of visitors to the house over the years. "Fish broth. Pan. Cumin seed bread. Oven. Tomorrow, lamb," she said at last, as if it had taken her that long to gather her thoughts and find words for them. He stood there for a while expecting more but she had done with him, pressing down on a damp handkerchief until it hissed and steamed.

They lived together like this for several months, Alice always away in the morning when he was awake, and in the laundry room when he returned from his priestly duties in the evening, cleaning every piece of cloth in the house she could lay her hands on. On the days he stayed indoors to prepare a sermon, she was nowhere to be seen. In all the time she lodged at the house he saw her for no more than a minute or two a day, if that, and then all she did was to grunt at him. To begin with he speculated anxiously as to her identity, even searching the loft when she was away for clues, but found nothing. She possessed nothing but the dress she wore on the first morning, which she supplemented with discarded clothing. He made discreet enquiries of his parishioners, but they had nothing to reveal. They merely assumed that the Church had provided him with a housekeeper, and the butcher and grocer supplied her each morning either as an act of charity to their priest, or in expectancy that he would settle his bills in his own time.

Speculation gave way eventually to acceptance of her presence, and then gratitude for a house always warm and tidy, meals truly tasty and clothes scrupulously laundered. Her daily notes to begin with directed him to domestic details – a leaking gutter or overgrown tree which needed the attention of tradesmen – but as time went on became more introspective, more revelatory of human character. The first such was harmless to read: "Father, tomorrow at 9 a.m. Tom the butcher will call upon you. He is obviously in need of your guidance, for he is delaying the opening of his shop, when he is most busy, to meet you." Father Harris thought nothing of the note: Tom had obviously asked her to pass on a message. Father Harris decided that he would be happy to leave her to organise his appointments, and would allocate three hours every day, after breakfast and morning worship, to see his parishioners. At present they would turn up at all hours at his door, much to his dismay, especially if he was immersed in his favourite Newman *Tracts*; his grumpiness and shortness with them grieved him afterwards, especially when their problems were merely trifling, or beyond his remedy, like asking him to pray for speedier breeding between February and April to augment their catch, or for some money promised by relatives to arrive before such and such a date when such and such a bill was awaiting payment. He condemned them silently for not being satisfied with their lot, promising them to intercede with God when he knew he would not. Now, under Alice's direction, he would be able to set aside specific times to such supplicants, then hurry back to his mind's pursuit of theological ideas.

It may be Alice intuited his denial of human feeling, or rather his hasty consideration, then discarding of their petitions, for her next note elaborated on the first. "Please remember that Tom the butcher will come today at 9 a.m. It is about foxes raiding his turkeys but do not heed him. Enquire instead after the welfare of his wife, Sarah. You will understand then his coming to you."

Tom arrived at nine. He looked unfamiliar in his spotless

woollen pullover. His freshly shaved chin was in odd contrast to haggard eyes which betrayed sleeplessness. Father Harris was accustomed to seeing him in his shop, his overall and his skin stained in the blood of his trade; he was always happy, always full of jovial small-talk, joking about the Lamb of God as he sliced and hacked away at a carcass. In church, though scrubbed and arrayed in his best suit, he still swallowed the wafer like a piece of nourishing animal fat. If ever Father Harris enjoyed a meal of plain steamed vegetables, it was after a visit to Tom's shop.

"It's the cursed fox," Tom opened, "no trap can match his cunning." He had tried to stay awake many nights with a loaded gun but the fox outsmarted him, waiting until he nodded off before raiding the pen. "I wake up to the screaming and the squawking, and I fire the gun into the darkness, but it's hopeless, hopeless, feathers floating in the air then settling on my head, crowning me a fool. I'm just a laughing stock to the fox." His voice dropped, he leaned over the coffee table to whisper to the priest. "Sometimes I think of turning the gun on myself." He remained bent over the table, waiting for words to bolster him, but Father Harris was at a loss as to how to comfort him.

"Suicide is a mortal sin," he said after a while, putting on his sternest voice, "you are to come to confession this afternoon and seek forgiveness through penance." Tom's face quivered on the brink of tears. He sat back with a grievous sigh.

"God is the very fount and inexhaustible ocean of forgiveness," Father Harris went on. "Don't worry, he's come across many many cases like yours before." Father Harris looked into his face seeking to find signs of relief but Tom remained sorrowful. "I will pray for your turkeys," Father Harris offered. Still no change in Tom's mood.

"Do you think she'll come back?" he asked suddenly. "If I change things and promise to act differently, what do you think? How can I change, please tell me..." His voice broke off as he suppressed the urge to cry.

Father Harris found himself embarrassed by the man's sudden desperation. How in heaven's name could the most common, the most natural, almost innocent activity of a fox bring Tom to the edge of despair, a hefty man accustomed to killing and gouging and gutting, a man moreover who could easily afford to lose half his stock of turkeys and yet enjoy a comfortable living?

"You can certainly change tactics," Father Harris suggested, "why not just cage the turkeys overnight, a sturdy cage, then there's no need to stay awake with a dangerous gun. Yes, it would change your behaviour for the better in God's eyes and the fox may well not come back to torment you."

Tom remained unaffected by his advice, and Father Harris's embarrassment turned to impatience. He was a priest of souls after all, not a dispenser of wisdom on livestock protection. "I'll pray for the fox," he offered as his final solution.

"Pray for me, not for that evil nasty... evil filthy..." He spluttered to find the appropriate curse, conscious that he was addressing a man of God. Father Harris got up and moved to the door, signalling that the meeting was over. Tom followed dutifully.

As he left the house Father Harris, remembering Alice's injunction, called after him, "Tom, give my blessings to your good wife... Sarah, isn't it, forgive my failing memory. Age, you know. Anyway I've not seen her at church for a while but my blessings all the same."

There was no meat for dinner the next day, nor for the rest of the week. At first Father Harris thought little of it: Alice was evidently preparing him for the coming Lenten fast. The house was as spick and span as ever. She laid out his washed and ironed clothes as usual. On the odd occasions he met her in the house she grunted in her familiar manner and retreated to the loft.

At the beginning of the second week his stomach grumbled ominously. He was beginning to tire of a diet of bread and vegetables. Lent, after all, was a full three months away. He suddenly realised that Alice had not left any notes, not since the butcher's visit. A commotion in the laundry room alerted him to her presence. He opened the door to find her thumping the iron down upon a shirt with uncommon energy, even in consternation. The steam escaping from the damp cloth seemed excessive and violent.

"Is all well with you Alice?" he asked. He expected her to remain with her back to him and utter a staccato reply, but she startled him by turning round and lifting her face to meet his. Her head was haloed in sunlight from the oval window above her. Her hair, profuse as ever, shimmered with such a fierce and unearthly quality that he found himself stepping back almost in fright. She reached into her dress pocket, handed him a piece of paper and gestured in the direction of his study.

"Tea. Read," she said, then turned her back to resume the ironing.

There was indeed a fresh pot of tea in the study. He ignored it, eager to read her note, to understand the oddity of her behaviour. The opening sentence so struck him that he had to sit down. "You have not paid heed to me, Tom is sick of heart as a result. You have failed him as a priest by not attending to my warning nor to what he had to say to you." Father Harris was flabbergasted by the imperious tone with which she chided him. Not since his time in the seminary, when his superiors would confront him with evidence of lazy thinking or muddle-headed interpretation of theology, had he been subject to such blatant accusation. He read and reread the sentence with rising resentment against her impertinence in addressing him so disrespectfully.

"Go and seek him out immediately before it is too late," the note continued.

Father Harris did her bidding. Armed with a Bible he set off for Tom's shop. It was closed. Father Harris knocked on the door with a sense of foreboding. He knocked again, this time so loudly that the windows rattled. He went to the back door and tried the latch, without success. The kitchen curtains were drawn. Normally he would return home, believing Tom to have gone off to visit relatives or to purchase livestock from the neighbouring village, but Alice's warning troubled him. He searched the exterior of the house for signs of violence, but there were none. The pen was full of turkeys dozing or scratching the ground idly. The fence holding them in was intact, not the slightest leaning or breach to suggest the predatory fox.

Father Harris set off to talk to Benjamin – Benji – the grocer. He was bound to know the comings and goings of Tom, his shop a meeting place and source of secular information about Father Harris's flock. It was his first stop when in pursuit of some parishioner who had not met his promised monthly dues to the church. Benji, taking one look at his slate, would supply information on the finances of the parishioner in question, and Father Harris would then know whether to persist in his chase, or to extend the man's credit with God.

"And how is Tom doing these days?" he asked Benji after a preliminary greeting. Benji's face soured. He was parcelling out flour. He dug the scoop viciously into the flour bag. Father Harris remembered why his spirit never took to Benji, even though the man always gave expansively – if ostentatiously – to the church. He gave for the necessary repairs throughout the year, and at the end he gave for the making of the Christmas Crib and seasonal decorations of the yew tree in the graveyard. When the authorities in Ireland instructed the Falmouth church to adopt the pagan colony of British Guiana, it was Benji who volunteered to organise charitable collections. He set up a small committee of fishermen which he named 'The Falmouth Relief Society for Heathen Guiana' and appointed himself its Secretary – rightly so, Father Harris thought at the time, though he distrusted Benji's ambitiousness, for Benji was one of the few villagers who could read and write. To begin with, Benji knew nothing of British Guiana, so set about collecting old rosaries and Bibles. These he parcelled with the same assiduity as he would corn or peas, and handed to whoever was due to visit family in Ireland, for deposit with the priests there, then shipment on to Guiana. The odd Church missive sent over from Ireland to Father Harris was passed on to Benji. He learned from these that Guiana was a malarial South American colony, mostly jungle and overwhelmingly Protestant. The English had allowed the setting up of a small Catholic monastery at the edge of the Demerara river and far enough into the interior not to disturb the affairs of the country. A retired Benedictine monk, Father Jenkins, manned the outpost, but with prayers and a little money he would begin to make inroads into the souls of the savages, mostly ex-slaves from Africa and native Amerindian tribal folk. Benji collected vials of fish-oil which the villagers used to repel gnats. He knew nothing of the diseases of savages, but the vials were blessed by Father Harris before being put into the parcel of rosaries and Bibles. He varied the parcel according to the contents of each new missive. Learning, for example, that the African diet during slavery consisted of salted fish, he persuaded the fishermen to put aside a small portion of herrings from each trip which he smoked and dried over a specially modified barrel placed prominently beside the entrance of his shop to remind the fishermen of their Catholic duty.

Father Harris resented this usurpation of his status, small as it was, insignificant almost, given the obscurity of British Guiana. It was hardly likely that Benji's efforts would lead to a full-scale armada and crusade to the colony, and earn him an honoured place in the annals of Church History. All the same, Father Harris harboured suspicion, especially when Benji acquired a donation of notepaper from a printer in Ireland, one of his relatives. The notepaper proclaimed the existence of the Falmouth Relief Society and, underneath the heading, 'Secretary: Benjamin Rogers, of Rogers Groceries, Falmouth village, England, purveyors of the finest quality of affordable goods'.

"And how is Tom doing these days?" Father Harris asked again, not looking Benji in the eye, glancing instead at a map of Guiana he had pinned to the wall, underneath a gleaming brass crucifix. It was a personal effort in green and black crayon, Benji mapping the place according to sparse information gleaned from the Church missives, supplemented by his own fancy. The colony was shaped like a puppy lying on its left side, with the profile of a limp ear, and paws drawn to his body. Father Harris recognised Scamp, Benji's treasure and companion, long missing, presumed drowned or stolen by a passing vagrant for its value, having the most unusual emerald-green eyes. In the middle of the colony, the place where Scamp's heart was located, Benji had indicated the monastery, marking it in bold black. Georgetown, the capital, was on the tip of Scamp's left paw. There were no other place names, just a smoothly crayoned spread of Scamp-eyed green, signifying jungle.

So, was this what all of Benji's effort amounted to, collecting in memory of his dog, Father Harris thought, uncharitably, as he looked at the map. He had often wondered as to Benji's motive in embracing the cause of Guiana so fervently; a man born in Falmouth, who never set foot outside the village except to replenish his stock, and who showed not the slightest inkling of wanting to travel overseas, much less to a lonely and diseased South American colony. God, of course, worked in mysterious ways and Benji may well have been seized by God's inspiration, though Father Harris knew his only previous passion to be parcelling out his goods, weighing them, pricing them and counting his take at the end of each day. He had no wife, a middle-aged man who found solace in the details of his trade and, a few years back, in Scamp, a puppy acquired from a villager in return for some seeds and coins. Scamp was not got for love, though Benji grew to fawn over the dog, feeding it choice bones, letting it roam through the shop even when it chewed through bags of goods in the agony of growing teeth. The villager, a drunkard, had come with the malnourished puppy so as to best present his plight. He wanted yet another extension of credit, but Benji refused. The villager offered Scamp as surety and Benji, not wanting a reputation for meanness, eventually agreed, handing over the mustard seeds (the drunkard had a choice of goods but for some mysterious reason insisted on mustard seeds) and a few shillings.

A fabricated map of British Guiana, a missing butcher, a dog stolen for its emerald eyes, mysterious seeds, a note from Alice warning of calamity... what was he doing here, Father Harris asked himself as he waited for Benji's answer as to Tom's whereabouts. Father Harris watched Benji measuring out his parcels of flour and was overcome by the hopelessness of his own condition. Benji's life was bracketed between sentimentality for a missing puppy and a vague attachment to a darkly imagined colony. His life was encompassed within these small movements of emotions which he steadied by daily calculation of income and expenditure. Father Harris's was no better. To begin with there was a sense of the world outside the seminary, tentacled by sin. The challenge was to prise it free from the grossness of human appetite, to wrest it from the gross sleep of the devil and return it in virginal form to the rightful possession of God. The prayers, the sermons, the canticles, the gleaming chalice, the incense, the lit candles, the stainless altar-cloth, all these were his weaponry against the devil. Once he had mastered their use, he would put on the garment of the priest. He would venture outside the seminary walls, a single vulnerable Knight of God, who, trusting his only weapons of faith, would do battle with the best of the devil's henchmen – a joyous cavalry of sodomites, child corrupters, addicts to the spectacle of shorn women, dispensers of baits and potions, prophets of arcane religions, purveyors of sacrificial rites... a procession as fertile and as endless as the mind's imagining of the variousness of pleasurable sins. Of course he would fail. He expected to fail, for to think otherwise would be to don the very cloak of the devil, which was arrogance. But the Church would succour his spirit, he would wrap himself in the raiment of Church History, the testimonies of saints, the cathedrals of sacred thoughts and deeds of martyrdom.

It was this hunger for the hugeness of the ruination of the world and the part he was to play in the endless process of restoration that sustained him in the seminary. But it was this hunger that his superiors feared in him. They had fed it initially, as part of his training for the priesthood, the long years of study and bodily deprivation needing to be sustained by the dream of questing. He never seemed to mature beyond it though, to awaken, as they did, to being rooted in a particular place, to the reality of the rehearsal of small acts of worship within the seminary, small acts of charity among the destitute outside its walls. The world outside was a village of peasants who performed their lives as their forebears had always done, planting corn, minding cows. They needed to be baptised, to be married and buried, with the necessary accompaniment of Catholic blessings. Occasionally, in times of adversity, they needed a consignment of bread. The idealism that gusted through them as novice priests, making them impatient to engage the devil in spectacular combat, waned. Dictates from Rome obliged them to humbler roles. They were to keep the flames of Catholicism burning in that part of Ireland, not fiercely, but with their hands cupped over the wick, protecting it from the foul breath of the English. The martyrdom of previous centuries was to give way to small unobtrusive strategies for the survival of a beleaguered faith. The devil was to be fought in different ways, and the time they lived in demanded appeasement.

Outwardly Father Harris was obedient to Rome's injunctions. He was steadfast in study and worship, and moved among the community of peasants, attending to their ordinary needs. But his superiors sensed his unease, his unwillingness or inability to settle for the less than grand, the less than adversarial. They would send him away, to tiny communities overseas, where the routine of caring for ordinary souls would blunt his vague longing for drama. New places, new characters and different landscapes, but he would soon learn that the Catholic faith was of the same fabric everywhere, his flock wanting no more than the comfort of the same ritual prayers, and a little charity when faced with hardship.

And so it was this morning, the 2nd November 1906 – his sixty-sixth year on earth – in Benji's shop in Falmouth, that Father Harris was more than ever convinced of his insignificance, in spite of his priestly robes. He was not one of the chosen few called to wield the sword of Christendom or defy the age's doubt and creeping godlessness through the force of intellect. Falmouth was as obscure a place as Guiana, even though the latter could be coloured according to odd outbreaks of fantasy, the colours however only projecting some familiar domestic detail or mood. They were all stranded at some point in the arc between the sacred and the mundane. The jars of food gleaming from Benji's shelves gave off false light. They were neatly positioned, each labelled with a price, but the order was evocative of a meanness of spirit. Father Harris remembered again why he so resented Benji. It was not that Benji was a middleman, profiting from the labour of others, buying cheaply and marking up the cost. After all, Benji was not particularly greedy, his prices were affordable and when the mood took him he offered discounts to the needy, albeit foodstuffs in the middle stages of staleness. No, it was the self-importance with which Benji arranged his goods on the shelves, his confidence in the material even as he sought sacred blessing each Sunday in church. Father Harris's prayers were received by Benji as a matter of habit; they propped up his faith in the order of things, like the simple wooden shelves bearing his goods. Father Harris watched Benji measuring out portions of flour and realised that the Church had sent him to England, to a nation of shopkeepers, to cure his longing for spiritual adventure.

He left the shop troubled by his unkind thoughts of Benji who had pressed upon him some tomatoes, shooing away his hand when he tried to offer money. There was no news of Tom but Benji had assured him that his worries were ground-less. "Look, here's the proof," he said, fishing out a piece of paper, neatly lined, listing each of Tom's purchases and pay-ments over three months. "He settles his bill every other Thursday, 8 a.m. sharp." Benji pointed to the entries, pausing at the odd one and studying it to verify the accuracy of his sums. "Tom is as regular as clockwork," he said, satisfied that the figures had proven Tom's reliability. "He'll be back soon, take my word. His next payment is coming up and he'll not miss it." Benji's confidence irritated Father Harris again, but he smiled weakly. "It's that Alice you ought to watch out for," Benji said, thrusting his head to Father Harris's ear and lowering his voice to a whisper. "She's odd that one, I wouldn't give her the time of day if she weren't your housekeeper." He made as if to cross himself but the flour was too thick on his hand. "You can always tell she's been in the shop, the air smells of salt for hours afterwards. And you must have noticed how scaly her legs are. She puts the fear of God in me, what with her jabbering like a fish gulping air. Last week she was in here for butter and two boys must have followed her in because as she was waiting at the counter one of them took from his pocket a piece of chalk and quickly drew a circle around her feet, then they ran off laughing and shouting how they had trapped the devil's dam but all the same they weren't staying to see whether their trial of her worked. And you should have seen her behaviour, she started to sweat and tremble, she wouldn't leave the chalk circle but started crying and begging me to rub it out. She wouldn't step out of the circle, staring at it and growing more and more hysterical, pulling at her hair and everything. Now Father, you know I'm not a man to get excited by anything and I'm not one for superstition, but what more proof do you need that she's not of this world, normal like you and me? The whole village is scared of her, but they don't tell you, she being your housekeeper and all. Here, have some more of these."

He offered his bribe of tomatoes as if wanting in return a prayer and blessing to protect his shop from evil. Father Harris gave neither. He was quietly appalled by the boys' treatment of Alice, but more by Benji's interpretation of it and by the desire of the villagers to endow Alice with darkly mysterious qualities when it was plain to him that she was only a simple woman frightened by a childish prank. She was a stranger to the village and to its superstitions. The chalk circle obviously reinforced her sense of being an outsider and she was naturally overcome by its unknown and potentially harmful meaning. The boys' taunts and Benji's fascination would have increased her panic.

So Father Harris reasoned, for he remembered the case of Miriam, a widow whose story had seized the imagination of the villagers and occupied them in speculation for many months until they had exhausted its excitement and resumed their normal lives. Miriam had stumbled into Benji's shop, blood staining her grey hair and running down her face. Benji dashed from behind the counter to support her. The two customers in the shop at the time ran off to fetch the nurse and the constable. Before too long the shop was crowded with the concerned or the merely curious. People muttered their sympathy as the nurse bathed her face and applied a bandage. After a prolonged period of moaning, Miriam managed to regain her sense, giving the constable an account of the incident and in such detail that he scribbled furiously in his notebook to keep up.

Miriam had woken up very early after a night of fitful sleep. Her husband John had entered her dream, warning her of some coming incident. Forty years dead, but not for a long time – not since 1899, or 1898, in the last century anyway – had he appeared in her dreams. He was warning her of – was it about her feet, the green spots which were spreading every-where, though she kept rubbing ointment on them? No, something else, perhaps something about the pear tree in the garden which had become infested with ants. Whatever it was, he kept her from sleeping; that and the screaming of owls made her arise early from her bed, light a fire and sit before it, wondering what had become of John, whether he was missing her, but if he was, why he had not come into her dreams before now. Barely two years of marriage, both of them just twenty, when he slumped forward from his chair, shuddered a bit, made a small cry, then died. Not so much as giving her a day's notice, not even an hour's. Gone. He ate his porridge, sat down before the fire to doze awhile before setting off for the fishing boat. Morning after morning after morning, the same routine, but not then. She cradled his head in her lap, wiped his mouth of the traces of porridge, then went to get help. But of course they would blame her, wouldn't they, his parents who never took to her, and who now looked upon her suspiciously, accusing her in their minds of causing his death. He was fat, grossly so, unhealthy really, some vein was bound to burst within him sooner or later what with the strain of having to support him, but no, his parents... The constable cleared his throat kindly, encouraging her to get to the point, but she was determined to have her say. She rambled on about herself and John, and the constable folded his notebook, taking up his pencil again only when she resumed the telling of the morning incident.

She had put on her blue dress. To begin with she had put on her yellow dress, then decided against it. Too bright. The blue was coming loose at the side but she wore it anyway. Call it whim, call it warning, but the yellow dress didn't seem right compared to the blue. Too gay. Blue was her mood that morning, faded and coming loose at the side. For some reason she decided not to wear a bonnet, setting off for Benji's shop bareheaded. She would clear off her credit of eight shillings and renew it with fresh purchases. Once a week she ventured out of the house with her money. The rest of the time she stayed indoors, as she had done since John's death, except for two annual trips to Gosport, sixty miles away by horse and carriage, to visit her parents. Christmas and Easter she spent with them, and when they died, she withdrew to the loneliness of her house, which she had cleared of all John's belongings, soon after his death, out of anger that he should have abandoned her without notice, abandoned her to the accusations of his family. He was born fat, he grew up fat, he was potbellied during their courtship and wedding, he fell heavily to the floor, full of porridge, and died. There was no more to it than that, no malice on her part, no resentment that made her want to be rid of him. Their marriage was an ordinary matter of mutual contentment, he bringing in the fish, she preparing it for the table. What else did his parents expect of her?

The constable broke the point of his pencil, deliberately, so that he could rest his hand. The onlookers in the shop were beginning to drift away, bored with her self-pity, when she hauled them back with a sudden exclamation. "A black thing from head to toe, black as a... as a... toad." The crowd murmured in excitement. "Oh he leapt at me, rolled me over with huge arms, pinned me to the ground, looked upon me with wild eyes. When I got up my head was bloody and my money gone. I remember him hopping back into the under-growth, on all fours, and that's all I saw before I fainted."

Father Harris was summoned to the shop. The villagers insisted he accompany them to the place where Miriam was assaulted. They were afraid to go on their own, no one volunteered to search the undergrowth into which the creature had disappeared. Dutifully he led them in prayer, pressing a rosary to the ground. They would never pass that spot other-wise, Father Harris reckoned, and seeing that it was on the main path through the village, their day-to-day business would be disrupted. So he said prayers to dispel their fear. Of course they were being foolish, Father Harris knew as soon as he learned that it was Miriam who was the victim. From the time he had arrived in the village people had told him of a woman who lived strangely, almost invisibly in her house. He visited her regularly but found nothing mysterious about her. The sadness of her life was apparent, the hurt at being deserted by her husband, and the shame of widowhood afterwards, made more unbearable by the hostility of her in-laws. She had decided to hide away from the world, to fret over her plight, but her self-imposed solitude over so many years was not puzzling to a priest accustomed to the tradition of denial. What was surprising was her sudden decision to rejoin the life of the village, to walk to them with loose hair and unravelling clothes, signs of carefreeness. She surrendered up her privacy even to the point of bleeding openly before them, and babbling, and having her life chronicled in the constable's official notebook.

Surprising, but Father Harris understood her sudden decision to put herself on display. The green spots colonising her feet and moving restlessly up her legs caused her distress. "I'm turning into a tree," she complained to him, and as if to prove the point she remained fixed on the spot as soon as she handed over a cup of tea to him. She stood over him rigidly. He shifted uneasily in his chair, between sips struggling to come up with a form of comforting words. "Birds will nest in my hair ferrying worms to their young," she said.

"Oh, you're still too young to die," Father Harris replied, unconvinced by his words. "It's only a minor infection, it'll go away, just keep rubbing in the oils. Think of our Lord's feet being anointed by Martha and be at peace with yourself."

"Death is waiting for me to turn wooden so he can more easily find the right place for his axe. The axe won't slip when I'm wooden," she said, refusing to budge from her morbidity.

The tea took on a bitter taste. Father Harris suddenly remembered some task awaiting him in the church, got up and left. "I'll bring you some holy water soon," he said, though he was sure of its inefficacy, for Miriam was too convinced of her coming demise to believe in miracles.

It was this sense of the impending closure of her life that made her open up to the village, Father Harris thought, blessing the site of the alleged assault but knowing that he was making a mockery of the Word of God. Still, no lesser a figure than St. Anthony had done the same. A young girl had been brought to him for cure. She had been tending her father's stallion in a lonely field when a dark-skinned monster surprised her. In the wake of his attack she became dumb, but St. Anthony had restored her speech and her impaired virtue. Miriam, like the young girl, was only seeking attention by the invention of a dark stranger who had leapt straight out of the pages of the Old Testament in the shape of the devil. Or out of the map of Guiana in the shape of a savage. On her visits to Benji's shop, he had broadcast the nature of the place, inventing details cunningly according to her circumstances to gain her support for his proprietorial role in the salvation of the place. To Nurse Knowles he spoke of a land of disease and malformed inhabitants and got a package of plasters and much praise for his work. Constable Jones gave a whistle for missionaries lost in the jungle. Miriam rifled through John's possessions which she had bundled up in the attic and gave trousers, apologising for their size but hoping that the naked inhabitants would still find some use for them, even if they ripped off the buttons and traded them as novel currency for food to ward off starvation, their habitual condition, according to Benji. She made tablecloths of John's capacious shirts, to encourage the savages to eat in a mannerly fashion.

The story of her attack, however, eclipsed the villagers' acts of charity to those dismal folk. Miriam, an obscure widow living obscurely by herself, was suddenly transformed into an object of pity and fascination. First and foremost, Benji forgave her her debts, indeed offered to supply her freely for as long as it took for her injury to heal. Second, villagers who hardly knew her, though she lived in their midst, sought her out. Before she was just an eccentric old woman, irrelevant to their lives, so they merely ignored or gave her a perfunctory greeting if she passed them on her way to Benji's shop. They greeted her, then hurried on, but now they insisted she visited their homes, preparing a welcoming meal for her as recompense for the years of neglect. They encouraged her to rehearse the incident, which she did with relish, prefacing her story with an account of her childhood, her marriage to John, the cruelty of his parents. In the telling and retelling of her life she learned how to be concise, how to distil and heighten this or that detail whilst downplaying others, how to pause at the correct time to allow her audience to dwell on what she was saying and to respond emotionally. The women plied her with pity and freshly baked cakes, taking her side against John for dying prematurely, even equating him with the dark-skinned molester. They combed her hair, hemmed her dress, made new remedies for her green spots. The men stared at the floor, slack-shouldered and defeated, taking on guilt over her suffering. The older ones vaguely remembered John as a harmless fellow fisherman, never complaining about the size of his catch, never making demands on their charity; an ordinary man going about his ordinary daily tasks, and though hampered by his body which made him clumsy at handling boat and net, never remarking on his lot. Miriam's narrative of woe made them see him in a different light, as bloated and selfish, caring only for the fullness of his belly.

John, long dead, and even when alive arousing no one's attention, was reincarnated and given the status of beast. Miriam, who lived on for decades, but given the villagers' neglect, might as well have been dead, became a legend, a story lodged in their memory in different versions according to her telling of it, or their apprehension of it. Father Harris found himself pitying the nonexistent behemoth who had rejuvenated Miriam, resurrected John, and renewed the spirit of the men and women of the village who would, for a while at least, attend to the romance of their original marriage vows. And what did the black man get but a meagre booty of Miriam's purse, the eight shillings she claims she was taking to Benji's shop? The devil always lost out on the bargain, creating great stir and dread in the human mind but remaining the same predictable non-changing creature of foul words and foul appearance. The villagers needed mystery in their lives and were getting bored with the devil's constancy. True, the devil drowned children and capsized boats but his deeds held forth no mystery, only cruelty and terror. The devil was set down in a book, he could not escape the staleness of the page. He had specific roles which bound him to specific words or deeds. Every day they lifted up their nets to amazing sights, queer foreign forms of sea-life, eyeless worms sniffing at the sky, fish with translucent bodies as if sculpted in glassy flesh, fish with pink gaudy lips, like those of a temptress, but the rest of the body repulsive with boils. And other life-forms, neither fish nor sponge nor worm, but pairs of ragged claws impossible to describe, so forever nameless. They stared awkwardly at the catch, partly excited, partly paralysed at the reality of other worlds which held no meaning to their own but which were incomparably glamorous, incomparably threatening. And though they threw them back into the sea, the mystery remained anchored in their imagination, scraping along at the bottom to give them pain, throwing up debris to cloud their reason. They resumed life in a show of nonchalance and practicality, drinking at bars over inane chatter, making love to their wives, playing with their children, repairing their houses and their nets, but the strangeness they had encountered mocked them with the sense of their ordinariness, their uselessness, mocked them with the possibility of miracle and amazement; the sea-life's movements, convulsions, cries, which made their Sunday worship seem so orderly, familiar, sedate. It was this mood of estrangement from themselves, Father Harris knew, which drew them to Benji's project in Guiana, and which led to the fantastic assault of the dark man. The excitement over the latter would eventually be exhausted, but leaving a gnawing void within them for novelty.

★

Alice seemed promising to their hunger for things other. Father Harris himself found her perplexing. She stammered out short broken sentences as if some catastrophe had reduced her words to rubble. And yet, though with infirm arthritic hand, she wrote with such fluency and authority. He would watch her sweeping his study, wondering at the idiosyncrasy of her speaking and writing. She would pause, pick up a beetle and hold it up to the light, examining it in amazement as it wriggled and kicked and glistened, as if recognising her own strange energy. Then she placed it back on the floor, gave it back its bizarre life, waiting for it to seek some dark corner before resuming her sweeping. As she lifted her head from the floor her hair fell voluptuously over her shoulders, disguising their hunch. All these aspects of her life he simply put down to eccentricity, no doubt brought on by age, and some loneliness which she would never confess to. In the early days he had made an attempt to engage her in conversation about her origin and past. She had merely stared at him, opening and closing her mouth like a fish shocked by air. Now he let her get on with her work, repressing his curiosity and judgement, even when she acted in inexplicable ways.

A few days previously he had woken up at dawn, and instead of taking to a book, he had set off impulsively to the beach. He walked along the shore with no particular thoughts in mind except a gladness for the revelation of God's hand in the light washing and stippling the sky; God determinedly making the day anew, awakening it to the delight of colour. Small waves splashed and chirruped on the sand, making him feel a child again, burdened neither by duty nor doubt. Later he would go back to the church and to his books, but at a time like this he was overwhelmed by God's certain presence. A sudden wild screaming of gulls shattered his wistfulness. At the far end of the beach, where the gulls were gathering, stood a figure, from her cascading hair visible even in the half-light, he knew to be Alice. The gulls wheeled malevolently over her as over prey but she stood her ground, staring out at the sea. Her calmness seemed to infuriate them, their cries grew more ominous, more desperate. She suddenly stretched out both arms to the sky and the gulls veered away in one distressed mass which then broke up in scattered flight. She lowered her arms and resumed her vigilance over the sea. The gulls regrouped and approached her, nervously, with diminished rage. She raised her arms once more, but slowly, gently, as if to lure them to her. The gulls moved away again, this time less in panic than in obedience to her gesture. After a while they ceased their noise, one loosened from the flock and alighted on the sand, at a respectful distance from her. The rest of them soon followed, singly, hesitantly, then altogether in one swoop of surrender.

They settled on their bellies and watched her drawing her long black hair out tight, stepping out of her clothes and moving towards the water.

An old woman bathing in the sea at dawn, nothing more, Father Harris mused as he gathered up Benji's offerings; she held as little mystery as the packets of dried peas and raisins lying on Benji's shelves, priced according to weight, weighed according to stock in hand. It was comforting after all, the simplicity of things, their ready acquiescence to a little reasoning, their secure place in the scheme of... of... he was struggling for a fresh word, when, pushing open Benji's shop door to leave, he came upon Tom's wife, Sarah. His eyes were immediately drawn to the gay orange ribbon woven into her hair. The cheer fell from her face like scales. She mumbled something and he mumbled back. He hurried past her as if on urgent business. He made his way home, unable to escape the image of her face suddenly whitening like the coating of flour on Benji's hand; her face draining of all mystery, becoming as empty as a chalk circle girdling Alice's fears.

And it came to him in a moment of quiet revelation that Sarah, in her pallor, was the ghost of Alice, that he had seen the ghost of Alice. He had seen what remained of Alice after she had broken violently from the past. Abandoning a husband? A family? What deed had Alice committed that led to her flight? Sarah at Benji's door was on the threshold of some transgression; she was yet to perform what deed? That lay in the future but when it happened she would be rehearsing what Alice had done. She would play Alice, become Alice, and he, Father Harris, had witnessed Alice's past in the evolving of Sarah's future. But it came to him, again in a meditative flash, that Alice had been sent to him so that he could bear witness not only to her past, which was projected unto as well as reflected by Sarah, but to his own presence on the threshold of an agnosticism evolving into faithlessness.

A fresh note awaited him when he reached home. Alice had expatiated upon the previous note. What was hinted at was now made explicit. 'Tom is in much sickness of heart, his thoughts turned to self-destruction. He hides away from the guile of his wife. She has been in an impious relationship with Benji for some time and they plan to elope. It will be the end of Tom UNLESS YOU FULFIL YOUR DUTIES AND DIRECT THEIR AFFAIRS ACCORDINGLY.'

The block letters were slaps in the face, a challenge to his ability to act, but her very boldness led him to doubt her intention. There could have been other explanations for Sarah's embarrassment at meeting him, ordinary reasons which once again revealed the simplicity of things as opposed to the messiness caused by visionary and intuitive disclosures. He went straight to the numbers in the church ledger and found, to his satisfaction, that Tom and Sarah had not donated what they had pledged, indeed, were three weeks behind payment. So that was it, he decided, solaced by the figures and by the thought that perhaps they had fallen on hard times and owed for their groceries too... another simple reason for Sarah's pallor, for Benji was notorious for gossiping about his debtors, calculating that they would pay up immediately so as to stop his slandering of them. Father Harris would ignore Alice's directive, but quietly seek out from his other parishioners more information about Tom's situation, so as to arrive at a reasonable view of the matter.

His trawl of small-talk and cunning questioning yielded nothing. The villagers' lives were as calm as the surface of the sea. Once more Father Harris found himself wondering at the character of the village, how it was formed by the necessity of the sea. It claimed lives occasionally, without warning or discrimination, caring nothing for this one who deserved to be spared because he was on the brink of first love, or that one upon whose existence depended an impoverished family. They grieved, retrieved their dead from the shore, buried them and resumed their lives as best they could, one day at a time for they had learned not to be ambitious lest they be left empty-handed; not to talk too loudly lest they be silenced; not to dwell on dark thoughts, provoked by the sight of the sea's lewd and deformed creatures, lest they could not be purified at the Confession. They came to an understanding that their losses were tributes due to the sea, and this helped to hasten the transition from grief to pragmatic acceptance of their fate.

"I've sought out Tom but there's nothing odd to report," Father Harris told Alice, but she remained bent over the sink, refusing to clear the hair masking her face. She scrubbed at a collar slowly and sullenly. Her silence was weighed with accusation. The next day, and in the following days, she splattered his desk with notes, each reinforcing and supplementing the previous one, though they were generated in such a litter of emotion that it was difficult to place them in a precise sequence. Tom, she claimed, was so afflicted with shame that he'd set off in a boat on the open sea, waterless, without food, rowing in no particular direction. Benji would profit from his disappearance, seducing Sarah so as to get to the contents of the shop, its carving knives, weighing scales and store of cured meats, and eventually to the property itself, on the pretext of monies owing. In this he was abetted by Frank, Tom's brother. Other notes gave a motive for Frank's behaviour: he was besotted by his brother's wife but had no money to speak of to keep her in her accustomed finery, and Benji (who had not the slightest desire for union with Sarah, though he would marry her after two years or so) would appoint him manager of Tom's shop, allowing him a share of its profits as well as free access to the widow. Benji could have managed the takeover of Tom's business on his own, but he needed a partner, to sustain his boldness but also to appear to be behaving in a humane manner. The brother would be given a portion of the property. Of course, after a reasonable period of time, Benji would move against Frank. He would dismiss him for some misdemeanour or the other, or pay him off with a paltry sum, with Sarah thrown into the bargain. They would have to leave the village and Benji would wear the mask of a cuckold, gratefully accepting the condolences of the villagers and gaining their admiration. He would be a picture of fortitude and forgiveness, refusing to speak of Frank as a thief and scoundrel.

Frank, however, had foreseen his fate and was concocting a counterplot. He would secrete a bloodstained knife in Benji's cellar. He would ply Jones, the village constable, with discounted goods, as a way of befriending him. He would do the same with Mrs. Knowles, the village nurse. They would come to trust his honesty, his generosity, and over the period of two years he would insinuate that his brother's disappearance was a darker story than they believed and that Benji was in some way involved. When the two years were up Frank would pre-empt Benji's moves by leading Constable Jones to the cellar and to the hidden knife. Benji would be arrested, pending further enquiries. Nurse Knowles would be called in to examine Sarah. She would find the bruises all over Sarah's body in various stages of freshness. Benji, Sarah would claim, had been abusing her from the time of their marriage a few weeks previously, out of guilt for what he had done to Tom. He had murdered Tom and married her, to ease his conscience, but his guilt could not be hidden. It was brutally visible in the bruises Sarah bore on her body. Like Miriam before her, Sarah would be succoured by the women in the village who would lavish pity on her, appalled by the reappearance of the devil in their midst. Benji's overseership of Guiana would be held against him. He had taken on the qualities of the very savages whose souls were in his custody. He had killed to acquire more money to provide for the savages. The collection of Bibles, rosaries and candles was only a cover for his increasing bewitchment with their impious habits, and what was worse, he had implicated the whole village in his scheming. The plan was now gospel clear: Benji would acquire and sell off Tom's shop, then his own, and voyage to Guiana to live among the capering redskins and yelping jungle folk, his fortune making him a god in their eyes.

Alice had involved – enslaved – them all in a drama of sin: nurse, policeman, butcher, grocer, husband, wife, brother, innocent villagers and foreigners each given a role, each of their actions leading to a tragic conclusion which only he, Father Harris, could deny by the fulfilment of his priestly function. Alice's notes were a clarion call to action which would make him the hero of the drama.

Father Harris put away her writings in sudden distress. An old woman whom he had allowed into his house as just another figure of destitution had revealed an aspect of the human imagination which, frankly, frightened him. Her cooking and cleaning of the house of God were ordinary enough but her careful minute attention to his clerical garments took on an ominous meaning. His sense of his ordained and appointed status, and the protection offered by the Church, strengthened him to resist complete surrender to fright. He put away her notes and took up instead his Cardinal Newman, as armour against her temptations and exhortations, but could hardly concentrate on the page. The clarity of the Cardinal's writing vied with the clarity of Alice's narrative. His mind shifted uncontrollably between the two and he found himself stuttering as if in mimicry of her.

VI

The pipe broke in Father Harris's hand, the sudden violence of his action stilling Father Wilson, who then cleared his throat as if to prepare it better for the passage of whisky. "The newspapers are full of rumours of war," Father Wilson said, staring at the broken pipe and calculating a way to resurrect the conversation. "The Germans are stirring things. Expect vile leaders and slaughter from them."

Father Harris ignored him, thinking instead of Alice, her abrupt arrival and equally abrupt departure. An apparition, to be sure, he mused, then chuckled to himself as he remembered the many peasants knocking impatiently on the door of the seminary in Ireland, each wild-eyed and barely able to speak. Each had seen something and wanted priestly confirmation of miraculous vision. Mist curling off a ram's horns and forming the image of the Virgin; a boulder smitten by lightning, the smoke clearing to reveal the face of the Virgin; a bull wounded in fight, the blood trickling to the ground and forming the outline of the Virgin's crown... such were the more imaginative of the apparitions, the Virgin otherwise appearing conventionally in the midst of sheep or by a running stream. If the peasants had their way the countryside would be littered with shrines, and the drunk or the plain crazy elevated to the status of visionaries. Pity the poor Virgin, Father Harris sighed, she seeming to have nothing better to do than wander through Ireland showing herself off to all and sundry. And pity poor village lasses like Bernadette, forced by their fathers to talk of sightings, to choose between a sound hiding and sainthood. No, Alice was no holy apparition, and he, Father Harris, no seer. Perhaps Father Wilson was right: mist off a goat's horns was mist off a goat's horns was mist off a goat's horns was not the Virgin, however poetic the expression of what was seen, or claimed to have been seen. Father Harris, however, would not give in easily to his adversary.

"Name me three women," he said suddenly, and leant threateningly towards Father Wilson.

Father Wilson was taken aback, he instinctively clutched the whisky glass to his chest, to guard it from capture.

"Well, go on, name me three women," Father Harris insisted.

"Em... I'm not sure what you mean," Father Wilson said.

"Women, you know, those creatures who are not you and men. They're called women. Just mention three." Father Wilson fell silent, his face resolutely refusing to betray any embarrassment. "Take them from our Church History if you will," Father Harris suggested.

"St. Catherine," Father Wilson offered, sipping his whisky in obvious relief.

"And?"

"St. Emmelia. Then there's St. Cecelia and St. Margaret."

"St. Veronica, St. Emmelia, I wager you know a dozen others," Father Harris said in a tone which put his adversary at ease. "But you only show up your regrettable self," he said, suddenly pouncing on Father Wilson. "The more names of women you call the more faults you name in yourself. Arrogance, stubbornness, bullying, cruelty, insensitivity, excess of power, shall I go on? It's not the Germans we should look out for, it's the like of priests like you." He paused to witness his friend's discomfort, then relented from the assault. "Me too, priests like me," he said in a conciliatory voice. "I would have done like you and named Veronica, Eustacia, and the rest, all martyrs to men's power. That's why we remember them and all we remember of them, the ways men broke them. We know little else about them and we're not even interested in knowing anything beyond their martyrdom at our hands." He fidgeted with the pipe, gluing the two pieces in his mind, then deciding otherwise beckoned to me, placed them with pained and deliberate care in my palm. I in turn laid them on his desk, among his tobacco tins of dissected insects or those waiting to be examined. Father Wilson, once more aware of my presence, tilted his head in the direction of the whisky bottle which Father Harris had left uncharitably on the cabinet, rather than on the table before them: it was his way of humbling Father Wilson, forcing him to ask for more hospitality and so reminding him that he had come empty-handed, apart from the ridiculously stuffed bird. I could have brought the bottle to Father Wilson, but I knew the ritual too well, which was to take his glass instead, fill it at the cabinet and return it to him. Such action on my part always pleased Father Harris, for it meant that I had understood his strategy without him needing to explain it to me. It made the two of us fellow conspirators against Father Wilson's craving, for after the first drink he became inordinately thirsty and would not leave the house without draining the bottle, prolonging the conversation though Father Harris made a show of his greater age, yawning or drooping a fatigued head on his shoulder; a show too of his superior power of concentration, for whenever Father Wilson began to lose the thread, he would jerk forward in sudden alertness and draw Father Wilson back to the theme of their discussion.

This time however, Father Harris made me fetch the bottle and when I hesitated in surprise, even betrayal, he looked at me with soft eyes as if seeking my forgiveness. He drank greedily, and Father Wilson gladly followed his example, finishing his glass and pouring another.

"Alice," Father Harris said, "now, she was a case in point, she was a right... a right..." He searched for the incisive word but he needn't have, for Father Wilson sunk deeper into his chair, preparing to surrender to his whisky and to whatever Father Harris had to propose.

"She was right alright," he said, encouraging Father Harris to continue. "Mind you, I don't rightly know her, this Alice, but do educate me."

"Two old men talking about women, that's what we are, and we don't understand the first thing about them. All you know are sainted victims, but I met Alice." Father Harris paused, considering whether to thrust further at his friend, but the game of argument and rebuttal suddenly seemed worthless. "Alice. Chalice. Benefice," Father Harris said.

"Surplice," Father Wilson added and helped himself to another drink in self-reward.

"True. Well done. Surplice, exactly. That's the way she spoke," Father Harris said, but Father Wilson was too engrossed in his glass to appreciate the rarity of the compliment.

"I should have run my hand through her hair," Father Harris said, the whisky seeming to inspire mournful lyricism. "What loveliness would I have harvested if only I had sought more than the ghost of her. That's my trouble. I stand before graves trying to imagine what the occupants were like, when I should have seized them when they were alive, got to know them in the present. I stand before graves, left with nothing but an imagining of what's past." And, inspired by his own words, and careless as to whether Father Wilson was following him, he launched into a monologue on Alice, ending on her abandonment of him. "I woke up and she was gone. Gone. Upped and left as abruptly as she came. Appeared. Disappeared. No meaning to it. And why should there be? Why should we always want things to follow, a, b, c, why always want things to make sense, to make a sequel and a finished story? To be sure she left a note behind, a kind of explanation, but who is to believe it? 'I am going to sea, in search of Tom. You have betrayed me and your Catholic duty since you have not sought him out. You have doubted me, so I will take it upon myself to go after Tom, to save him from the sin of suicide.' And all I could think of was that she had broken from me as abruptly as she bad broken from her past of a nameless and cruel husband. In my mind I had given her a husband, even a family, so she could flee from them and come to me. I had made a martyr of her, Veronica,

201

Eustacia, Margaret, I had made of her a legend of the Church. I had given her a dead story. That's what we do, you and I, two old men, two old priests who know not women in the present and in the flesh. They might as well be stuffed birds." The finality of sorrow in his voice was wasted upon the half-snoozing Father Wilson, so he turned to me for confirmation of his failure to appreciate the texture of Alice's life, repenting for his fabrication of her as victim and martyr.

"Alice. Borealis," I said, the rhyme coming to me strangely and spontaneously. Father Harris looked upon me as if awestruck by my wisdom. He opened his mouth in praise but changed his mind.

"Wake up that piece of impiety," he said, kicking his foot in Father Wilson's direction. He would not speak of me except in Father Wilson's hearing. We were to resume our fellowship and conspiracy. I swished the liquid in the bottle and held it to Father Wilson's nose. The vapour was like smelling salts to the faint, he lurched forward from his chair, holding forth his glass for replenishment.

"Alice poor Alice, Alice the poor, Alice and Benji the boor, Alice on the seashore," he said drowsily.

"You're drunk," Father Harris barked, insulted by the silliness of the rhyme. "This boy is a blessing compared to you and your stuffed bird."

Father Wilson's eyes looked vaguely and glassily in my direction. "He is indeed an excellent specimen, but we must wait. Wait. Patience. We must be patient. He's young, we'll never know how he'll fill out. Please, my dear friend, allow me the last word in taxidermy, the last deed of glue and wire, and I'll make something of him prouder than your present living estimation."

"You're drunk," Father Harris barked a second time, and Father Wilson made an effort to steady his mind and stay awake to his host's need to talk. "This boy's our future, he'll know the truth of women's lives one day. He's bright and he'll redeem us."

"Bright, how bright?" Father Wilson asked, looking me up and down suspiciously for signs of the new order. "It was he who speculated that moth and German cockroach both had chitinous teeth."

"Ah, a worthy proposition from one so young," Father Wilson said, relieved at the prospect of leaving behind the subject of women which not only bored him but which also exposed his ignorance. He was on safe and pleasurable grounds with insects. "So we have an entomologist in the making."

"No, a poet and a philosopher," Father Harris corrected him.

"Come, come my friend, you sound so backward and dotish," Father Wilson replied, sobering up as best he could and sitting straight in eager anticipation of battle. "There's no philosophy to the being of an ant, no poetry in the way it crawls over rotting food. Modern science describes its mechanics, anything else is medieval mysticism."

Father Harris would have none of this, arguing about complex gut systems, feelers and the like which in their minuteness were manifestations of the grandeur of God's mind. God's mosaic vision was mirrored in a spider's several eyes which looked simultaneously in different directions and in different foci, or in thousands of lenses in a dragonfly's eyes. And as to the miracle of flame and shadow, what greater revelation than the water-fly gathering to the light on the surface of a pond, whereas the lava of the elephant hawk moth burrowed down on the bottom-stems of the willowherb, awaiting dusk. "All are bound together in one process of living, immeasurably various as it is." He paused on asserting this, remembering the commingling of the bones of Stephen Yardley, Mark Yardley, Christopher Reece and John Taylor in their mass burial; on the surface different men but identical in the foundation of an earthen grave. He thought of Alice's story of Tom and Benji that could be drawn out endlessly, and even configured differently, each character playing other roles, even exchanging roles among themselves, but with the theme of sin and salvation remaining the same. It was what Alice saw when she held a beetle up to the light, a design of infinite complexity.

Father Wilson resorted to laughter to deflate Father Harris's enthusiasm. His mind was still too groggy to engage in difficult conversation. He merely restated his conviction that, apart from man, nature was a machine, the exclusive province therefore of the scientist. "Poetry and old wives' tales are the only things that are one and the same," he said scornfully. "An ant is an ant is not a moth is not a fly, even in wet weather when it sprouts wings. Only when you dissect and stuff a dove do you discover how separate its structure is from a hawk's. That wretched fellow Darwin has got it wrong, he's not a scientist but a prophet. A prophet I tell you and a false one at that." The repetition of the word 'prophet' made him remember me, how Father Harris had called me the new redeemer. His anger at the new cult of Darwinism waned and he turned to me in a mood of kindness. "Come, boy," he said, and as I approached he dug into his jacket pocket and fished out a present. "Now, this is a single lens in an ebonite handle, a Leitz lens. Not as good as the Steinheil achromatic lens, but it will do for your young eyes, what do you think? The Germans will make wicked and murderous war on us, but by God their lenses are the best, whatever the race or nationality of your eyes! Go on, take it, go study your German cockroaches for their chitinous teeth." I took it from him then hesitated, torn between a sense of worthlessness and an intense and joyous pride. It was the first precious thing I possessed of my own. Father Harris, himself moved by his friend's act of kindness, gestured to me to accept it. I mumbled my thanks, unable to find more appropriate Christian expression. "Now that you're armed we must give you a title befitting your new status. What shall we call you?" His brow creased in concentration. He pressed his tongue to the roof of his mouth, awaiting inspiration. "That's it," he chuckled. "We'll make you a member of the Order of the Mites of St. George."

"St. Patrick," Father Harris snarled, pouring out the last of the whisky in preparation for a final joust of worldly and divine disputation on the being of ants.

★

"A sorry old man, a slave to Reason, don't heed his cynicism," Father Harris told me as we walked in the garden, or rather struggled through it, for it was dense with weeds, the flowerbed laid down by a previous tenant turned into wasteland and the elm trees long dead, strangled by creepers. Father Harris forbade me to touch anything, not even to rake up dead leaves. He had given me charge of the garden, but only to witness its growth.

"That's why your grandfather is sick," he said, "all that digging and slashing and laying down of bricks. Nature lets you clear and build but only so much, for then you will wound it beyond recovery, so it will have to retaliate, not out of hatred but to let you and your kind survive in it, through it. So many hundreds died shovelling out the Coventry canals in the old days, not so much out of hunger, though you wonder how they lasted at all on the little wages they got paid for backbreaking work whilst the rich looked on, waiting for them to drop and rot so that they could suck their bones, having already sucked their flesh."

We paused at the pond for Father Harris to catch his breath and recover his calm. He rested his hand on my shoulder, then pressed down on it so I could feel the weight of his anger.

"And they're doing it again. They've shipped over your grandfather and hundreds of the poor Irish to extend the canals, yes, paying them a bit more, because times have changed, they're afraid of riots and stoppages, but it's the same disdain for nature. In the old days the earth breathed out spores and germs and animalcula – mark that word, a lovely word for nature's shock troops." He spelt it for me and I repeated the word and its spelling. Satisfied with my mastery of it, he continued.

"The animalcula bred all manner of sickness in the stomach and bowel but it was done not out of spite but to stop the extinction of the earth upon which all life depends. It's like God sending his plagues and floods now and again to wipe out evil men and make space for new beginnings. He warns them first, through prophets, but they kill the prophets. Then He sends them dreams but they only wake up and rub their eyes in forgetfulness. Floods and plagues are the last resort."

He relaxed his hold on my shoulder and led me to the edge of the pond. With great effort he squatted on his haunches and gazed on the surface of the water as if into a prophetic dream sent by God. The morning wind was wet with frost, I stood beside him shivering. The dead elms loomed above me.

"Oh I was never one of them, in spite of my belonging to the order of training and study and worship," he said, and with such energy that he nearly toppled over. I went to steady him, but he recovered on his own, sat down on the wet ground, stretched out his legs and dipped his shoes into the water like an old man at the seaside, careless of the soiling of his clothes.

"That's why Father Wilson comes to see me. We grew up together in the seminary, but I was always the odd one out, I left and he stayed. All his life he stayed indoors until a few years ago when they put him out to pasture in a home for old priests in Wolverhampton. He would have stayed in Ireland but for me. He needed to be near me, though I hadn't seen him for all those years. When we were young in the seminary I hardly noticed him, just another pious shaven face like mine mouthing medieval prayers and the wisdom of Church Fathers. But he must have taken secretly to me, why, I don't rightly know. He must have thought I'd turn out disobedient. Now I can't get rid of him. He comes to pick a quarrel, or so I used to think, to bring me back to the fold of everything he was schooled to believe in. Now I'm not sure, I wonder whether he comes awaiting some kind of conversion."

He reached for my hand, drew me to him and made me sit down at the water's edge.

"He's too old, too set in his ways for me to make a proper follower of him, and I'm too old myself, I don't even know what I believe in, only what I don't, which is God the Father Almighty."

He suddenly kicked off a shoe and it fell into the water. I rose automatically to retrieve it but he held me back. He laughed as he watched it floating, then filling up with water and slowly sinking.

"Give me the mite any day rather than the Almighty, give me the widow's mite," he said, watching the pond life gather curiously and excitedly at his shoe, some clinging to its lace as it floundered.

"The Jews will be all our downfall," he said mysteriously as the shoe gurgled a last breath and disappeared. "They own the canal and will kill your grandfather. They own all of Europe and will profit from the coming war. Father Wilson will never be my follower, but you will. After the coming Flood, when the waters subside, we'll wade through the mud and recover statues of Jesus and Mother Mary and the icons of the saints, only female ones mind you, and we'll wash them down, restore them as best we can, and you'll take them to a new land, a place called Guiana, among new people who will worship them in ways you teach them. But first I must teach you. Come, give me some help."

He struggled to his feet, I placed my hands under his arms and heaved him up. He hobbled off on one shoe to his study and I followed, walking as exactly in his naked footprints as I could.

"First learn the pathways of the dead," he said, sending me to fetch pipe and tobacco. He scratched a match then decided against lighting up. "Fetch me the King James Bible," he commanded instead.

I climbed the ladder and prised it out from the topmost shelf. I descended carefully, for the Bible was in a fragile state, its covers coming loose.

"Open it on the first page, what do you see?" he asked as I sat on a stool at his feet.

"To the Most High and Mighty Prince James by the Grace of God," I read, but he interrupted me.

"Fine. Fine. But what do you see?" he asked again.

"Great and manifold were the blessings, most dread Sovereign, which Almighty God, the Father of all mercies bestowed upon us the people of England when first he sent Your Majesty's Royal Person to rule and reign over us."

"I ask you a third time whether you will stay awake for me and tell me what you see," he said with barely disguised disappointment. "Here, give it to me."

He took it roughly from my hands, not bothering when the covers fell to the floor. He looked triumphantly at the denuded text, at the threads of its spine weakened and stained with age. "The rascal James and his Jewish patrons who funded his Court and his Protestant Bible!" He placed the Bible in his lap and lit another match, moving it to the spine, and when my face flared with alarm he blew it out, leaning back on his chair to watch the smoke curling blackly towards the ceiling.

"Be not afeared," he said as the smoke thinned and disappeared. "You and I will not be called to account for the fate of the Jews. They will destroy themselves at the hands of others. Your duty is altogether different." He took up the Bible again and held it before me. "Look at the holes," he said, pointing to the evidence of bookworms. "All my other Bibles I have treated with powders, but not this one. I have left it as a breeding ground for insects, so that I can learn from the pathways they make through it."

He handed the Bible to me. "How many holes can you see in Genesis?" he asked.

There were three.

"Read the lesson of the first worm," he said, "read the very sentence it begins its exegesis. And mark that word, e-x-e-g-e-s-i-s, which means the interpretation of the Bible."

I repeated the word, spelt it correctly and began to read the portion of the verse punctuated by the worm. "And God saw that it was good." I hesitated, but Father Harris waved me on. "And God said, let there be light in the firmament of the heaven – "

"No, no, no," Father Harris stopped me. "Be guided by the worm. Don't read across the page, read down, vertically. Follow it. It started in Genesis, now find out where it stopped."

I flicked page after page which the worm had bore through cleanly, the hole ending at Leviticus.

"Read, read," Father Harris said impatiently.

"And this is the law of the sacrifice of peace-offerings which he shall offer unto the Lord."

Father Harris twisted his mouth in contempt. "I know the passage well," he said. "It's about choice cuts and blood and fat, what's to be offered to God as sacrifice, what's not. Read it to me."

"And he shall offer of it all the fat thereof; the rump, and the fat that covereth the inwards, and the two kidneys, and the fat that is in them, which is by the flanks, and the caul that is above the liver, with the kidneys, it shall be taken away."

Father Harris signalled me to stop. "All these rules, as if God exists for gobbets! This bit clean, that bit unclean, the other bit to be roasted in its blood... Leviticus is all law, you can't raise a simple piece of meat to your mouth in peace without Moses or Aaron slapping your hand away with a haircloth napkin. Poor worm, no wonder he expired where he did. He starts off excitedly, believing that Creation was good, but by the time he gets to Leviticus he's squashed by Moses' tablet. Or perhaps he just gave up, totally confused by all the dietary regulations. Perhaps he preferred to starve to death."

"But to get to Leviticus he had to pass through Exodus, and that's full of laws," I said in mild protest.

"Admirable, boy, you're perspicacious." He paused momentarily, but the excitement of his thoughts made him decide against spelling the word. "You belittle the worm though," he chided gently. "You underestimate the wisdom and the hopefulness of the worm. What does Exodus mean, tell me?"

I looked ignorantly at him.

"It means 'going forth' or 'flight' or 'migration'. So you see now the motive of the worm?"

I fidgeted with the Bible, unable to answer.

"A worm, bless his mandible, is a faithful creature. He sets off at the beginning in a freshly created world, inspired by God's Word made flesh... ooooh, such delicious sacred flesh which he can't get enough of, munching, crunching, licking and sucking, for it's the First Supper, Jesus is not yet strung up, it'll be many books and hundreds of pages before the Jews kill him. Of course the worm is not to know what's to come, but the more he goes through Genesis the more the earth hardens, hurting his mouth, filling it with thorn and briar. Although he is confused and foreboding comes upon him, he persists, plucky little faithful thing, and gets to Exodus, where the dew of Creation slowly evaporates and the first light fades, but though he thirsts and the darkness closes over him and the ground becomes rock, he believes that he'll soon pass through this time of trial, migrate to another shore where he will find once more the bright first fruits of God, the taste of the original pages. After exemplary fortitude and the effort of the true believer he exits Exodus, hoping to find a spot to settle, to procreate, when bam! the tablet of Law flattens him. No more delving for him, no more penetration of God's matter, no more vertigo of nervous expectation and challenge as he looks down from the snowcapped domes and the gorgeous towers of God's imagination. He's been stamped to the ground with all of God's structures. The earth is as flat as the line of Law." He looked vexedly at the Bible, swallowed in preparation for another assault on Moses, but he quickly grew exhausted and clamped his mouth like the rueful worm on stony ground.

After he had retired for his afternoon nap I went back into the garden, taking with me the King James Bible, my Leitz lens and a sample of German cockroach. I had thought to embark on some adventure of science but the sight of the dead elms weakened my resolve. A vague anger rose up in me for no apparent reason. Perhaps it was the endless and pointless talk between the two men which I had had to endure, talk that revealed tension between them; talk too, though not explained to me properly, of Germany making war and Jews to be massacred, with Father Harris saying they deserved it because they killed bookworms, funded the Protestant Bible and owned the canals of Coventry. German lens, German war, German cockroach, stuffed birds, germs, worms, Jews... it was all foolish, I told myself, though it came from the minds of learned priests. Anger turned briefly to self-reproach for daring to dismiss Father Harris and Father Wilson, me, an unformed and unlettered thing. Better to listen unquestion-ingly next time to my superiors and repeat whatever they said. "A-n-i-m-a-l-c-u-l-e," I spelt aloud, then again, like a mantra of obedience, but the anger would not wane. I placed the cockroach upon the Bible as upon a catafalque, draped it with a dead leaf and held the lens above it to focus the light. Many minutes passed, the leaf would not catch fire, not being dry enough. I tore a page from the Bible and crumpled it up, but though I twisted the lens this way and that, a flame would not form to burn the Jews, the afternoon sun being too weak. I grew so desperate that I flung the lens away from me. It fell into the pond with a plop so final that my heart sunk. I though immediately of Father Wilson's kindly face as he presented me with the lens. I rushed to the shed, found the fishnet and trawled it along the bottom of the pond. I located Father Harris's shoe and pulled it up. When the water drained from it I could see a dozen insects under the tongue of the shoe, in holes meant for laces, in the cracks in the heel. Although the shoe had been a mere hour or so in the pond they had sought to colonise it, to turn it into a permanent home. I went to shake them off, and put the shoe out to dry but stopped, hearing Father Harris addressing my mind. "Leave them be," I imagined him saying. "The shoe fell from the heavens like a miracle and landed in their midst. They took to it without questioning, without murmurings of discontent, without secretly wanting a bigger size or leather of a different colour. Learn the lesson well, boy: submission, obedience, meekness." I waited respectfully until his voice ceased to echo in my mind, then threw the shoe back into the pond. I trawled again, and happiness of happiness, found my lens! It was coated with insects. I tried to flick them away with my fingernail but they clung on to the glass as if mesmerised by some image they beheld through it. I flicked again and again, hurting their bodies, but they remained steadfastly rooted in vision. Father Harris would have scolded me, telling me to let the creatures be, let them gaze and be transfixed by what they perceived, but he was still asleep and I would not heed his imaginary voice. I wanted *my* lens, *my* gift for putting up with the nonsensical exchanges between him and Father Wilson. I took up the page torn from the Bible and with deliberate cruelty wiped away the insects. They lay smudged and squirming on the paper which I cast into the pond, oddly satisfied with the thought that though I failed to burn the Jews I could still destroy the animalcula, injured beyond recovery, who were the Jews' lackeys and novices.

The years, the passing of so many of them, have dulled my mind so my writing now is steeped in error and contradiction. I claim that Father Harris demanded of me obedience, submission, meekness, but perhaps I have forced these words into his mouth under the pressure of the telling of my tale. To tell is to pretend to resurrect and give shape to what has gone irretrievably, sunk into nescience. And were it not for his injunction to write, I would have made of my pen the dereliction of my memory and put it away. Write *disobediently* he commanded, though I now find myself cloistered in sentences instead of scattering them to the wind. The need to make sense creates a prophet of him, one who demands of me obedience, submission, meekness, one who instructs me to hate the Jew when, in truth, it was the Law he abhorred, the settled word, the bargain struck between men of money and banal souls. "Never mind Father Wilson," I seemed to remember him urging, "we have to learn to read and write in new ways, for it is a new century. The enemy will always be at your elbow as you write, he'll be nudging and shoving you to get you back to a preordained line, but name him Jew and banish him with curses." And so I was pressed into reading the Bible bizarrely, seeking connections between arbitrary passages marked by the beginning and finale of wormholes. Of course nothing made sense, but that was the point according to Father Harris. He waited patiently as I struggled to connect one worm's entrance into the Bible in Deuteronomy ('The Lord will smite thee with the Egyptian scab, and swelling in the groin, and the itch') and the same worm's expiring in the First Book of Kings – ('With harp and tambour, flute and zither at their head they will be uttering words of prophecy.')

"Try cross-referencing," he offered when I was on the point of despair. "Link up one worm to another and see where it gets you."

Gladly I abandoned my difficult worm and went to his fellow who had also started in Deuteronomy. "When the whole people or some one Israelite offer sacrifice, be the victim ox or sheep, the priest can claim the gift of shoulder and maw; they can claim the first fruits too of corn, or wine," I read.

"And where does this wise one end?" he asked headily.

It had been truly voracious in its piety, exiting some four hundred pages later, at Ecclesiastes, a veteran of eighteen books no less.

"Food will cheer, the wine bring thee gladness, but money, it answers every need."

"Well?" he said, waiting for my exegesis.

After a long period of contemplation under Father Harris's hawkish vigilance, I surrendered. "Is it to do with men catching diseases and getting drunk and becoming greedy and spending money?" I asked weakly.

"No no no," he said, "that's too reasonable. The whole of the Old Testament is full of itching scratching gluttons with their pockets full of other people's coin. The worms are exact on this, but look again, find the moment of redemption they point us to."

I reread the passages and cogitated more. Father Harris was about to snatch the text from my hand when in a moment of inspiration I said, "Prophecy". As I spoke the word I looked up at him, identifying him with it. "The worm is telling me about you as a prophet," I said, wanting to remain at his feet forever as he spoke, at his elbow as he wrote, beside his shoulder as he read: to be both shadow and vessel, unworthy and insubstantial yet catching and preserving all of his wisdom in a structure invulnerable to time. My face was lit with adoration but he denied me, abruptly and harshly.

"Nonsense, boy. I am none such," he said, his denial causing me such instant hurt that even now, years later, my pen hesitates to record it. It is a true memory of childhood hurt, his refusal to accept the gift of my obedient, submissive and meek self.

"I am no prophet," he repeated with cruel emphasis, "but all the same hearken unto me and learn, but not parrotwise. When I speak I want you to cock your ear at an odd angle, so that you don't catch all that I say, or you mishear the odd word so you have to guess, ponder, remake. You will never be other wise if you don't do so. Now, recite that verse about prophecy and make of it your motto, emblazon your mind with it, little noble Knight of the Order of the Mites of St. Patrick."

The attempt to smooth me with flattery failed. I would resist him even as he resisted me. I recited the verse but without appetite: "With heart and tambour, flute and zither at their head they will be uttering words of prophecy." I could have yielded to his desire for interpretation but I would not, falling silent in feigned ignorance. He cupped his hand at my mouth, wanting to gather my words and when nothing came he spoke instead, but in gloom.

"The words of prophecy are like winged insects," he said wearily. "The music of the heart soars and cannot be drawn back by the gluttons and drunkards and merchants. They belch or retch curses after it, or else the cunning Jew gestures after it, holds up a counterfeit coin, but the heart will not be tempted by their foulness or their fools' gold. Words of prophecy are like maggots, they are born in flesh that has died in sin but they will not be trapped in flesh. They sprout wings and rise in an upsurge of melodious sounds. Words of prophecy are like – "

I stopped listening, though I made my eyes shine with keenness and set my mouth in an attitude of studiousness. Similes would swarm from him now that he had returned to the subject of insects. He had made beads of greenflies and beetles and threaded them into a rosary of tedious rhetoric, tedious exclamations. I was too young then to understand my boredom of him but I well remember my alarm when I suddenly realised that I was trapped in his presence and that I must make preparations to escape. I wished him dead, to be free of him, free as the melody of inspiration or the horrid sound of a page ripped from the Bible, it didn't matter which. I would practise to wait. He was infirm, death would take him soon. I made a show of waiting at his feet as he spluttered out comparisons between the world of words and of insects, the sincerity and passion in his voice an indictment of my willed deafness, willed dumbness, but whatever guilt arose in me was quickly clipped. I decided there and then, with the barren resolve of a child, which yet brought forth an urge to cry and a wanting, that he would never be my father, and most of all, never be my mother.

My lessons were as varied and disconnected as they were useless. I was taught to pun, to yoke ideas together. Words were as infinite in capacity as insects. "Entomology and etymology: let these terms be sovereign over all you think and do." He made me write the two words down a hundred times. When I finished he took up the paper and examined it, admiring my effort.

"Now write them backwards on the other side of the paper," he said, returning it to me.

I did as he bid, suppressing my irritation at the tediousness of the task. Two hours later I presented him with a messy picture, for I had crossed off the many false starts and errors, or else my palm had accidentally smudged the ink as it made its passage across and down the paper. To my surprise he was not in the least reproachful. Quite the opposite – he smiled approvingly at my handiwork.

"If only the Jews were as untidy, the world would be free of blood," he said enigmatically. When I looked puzzled he launched into an attack against the Old Testament which I could barely follow. He railed against the idea of 'Chosen People' and the separation of things into opposites. "Saved: Damned. Jews: Gentiles. We: Them. Birds: Insects. Man: Fish. Every living creature divided from every other. I'd rather be a Hindoo than take on Father Wilson's way of thinking. Deep down he's a Semite, a versus man. Oh how I pity a man who strips verse of rhyme and cadence and play, for he makes an adversary of me."

He nodded in the direction of his desk. He didn't need to elaborate for I anticipated the task and took up a fresh piece of paper, proceeding to fill it with the words 'verse', 'versus' and 'adversary' to which I added my own, 'veracity', much to his delight. It was easy to please him, I thought, as I turned over the paper and began to write the words backwards, and then, for variety, with my left hand, not bothering to make corrections. I handed it to him, pitying the predictability of his response, hardly listening as he started once more to berate Father Wilson.

"I'd gobble up the lot, I'd riddle all the pages of the Old Testament with holes," he concluded at long last. "There's nothing but horror in it, screech owls and unclean dogs, not a kind word about God's creatures. Gadflies are pests, spiders are symbols of mischief-makers, bees and locusts are enemies of goodness. And do you know, ants, among the most harmless and beneficial and diligent of God's creatures, are mentioned only twice in the Old Testament, and then only in the Book of Proverbs. Twice! Imagine that!"

I didn't know and I was disinclined to let my imagination roam over the fate of the sparsely-cited ants. I yearned for some practical outcome to my lessons, the acquisition of some skill that would equip me to lead a life independent of the Church's charity and the company of weird priests and their attendants. At first I was enchanted by the crushing, the restoration and painting of eggshells, as I was by the word games he set to befuddle my mind: acrostics, puns, neologisms and the rest. "Mind your Ps and Qs, never waste a letter or let it lie fallow," he urged, showing me how the world was made and could be made even more wondrous, by the twisting and twining of syllables. The sheer repetition of such exercises though, accompanied by his rambling philosophising, exhausted and bored me.

Even our science classes were exhibitions of magic, Father Harris releasing a liquid from a pipette onto a crystal and stepping back to marvel at the fury of the reaction, vapour pouring forth from the test tube or else a sudden flame blackening it. I yearned for a simple explanation of the principle of the chemistry, but none was forthcoming. Father Harris merely sighed in deep contentment as the crystal bubbled or whistled or sparked.

Our mathematics classes were the same. Father Harris stood before the blackboard for what seemed an eternity, writing down numbers, crossing them out, connecting them with arrows, enclosing groups of them in circles, the meaning of his calculations evident only to himself, for once he started he seemed to forget me, turning around only occasionally to frown at the sunlight streaming through the window behind me, then taking up fresh chalk and resuming his work. It was a mighty effort on his part to be upright for so long, for his limbs were doddery, but the excitement of playing with numbers sustained him. Only when there was no space left on the blackboard would he seek out his chair. I fetched a glass of whisky to aid his recovery. He swallowed it in one go, then sat panting and staring at the numbers. Sometimes he would wag his hand at a particular spot on the blackboard and turn to me as if wanting confirmation of the wizardry of his calculations, but more often than not he just sat there, immersed in his own thoughts. The excitement gradually waned, his breathing regained its evenness, and it was then that he would slump deeper into the chair, wanting to be alone. I sensed his changed mood and without needing to be told I left him to his despondency, retiring to the kitchen to prepare the evening meal.

These days he hardly bothered to eat, picking absentmindedly at the simple food I served him – boiled potatoes, cabbage, slices of cured ham. Nor did he care about his appearance, wearing the same shirt on successive days. I continued to clean the house as diligently as before, to cook, to manage his laundry, but he no longer commented on my dutifulness as he did at the beginning of my stay with him. More alarmingly he opened his door to all corners, out of apathy more than an expanse of charity. At first he guarded the privacy of our space, spending all his time converting me to his ways of thinking, resenting any knock on the door which interrupted my initiation into the conundrum of words and numbers.

"Show whoever it is to the cellar and don't linger in worthless conversation."

I did so, returning speedily to his company. When the lesson was over he would remember the newcomer and ask, "Family, alcohol or police?"

"Alcohol," I said, for the stranger's breath was fiery and though the evening air was keen he wore no jacket, no doubt having pawned it for drink.

"Good. He'll sleep it off and be gone in the morning. See him on his way with a handful of carrots. Perhaps he'll smell their freshness and be all sentimental and hurry back to his allotment in Kerry or wherever. No point me preaching to him, but the smell of earth may bring him back to his senses."

There were only three categories of guests allowed into the house, and these only for a few days at the most. 'Family' were those men and women afflicted by some domestic trouble: a wife discovering the adultery of her spouse; a husband recently widowed who found it unbearable to be in the matrimonial home among his wife's possessions. Father Harris permitted them space to grieve – men in the cellar, women in the loft – and gave them a specially blessed candle on their departure. 'Alcohol' referred to those who had climbed into the bottle and become one with its contents, corking it from the inside so as to secure their solitariness against gospellers, reformers, benefactors or mere scolds. Father Harris respected their spirit of resistance and gave them vegetables bearing traces of earth to remind them of the Bible's reverence for those who tilled and ploughed. 'Police' were a gallimaufry of pickpockets, burglars and dealers in smuggled or stolen goods seeking temporary refuge from English sentencing. These were provided with a list of names and addresses of Catholic sympathisers in obscure and unsupervised ports from which they could escape safely from their pursuers; a list Father Harris wrote out with relish and painstaking accuracy.

No one was allowed into the house who did not belong to any of these categories. Father Harris gave me full sanction to question petitioners at the door, to accept or reject them. And so it was that the slight boy that I was would turn away huge and fearsome men, scarred, unshaven, smelling of freshly used daggers, of ditch and prison-house. Cloaked in the authority of my priest I denied them and went back to the privacy of our study.

Now, three years or so into my housekeeping, Father Harris no longer appreciated my boldness nor my strict adherence to the rules of refuge and hospitality he himself had laid down.

"For God's sake let them in, anything for a little peace," he said angrily after I had refused a man entry but he had remained banging on the door.

"But he has no reason to stay," I complained.

"Reason, what's that to do with it? Just let him in, otherwise he'll wake up the dead with his noise."

Every Tom, Dick and Harry now demanded my services. The cellar began to stink. They left phlegm on the walls and puddles of urine on the floor. They kicked over the trays of watercress I had placed with such care in the dampest corners. The true refugees – even the most drunk – were always conscious of being in God's house, clearing up the debris of their lives and folding their blankets before they left, the odd one even gracing me with coin; the women especially, destitute as they were, would search through their bundles and give me a farthing, or failing that, press me to their bosoms, fondle my hair as if departing sorrowfully from a loved son. These I missed, hoping they would return, but they never did, grateful for the brief respite from distress, the calm hours under God's roof, in proximity to God's priest and disciple. They made little demand on our meagre provisions and left as soon as they could to make space for others as unfortunate as they, their spirits considerably lightened by Father Harris's symbolic gifts.

The new occupants cared nothing for cleanliness, much less the sacredness of their surroundings. The men played cards and drank throughout the night, waking up in the middle of the day to order me to make them food. They suffered from no physical or mental ailment, they were plainly too lazy to find work but would take advantage of free board and lodging before moving on to the next charitable shelter in another part of the city. Before leaving our house they stole whatever could be sold on, spoons, plates, candlesticks. The new women were also a different breed. When night came, instead of staying respectfully in the loft they made their way to the cellar, seeking out the company of the men. Their laughter kept me awake, but the lewd and haggard looks they gave me in the daytime made me afraid to address them. They took over the kitchen, cooking whatever they could scavenge and expecting me to wash up after them. In good weather they'd trespass into the garden, spread blankets, loosen their blouses and fall asleep in the sun, stirring only to order me to fetch them glasses of water.

It was difficult to maintain order in the house. Whatever or wherever I cleaned was soon soiled by their presence. The garden pond began to fill with dead leaves for I was reluctant to pass by the women in their condition of shameless undress. Father Harris didn't seem to care for my distress. "They steal things from us," I said, but he shrugged off my protest. So long as his library remained untouched, and the jars of insects on his desk intact, he was content. Books and cockroaches held no commercial interest to our guests, so the raiding parties never ventured into the study. They never entered his bedroom, his clerical garments impossible to sell. Father Harris restricted himself to his study and his bedroom, rarely encountering the new rabble, and it was understandable that he was unresponsive to my complaints. Still I persisted, determined to purge our surroundings and to restore the exclusivity of our relationship.

"The ones upstairs leave the window open, pigeons come in, there's mess everywhere, the loft is a jungle like the garden pond."

"A jungle?" he asked, not bothering to look up from his newspaper.

"The garden pond is wild, the pigeons are building nests in the loft and you should see the plates! The women take food up there, and what they don't eat turns green and the plates are thick with green mould. It's jungle everywhere."

The repetition of the word 'jungle' seemed to awaken him from his apathy and I pressed home my argument.

"And there is blood too," I said, my voice darkening theatrically.

"Blood?" he lowered the newspaper and looked strangely at me.

"Yes, on the sheets and underneath their mattresses, rags with dried blood. Why are they making blood in our house?"

Father Harris made to reply to the sincerity of my question. He thought for a while. He rubbed his tongue along his lower lip, formulating an explanation, then decided otherwise.

"Oh, it's nothing, just give them fresh sheets," he said, retreating behind his newspaper. I stood my ground, refusing to yield to his desire to be left alone. After a minute or so, oppressed by my presence, he lowered the newspaper again.

"Women's blood is as innocent as the blood of the Cross," he said, but in a tone of voice that hovered between conviction and scepticism – conviction because he was resorting to the imagery of the Gospels; scepticism because the imagery could not be applied to the crude and sickly stains left behind by the women, real stains, true stains, for however vigorously I scrubbed the sheets they still left behind a ghostly presence. I might as well try to wash the printed words off the pages of the Gospels. He had schooled me to make the most illuminating unity between things most diverse and seemingly resistant to connection, but now, as he spoke hesitantly to me, offering a hesitant explanation, I began to doubt the wisdom of all my previous learning. He sensed my confusion, my slippage from him, and sought to recapture me with angry words, donning the mask of a prophet and railing against the stupidity of humanity.

"Why do you arraign me with the doings of a few women when the earth will soon be deluged in blood so flowing and final that even God will be drowned in despair and despatch no ark to start the world a second time. There will be no Second Coming, this war will see to it."

He waved the newspaper in my face as if to ward off some small irritating insect distracting him from the colossal events of the world. The suddenness and the scale of his condemnation robbed me of conviction and I found myself on the edge of tears. Having broken my spirit he sought to retrieve me with a joke so feeble that even when he spoke it there was no levity in his voice.

"A jungle, eh? Father Wilson's stuffed birds will be happy then, what do you say, all lonely in a barren loft and then all of a sudden the women make a jungle of the place. They've probably found new blood and breath and flown away by now, what do you say?"

"They've gone," I scowled.

"Gone?" he asked in surprise.

"Yes, gone. Stolen. The stuffed birds had been taken away to be sold, like our spoons, plates, linen, brooms, anything that can fetch a farthing or two. Soon there'll be nothing left in the house and we'll starve, and that will be that, and that will be the end."

This time it was his turn to be alarmed by the rudeness of my outburst. He opened his mouth to reproach me but before he could recover control of me I turned away from him, hurried from the study, slamming the door so violently that I imagined his books loosening from the shelves and toppling to the floor.

Going forth. Coming back. I would escape from him, but whither? And how? With the rogues populating our house, moving from one shelter to another? A servant to one of the women of dubious character? No, it was unthinkable. I would be drawn back to Father Harris's company, not out of need for his tuition, but out of his need for my service. True, the house ran largely by itself, newspapers being delivered every day, meat and groceries every Saturday and coal at the beginning of the month. The Church had made these arrangements for him on his retirement, paying bills directly to the tradesmen involved. As for cooking and cleaning and gardening, the Church could easily put a housekeeper in place, though Father Harris no longer concerned himself with these. But he needed me still, I convinced myself, not as a prop to his failing health but as a presence as he knelt every evening before the make-shift altar in his study; a presence that betokened the community of worship. He needed me to look upon the spotless white robe he wore for evening worship and believe in the sanctity of the garment, believe in the beautiful words of the prayers he uttered even as he looked upon the Cross in an agony of self-doubt. It was not agedness which gnawed away at his strength, hobbled body and mind, but a slow awareness that the world was to be concluded because of the callousness of men, their refusal to see into the life of things.

It was among my earliest lessons, his teaching about a spirit that excited and animated everything. We took a train to the seaside, strolled along the shore and paused to watch the fishing boats bobbing prettily in the distance. Gulls swooped and dived or else spread their white wings and glided so abstractly and with such surrender to the immateriality of the air, with such unawareness of their own weight, that Father Harris could not summon words to address me. He had to turn away from the scene before he could do so. The two of us stood with our backs to the sea, facing a huge boulder which had broken off from the cliff. With the passage of centuries and the action of the sea it had become shaped into a pillar.

"Once upon a time Adam stopped at this spot, before this cliff which was whole then, and suddenly longed for someone else to be with him so that he could speak it, paint it, or simply gaze upon it quietly. Now the cliff's in a fallen state and Adam's gone, but you and I are here. In twenty years and in fifty and forever, others will take our place, stand in the ghosts of our footprints and stare at this cliff."

"But the boulder will have gone one day?" I asked, answering his call for a communion of voices. He spoke again, prompting me to respond, which I did, each utterance an ever-expanding and ever-soaring antiphon like the movement of gulls, gathering, lifting, dispersing, gathering again at a greater height.

"Another will have sheared off to take its place," he said.

"But will it roll to the spot where the original boulder lay?" I answered.

"It will, and with time it too will be shaped into a pillar, then sink without trace, or the sea and the wind will break it down to pebbles."

"But will a third fall and settle over it?"

"The third will be the last, the cliff will give birth no more, only bare sand will be left. There'll be nothing beyond the pillar for the cliff itself will crumble to dust."

"But will the sea remain, the fishermen and their boats, and the birds crying out to them?"

"Once upon a future time when the shore is barren so will the sea empty itself and vanish."

"But the sea is everywhere, how can it not be here?"

"It will withdraw elsewhere, to another shore, for new men and women to harvest it with their eyes and souls."

"But what about us, the village, the fishermen, what about our livelihood?"

"All would have died by then," he said, bringing our song to a sudden end.

I turned from him, rebelling against the prophecy of my death and faced the sea defiantly. I expected him to chide me, but instead he too turned, resting his hand on my shoulder as if to acknowledge his growing frailty and need of me.

★

'The Peace that passeth all Understanding' – how often had he concluded evening prayers with these words which never failed to arouse me, so that afterwards when I sat quietly beside him, trying to read, I could not, for they pealed in my mind. I was restless in bed, however late the hour, for the words had taken possession of me, denying me sleep until I had rehearsed them a hundred times. Now the words held no allure. Now he rose despondently from prayer. I guided him, led him to his chair. He took up the newspaper he had been studying all day to pore over it again. It was packed with stories of military preparations in Europe, recruitment of soldiers, the conferences of diplomats. He spoke nothing to me but I read in his face, and in the way he fidgeted and sighed, a dreadful unhappiness.

"Stupidity," he muttered to himself, repeating the word intermittently as the evening drained away. Although he seemed to ignore me I knew that the word was uttered for my hearing, to draw me back to that day on the beach, when I was being taught the holiness of my presence in the world, however brief the allocation of time. He, born in 1840, would be given a few more years at the most; I, born around 1897, might go on, by God's grace to the 1960s. Others would replace us, as we had replaced others. The ceaseless coming and going forth, each occupying a little space, but the brevity of our lives didn't matter. We had to give way selflessly so that others could have a chance to marvel at the light freckling the sea or at the boulder that once split proudly from the cliff, crashed in rage, but with time grown into a slim smooth pillar of stone; and so becalmed that birds alighted to sip fresh water collected in the indentations of its head, to nest and lay eggs and depart in gratitude for the protection its height gave against land predators, but always leaving behind a scent or invisible mark, so that their young could be drawn to it the next year to roost in turn.

"The war will come because we've killed off our sight," I imagined him saying behind his newspaper.

"But we'll outlast the war, I'll go on painting, Father Wilson will stuff and admire his birds, you'll dissect beetles and pick fights with him and wrestle with God," I protested.

"After this war there will be no spirit... The wasteland left behind will not be worth dwelling on, never mind dreaming of."

A sudden cackle from the cellar, from a female mouth, disrupted my inner conversation. The agitated voices of men followed, and I looked to Father Harris for guidance but he was deaf to the uprush of noise. I resented them again as Gadarene swine, creatures of unclean character. To think that a dragon-fly, for all the beauty of its furious wings, lives only for a few days, or the pheasant brushed in scarlet and gold less than a season, whilst such people dragged on through years and decades, taking up precious time, and content to be hidden from light in a cellar. Let the war come, let them be sent forth to some foreign shore to be slaughtered, let them not be replaced, I said to myself, happy that Father Harris was too steeped in miserable thought to hear my execration.

★

The coming and the going forth. The approach of war, many thousands to be marshalled and despatched from England to Europe, the newspapers said, but smaller things preoccupied me, the making of soup in the kitchen and the taking of it to Father Harris. He had given up meat, wanting the most meagre broth, and even then he supped on it without relish. Previously I took pride in feeding him, concocting various sauces to accompany the roast, handling the carving knife as deftly as a Crusader his weaponry. Soup demanded neither skill nor imagination, yet the making of it retained an element of the heroic, given the loathsome presence of women in the kitchen. "Give us a bowl darling" or "Pepper it well, the old man could do with a bit of fire in his belly", they called out to me and when I ignored them they fulminated, threatened to dash me against the rock of their wrath.

"Leave him be, he's only a boy," one squeaked in my defence. It was Corinne, the one who bled the most, but the only one who offered to wash her own sheet when the others bundled theirs up and shoved them at me. Thin as the wick of a candle, the teeth in her mouth long wasted, she spoke in a high-pitched voice which started off with great effort then waned quickly in exhaustion. Her voice was as wiry as her body, and I knew, the moment I saw her, that she was destined for an early death. The other women sensed this too, allowing her to interrupt them, listening sympathetically to whatever she said, giving her the choicest space in the loft, directly below the window where the light was strongest and the air more easily purged of the smell of collective sweat. At first I knew little about her – they were all guarded, hardly speaking of themselves – except that the man thumping at the door at all hours, demanding to see her was related to her, but she would not elaborate beyond naming him Enoch. I never allowed him in, on account of his intimidating appearance. He was much more disquieting than the men frequenting the cellar.

"Keep him from me or else he'll murder me," Corinne begged and the women gathered protectively around her as she wept. Her desperation led me to warn Father Harris of danger looming. She was brought before him, but would divulge nothing.

"Shall I summon the constable to arrest him?" Father Harris asked. She began to tremble, obviously terrified by the prospect of incensing Enoch beyond his normal mood.

"Give him some money next time he comes," Father Harris instructed. "Warn him not to return, otherwise he'll have to deal with me."

I gave Enoch a shilling. I expected him to behave like the others when they were turned away. They would spit into my palm but take the coin anyway, swiftly pocketing it but still lingering at the door, hoping to be let in.

"She's not here, she left yesterday," I lied.

Enoch said nothing. His eyes stared through me as if hoping to catch sight of Corinne.

"If you don't go away you'll be done for, Father Harris will see to that," I advised him, adopting an attitude of friendship, even conspiracy. "You wouldn't want that, now would you? He's gentle but just arouse him and you'll regret it." Normally such a threat was sufficient to see them off but Enoch seemed beyond fear of the authority of a priest. I felt I should stay his wrath against us by inventing greater powers for Father Harris.

"He'll write to the Cardinal, even to the Pope if needs be," I said, to excite his cowardice. "If he does, there won't be a spot anywhere on this earth where you can shelter, not even... not even... Guiana." The word slipped readily from my mouth for between talk of war, Father Harris had been telling me – a scrap mentioned here and there, without elaboration – about that faraway place. Enoch remained still, heeding the word inwardly as if heeding the word of God. "Not even Guiana," I repeated, thrusting the word again at him. He turned away and left the house like a wounded animal.

A day or so later, Enoch came back, but meekly. It was easier to rebuff him, but when I offered a potato as compensation he didn't even acknowledge it.

"Corinne's long left, sailing to America she told us," – and to elaborate upon the lie, give it convincing and poetic detail, I added – "she mentioned she'd go to sea. After Coventry, which is all puddles and gutters and canals, she longed for the pure expanse of the sea. There's a monastery there, in Virginia, Father Harris gave her a letter addressed to Brother Lance who is in charge of the Community of the New World, requesting that she be given a place in the grounds, cooking for the orphans there, or seeing how she loved our garden, tending to the orchard which is full of stones and hungry birds. Father Harris supplied her with forty shillings for the sea-passage and an ample bundle of provisions – carrots, peas, cured meat. She'll reach land in a month's time, Virginia is where you need to seek her out."

Corinne was so grateful for my intercession that she began to make attempts to reveal herself to me, though in fragments of jumbled information which were difficult to piece together. "When I was a girl I used to climb over fences, that's why my legs have scars." She raised her dress and pushed out a leg for me to examine, then withdrew it shyly, giving me no time to confirm the truth of her scars. An embarrassed silence followed. I leaned across the kitchen table where we were sitting and poured her some more tea.

"Where were you born?" I asked, wanting a simple beginning from her.

"The rich people built big houses and put up fences everywhere and lined the tops with spiky wire but I climbed them all," she said.

"What did your mother and father do for a living?" I persisted.

"In August when the plums were ripe I used to raid the trees," she said.

"Do you have brothers and sisters?"

"In all her years of service my Ma took nothing from Lord this and Lady that, not a spoon nor a piece of cheese she'd steal. Oh I used to love the smell of cheese in the pantry but she wouldn't let me have what didn't belong to me though they were in huge chunks, so I made my mind up there and then to become a poacher when I grew up."

"Your folk, are they still alive, where are they now?"

"The hare, the deer, the lot I'd go after, but the thought of a trap shutting over their little feet and having to wring their necks changed my mind and then I just didn't know what the years would bring and what I would become..." Her voice trailed off as she sought to relive an aspect of her past.

"But then, just like that and out of the blue I saw myself with a herd of goats on land that was my own, a small herd mind you and the land only as far and wide as you could spit out a peach stone if you stood on tiptoe and craned your neck as far as you could without toppling over, and made a slingshot of your tongue." She giggled as she pictured herself as a girl spitting out a peach stone to measure the extent of her land.

"What about your brothers and sisters? Did you have any?" I asked again, but she brushed aside my attempt to establish a sequence of simple facts.

"My mother sewed me a frock with two pockets. The one on the left I kept empty for the day the mushrooms she sent me to pick for our supper turned into pieces of gold when I touched them. I can't remember what I put in the other pocket. Perhaps I put my right hand there, to keep it safe from murderers. If only people got to know that my hand could make gems of pebbles and gild mushrooms they'd lop it off for themselves. I was so afraid for my right hand that I couldn't sleep for the thought of people coming to me with axes and sickles. I prayed hard to God to take away my gift to make miracles, I promised Him I'd be glad to remain poor, to use my hand instead to scrub in the Lord-and-Lady-whoever kitchen. Otherwise who'd marry me if I was crippled, how would I tend my goats?"

She held out her hand and presented it to me, spreading her fingers to give me the fullness of it. I hesitated, drawing back from her.

"Go on, feel it and tell me the gift is no longer there, that no one will come to kill me." She addressed me with such yearning that I wanted to surrender to her, to place my hand upon hers, to fold hers around mine and to trace the lines and curvages of her palm, but she withdrew it abruptly, bursting into scornful laughter.

"He came to me with a bunch of cherries, oh how I wanted to snatch it from him and run away, but Ma always said, 'Take what you're given, don't forget to curtsy.' A huge man he was, a Marquess or one of that lot, my mother kept his house clean. It was summer and he came to me with cherries. 'Close your eyes,' he said, but I wouldn't, and I wouldn't stretch out my hand either, and my mother slapped me hard afterwards when she found out. She was gone to market and when she came back the Marquess dismissed her because of me, for I didn't take from him. I never never would, even if he promised to fill my hand afterwards with coin, it was of no worth compared to what I could make by my own power. So I kept myself in my pocket, because if I took the cherries they would turn right away into treasure and he would then know my secret, and rich as he was he'd still chop off my hand, so that nobody would want to make of me a bride."

She would have meandered on but for the three women who slammed the garden door shut and barged into the kitchen. They were of her age, I guessed, in their late twenties, for they were still alert to the quality of their person, powdering their faces, tying their hair with bright strips of cloth and wearing tightfitting dresses to show off their figures. Corinne, though she kept herself clean, was otherwise indifferent to her body, clothing herself with whatever came to hand. She was brittle beyond the attention of men, and it was perhaps the unattractiveness of her skeletal face that made the women protective of her, for she aroused no jealousy in them.

"What are you saying to him?" one of them demanded, rubbing one bare foot against the other to loosen the garden dirt. She looked sternly at me, then shook bits of leaves and twigs from her dress. I fetched a broom to remove the mess, not wanting to incite them to vulgar language.

"Don't tell him your business, he's only a boy, he'll grow up and find out for himself," another woman said in a voice tempered with pity.

Only a boy who will grow up and find out for himself, but what? At first I thought that they would prevent Corinne from speaking because the revelation of her history was a revelation of theirs, differing in detail but identical in substance. With grown men they could profit from the looseness of their character, but not from the mere boy that I was. It was not that her confession would bring shame to them, but that it would bring no monetary benefit. It was literally none of my business. So I thought at first, until I heard a protectiveness in the second woman's voice, and then it came to me that when they surrounded her like bodyguards, trying to keep me away from the sight and sound of her, it was as much to cordon me from knowledge forbidden to a boy, much less a priest's apprentice. I was obviously aware of the existence of prostitutes from my reading of the Bible, but I was not privy to the details of their trade. I could know of them in abstract and general terms, but the particularities of their impure deeds were to be withheld from me. The women were suddenly transformed in my mind, because of their kindness, and I remembered, with a rising sense of illumination, Father Harris's injunction to me to always find a redemptive moment in any situation. I swept up the dirt they made on the floor with a new willingness, promising myself never again to burden Father Harris with complaints about their behaviour.

VII

Corinne became my sanctuary against the mayhem of Father Harris's teaching. It was in the laundry room that I accidentally discovered a way of drawing out her story. Apart from Corinne, the guests in the house were too lazy to deposit their soiled clothing there, preferring to wait on me to collect their washing from wherever in the cellar or loft they had discarded it. The two of us found ourselves regularly in the laundry room, the privacy of which took on the space of a confessional.

The trick was never to question her but instead start her off by making a bland or neutral statement or observation which bore no connection to her life. Men – magistrates, constables, wardens of almshouses, usurers of her body – had interrogated her throughout her life, but she had deceived them all, taking their chastisement or their charity without ever yielding up her true self. Corinne was a stone dislodged with a thoughtless kick, turned over in anticipation of the sight of crawling things, but they uncovered nothing to appal or excite them.

"That's a true Coventry blue," I said, soaking someone's shirt in the water. "My favourite colour. I bet yours is red."

"I was born in Yorkshire, in a village called Ashlow, eight miles east of the city, an hour's ride by wagon or four on foot through rape and barley fields. I got there anyhow just to climb the walls that were from Roman times. I'd lean over the walls and pretend to chuck a spear at those beneath, like the Romans used to do, but I didn't mean harm to anyone, it was only make-believe. I wanted to be a Roman soldier, not me, anybody but me. I must have been eleven or twelve, I can't tell for sure except I hated myself and wanted to be a Roman soldier, a man, lots of strength and muscle and armour and a spear to fling against my foes."

Her outburst pleased me, though I couldn't think how to respond, but without prompting she continued to unravel her life, starting with a description of the cottage they lived in, in the grounds of a Great House, then having sated my appetite for simple details, threw me into confusion with a dreadful recollection:

"The Lord man, I wouldn't foul my mouth by speaking his name, but he was a Marquess or one of that lot, he threw my mother on the floor and had his way with her. She and me were in the kitchen slicing up cheese. When he was doing it to her he pressed his hand over her mouth, but I was small, like you, so I just let it be, and because he was not looking at me I slipped a piece of cheese into my mouth, and another, and wasn't it lovely, I swear to God it was the most tasty cheese I'd ever eaten, so I broke off a chunk, put it in the left pocket of my dress my mother made me, and I left the kitchen so quietly that he didn't notice me, though my mother turned her eyes to me but couldn't speak because of his hand, otherwise she'd tell me to curtsy and say thank you to him. She looked at me, and tears bled from her eyes, but what did I care? She could slap me later for not curtsying to him, but for now I had the cheese, I owned it, it was mine, I could go under one of the beech trees in the grounds, lean against it, spread out my legs and eat to my heart's content. Mind you I was never cruel to the birds. When I got up I emptied out on the grass what was left in my pocket. Odd that, how the birds never bothered to feed on it. When I went back the next day the bits of cheese were still there, turning green. Tell me, do birds eat cheese? I used to worry so much that the birds didn't like me, that's why they wouldn't take my present, but I bet it was just that they don't eat that stuff, even though the bits were as white as worms."

Cheese white as worms but do birds eat cheese? The question ignited in my mind, I would have to ask Father Wilson for an answer. All his wisdom in twisting wires, gluing feathers, polishing beaks and mounting birds in attitudes of rest or flight, which once brightened me with awe, now seemed lesser than the need to answer Corinne's question.

"The elms block out the sunlight, I should get them felled," I said, looking out of the laundry room window to the garden of dead trees.

"I wouldn't have his cherries, though he ordered me to, then begged, then threatened, then begged, but I wouldn't, until one day he lost his head, grabbed me by the hair, squashed my cheeks and shoved them into my mouth. He could have done it like that in the first place, but no, he wanted me to have them by my own choice, but I wouldn't, so in the end he had to force me. 'Take,' my mother told me, 'take from him,' she said, shaking me, shouting at me, because she wanted to be left alone. If I took from him she'd be let off from what he kept doing to her, he'd leave her be..."

"Once the trees are gone I can bed down watercress, they'd thrive in the sun for sure." The words tumbled out, I struggled to rein in my sadness and excitement at the prospect of her self-exposure.

"My father died the day I was born, can you believe! It's normally the reverse, the woman dying in childbirth, but he was odd that way. My mother told me, 'He was always odd, everything he did turning out the opposite.' He was gardener for the Marquess, but what a mess he made of the place! My mother told me, 'he'd prune back the apple trees but instead of blooming afterwards they more or less refused and the fruit was sour and deformed. Any other man would have harvested barrels by the dozen but not our Jack. Every living thing seemed to hate him, at the height of summer barely a bird to be seen on the trees, they'd go elsewhere rather than eat from his fruit trees. And he hated every living thing in turn, that's why he buggered off the day you were born.' I asked her, if he was such a malady, why the Marquess didn't get rid of him. She told me, 'Because the Marquess wouldn't let me go. I was the cause that your father was kept on, the Marquess needed me in his kitchen. The men employed in the house laughed at your father behind his back, and some of them to his face, but it didn't bother him a whit, he just took it out on the trees, poor things!' One day, mowing the grass, his scythe made a nick in his heel. My mother told me, 'any other man would have healed, it was a little cut, but not him. The more he bandaged and nursed it, the more it swelled, till the whole of his foot was blown and coloured blue and stinking. The wound festered, that's how he died, smelling to high heaven.' My mother told me, 'When you arrived and the midwife washed you, returned you to me, I put you to my nose and you gave off such sweetness that I knew you'd be trouble but it was your first hour, so I just sniffed the bud of you and was taken with strangeness that out of my sick belly came such bouquet.' But I didn't trust her, I cried when she told me, because I didn't believe her, because she made me go to the Marquess, and I wanted to belong only to her." She stopped to dab her eyes. I pretended not to engage with her emotionally, letting silence preside before looking out vaguely at the garden and offering another inappropriate comment about the need for good husbandry.

★

In the three weeks Corinne stayed with us I was able to gather her story, albeit haphazardly. As the priest's shadow in the confessional of the laundry room, I'd not look her in the eye, focusing instead on the soiled clothes in the washing tub. I would initiate the sacrament (a scandalous term to use, I know now, but at the time I wanted to believe it) by an innocent remark addressed seemingly to myself, and she would proceed to unveil her life, divesting herself of the apparel of pride and stepping out of the undergarment of self-consciouness. To be with her, I knew, was to transgress against the office of my youth, for what she divulged to me was material fitting only for the ear of a grown priest, but I listened anyway, or rather pretended not to, dutiful instead to the washing before me.

She had run away from the Great House and found refuge in an alcove in the Roman walls of York, where she subsisted on rainwater and the charity of passers-by. One night, when the skies were pouring down, a man came to her with an oilskin sack containing soap and a blanket. After she had washed to his satisfaction he took her into the alcove, spread the blanket and contented himself with her. When lightning flashed she panicked; it was as if God was taking a photograph of her, like those of the Marquess's wife and daughters hung on the walls of their drawing room, except that God was making a picture of her so as to remember her among the hundreds of thousands of others disobeying His commandments that very night all over the world. Was God choosing to remember her for His special mercy, or would the photograph be produced on Judgement Day to condemn her? The lightning flashed again, catching the man with his tongue flicking snakelike at her fledgling nipple, but this time she flaunted her disobedience, squeezed her flesh to make it fuller in his mouth.

"He hitched up his trousers and said he was a rich widower and if I went with him he'd see me right. He said my milk was sweet, that he liked me, but I didn't believe him either, though he presented me with a bright florin. He returned after a few nights and said I'd given him a sickness, and he chastised me with his walking stick, across my head and chest and legs, and would have killed me, but praise God, was too elderly to continue the beating. I felt pity for him, and when he got back his breath, I propped him up on his stick and sent him on his way. I lay upon, not under the blanket that night, though it was freezing cold, so that God could take photographs of the blue bruised pulp of my body. I figured the Marquess had bequeathed a sickness which I had passed on to the poor man."

He never came back, but others did, bearing gifts of scented oils, combs, pretty blouses, stockings, and they bathed her in fresh rainwater, brushed her hair, rubbed fragrances in her skin, dressed her. Then the merchants talked to her for hours about clever deals they planned to make which would give them a fortune, the lawyers rehearsed before her the arguments they would present to juries, the private tutors complained of the rich brats who scorned their instruction, but whose parents would yet be persuaded to part with their money. All of them confided in her, as if she was a trusty wife, her silence taken as approval for their various schemes instead of the enforced patience of the needy or the incomprehension of the young. Their monologues done, they undressed her, made her hair once more unkempt, licked off the scent and left the spittle of their cunning on her body.

"The lesser the coin they gave me, the more forceful they said how they liked me, so I soon learned how to measure a man's heart. And I gave them blight in memory of my father, for just as whatever he tended to withered, so I tended to them. No more did I keep my hand in my pocket in case it gilded things, for I knew then that my gift was contrary. When they had tired themselves in me and lay there wheezing I'd trail my fingers over their belly, and below, and they thought I was teasing them for more, but I was passing on the sickness of the Marquess."

As she said this I dipped my hands under the water, hiding them under the scum and soapiness, trying to formulate a meaningless statement but could wring nothing from the shirt I seized. I was saved by a thumping at the front door. "Enoch," she said, pressing her hand to her mouth in sudden alarm. "Guard me from him," she whispered, her face soiled with grief where she had touched herself.

★

Enoch, I was to learn from future meetings in the laundry room, had turned up under cover of darkness like any other suitor, or so it seemed as he made his way into her refuge without asking her consent.

"I was just lighting a candle when he came in and as soon as I held it up to him I could see he was different. There was a mark on his forehead in the shape of a star. Without thinking, for being with men had made me bold, I reached out to touch the star but then I caught myself and withdrew. He didn't say anything. The others would have thought I was being inviting, but not him. He just sat down, wrapped his arms around himself to comfort himself and seemed to fall asleep, though his eyes stayed open. It was as if he was travelling for days and weeks to the spot where I was, following the star on his brow, but when he reached it he had nothing to offer but his own fatigue. He wrapped his arms around himself and gave himself to inner sleep."

Enoch stayed with her for what seemed an endless season of companionship. Each morning he left her hovel soon after she awoke, returning at night when she had already prepared for bed. His movements during the day were an enigma to her. It could not be that he was at work, for he had nothing to show for it, no possessions apart from what he wore, not even a comb in his pocket. And yet he was always spick and span in appearance, not a stubble on his face, not a reek from the clothes which never left his body. Nor did she ever see him eat or drink anything. She guessed his age to be a few years above hers, eighteen perhaps.

"In truth I couldn't tell. Sometimes I'd open my eyes and there he was, sitting with his back to the wall, staring at the opposite wall. Thinking what, I used to wonder? I'd stretch and yawn loudly to signal I was awake, and he'd turn to me, knowing it was time for him to go, and sometimes his look was shy and boyish, he could have been twelve or thirteen then, but at other times he'd look at me as if he was scowling, his lips like they were puffed with blame, and then he could have been twenty, even thirty then, a big brother or a husband wanting to bully me and make me tell what mischief I had dreamed. His age changed according to what I was dreaming, as if he could enter my mind when I was sleeping and peep at all the pictures of what I was doing. If a night was a field of my beloved herd, my own goats on my own land, me milking or making cheese or pulling thorns from a paining hoof, then I'd awake to his awkward tender face. When I dreamed of giggling and sighing in my nakedness, he'd age overnight and greet me with eyes worn out from watching over me. Only the star on his forehead remained the same, whatever the nature of my dreaming. It was fixed there, like a third eye, seeing within and beyond my sleep; neither blaming nor forgiving, just drawing me to it as the first thing I saw when my eyes opened."

Enoch, at first welcomed for the protection he offered her

against intruders, began to irritate her. It was not a consequence of any particular act on his part. It was just his being there, the constancy of his presence. His face mirrored the mood of her dreaming but after a while she tired of her reflection in it, wanting to be her own self, especially at nights. Because of him she could no longer entertain men. Her income from them withered, and she had to fall back on the scraps of charity from passers-by in the daytime, mostly women caught between pity and outrage at her youthfulness who, in return for some paltry gift, expected her to listen to their advice and their reproaches. 'Haven't you a home to go to?' they would ask, or, 'Does your mother know that you beg on the streets?'

"A right prim and superior lot who would direct me to Sunday school or threaten to bring a constable upon me. At least the men treated me kindly and before they left told me how much they liked me, and the odd lonely one said he would have happily married me but for my age."

She grew dirtier and shabbier as time passed, what with no replenishment of soap or oils from men.

"I was wilful in my messiness mind you, hoping to repel Enoch so much that he'd go. I even took to fouling the place, puddles of stink near where he would sit." Her voice faded as she remembered in quiet embarrassment the way she felt forced to turn her refuge into a pit. "He wouldn't go, he wouldn't budge," she resumed, struggling to suppress her complaint which was still fresh after so many years. "He just gazed at the wall opposite or at me, not a word passed from his mouth. I wanted to pelt something at him, to see him off."

Enoch's serenity only bred more spite in her. For the first time in their being together she attacked him with obscene expressions.

"I used to talk to him all the time, like I talk to you, but he didn't seem to listen. I started by asking him his name, and after four or five times, when he wouldn't answer, I called him 'Enoch'. Don't ask me why, the name just came to me out of the heavens. I suppose it was that it rhymed with rock, which is what he was, sitting against the wall as quiet as a carving. But

238

I soon found nastier rhymes for his name and threw them at him like muck. I used to ask him tenderly about his family, his village, the scar on his forehead, but in the end I gave up and just let loose a stream of nastiness at him, which only washed over him and drained away and left him as be was, not a stain or mark on him. The Roman walls were full of carvings, Roman faces with noses broken off or worn down by the weather, or sometimes the whole face was pocked and eaten away as if from leprosy, but Enoch was a whole statue unto himself. Come rain or shine or bolts of lightning, he just wouldn't ruin. Even if he entered me, I knew he'd resist my disease."

So, at last, the real reason why she despised him? That he was beyond her power to corrupt? In her youth, it was her only defence against the depravity of men, this ability to taint them.

"For the second time in my life I ran away," she said. "I was sixteen then, a plucky little thing, you should have seen me in the coach with my lipstick on and my red shoes with heels."

She smiled to herself as she recalled her earlier adventurous self, a girl in a fresh frock and fragrant as a bride setting off on her honeymoon.

"And the words in my mouth were still choice, even after three years on the walls, the men could never take them from me. That's what made them crazy for me, the way I talked like a lady."

She proceeded to tell me how the Marquess had taken paternal care of her after her own father had died. Her earliest memories were of nestling in his lap as he read to her from books which once belonged to his daughters.

"They grew up and got married, his wife died, there was only him left and my mother and me, so he gave me all his interest. Every morning my mother would wash me and send me upstairs. The drawing room was marble and porcelain and lace and paintings and all the most precious old objects in the world, old vases and statues and silver trophies and velvet sofas. Even the doorknobs were coated in gold. Imagine, gold doorknobs! My mother said the family used to own slave plantations across the seas, that's where the money came from but I didn't mind, I just was dazed by all the richness surrounding me. And the words he read me from books were lovelier than all the treasure surrounding me. He brought me a child's violin and showed me how to make different sounds by dipping or raising the bow, but I preferred the sound of words and would beg to learn to read them on my own. I was happy then, the day I could read, and when he taught me to write. That's how I spent all my time, practising with the best words which shone from the page more brightly than the polish and wax of things in his room. You'd think he'd be happy for me, but he didn't like that I wanted to be by myself, for once I could read on my own I shunned his lap. Sure, I'd go to him, my mother told me to, and he read to me, but I'd wriggle off and snatch the book and run away as fast as I could. That's when he pressed the violin on me, and forced me to play the piano, and I could feel his mood hardening as I scraped at the strings halfheartedly and got my fingers all confused on the piano, always going for the black keys when I knew I should be playing the white. I hated white, I wanted to be with the blacks, shiny, single. The blacks were higher up and lonely-looking, that's where I wanted to be, higher up and by myself. That's why after I escaped from the Marquess and he took away the books I'd go and climb fences instead. Then he forced my mouth open, so I ran away to the high walls of York, and now I'm living here, no money, no fine clothes, but I no longer care for anything but my space in the loft. Never in my life have I slept in a ditch or hovel or plain ground and never will."

She spoke with such fierceness and finality as if hammering nails into her body, seeking to be borne aloft on a Cross from which she could look down spitefully and triumphantly at the world at her feet, a world which she had touched with disease and suffering.

"How many marriages I broke up, how many blighted wives because of me, how many orphans I made, how many suicides, how many ruined estates and spoiled inheritances, I can't begin to number or weigh or conceive in words. I wore down the world to the skeleton you now see when you look at me."

She moved from behind me and stood before the laundry tub. She stretched out her arms, forcing me to look at her.

"Tell me what I am," she demanded.

I couldn't avoid answering her, for she blocked my access to the tub. I saw a Cross leaning to the ground. I saw a woman slipping off it as the nails came loose. I saw a hole in the earth prepared for her.

"Aah, you should have seen me then," she said, brushing aside my thoughts. "I had on lipstick and red shoes to catch their eye. I went from this hamlet and village to that, living in barns, out of earshot of their wives, so that the farmers could snort freely like their animals, and be plentiful afterwards with turnips, potatoes, cheese. I fattened up again but Enoch followed me. I thought I was secure from him, I spread out comfortably in the straw to get some rest, then a honking and caterwauling from afar, like geese about to have their necks wrung, or chased by a fox which had broken into their pen. I hid under the straw, I curled up to make myself smaller, I held in my breath and let it out softly, and as soon as daylight broke I left for somewhere else. Many days and nights would pass, there'd be no sign of Enoch, then all of a sudden, in the middle of my sleep, the noise of beating wings and bird-cry. I paired up with other girls for safety – there were dozens of them like me roaming the land, but you'd have to be desperate to bed down with them. The farmhands took them in return for a bunch of vegetables but I was prettier than they and well-spoken, I only traded with farmers. But I was forced to pair up, so I chose a girl with ambition, you can easily tell by whether she wore shoes or not, never mind the squall of words that passed from her Yorkshire mouth for speech... 'Eh up an nowt an laatin an scrattin aboot'... 'Mack hast an hye thee ore to' th laer to me'... She and me would share bed and bounty, and next day we'd leave the farmer and go exploring somewhere else, but after a month she'd get greedy and go off and seek her own fortune and adventure. That's when Enoch would come, when I was in my loneliness, flapping and calling from afar, so I'd have to match off with another girl the very next morning to keep him at bay. The two of us followed the sun, or we headed south, or we walked in a wide circle, or we went wherever a passing cart unloaded us, but for all the turning and returning

I knew he'd catch up with me the moment I was forsaken. To murder me. Out of jealousy. Or because he's an angel come to avenge all the sins I've visited on mankind."

Another noise at the door made her seize up, but it was only one of the dwellers in the basement. She would remain still for a long while, the silence was irksome and I wanted to physically prod her to go on. I began to understand the frustration of the farmer: one moment he was aroused by her suppleness, the next cheated of excitement as she froze to the distant sound of geese. I imagined he would shake her, question her, but the more he showed rage the more the life of her stalled. I knew I would have to act otherwise, assuming an air of indifference, waiting with my hands in the water for as long as needs be, though the skin of my fingers crinkled and the soap made them sore. I waited on her with a rising sense of martyrdom, however minute my suffering compared to St. Veronica's, St. Eustacia's, St. Margaret's, the ones Father Harris said embraced the fire of chastity rather than surrender to the shaking and the questioning and the probing of men.

★

She went back to her mother. She figured that was why Enoch was shadowing her. Father Harris agreed: "He was directing her away from a family of fallen girls to the forgiveness of her mother. Enoch's a kind of guardian angel by the sounds of it, she should count herself lucky."

"It didn't work out that way," I said, disappointed by Father Harris's simple interpretation of Enoch when he always insisted that I should probe and imagine so as to arrive at some original truth.

"There's never pleasing women," he said. "Why didn't she just knuckle down and get on with her life instead of hopping here and there. Is she still lodging with us or has she strayed off?"

The lack of sympathy in his voice wounded me. He had drawn in all his feelers in preparation for war. He had become an insect I could not recognise, nor did I have the slightest interest in studying him. We were truly drifting apart, his preoccupation with the war eclipsing the love in our previous relationship. I was more drawn to Corinne than to him, whatever her previous indulgence in dirt.

"She's still here but she's fallen badly ill," I answered, but Father Harris was unperturbed, delving into his newspaper like an obsessive worm.

The going forth and coming back: Corinne had cleaned the lipstick from her mouth, given away her red shoes and returned to her mother. It was a purposeless journey, she didn't know what she was seeking from her mother except perhaps some regret for surrendering her to the Marquess. She found her mother in her usual place in the kitchen, making bread. A girl, three years old or so, was beside her, her hands dipped merrily in dough. The girl had fair hair like hers. She wore a frock of rich satin and her shoes were dainty and elegantly laced. She looked at Corinne with hostility, stopped playing with the dough and sidled up closer to Corinne's mother, reaching for her reassuring hand.

"So the devil has sent you back to us," her mother said looking Corinne up and down, measuring her growth during the years of absence. "You left barefoot and you're still the same." She took up a lump of dough and began to knead it, rolling back and forth as she remembered Corinne and searched for words to say.

"Your father left us nothing. Two or three hours after you were delivered I had to go back to work. I gave you over to my mother. She squatted on a piece of land at the far end of the estate, in a house of mud and wattle she made with her own hands. It was a good hour's walk, more if it was mud or snow, but I visited you every night. You were sleeping by the time I reached. I just put my hands over your forehead, warming them up with your new life, then I arranged the blanket so that you were snug, ever so secretly because I couldn't bear to wake you. 'Sleep,' I whispered to you, 'sleep, sleep, sleep, never open your mind to me until I've bettered myself.' In those five years I only saw you lying in your crib, asleep. I never saw you growing upright, only longways. I'd measure you with my eyes, noticing how you were stretching and stretching from month to month, till your feet reached the base of the crib and Mum had to make you a bed on the ground to give you space to grow."

Things were different now. The Marquess had dismissed her on account of Corinne's behaviour, but had taken her back when she found herself with belly for him. Her livelihood was secure, and her work lessened to odd kitchen tasks of her choosing. The Marquess had lifted her burden by employing other servants. She now had money and sufficient clothing.

"I opened my mind to how she had bettered herself but there was no longer a place for me. She hugged the little girl to herself instead. I looked at the two of them pairing up to get through the days and nights with provisions ample enough to make life bearable, as I used to. I turned away so they couldn't see me reddening in my eyes. I looked down instead at my feet and missed my pretty shoes."

★

In her final days with us Corinne was too feeble to raise herself from her blanket. The women cleaned her with towels and kept watch over her, night and day. I made food for her but she could keep nothing down, not even soup. There was nothing I could do but wet her lips with water. Every hour or so I went upstairs with a fresh bowl of water and towels.

"Will you be taking me to Land's End?" she asked piteously as I dabbed her brow.

"We'll take you to wherever you want to go, but you'll have to get better first."

"I want *you* to take me," she said petulantly and in a mood of stubbornness. She twitched her limbs as if to work up a childish rage.

"I'll take you," I said to becalm her.

"Only you, I want only you."

"Only me," I said, wiping her chin and neck of dribble.

"And not anywhere but Land's End."

"Land's End is where we'll go," I reassured her.

"Why do you want to go to Land's End?" one of the women asked, not so much out of curiosity but to keep her company in conversation. She wouldn't answer them but gave me a conniving look instead. I read her intention and leaned my head to her mouth.

"I told my mother that's where I'd go, as far away from her and my father," she whispered.

"What's she saying to you?" the woman asked, a little piqued by Corinne taking me into her confidence and ignoring them. Corinne turned her head to face them.

"I was telling him I want to climb a rock and look out at the sea."

"Ah, the sea," another sighed. "The breeze smelling of blue porpoises and living crabs and starfish and the inside of shells shining like looking-glass."

"Mind you don't go too high," the first woman cautioned. "The rock's bound to be slippery. Hold tight in case you fall."

"Don't be a spoilsport, let Corinne go all the way to the top," the third woman interjected. "What's the point of her being middling when the sea's calling out to her?"

The first woman desisted but added all the same, "She should crouch low when she's at the top, not stand up, else the wind might swipe her away."

Corinne beckoned to me again with her eyes. "When I left, my mother hurried after me and pressed a purse on me but what's Judas' silver to me, I could make twice that in a night. I brushed her away. She tried to hug me but I shrank from her. I set off for Land's End because there would be nowhere else to run. If Enoch trailed me there I'd just jump into the sea, swim and swim until I'd reach a boat going to a new country. I'd buy slaves there and become richer than any Marquess."

I nodded sagely even though she spoke in a muffled voice which I could barely follow. "What's she saying now?" the first woman asked.

"Is she still intent on Land's End or has she changed her mind?" the second woman asked.

"She'll have to find her feet first, it's a far way to go," the third opined.

Corinne turned her head to face them again. "I have money,

I'll hire a chariot with six strong stallions, I'll reach there in no time."

"No time, eh? I wouldn't be too sure dearie, there's deep winter snow down south this time of year, not to mention highwaymen to stop your passage."

"Let her be. We'll pack a month's provision for her and the boy will guard her with pistols."

"If I had not fallen in with you lot I'd have got there by now," Corinne snarled, her outburst bringing their chatter to an abrupt end. "I set off ever so long ago, but you three got in my way and made me stay. You're the death of me, never mind that man Enoch harassing me with his nightly calling."

The women, hardened by their profession to accusations and rebukes didn't bother to respond. The more she frothed the more they showed kindness to her.

"In a week or two I'll finish knitting you this cardigan," the first woman said, taking up her needle with renewed resolve.

"Leave the buttons for me to sew on, I've chosen them already," the second woman urged. She held up one of her own blouses to show Corinne where she had ripped off the buttons as a gift.

"I'll do the dyeing of the wool, I'm best at that," the third woman added. "I'll make it blue, dark blue. No, I'll make it light, or should I go for a daffodil yellow? It'll be spring soon, yellow will set you off against the daffodil fields nicely, what do you think?"

Corinne didn't answer. She was listening instead to noises in her head, the squalling of geese trapped in their pen, even though it was not yet dark and she had long renounced the society of men.

★

It was time for the going forth of her. We had given her a little space to rest in God's house. The women did their best, trying with their cheerful banter and promise of a bright garment to keep her spirit from miscarriage. I went up and down the stairs with water and towels like a servant to their midwifery. One

246

morning her body convulsed and seeped beyond control. The women made a cradle of her blanket and brought her into Father Harris's study. As soon as he saw her he made me hurry to fetch crucifix and candle and holy water and clerical vestment.

"How long has she been suffering?" he asked when I returned, reprimanding me for not alerting him earlier to her condition.

"How long has she been suffering?" he asked again as I helped him put on crucifix and surplice. I was at a loss for a truthful answer, the details of her life having only been partially revealed to me. Should I say two weeks, at the beginning of her deterioration when her body refused to retain food? Or from the time the Marquess fed her cherries? The acquisition of her first pair of shoes? Enoch's coming? The giving up of her dream of goats in a fenceless land which was hers? There was only a flimsy plot to her life which Father Harris's questioning and my inability to answer made apparent.

The donning of priestly symbols transformed him from the introspective and forlorn character I had grown to disrespect into a servant of God hallowed by possession of scriptural interpretation and knowledge of ritual. In the presence of death it was upon these resources he fell back. I watched him sign her forehead with holy water; the fixed sign of the Cross, with its utterable and certain meaning, not the two beams he used to teach me the Cross was, urging me to prise them apart, reassemble them with shapeless imagination, or to take up a dislodged nail, grind it against a piece of stone to make spark and fire which would consume the biases of the elderly, the chastened, the officious, the scripted. He read dutifully from the prayer book, word by word, sentence by sentence, pausing in observation of commas and dashes and full stops. In the presence of death there was no place for the play of worm-holes, for the blasphemy of breaking the spine of the Bible, loosening the pages, tearing them up and re-pasting them indiscriminately. Once more he became the priest I revered, the intonation of his voice at prayer ravishing me, making me feel extravagantly alive even as the women wept at the sight of Corinne, the distress of her body speaking to them of the consequence of their own trespasses.

The performance of the last rites was disturbed by a knocking at the door. It was the coalman coming to deliver his monthly sacks.

"Tell whoever it is to wait," Father Harris said, irritated by the interruption.

"I'm already late boy, just open the side gate for me to leave your coal," the coalman complained.

"We're in the middle of service, Father Harris says you'll just have to wait. And we want you to take a sick woman to hospital."

"Hospital? Boy, I can't do this, I've got a whole day-load of work in the wagon. And there's no space, look how high it's piled up."

"When you take out our four sacks she'll easily fit in. She's only that size," I said, holding my hands apart to give a measure of Corinne's body, and at once was shocked by the realisation of how diminished she had become. The coalman made to complain more but I could smell the whisky on his breath. The bottle in his back pocket had obviously run dry, he was only anxious to reach the nearest tavern. His face was coated in coal dust. He looked like a drunken savage.

"Father Harris wouldn't shorten the service," I said, putting on a face of disgust and disbelief when he asked me to go indoors and tell Father Harris to hurry up his worship. "Either you stay or else forgo his prayers for your sins." It was a trick that worked with everyone making rude demands on our time and resources. The coalman was instantly stilled by the prospect of damnation.

The women lifted Corinne into the wagon. They perched on the sides, watching over her; her praetorian guards, though the scene lacked all nobility. No chariot and stallions for her but a skinny dray horse whipped drunkenly all the way to the hospital, the women coughing in coal-dust, the driver cursing his fate. As the wagon set off I remembered we had not given her the customary gift of candle or carrot or coin. I ran back into the house to fetch one of these, then changed my mind. I went to Father Harris's library and took out the story of Andromeda, my favourite book among all the pagan and classical ones he encouraged me to read. It told of love and salvation, neither of which would come to Corinne but I placed it in her hands anyway because of its red cover. She was on the brink of unconsciousness but I folded her hands over the book, hopeful that she would feel the candour and the excitement of red.

VIII

"A remarkable face, Corinne's, sear and bony and angular, yet as virtuous as a kid's to touch. I've never seen such a death mask before, so caprine." He automatically spelt out the word for me. "Caprine: of, or like, or pertaining to a goat," he explained, and though Corinne's absence grieved me I was glad that Father Harris was restored to his former self, albeit temporarily. His own fading health and the dawning of war would soon depress him, but for now he was buoyant with speculation.

"The Colorado beetle has caprine features. Come to think of it so has the head of the Roman mosquito. Now isn't that something?" He shuffled off to the bookcases to fetch a reference text but collapsed on his way. I hauled him up and placed him on the sofa.

The agony of Corinne's dying was lightened by his musings, but out of conventional pity for her I resisted speculating too strenuously on the connections between death mask, goat, beetle and mosquito, as Father Harris wanted me to. He sensed my unwillingness and let me go, but first making me repeat the word 'caprine'. I gathered a handful of books from the shelves, indiscriminately, according to their red covers, and sought out the solitude of the loft. I flicked through them – Pliny's *Natural History,* Charles Lamb's *Tales from Shakespeare, Sir Gawain, Hindu Myths* – searching out the illustrations, for I was unable to concentrate on the words. A cold wind gusted through the open window. I spread out Corinne's blanket but lay upon it, in the path of the wind, refusing the urge for warmth. I spent hours there, shivering, waiting for darkness to gather around me; to be like Enoch in the refuge of the Roman wall, keeping vigil as she slept, certain that she would awaken.

I stared at the wall opposite, hoping to blot out my thoughts, to repress the words from fermenting in my mind, to arrive at Enoch's stillness, but the words would not obey my will. The words took inner shape and sound against my will, mocking my frailty and my powerlessness. Hard as I tried for silence, hard as I clamped my mouth, the words would speak to me inwardly. And to my shame they spoke my desire for Corinne, the way my eyes used to trace the pathways of her veins which gusted with blood and the excitement of blood, resisting the shrinkage of flesh and the final evidence of bone.

"Enoch's supposedly the first man to speak with God after the Flood," Father Harris explained. "Some said he spoke a kind of gibberish but others claimed that if your mind was magnificently attuned, it sounded like a beautiful carolling."

When I looked perplexed he gave me an impromptu example. "Enoch never bothered with the properties of common sense. If I said to you, 'Not too long from now I'll send you to British Guiana' Enoch would utter something like this: 'Lightning provokes the growling of the dog-star which is the voice of thunder, and betwixt the gleaming blade and the swelling throat a youth garbed in the innocence of white will voyage by my will to a muddy shore.' Something like that, abundant with images, hurtling ahead, turning back on itself, spinning, chasing its tail till it grows dizzy and flops down on all fours, but never as a game or silly play with the shadow of words."

Biblical Enoch, he confessed, was once his mentor and guide. Biblical Enoch could read the patterning of stars, he heard prophecies in the mouths of caves, in water crashing against stone. Enoch stood by a pond to watch fish making bubbles on the surface, each bubble a testament and a psalm. He knew the language of fish and stone and star. Enoch begged God to forgive the fury of the angels, for he could sense a carolling deep beneath the obscene noises they uttered in the form of typhoon and hurricane.

After Father Harris's explanation I tried to see Corinne's Enoch in a new light. I had banished him from her door whilst Corinne stayed with us, and he had gone away obediently, reappearing the morning after the wagon had removed her. It was Sunday, the beginning of the week when I would go to visit my grandfather. I pushed open the gate to find Enoch squatting with his back against the fence, staring out at the path that led to the road which the wagon had taken to the hospital, and which would take me to my grandfather's almshouse. He made a little whining noise when I discovered him, and I knew instantly that Corinne had fallen. She had clung to slippery rock and climbed, but a few inches from the summit which she could easily reach, she had let go, disdaining the sight of the sea. I heard in Enoch's whining the sound of waves crashing against stone, telling me in plain words, which my sensible mind was attuned to, that Corinne had died.

Caprine. Caprine. Caprine. If I repeated the words sufficiently would the magic of association restore Corinne to the present? The goat's head recalled the beetle's, recalled the mosquito's: nothing was fixed beyond recall. Is that what Father Harris meant? Could Corinne be recalled from the other side of the grave? If one day I dug up her thighbone and fashioned it into a flute and blew into it with true spirit and longing, would the melody be the redness of her which death did not fade? I trudged along the muddy road leading to the almshouse, weighed down by questions, trying to make sense of things even though Father Harris warned against such efforts at clear-headedness. Caprine. Caprine. Caprine. I walked to the rhythm of my incantation, as if by achieving symmetry of body and mind some answer would be revealed. Nothing came and I repented of my boldness in wanting to compare myself to St. Paul. I changed my gait to the rhythm of the Lord's Prayer. Father Harris himself had reached out for the Lord's Prayer as he attended to Corinne, casting aside all previous talk of the melody of gibberish, the need to be unmindful of the properties of things. He had cast aside Enoch and found solace in the clarity of Jesus' prayer. 'Our Father Who Art in Heaven': millions and millions before me had uttered these words, kings and shepherds, no matter how different, had found comfort in the same words. 'Our Father Who Art in Heaven': there was an eternal Person, there was an endlessly spacious Place even though on the surface it looked as if Corinne had shrunk to nothing and was placed into a definite measured hole in the ground. I rehearsed the Lord's Prayer inwardly, desperate to believe in its clarity but my mind kept stumbling against the word 'art'. An innocent Biblical version of 'are', that I knew, but other aspects of the word came unbidden to mind. Father Harris's eggshell which he made me crush and remake, keeping the cracks visible by bright lines of paint. And Corinne, when I once shyly asked her whether she had children, and she broke into a cackle that sounded like a fowl squabbling with another, then her voice softened, she spoke to me as if singing me a lullaby, 'Little boy, I cannot lay. I'm not for making more than play.' And she reeled off a list of names of men, single, married, widowed, farmers, farmhands, priests, magistrates, fugitives, she had been with in barren consort. "All sorts, all of different status, all at different stations of the Cross, but none of them could breed me, though they all hoped to. Why did they, I used to wonder, why weren't they content to own me for a night but wanted to visit me with a lifetime's child? Did they in kindness want to give me something lasting, not just a frock or a few shillings? Or was it to mark me out for themselves, like how a farmer puts a brand with his initials to his animal? I used to lie there with the question howling within me, like a calf he had pressed to the ground, trussed up its legs and burned with hot iron." She wanted to continue but realised by the reddening of my face that I could not bear to listen to her experience of men.

"Little boy, you're Joseph's self," she said, seeking to pacify my jealousy. "Only God could have made Mary hatch, and only God could do the same with me. Poor Joseph, I bet he didn't believe Mary, even when God sent an angel to explain the hatching to him. From now on you'll be my Joseph. If I call you that, will you answer to the name?"

I ignored her, not out of rudeness, but because I suddenly remembered Lance opening his mouth and raising his tongue to reveal an egg no bigger than a pebble. After our morning bath, and on our way back to the dormitory to dress for morning worship, he had slipped into the orchard and raided a wren's nest. He had taken the egg under his tongue to chapel, keeping it intact through prayer and hymn. I didn't understand the glee in his eyes when, alone with me in the kitchen, he revealed the egg. He took it from his mouth and offered it to me but I refused, disgusted with the unnaturalness of his deed. "Put it back where it rightly belongs," I cried, but he giggled at my unease, made clucking noises as if to mock me, then with a triumphant flourish placed the egg back under his tongue.

Art. Painted eggshell. Corinne's lullaby. Lance's bright tongue. I should have blamed Father Harris for teaching me to loosen my thoughts, let them roam or gather without need for control, but a more distressing realisation overcame me, that I had suppressed what should have been my most memorable experience of Lance and that I would do the same to Corinne. One day, if not right now, on the way to my grandfather, and before I reached him, I would forget the glee and wretchedness of her life, for if I did not I would be captured by the excitement of art, even though I fought to dwell steadfastly on the Father and the Heaven of the Lord's Prayer.

I followed the bend of the road, seeking relief from my confusion, and it came as I caught sight of a field swarming with boys of my age. They were kicking a ball along the snow, scooting ahead, swerving, running back, tripping over each other, a joyous muddle of bodies. They were the children of the poor, living in makeshift dwellings within sight of the almshouse, but neither their ragged condition nor the snow could slow their feet. I was of their age but I felt elderly in comparison, weighed down with anxieties and questions that rightly belonged to grown men. As I watched them play I resented my grandfather, Lance, the priests in the monastery of my childhood, Father Harris, all those who had in innocence or conspiracy made me the force-ripened yet unhatched thing I was.

★

"He'll be off to Guiana soon, to serve Father Jenkins, I'm arranging it with the Church in Ireland," Father Harris announced as I came into the room with the customary bottle of whisky. He had long since given up on Biblical Enoch's convolutions and on the clarity of Cardinal Newman. Only newspapers would do. Dozens of them were heaped at his feet as if in preparation for his martyrdom, as if he was determined that the conflagration in Europe would also engulf him. Father Wilson didn't seem to care a fig for the coming war, though as a precaution he had decided to leave Wolverhampton and return to Ireland where he could practise his taxidermy in peace until the troubles blew over.

"Why not return with me?" he told Father Harris, but the offer was refused. Father Harris was resolved upon the nurturing of his pessimism. I pitied him again, because for all his age he still lacked the gravitas of a patriarch of doom. For a start his spectacles kept slipping off his nose and falling to the floor, beyond his ability to retrieve them. Every time I picked them up for him I thought of how supreme Biblical Enoch was in comparison; Enoch staring out at the desert with eyes as fierce as an eagle's, eyes that scorned the prop of a looking-glass; Enoch of stern jaw, ruminating on the end of a world, whereas Father Harris's sagged, its tired muscles telling of the ending of his individual life.

"I'm sending him away to Guiana," Father Harris repeated, for Father Wilson was too engrossed in assessing the quality of his whisky to reply. He swilled it around his mouth, then satisfied with its taste, he swallowed, holding out his glass for more.

"Guiana, eh?" he wheezed, surprised by the strength of the drink. He squeezed his eyes tight and shuddered in pleasure.

"He's a talented boy," Father Harris said, gesturing to his library, drawing Father Wilson's attention to all the classical and pagan books I had read over the years I had studied under him. "He has the makings of a genius, I'm convinced of it," he continued, thinking to pre-empt any contrary opinion from Father Wilson. I was, after all, still an untested youth, as far as Father Wilson was concerned, a mere novice at the anatomy of the dead. I had yet to present him with a perfect example of a dissected and preserved thing, though it had been months since he had made me a gift of the Leitz glass.

"If he has the makings of a genius, bless the codling..." (he reached out and tickled me under the chin) "...then you'll of course ensure that he never trains for the Church. You wouldn't turn him into a drooling specimen of a priest, would you?" He turned his attention to his glass, admiring the rich colour of the whisky, whilst Father Harris muttered impotently at him. Satisfied that he had made the first wound, he relented, inviting Father Harris to a new tilt, but lazily, for he merely sat back in the chair and asked, "Guiana, eh? A slave colony, isn't it?"

Father Harris was keen to boast of my powers. "Of course there'll be all kinds of dangers, but he'll brave them out, I'm sure of it." He gestured again to the books, and Father Wilson sat up, peering in the direction of the library, more out of courtesy than conviction. "He's read the ways of the Hill Coolies of India, the tribal doings of South Sea natives. He's read of earthquakes and volcanoes, of jungles choked with vines and rivers which deceive with hidden currents and rocks. Guiana will be an orchard by comparison to a boy so brave and prepared."

"What's in a book and what's on the earth are opposite truths," Father Wilson replied, attempting wisdom and concern.

I topped up Father Wilson's drink by way of acknowledgement of his interest in me. I wanted him to win the debate, for truly I was terrified at the prospect of Guiana, not so much because of its crocodile pools or painted savages, but because I had not even got acquainted with the city of Coventry. What I saw of it, when I got off the boat and walked with my grandfather to Father Harris's house, had frightened me. My grandfather strode ahead with false courage. It was his first experience of the bigness of a city, the houses joined to each other in an endless march of bricks, roads packed with wagons piled high with goods and men riding bicycles. He paused to watch the men ride past, marvelling at the ease with which they balanced on the thinnest of wheels without the least sign of discomfort, never mind peril. He caught himself and moved on, not wanting to betray his wonder to me, a small boy in his care, a small boy who was not to sense his anxiety and loss in this strange new English reality of brick, asphalt, metal. The Proprietor's shop with its expensive contraptions to plough and harvest had once made him feel poor, unworthy. He would not now let his grandson glimpse his inferiority, so he pretended to be purposeful as he headed to Father Harris's house. I walked a yard or so behind him, giving him space to act. I pretended not to notice his humiliation as he was forced to stop a passer-by to ask directions, in as few words as possible so as to disguise the accent of his origins in an obscure village in Ireland. Nor would I betray to him my overwhelming desire for the quiet simplicity of the monastery he had removed me from; my terror at the hideous rumble of wheels, the hollering of drivers and brutal whipping of their horses especially when the wagons lurched and spilled some of their contents.

The church's house became my refuge, I only ventured out on a Sunday, to visit my grandfather on his sick bed. I only saw boys kicking a football in an empty field, for we lived on the green outskirts of the city. The boys never acknowledged me, I passed them by in loneliness.

Five years of solitude in Father Harris's care, apart from the imagined world of his teachings and his books, a world made more intangible by the huge and spacious words he introduced me to. The vagrants who yelped or grunted in the cellar contracted that space, grounding me in the memory of the noisiness of Coventry. Five years of an expanding and contracting self, but just as I was being reconciled to the fact of its contrariness, Father Harris decided to send me to a third world.

"Poor thing, he's only a pupa, if that," Father Wilson said, the whisky apparently heightening his awareness of my distress. "They'll devour him in that ungodly place."

Father Harris, though, insisted on my preparedness for Guiana. "It'll be an orchard for someone so... so... so impavid." He was certain that he had found for me a word that defied common usage, which proved that I was of unusual character. He would not listen any more to Father Wilson's halfhearted slurred objections to my exile. After the fourth drink Father Wilson abandoned speech altogether, rested his head on his shoulder and took to snoring. I eased the glass from his hand and bade him a silent goodbye.

Enoch was nowhere to be seen except on Sundays when he appeared at the gate as if by magic, at the very moment that I left the house to visit my grandfather. He never accosted me but squatted always with his back against the fence, gazing out at the road. I mumbled a greeting to him but he seemed not to hear me. I looked hard at him, trying to find the star on his forehead which so beguiled Corinne, but if it was there it was covered over with dirt. Corinne used to wonder how in all the weeks he spent in her company he remained immaculate in appearance, though not owning a piece of soap and always in the same clothing. Now he was filthy to behold and whined like an abandoned dog.

The following Sunday Enoch was a changed man, his face scrubbed clean (though still secreting its star), his hands clasped before him, glowing like marble. His hands were not locked in an act of prayer but in resolve against the cold, yet the attitude of worship and the loose-fitting sleeves of his coat gave him the appearance of a carved angel, the kind you see poised over a recent grave, the brightness of the sculpture telling of grief still fresh, yet to be faded with time or sedated by the Christian platitude inscribed on the headstone. That day I read passionately to my grandfather, wanting him to stay alive and not slip into unconsciousness because of a tiredness in my voice or a triteness of words, even though it was the umpteenth time I was reciting for him the story of Jack and the Beanstalk. As I described the illustrations I kept my voice fresh with emotion by imagining his coming death, by making him Jack climbing higher and higher until he was lost from my sight in a heavenly mist. I made myself imagine that he would never reappear and the forcibly anticipated grief made my voice tremble and break so that my grandfather interrupted his mutterings about wire and listened keenly to me.

On another Sunday Enoch was soiled again, his face twisted, his open mouth issuing spittle as if he were a gargoyle. There was a look of murder in his eyes. I hurried from him, glancing back in case he bounded after me on all fours, but he remained settled on his haunches like a feeble savage put out to die because he was of no use to the tribe. My grandfather too looked loathsome, as if he had fed on unclean meat, his lips riddled with boils. I hid behind my book and read to him. When it was time to go I could not bring myself to kiss him.

The last time I saw Enoch he looked like a common field-hand resting against a bale of hay to catch his breath, staring out impassively at a field that he had only begun to plough. There was no emotion on his face and no sign of the fabled star. He was like a common field-hand inured to work. From the time he was strong enough to lift a fork that was all he did and expected to do. His life was measured by seasons of labour. Neither complaint nor self-pity would shorten the seasons or lighten the labour, so he merely rested, his face expressing no thought. I left him a potato on the ground as a gift and went to my grandfather, expecting to find him in Enoch's condition, and he was, lying in bed so stiffly that had breath not rasped from his mouth I would have believed him dead. I read about Jack, but he was unmoved. The story of Andromeda had no effect. I grew desperate and for the first time described to him the picture of a woman spread brazenly against a stake by the edge of the lake. I spoke Andromeda's nakedness in vivid detail, her dishevelled hair, the swelling of her breasts, their cherries full and naturally ripened for the appetite of the monster emerging from the lake. My grandfather would not be roused by my power of description.

I left him for the last time, embittered by his silence which to my mind betokened my failure to minister to him. Perhaps I should have held up a picture of the Virgin Mary to him instead of Andromeda on the brink of violation. The nun in charge of the almshouse seemed to read my thoughts. She opened a door to let me out, and said, in a stern voice, by way of valediction, "Pray for his soul and pray for your own and remind Father Harris to pray for mine." Her words passed me by, I found myself gazing shamelessly into her face, wondering at her age which was disguised by her wimple and habit and which could only be revealed were I to strip her.

Prayer was the last thing on my mind as I departed. All I

could recall of my grandfather was the filth of his sheets, bits of food hidden under his pillow. I imagined him gobbling like swine, disobedient of the laws of Leviticus which I now found myself revering in spite of Father Harris's contempt. The trees lining the road were stripped of all life. They stuck out their branches at me, accusing me, but I blamed my grandfather for their bleakness. It was he who had maimed the earth, making unnatural canals. He had tossed aside the earth, careless of the spores his shovel awakened to vindictive life. He had brought disease upon himself, which would spread all over Coventry and beyond. The coming war in Europe was a sign of his doing. Father Harris knew it, that was why he would send me to Guiana, beyond the reach of plague. There, in a fresh place, I would plant anew the seeds of the Catholic faith, and allow its unfettered bloom, like our garden profuse with growth which I was forbidden to uproot. I was being sent to Guiana to plant myself and what I bore would be lush testament to Father Harris's teaching.

I turned the corner for the last time to be greeted by boys crying in merriment as they chased their ball, skidding, tumbling to the ground, rising up instantly, shaking off their hurt for the sake of play. The life of the trees was not lost, it had drained into them. I halted out of guilt, suddenly knowing that it was I who was at fault, it was I who nursed my hurt and made it a thing apart from theirs. I had kept to myself bleakly, hiding in the shadow of Father Harris. "Come out from under the shadow of the Cross," they wanted to call out to me, but were afraid because of their ordinariness as I was afraid because of my status as the priest's apprentice. They believed that I was from the priest's house, and therefore forbidden from play, marked out for a life more lofty than theirs, and so they let me pass by in loneliness. And I chose, out of pride, to remain invisible to them when I could have gone up and revealed myself to them, asking like any normal boy to join in their game. I suddenly knew why Enoch appeared to me as he did. I had scanned his forehead for a special sign, but he had chosen to show me his ordinary being, so that when I sought out my grandfather I should not, in that final hour, burden him with my selfish wants. The common thief or penitent murderer crucified beside Christ asked nothing of him in the final hour, sharing instead in his hurt. I had demanded of my grandfather the name of my father, the fate of my mother, when I should simply have tended him in his sickness, for how could he influence the direction of human lives, an ordinary peasant practised only in sowing and reaping, subject to the whims of a sky barren or plentiful of rain? The theft of his wire and the following drought had broken him down to nothing. He had sought, by the enclosing of his land, haughty ownership of himself, his wife, his goods, but God had chastened him. He lay on his deathbed surrendered to the sickness of his body, unto whatever blessing came out of duty from the nun's mouth, she who saw her officiation over such men as punishment for her own misdeeds. I should have waited quietly beside him, grateful for the example of his going forth in poverty and humility. I should have accepted Lance's mocking assertion that my father was a passing vagrant who had espied my mother in a lonely field and had his way with her. My mother was then sent afar to be devoured by the monster of shame. Neither my longing for her, nor my prayers, would restore her to my presence.

I would submit to Father Harris's plan to send me away to Guiana, far from the sickness soon to destroy the Christian world. In Guiana I would accept whatever befell me, I would serve Father Jenkins faithfully until I was recalled to Coventry or wherever else Father Harris determined upon. When I reached the gate of God's house, Enoch was gone, but my sorrow was immediately lightened by the sight of the potato. He had refused it, preferring to keep company with his nothingness, instead of hungering for a miracle as my grandfather had when his mouth fumbled for the morsel from Arthur's hand. I had questioned Father Harris repeatedly as to Enoch's identity, but now I knew by my own understanding, which was still not mine to possess, that he was the common thief who stayed awake for Christ's dying, under a sky jewelled with stars, so that having borne witness to the miracle of grace, he too could depart in peace.

ALSO FROM PEEPAL TREE

Slave Song
ISBN: 978 1 84523 004 3, 72pp, £7.99

Slave Song is unquestionably one of the most important collections of Caribbean/Black British poetry published in the last twenty years. On its first publication in 1984 it won the Commonwealth Poetry Prize and established Dabydeen as a provocative and paradigm-shifting writer.

At the heart of *Slave Song* are the voices of African slaves and Indian labourers expressing, in a Guyanese Creole that is as far removed from Standard English as is possible, their songs of defiance, of a thwarted erotic energy. But surrounding this harsh and lyrical core of Creole expression is an elaborate critical apparatus of translations (which deliberately reveal the actual untranslatability of the Creole) and a parody of the kind of critical commentary that does no more than paraphrase or at best contextualise the original poem. Here, Dabydeen is engaged in a play of masks, an expression of his own duality and a critique of the relationship which is at the core of Caribbean writing: that between the articulate writer and the supposedly voiceless workers and peasants.

This new edition has an afterword by David Dabydeen that briefly explores his response to these poems after more than twenty years.

Turner
ISBN: 978 1 90071 568 3, 84pp, £7.99

David Dabydeen's "Turner" is a long narrative poem written in response to JMW Turner's celebrated painting "Slavers Throwing Overboard the Dead & Dying". Dabydeen's poem focuses on what is hidden in Turner's painting, the submerged head of the drowning African. In inventing a biography and the drowned man's unspoken desires, including the resisted temptation to fabricate an idyllic past, the poem brings into confrontation the wish for renewal and the inescapable stains of history, including the meaning of Turner's painting.

"A major poem, full of lyricism and compassion, which gracefully shoulders the burden of history and introduces us to voices from the past whose voices we have all inherited" – Caryl Phillips

The Intended
ISBN: 978 1 84523 013 5, 246pp, £8.99

The narrator of *The Intended* is twelve when he leaves his village in rural Guyana to come to England. There he is abandoned into social care, but seizes every opportunity to follow his aunt's farewell advice: "...but you must tek education...pass plenty exam." With a scholarship to Oxford, and an upper-class white fiancée, he has unquestionably arrived, but at the cost of ignoring the other part of his aunt's farewell: "you is we, remember you is we." First published almost fifteen years ago,

The Intended's portrayal of the instability of identity and relations between whites, African-Caribbeans and Asians in South London is as contemporary and pertinent as ever. As an Indian from Guyana, the narrator is seen as a "Paki" by the English, and as some mongrel hybrid by "real" Asians from India and Pakistan; as sharing a common British "Blackness" whilst acutely conscious of the real cultural divisions between Africans and Indians back in Guyana. At one level a moving semi-autobiographical novel, *The Intended* is also a sophisticated postcolonial text with echoes of *Heart of Darkness*.

Disappearance   ISBN: 978 1 84523 014 2, 180pp, £8.99

A young Afro-Guyanese engineer comes to a coastal Kentish village as part of a project to shore up its crumbling sea-defences. He boards with an old English woman, Mrs Rutherford, and through his relationship with her discovers that beneath the apparent placidity and essential Englishness of this village, violence and raw emotions are not far below the surface, along with echoes of the imperial past. In the process, he is forced to reconsider his perceptions of himself and his native Guyana, and to question his engineer's certainties in the primacy of the rational.

This richly intertextual novel makes reference to the work of Conrad, Wilson Harris and VS Naipaul to set up a multi-layered dialogue concerning the nature of Englishness, the legacy of Empire and different perspectives on the nature of history and reality.

"An electrifying array of surmises about how the imperial past has affected everyone in Britain today" – *Scotsman*

The Counting House   ISBN: 978 1 84523 015 9, 180pp, £8.99

Set in the early nineteenth century, *The Counting House* follows the lives of Rohini and Vidia, a young married couple struggling for survival in a small, caste-ridden Indian village who are seduced by the recruiter's talk of easy work and plentiful land if they sign up as indentured labourers to go to British Guiana. There, however, they discover a harsh fate as "bound coolies" in a country barely emerging from the savage brutalities of slavery. Having abandoned their families and a country that seems increasingly like a paradise, they must come to terms with their problematic encounters with an Afro-Guyanese population hostile to immigrant labour, with rebels such as Kampta who has made an early abandonment of Indian village culture, and confront the truths of their uprooted condition.

"Beautifully written... Dabydeen's grace, as a poet turned novelist, is to give his characters' imaginations and inner lives voices in prose... This is a marvelous novel" – Michele Roberts, *Independent on Sunday*

ABOUT THE AUTHOR

David Dabydeen is the distinguished author of six novels, three collections of poetry and numerous works of non-fiction and criticism. He is co-editor of the celebrated *Oxford Companion to Black British History*, and is Professor at the Centre for British Comparative Cultural Studies, University of Warwick; a member of UNESCO's Executive Board and winner of the 2008 Anthony N Sabga award for literature, the Caribbean equivalent of the Nobel prize.

PRAISE FOR DAVID DABYDEEN'S PREVIOUS WORK:

"Magnificent, vivid and original" (Hanif Kureishi)

"Dabydeen's writing vibrates with passion, energy and splendid rhythm" (Anita Desai)

"Painfully beautiful and true" (Maya Angelou)

"It is everywhere apparent that Dabydeen has an imaginative mastery of the period, and can render it a hundred ways" (*The Observer*)

"Dabydeen presents his scenes of cruelty and vice in an assured and elegant style, but he goes much further by imbuing his story with a resolute humanity, and a warm and defiant sense of compassion and fun" (*The Guardian*)

Ed. Kevin Grant
The Art of David Dabydeen   ISBN: 978 1 90071 510 2, 231pp, £12.99

In this volume, leading scholars discuss Dabydeen's poetry and fiction in the context of the politics and culture of Britain and the Caribbean. The essays explore his concern with the plurality of Caribbean experience; the dislocation of slavery and indenture; migration and the consequent divisions in the Caribbean psyche. In particular, the focus is on Dabydeen's aesthetic practice as a consciously post-colonial writer; his exploration of the contrasts between rural creole and standard English; the power of language to subvert accepted realities; his use of multiple masks as ways of dealing with issues of identity; and the play of destabilizing techniques within his narrative strategies.

"Part of the usefulness is that the essays overlap, build on, and disagree with one another. They bring out Dabydeen's recurring themes, autobiographical material, and the links among his scholarly publications, interviews, and creative writings." – Bruce King, *World Literature Today*

Eds Lynne Macedo and Kampta Karran
No Land, No Mother: Essays on the Work of David Dabydeen
ISBN: 978 1 84523 020 3, 236pp, £12.99

The essays in this collection focus on the rich dialogue carried out in David Dabydeen's critically acclaimed body of writing. Dialogue across diversity and the simultaneous habitation of multiple arenas are seen as dominant characterics of his work. Essays by Aleid Fokkema, Tobias Döring, Heike Härting and Madina Tlostanova provide rewardingly complex readings of Dabydeen's *Turner*, locating it within a revived tradition of Caribbean epic. Lee Jenkins and Pumla Gqola explore Dabydeen's fondness for intertextual reference, his dialogue with canonic authority and ideas about the masculine. Michael Mitchell, Mark Stein, Christine Pagnoulle and Gail Low focus on his more recent fiction. Looking more closely at Dabydeen's Indo-Guyanese background, this collection complements the earlier *The Art of David Dabydeen*.